Figures in a Mirror

Z.D.M. Strong

Wordrunner Press

Figures in a Mirror
© 2020 by Z.D.M. Strong

ISBN: 978-1-941066-42-3

This is a work of fiction.
Any resemblance to persons
living or dead is coincidental.

Wordrunner Press
Petaluma, California

I *must before I die*, find *some way to say*
the essential thing that is in me,

that I have never said yet —
a thing that is not love or hate or pity or scorn,

but the very breath of life, fierce and coming from far away,

bringing into human life the vastness
and fearful passionless force of non-human things.

—Bertrand Russell (letter to Constance Malleson, 1918)

Contents

Figures in
a Mirror

PART ONE

Drawing Fire

The road of excess, having trampled the ground of innocence,
Might yet lead to the palace of wisdom.

— William Blake (proverbs)

1

Beautiful Lies

Mayday, 1990
San Francisco Bay Area

A loud crick-cracking, like narrow bones breaking, threaded into the darkness and disorder of Jake's dream. He was moving in slow motion, tangled in a rope that kept him from stepping over the edge of something vague and treacherous. The cracking mixed into his dream and broke it. He found himself in his bedroom lying as though under a pile of broken things, listening to the desperate flapping of a bird banging against a window pane to his right. As full consciousness flooded in, he realized a robin had flown in through the open slant of his window and was now hurting herself trying to get out.

His first impulse was to show her the way out by pointing a finger into the slot, but that might scare her off into the main body of the house where he'd have to open all the doors and window in hopes she'd fly out one of them without hurting herself. She needed to calm down enough to to feel the airflow in the window slot.

He knew any movement on his part would draw her attention. Somehow he sensed if she did not feel him as a threat she would allow him to approach.

Careful to avoid any sudden movement, he gently pushed the bedding aside, watching the bird as he did so. The robin stopped fluttering and looked at him, tense but still as he gently placed his feet on the floor. When she did not fly off as he stood up, he sensed she might actually allow him to approach. All he had to do was clear his head to keep his energy right, which meant not to think or feel in any way threatening toward the bird. The robin fluttered, and he sensed thinking about not thinking had somehow affected the manner in which he moved his body. He stood still for a moment; turning his thoughts off, to feel only the presence of the bird and his wish to help her. As he started toward her, he noticed how graceful his movements were, and how unlike him that was.

The bird fluttered nervously. She had felt the heat of his negative thought. He emptied his mind and she calmed down. Their eyes met. At that moment he knew she knew he was not a predator and he wanted to help. She followed the graceful sweep of his fingers toward the open slant of the window.

Then out she flew, her feathers brushing his fingers as he pulled them back.

"Good-bye, little robin," Jake said, awestruck by what had just happened. "Have a nice life."

JAZZ DUPREE glared down at the black four-wheel drive pickup pulling up below. Her wide mouth twisted into a scowl.

"See what I haf to put up with, Jean-Luc?" she said to a floppy-eared, black and white bunny hopping on the floor. "Blowing his damn horn like I'm some lowlife in the projects. Shit. Can't be bothered getting his lazy White ass out of his damn truck to knock on my damn door. Wouldn't treat me like that if I was a White bitch. Well, he's gonna have a long wait 'cause this girl's not going nowhere 'til she's damn good and ready."

JAKE REMOVED his glasses and rubbed his eyes as he slowly lowered his head to the steering wheel. On the drive over he'd drifted in and out of a mental fog so dense he had to stop several times to figure out where he was, where he was going, and why.

He raised his head to adjust the rear view mirror to look at the face that had once been a boy named Danny.

Danny became Jake when he got involved in making porn films in an effort to stave off the shame he felt from being sexually assaulted in the Army. The first time was in basic training after he got drunk in the barracks and passed out. When he woke up with a butt load of cum, he knew several members of his platoon had raped him. He also knew it was in his best interests to pretend his hangover was too intense for him to notice what came out of him when he got off the toilet. Then he went on sick call to see if he could get an appointment with a psychiatrist. His clerk advised him not to seek help of any kind because the psychiatrist and chaplain were required to immediately report it. If the word got out, his life would be in jeopardy. A case in point was the boy in Company A who was believed to have committed suicide. He had actually been beaten to death by members of his company, then thrown into a ravine.

Seven months later, at his post in Landstuhl, Germany, Danny was sexually assaulted by three MPs then hospitalized for three days. His doctor advised him not to report the rape because, if he did, he'd be punished more severely than those who assaulted him. After his hospitalization, he was transferred to another post and placed among Airborne troops who'd recently returned from Viet Nam. They said they'd routinely fragged (killed) fags in Viet Nam. Danny told them he was not a homo, but they chose not to believe him.

He woke up in a hospital, unable to remember anything. Twenty years later, he found the incident in his medical records. The file was vague as to the cause and extent of his injuries, but it was serious enough for him to have been hospitalized for two months.

After his release from the hospital, he was put on orders for Vietnam. He decided to go AWOL. Eight months later, he turned himself in at the Presidio in San Francisco and was jailed in the stockade.

Two months prior to Danny's imprisonment, a guard had shot and killed a seventeen-year-old inmate who'd kept whining about wanting to die. In the presence of other inmates on the detail, the guard told the boy all he had to do was walk away from the detail and ignore his orders to stop three times, and he'd be shot dead. To be sure the boy knew he was serious, he told him he hated San Francisco, and the army would reward him not only with a promotion, but also with a transfer to any post he wanted.

Twenty-seven prisoners sat-down in a peaceful protest against what they considered cold-blooded murder. The army considered their action mutiny and brought in marines from Treasure Island to turn the stockade into a living hell while the army sought the death penalty for the protesters. Prisoners were routinely beaten, tortured and sexually assaulted. The absolute worst punishment was to be sent to the marine base where they were given *special attention* over a thirty-day period. Anyone sent to the marine base was no longer sane when they returned to the stockade.

Danny decided to get the word out on what was going on. He informed his army psychiatrist, his civilian and military attorneys and the stockade chaplain. Having done so made him a target for assaults. After a severe beating, he was left alone for weeks with a concussion. A sympathetic sergeant told him they could not send him to the hospital because too many prisoners had been sent there with concussions. The Inspector General had to order them to stop sending more.

When Danny got out, he went to the War Resisters League to seek help for the prisoners after their release. His (and others') efforts contributed to the eventual shut down of the stockade. Within a year after their discharge, most of the Treasure Island victims had committed suicide. His efforts to help them had exacted a heavy toll on him.

At one point, after his discharge, he asked his best friend Jack, a Viet Nam vet, if he thought he was crazy. He said, "Yeah, you're crazy alright, but it's cool. We all are, in one way or another."

Some months later, when he got into pornography, where sexual shame was considered a turn on, he let go of being Danny. He became Jake.

"I wish," Jake mumbled at his sad reflection in the mirror. Not so long ago there'd been love in that face. Enough time had passed for him to adjust to Cedar's absence on her side of the bed, yet a part of him could not accept the end of a beautiful dream. For her, he'd quit the porn business.

"Beautiful lies you can live in," he sighed. Seven years together. Cedar was gone. *A beautiful wish-fulfilling illusion.* The pain would not go away until he somehow processed the fact his trusted mate had rejected his love (the most beautiful thing he had to offer), and given away everything he'd ever valued to strangers. Being rejected by those you love is the most profound sense of failure. A kind of death.

"What once was, is no more," he sighed. One day it would all be over. Then he noticed a crack in the rear view mirror, and wondered how and when that happened.

JAZZ SLAMMED the door shut, then clumped noisily down the concrete steps.

As she approached his truck, she glared at the forty-something White boy's frayed aviator jacket, then snorted at the stupid cap she detested *and* the lint on his knit tie. After all the trouble she went through borrowing Yolinda's fancy red silk dress and wolf fur jacket so he'd feel proud being seen with her, he shows up wearing whatever he found on his bedroom floor. He didn't know the meaning of the word pride.

"It wouldn't kill you to open the damn door for me," she snapped. He took a map off the seat then reached over to push the door open.

She climbed in with a contemptuous snort when she saw his faded black pants and smudged burgundy shoes. It made her all the more determined not to give him so much as a glance until they reached the shoot. Let him figure it out.

DR. BENJAMIN Adler, a five-foot-five, sixty-four-year-old psychotherapist, had a strangely split face. The upper part gave the impression of an intelligent, mature, strong man whereas the lower part was like a boy of eight, the expression of his mouth completely immature. His naïve child's mouth and thin little chin suggested something weak that, like a child, there were certain tensions he could not tolerate. From a distance he looked boyish. Up close, in the right light, he could pass for being in his forties, *if* you failed to notice the tightness around his eyes and the inky dullness of his dye job. He'd recently had plastic surgery to minimize the bags under his eyes and to tighten his eyelids.

Ben had come down two flights of stairs from the deck to the backyard patio to hide under the deck, where he'd closed his eyes. He needed darkness and privacy to calm down and think, to center himself. He feared he was becoming like his father Irving who, if someone were to ask him a question at a social gathering, would look back at them like a deer caught in headlights. Or he'd wince himself into a foolish nodding grin, then go into a fit of jabbering nonsense if they persisted. Or he'd cover his face and walk away, rocking back and forth muttering things like "Stupid! Stupid! Stupid!" As a boy, Ben had felt personally humiliated and shamed by his father's antics. People put up with Irving only because he was highly regarded as a mathematical genius.

"Got to do," Ben mumbled, his lips clamped between a finger and a thumb to keep from speaking out loud. "Got to! Got to! Got to do!" His eyes shot open.

He looked around to see if anyone had come down who might have heard him. No one on the deck above would have, because of the loud thumping music. What he feared most was someone might have overheard him muttering something about his missing-for-thirty-years-presumed-dead wife. The love of his life. Not a day had passed since her disappearance without his mumbling (or, more and more often now, bellowing) *I loved!* or *I wish!*, expressing his love and longing for her. Having reached the point where he felt not even death could put an end to it, he'd all but given up trying to stop.

All too often now, he caught himself spontaneously muttering those words in public. He feared he was becoming like the homeless drunks who wandered the streets shouting out nonsense. Had his love devolved into madness and shame? Lately he'd catch himself bellowing *NO!* in the privacy of his home where he knew no one would hear. *NO!* was aimed at his dirty mind, his personal shame.

He feared he'd end up shouting NO! in public.

Exactly what had upset him, he wasn't sure. Whatever it was, it started after Mindy (the director of the porn film) informed him the pre-pubescent boy he'd objected to hanging around a porn set was in fact a nineteen-year-old girl. Julie. The cameraman's assistant. The purple highlights in her short, reddish spiked hair and the crucifix around her neck had caught his attention. His sudden interest in her butt after Mindy told him she was a girl had stirred *something* in his mind that was hard to define. Something tainted with more than a tinge of depravity. Exotic young women with hour glass figures and big butts gave him fever; slim, boyish butts on boys or women did not. Yet he'd *definitely* felt the burn of Butt Fever. He couldn't stop himself from watching how her firm, compact butt filled out her form-fitted jeans. In the thrall of Butt Fever, he always found it hard to think straight.

Then the girl with a boyish butt suddenly turned around and glared directly at him, and he found himself dead center in a fever of conflicting currents of depravity.

Turning away, trying to appear as if he were looking for someone, he was afraid he may have looked at her like a deer caught in the headlights. That shamed him onto the verge of blushing with shame. Then he spotted Joaquin, the cameraman, mounting his camera on a tripod. He approached him as if he'd been looking for him all along to ask how long it'd be before they'd start shooting. Joaquin answered him while Ben, absently nodding, tried to think of something to ask him about the boyish girl.

Depravity, in one guise or another, had always haunted him. He'd written a best seller on sex crimes and the minds of those who committed them. Like most people, he'd religiously avoided recognizing depravity in himself, especially when overwhelmed by Butt Fever. Or, when someone glared at him like the Boy Butt Girl had. She had the clear creamy white complexion he associated with redheads, and probably their gloriously pink butt hole, as well. He tried to put a stop to that line of thought by shifting his attention to Joaquin. Then something tugged at his mind, and he turned around and saw Julie glaring directly at him. A sudden surge of shame overwhelmed him, like a yawning dizziness. Hoping she hadn't noticed any weakness on his part, he excused himself to Joaquin then headed down the stairs to the backyard to hide underneath the deck, where he would try to clear his dirty mind.

JAKE parked across from a ranch house with a driveway full of cars.

"That it?" said Jazz, sounding more cordial than she intended.

"Yeah," Jake mumbled as he opened his door.

"Wait a minute," she said.

He frowned, thinking she'd changed her mind at the last minute. "What's the matter?"

"Nothing's *the* damn matter!" she snapped. "I don't know anybody here, that's all."

"You know me and Jack, and Mindy."

"That's right, I know *you*." She glared at him. "I *know* you're gonna ignore me like you always do at parties."

"Hold your horses, this isn't a party. It's a movie."

"That's another damn thing!" she snarled, annoyed by his tone. "I've never been in a porn movie before and I don't feel comfortable. Is that fucking all right wif you?"

"Come on, we're extras in a McNothing production. You're a singer, you perform before good-sized audiences. This is nothing compared to that."

"Easy for you to say, you won't be the only Black person there."

"You've been the only person of color virtually everywhere we've gone," he said, thinking if one of them was going to draw fire it wouldn't be the long necked, hard bodied, twenty-eight-year-old Black beauty. It'd be the old, frumpy, White fart she was with. "You should be used to it by now."

"Well, I'll have you know, Mr. White-is-Right America, that is something I'll never get used to. And another thing, I *haven't* been comfortable in every damn situation we've been in."

"Yeah, sorry, okay," Jake shrugged.

"Thank you!"

"Listen," he said, softly. She gave him a suspicious look. "We're doing this as a favor to Mindy. No money's involved, so we don't have to get naked and we can leave anytime we want. No big whoop. Besides, you've been to real orgies which I think would be a damn sight more intimidating than a movie orgy."

"I didn't say I wasn't gonna do it! I'm not comfortable, that's all. And thank you for your damn sympathy!"

He smiled at her alleged shyness considering her dress was cut so low in back it showed off most of her butt crack.

"Don't leave me," she said, looking vulnerable.

"Stick with me, kid, and I'll show you a good time," he said, wiggling his eyebrows.

"I'm not gonna follow you around!" she snapped. "You could check on me every now and then. You know, to see if I'm okay."

"Sure," he shrugged as he got out of the car.

"I must be crazy being in luf wif you," she muttered. "Goofy White boy, ha!" He opened her door. "What's this? *You* being a gentleman?" she said, with a haughty smile. "You should always treat a lady like a lady." She gracefully swung her legs out then stood up, a good six foot high in heels, three inches taller than him. "I can't believe your precious little wife let you get away wif the shit you do, but then again I can't believe she'd let you out of the house dressed like that either." She snorted. "You think that shit look good? You look like an absent-minded professor tryin' to be cool."

He hesitated. "The jacket?"

She examined him contemptuously. "You should definitely lose the jacket."

He took the aviator jacket off and tossed it in the truck.

"That tie, hmmmph! Did your darling wife pick it out for you? She must've hated your ass."

"What's wrong with the tie?" he said, irritated.

"Nothing," she mocked. "Nothing at all."

As he examined the beige knit tie he noticed his no iron shirt needed ironing. A wrinkled shirt would make him look like a dirty old man with an expensive Black girl. He took the tie off but put the jacket back on to help hide the wrinkles.

She shook her head. "You gonna wear that damn hat?"

"Yeah," he said, defiantly.

"Why you wear that thing for? Don't you know how stoop-id it makes you look?"

"Look, you know I always wear a hat."

"Least you could do is wear it right 'stead of backasswards."

"That's how filmmakers wear this kind of hat."

"Shit, only a wooz'd wear a hat like that. And you think you be so hip."

"Hip is not a fashion thing," he grumbled. "Anyway, I don't give a damn about that crap."

"You telling me," she muttered, shaking her head.

He locked the car door. "Okay, okay, let's go, we're late."

"No, it's not fucking *okay!*" she yelled as he started across the street. "I'm nervous and I expect you to treat me wif respect." She stumbled as she started after him. "Damn! Hold on a minute, will you. I'm not used to runnin' in high heels."

Jake sighed, and waited.

"I wanna make a decent impression," she said, reaching for his hand. "I don't want to feel like some lowlife. A little class is all that's called for."

"Fine. Now let's go." He pulled her toward the path alongside the house.

She snorted several times before they reached the gate to the backyard.

"I'm serious, don't make me feel like trash. It's bad enough we're two hours late, for which it's not my fault. *I* was ready."

"It's no biggie," he said, then winced. That was something his ex, Cedar, would say. "I'll eat my wooz hat if they're on schedule."

JAZZ IMMEDIATELY caught Ben's eye when she and Jake came through the gate into the backyard. Her braided hair, wolf skin jacket and sheer red silk dress gave him the impression of a fashion model on a runway. Big Butted Black Beauties had always hit Ben's hot button, but this exotic Black Beauty locked it in on sizzling heat. Butt Fever!!

Julie noticed Ben's rapt attention as she started down the stairs with a plate of food. Then, like everyone else in the backyard, she looked over at Jazz.

"Yo! Jake! Jazz!" Joaquin yelled down from the top floor deck. "The legendary Jake Zakheim timing. We just broke for lunch. How do you do it, bro?"

Jake waved in response then did a quick scan of the people in the backyard, all of whom appeared to be middle-aged. Not a good thing for extras in a porn feature. He recognized Dr. Ben among them. He'd met with him as a potential investor many years ago. The head shrinker wanted to work his perverted rape fantasies into a project and Jake had given him the brush off. Then he heard Jazz, who was fully aware all eyes were on her, mumbling under her breath that she'd give them something to really look at. She slipped off her wolf skin jacket to expose the backside of her silk dress, which was cut so low it exposed most of her bare butt cheeks.

The unexpected exposure of the exotic Black Beauty's butt cheeks flexing as they ascended the stairs ramped up Ben's Butt Fever. Firm flexing Big Butts were his thing. He considered butt cracks to be much more erotic than cleavage. Her ass was not the only thing that attracted him. Everything about her face and the way she moved excited him, as well. He had to fight the urge to jump up and follow her Butt up the stairs.

THE FIRST THING Jake noticed about Joaquin, the name Jack preferred his friends to call him now, was his crisp, clean clothes looked as if they'd just came off the rack that morning. His face, though, looked worn out, his ears red, his gray hair messy, his short beard in need of a trim. After twenty-two years of friendship Jake was still accustomed to seeing him as a youthful bohemian. Today, though, at forty-five, he looked old.

"Had a hard night, Joa-Joa?" Jazz asked. "Your nose looks like a red light." Then she eyed the bottle of beer in his hand. "Where'd you get that?"

"In a cooler on the kitchen floor," he said, gesturing with the bottle to the sliding glass door that opened on the dining room.

"I'm hon-grey," she said, taking his beer from him. "Where's the food?"

BEN ENTERED the dining room to look for an opportunity to approach Jazz when he spotted Will at the kitchen doorway. William Worthingham, a sixty-six-year-old criminal law attorney, used Ben as an expert witness when one was needed involving sex crimes. He also referred pathological sexual cases to his clinic (the ones considered a danger to others as well as to themselves). Will's eyes, shielded by a heavy brow, were focused with bright blue scrutiny on Jake at the buffet table, stuffing food in his face.

"Well, look at what the cat drug in," said Ben. Noticing Will's sour expression, he added in a friendlier tone, "You been hitting the sauce?"

Worthingham frowned. "A couple snorts."

"Enough to make you mean. A few more and you'll be stupid."

"Who's the pig?" Worthingham said, nodding toward the buffet table. Ben glanced at Jake loading his plate. "That's Jake Zakheim."

"So that's the genius who gave the world Visions of Claire, Blondes on Blondes and Sin City Cycle Sluts?" He reached for the flask in his suit pocket, but managed to stop himself short.

"Jake's father was an alcoholic. First impressions are critical," Ben said as he handed him a little breath spray bottle. "Use this to mask the smell."

Worthingham glared down at him, his eyes varnished with a hard gleam of scorn. He wanted to remind the little squirt of the major cases, spread out for going on forty years, he'd won with a buzz on. Kept him *focused*, one-sided. But talk would get him nowhere with Ben, so he bore down on him with his stare.

Ben looked Worthingham in the eye, his thin chin down. "What happened?"

Will suspected he was referring to the Katie situation, but under the circumstances he figured Ben was referring to his drinking. Truth be told, he had no idea what specifically triggered the restless agitation that required self-medication. Sometimes it just happened. In any case, the last thing he felt like doing with a buzz on would be to talk about Katie *or* his drinking. He signaled Ben with the blaze in his eyes to drop it, as if the fierceness of his gaze could convey the message words would fail to deliver.

"I know you don't like his films," Ben said, trying to keep things simple. "And you probably won't like him as a person either. But Mindy says his participation is important."

"Hey, Will," said Mindy Rosensweg, a tiny woman in her early forties with a halo of kinky, black hair. "Glad you could make it. Before I forget, Peter called to ask me to let you know he's arranged to take Katie over to meet with Riley tomorrow morning."

Worthingham glared at Mindy. "Can't stay long. Just checking things out."

Mindy grimaced, knowing that wasn't true. "I'm glad you're both here because I need to talk to you both about putting up more money. We need more young women."

"WE'VE BEEN HERE since seven and haven't shot a damn thing," Joaquin told Jake at the buffet table. "You should give Mindy a talking to, boy."

Jake glanced over at Mindy. Her faded jeans and torn t-shirt made him feel better about his casual clothes. She was talking to Dr. Ben and a man who appeared to be in his late sixties, dressed in a well-made gray worsted suit. "Who's the suit?" he asked.

"Will Worthingham, Mindy's principal investor. Your favorite kind of predator. A lawyer. He's Riley Thierault's attorney. The other guy's Thierault's shrink."

"Should I know who that is?"

"You're putting me on. The king of splatter? He did that bogus snuff film everybody was talking about back in the seventies."

Jake frowned. "You know I don't watch that crap."

"Neither do I, but I had to check that one out. You have to admire the mileage he got off a bonehead rumor. The disembowelment scene was so phony it was funny, but not as funny as the custody battle afterwards. You at least heard of that, right? Holy Roller fights Demonic Director for a little Orphan Girl's soul? Tabloid fodder some years back."

"I don't read tabloids, either."

"Not even the headlines at the checkout counter? C'mon, bro, one of life's simple pleasures. Okay, so the orphan's Riley's niece. The Holy Roller's her grand pappy, and Riley starts a rumor that he's hired ghouls to hang out at bus stations to kidnap runaways to turn into zombies. You know, for his next movie. So a reporter asks Gramps about it, and he *allegedly* says he thinks Riley turned his granddaughter into a zombie. So Riley holds a press conference, then brings out little orphan Katie looking like a zombie. And she answers every question in a scratchy goblin voice with the same word, terrr-EEEEE-bluh. She's trying to say terrible but it comes out in goblinesse as terrr-EEEEE-bluh, ha! ha! ha! Oh, and she did her own make-up. Turns out she has a knack for making sluts look like angels and angels look like devils."

Jake grinned. "Then what happened?"

"The story got so much play, Gramps ended up letting Riley have full custody," he said quickly when he saw Mindy approaching. "Here comes our fearless director. Say something to her, will you? I don't want to be stuck here all night."

"I doubt if anything I have to say will make a dime's worth of difference, seeing as how much she's heeded my advice so far."

"I'm so glad you made it, Jake," said Mindy. "Did you bring Jasmine?"

"Yeah, she's around here somewhere."

Mindy looked worried. "Will she do a sex scene?"

"If you pay her, sure, why not."

She grimaced. "How much? We're way over budget. Do you think she'd do it for fifty bucks?"

He looked doubtful. "You'd have to ask her."

"Could you ask her? Maybe coming from you she'd see how important it is. We *really* need her."

"Hit your investors up for the extra bucks." Jake scanned the room. None of the women he saw were, by porn feature standards, attractive. "Call it cheap insurance."

"I can't do that. I've asked them for too much as it is. Maybe she wouldn't mind if we just used her mouth? She has such an incredibly sexy face."

Jake shook his head. "She's an ex-prostitute. She equates blowjobs with money. Won't do it for anything else, not even with me. You know how it is, nothing wrong with sucking a John's dick, but kiss him on the lips, no way. Kisses are too intimate."

"For real, bro," said Joaquin. "Kisses *are* more intimate because no two people kiss alike. No two people fuck alike either but a kiss is more personal, more individual than a fuck. Know what I mean?"

"Could you maybe at least talk her into taking her clothes off?" she said, hopefully. "No sex, just a little nudity."

"Try to understand my position," said Jake. "She thinks you turned her down for the lead because she's Black. So if I, the object of her infections, were to suggest she give it up to you for a token, she'd make sure I paid the balance."

Mindy sighed. "I see what you mean, Jake, but I'm in kind of a bind. You warned me about having only two women in the movie so the extras in this scene were suppose to make up for that. I thought I had it down since my investors said they knew all these beautiful women in the swing scene who'd love to be in an erotic movie." She glanced around the room, a pained expression on her face.

Joaquin chuckled. "Mutton dressed as lamb."

"There you go, they let you down," said Jake. "It's not your fault. They should kick in the extra bucks in penance."

She shook her head sorrowfully. "I can't tell them their girlfriends are dogs."

"Okay," he said, biting his lower lip. "Tell them the scene needs a sexy twenty something and there just happens to be a bootyful one available, but it's gonna cost 'em."

Mindy sighed. "Maybe she'd take a deferral?"

"I doubt it."

"This is a quality project, Jake, one she can be proud to be part of. Everyone's deferring all or part of their salary. Even Shannen, and she's a major star who never defers."

"As far as Jazz is concerned, a deferral's a fart in a glove. She doesn't think you'll make money, and she's probably right since making money doesn't appear to be your objective."

"We're doing it because we believe in it, Jake."

"Right," said Jake, distracted by the entrance of a bejeweled platinum blonde in her mid-twenties. "Who's that?"

"You can forget about her. I've been trying for the last hour to get her to sign a release but she refuses to go on camera. She and her twin brother just came to watch."

"Geeez Louise," Jake groaned. "You're letting everyone walk all over you. You have to control these people. Appeal to her vanity. Tell her you need a beautiful young woman in the midst of these senior citizens to give the scene—"

"Body," said Joaquin.

"Who knows, maybe she'd go for it, and once that barrier's crossed her perverse side will kick in and she'll give you a free ride. Tell her to sign the release or get the fuck out."

"I know what you're saying. I'd have done that long ago but the extras are turned on by the idea of them watching."

A close cropped, effeminate blond young man approached the buffet table. "Is that her twin?" asked Jake.

"Yeah," said Mindy. "And they have little incentive for being here other than as a favor for one of my investors."

They both appeared to be uncomfortable, the brother somewhat more so than the sister. He noticed her jewelry. *Maybe she's worried about the safety of her valuables.*

Mindy grimaced. "Wouldn't the audience resent it if the dogs took their clothes off and the good looking women didn't?"

"Yeah, I'll say," Joaquin laughed. "Jake did that in one of his flicks. Like to drive a man out of his mind."

Jake's glared at Joaquin. "I did it because I had no choice. Anyway, a lot hangs on the editing."

"What about you? Would you do a scene?" asked Mindy. "Have you checked out the guys? They're nothing to crow about either."

"That's right, bro," Joaquin laughed. "If Jazz ain't gonna show us her fine Black ass, the least you could do is give up your forty-nine-year-old White buns."

Jake noticed a young man with shoulder length hair talking to Worthingham and Dr. Ben. "What about the tall kid in the baggy pants?"

"You think he's attractive?" said Mindy, surprised. "I doubt he can get it up. Lars is pre-op. He's on all kinds of drugs."

"You're kidding?" said Jake. "A sex change? He's what, six four?"

"Does he have tits?" asked Joaquin.

Mindy frowned. "Yes, small ones. Not enough to be a turn on, for me anyway. Don't you think he'd ruin the scene? His dick is rather small."

"Be different." Joaquin shrugged.

Mindy noticed Worthingham leaving the room. "Excuse me. I have to go."

"Don't wait too long after the extras eat," said Jake, "or you'll lose them."

MINDY JOINED Will on the deck. He was watching Jazz following Joe, the male lead, down to the backyard with a plate of food she was swinging about while she talked.

"She is expensive," Mindy said.

Worthingham fixed his face into a grim little look, as if he had just realized his roof leaked. "We'll get her for nothing."

"What if we don't?" said Mindy. "After what Lars said about the twins, we have no other choice. Jake says—"

"Forget Zakheim, he's a mark. He doesn't know his ass from a hole in the ground."

Joe struck Jazz as a fine looking White boy. Wavy blond hair, perfect teeth, movie star blue eyes, all fancied up in a financial district stripped shirt and gray cotton herringbone slacks, looking like he just stepped out of a Macy's catalog.

"Damn!" Jazz jerked back when a lump of lasagna slid off her plate onto her dress.

"Here, let me help," Joe said, brandishing a napkin.

"I better put this away before it kills us both," she laughed when the rest of her lasagna flew off her plate onto Joe's shirt.

ALL YOUR *DREAMS TURNED FANTASIES.* Oliver had used words to that effect. Ben had never thought of it that way before, but Ollie was right. Ben's ambition in high school was to become a groundbreaking, world famous blues singer. Eventually he came to realize no matter how good he got technically, he lacked the ability to impart the feel or nuances reflecting what he felt in his lyrics into his instruments or his voice. The songs he wrote were okay. His mother managed to get him to agree on being filmed performing two of them. To his embarrassment, she invited a number of people over to watch it. They all said they liked it, but he felt otherwise. He sounded and looked like an immature adolescent who thought he was hot stuff, and his songs came off as just plain dumb. He destroyed the film to avoid any further embarrassment.

He also wanted to dance like Fred Astaire. Astaire wasn't that good a singer, or even good looking, and rather scrawny as well. But people didn't seem to mind any of that because of his dancing. Ben took lessons and the instructor praised him. Then his mother filmed him at a recital. She was so proud and wanted to show the film to her friends. But this time, before she got a chance, he looked at it then destroyed it. He looked ridiculous. Studied, mannered, not at all displaying the grace or flow he felt while dancing. And the dumb look on his face, mostly his stupid mouth, like he thought he was being artistic or some crock of shit like that. He was fifteen at that time, but he still looked like a kid. He'd have to wait until he looked older, and had more experience.

In college, he majored in music and psychology. He played some of his songs in coffee houses, but his audience always prefered standards. He got better, but not good enough. Unless he felt the sound matched what he felt, it was pointless to continue.

"Why were you messing with Joaquin?" Julie snapped at him.

Ben became abruptly aware of Boy-Butt Girl's eyes boring down on him.

"Joaquin?" he said. "What? Why?"

Julie looked impatient, annoyed. "Jack! The cameraman! I saw the way you were looking at him. Don't waste your time trying to hypnotize me. It won't work. Not on me!"

His brow furrowed as he scrutinized the striations in her green eyes, like bevels in a pair of intricately cut emeralds. "What makes you think I'd try to hypnotize Joaquin, or you for that matter?"

"I know who you are and what you do. I'm Julie Jodorowski, Oliver Jodorowski's daughter. Fucking with people's heads is like his main mission in life."

"Oliver's daughter?" Ben said with a mixture of surprise and alarm in his voice. He didn't know Oliver had a kid. "Does he know you're working here?"

"I don't know, doc. Does he?" she snapped as she parked her butt on the chair facing him. "Since I left home I've kept my private life to myself. I don't want him knowing anything about what I do, unless I tell him. And we don't talk."

"What'd he do to deserve that?" he asked, watching her ruby red lips puckering up. He felt himself being very much aware of and interested in her life force.

"That's private."

"Okay. I respect that. Would you mind if I asked him?" he said, breathing with his mouth open, what he realized was her natural body odors. Clear. Clean.

"Like he'd ever tell *you* anything about his private life." Her lips curled down, and her eyebrows furled as she thought something through. "He pulled one of his freaking archetypal field dramas on me and my friends. It ended badly." She pursed her lips as she glared at him. "My friends! Afterwards I told him to leave my freaking friends alone, okay!"

What was it with her lips? Why hadn't he noticed them before. Of course, at the time he was more interested in her butt than her face. He watched her chew on her lower lip, her eyes looking down, away from him. He wondered if she was trying to draw his attention to her full lips. Her lips and eyes were the most striking things about her face, and she no doubt knew it.

Then, her face screwed up into a grimace. "You know about his stream of time thing, right?" Her lips relaxed for a moment, then tightened into a sneer."

"No, I can't say that I do," said Ben.

She looked doubtful. "I think you do. Maybe you know it as something else."

"Could be."

She frowned, then began in a tentative tone, "We exist in a stream of time, but very few of us are aware of it. The stream is circular. No beginning. No end. The past and future are fluid, connected by the present. When I was little, he told me I was born aware of the stream, that I could sense the waves of past and future in ways that my awareness could direct events in the present. He pointed it out to me whenever he saw me do it. He said he had little to do with what happened to my friends, other than having constructed a field where I had the power to shift events at any time. All I had to do was to look for the forces behind what was going on, then allow my instincts to alter the current at the right time." She looked frustrated for a moment. "Did he send you here to *observe* or to act?"

"He said something would start here today. That I should draw its attention by making a fool of myself at critical points. In a way, sort of like what you just said." Then it dawned on him, she could prove to be useful. *If* he could get her to drop her act.

"So it *is* a set up. I knew it! I fucking-A knew it! He always sets up someone capable of recognizing the god in the machine. Would that be you by any chance?"

Ben considered how to answer her. "It'd be the goddess in the machine, being as pornography lies in the realm of goddesses. So, yes, I'd know. What about you?"

"Duh, yeah," she muttered. "But I don't want to know! I never wanted that kind of life. My dad says that's why I failed to do what I had to do at a crucial moment with my friends. Who I don't have anymore because ..." She stopped herself from saying more.

"Living the myth is what it's called, by making yourself available to it," said Ben.

"Why the fuck would you want to do that?" Julie snapped.

"To be in play with gods or, as in this case goddesses, is a special kind of adventure," Ben said, watching her intently. "Risky, sure, but it's an opportunity to gain insight and depth. The vast majority of people who find themselves in an archetypal field rarely have any idea that they are in one, much less that gods and/or goddesses are behind what appears to them as ordinary reality."

Julie sucked in her lips, glaring at him in a way that made her look even more boyish. He wondered if she'd sensed she was turning him on, that he wanted to taste her flavors. As soon as he had that thought, he felt badly about it. Definitely not a story he should slip into. Psychiatrist's daughters, like preacher's daughters, tend to be nasty. Especially if they have daddy issues. He liked that kind of nasty. But Ollie's flesh and blood? That would be asking for trouble. Which would be why she'd do it, and why he should not. The way she worked her face as she thought excited him. There was a time when he would have taken the risk with no misgivings, but after the disaster on Riley's last film he'd become more circumspect. He would resist the urge by seeing through it.

Then he heard himself say, "Let's talk again, when you're ready to drop your act." She looked startled, then her face talked to him. He'd never seen anything quite like it, except on lunatics who were totally unaware of what their faces were doing. She knew, though, and stopped her face as soon as she realized he was reading it. Without saying another word, she walked off, too self-conscious to control the anger in her gait.

He knew she'd eventually come around to talk again, and knowing that somehow empowered him. He was no longer afraid or nervous. Game on.

JAKE TOSSED his paper plate into a huge trashcan in the kitchen then grabbed a beer out of the ice chest. "I haven't seen the script," he said to Joaquin. "Is it any good?"

"Seems to be about sex as a religious thing," said Joaquin. "Especially extreme sex, because God is sexual, and bi-sexual at that. You know, the way I see it, sex is by itself *the* great creative activity of our time. Think about it, bro. Where else do people give their imagination such free rein to spur their inner artist on to brilliance? Come to think of it, making movies is a lot like making love. Neither one's much fun without fantasy."

Jake listened to the "pop" of the bottle cap. "Beautiful lies," he said, smelling the acridness of the first stream of vapor as he raised the bottle.

"Say what?"

"Sooner or later ugly realities make it hard to keep churning out fantasies."

"Hey, who knows, maybe Mindy will pull it off. Stranger things have happened."

"How much disbelief was it necessary to suspend to reach that confusion?"

"Remember how when we were partners we got so pissed at each other we wrestled," said Joaquin. "You remember what that fantasy was about, bro?"

"Money, probably. That was during your revolutionary period when you thought making money was counter-revolutionary, since money corrupts and all."

"I could stand with a little corrupting right about now," Joaquin laughed.

"How much you deferring?" Jake asked.

"Only half, thank god. I know it's probably a lost cause, but I don't care. I plan to keep churning the fantasy fires for as long as I can get away with it."

"Still governed by passion, eh?" said Jake.

"It's more like a dictatorship," said Joaquin.

"Yeah. If only I didn't know now what I didn't know then," Jake said, watching a beautiful brunette in her early twenties enter the kitchen in a long, gold sequined t-shirt that hung down from her large breasts. "I feel like if I got back in the biz it'd only bring me grief."

"That's gold on them thar hills." Joaquin wiggled his eyebrows at the girl's boobs.

An amused sparkle in her eyes attracted Jake. "Who is she?"

"Moira Vandergrift, the second lead. It's her first porn gig. I love working with first timers. Gives things an edge. You're going to love this. She's the attorney's niece."

"The goblin?" Jake said, startled.

"The goblin?" Joaquin looked confused. "Oh, you mean Katie, the zombie. No, no, that's Riley Theirault's niece, the make-up artist. This one's Worthingham's niece."

"You're putting me on." Jake made a face. Moira glanced over at him. He turned to Joaquin, whispering, "His niece?"

"Not a blood niece. She's adopted."

"Ah, but come on, still," said Jake.

Joaquin looked surprised. "You did a project with an investor's son in it. Does that mean you don't care as long as it's a guy?"

"Oh no, believe me I was pissed when I found out. I wouldn't have done it if I'd known beforehand he was her son."

"Hey, bro, lighten up. I think it's great her people are behind her.

The number of actresses who let family in on what's going on is practically zilch, am I right? It's a refreshing change. Look, for all we know, she talked her uncle into it."

Jake glanced at Moira, her back to them. He noticed the childlike way she arched her back and flexed her buttocks as if she knew that was what he wanted to see.

"You're not getting weird on me in your old age are you, bro? Her uncle also got her a part in Thierault's new flick. She's scheduled to be gutted and filleted by a mutant in a few days. Is that any better?"

MARCIA O'Connell always arrived on porn sets looking nothing like a porn star, wearing no make-up, dressed in old jeans, her hair tied in a ponytail. After immersing herself into make-up, hair-styling and fuck-me clothes, she'd transform into her uninhibited Shannen Bardo sensual persona. Today, she knew Marcia had to shine through the mask because Riley Theirault, her favorite director, preferred wholesome looking women for his victims, a bill Marcia fit much better than Shannen. Will, Riley's attorney, could arrange for an audition, but he was with Mindy at the moment, and he looked displeased.

She decided to wait until he was alone.

Jazz and Joe came running up the stairs from the backyard. When Marcia saw Mindy walking toward them she recognized it as an opportunity, but hesitated when she noticed Worthingham seemed interested in what Mindy was up to.

JAZZ TRIPPED at the top of the stairs. "I know, I know," Jazz laughed with Joe. "I'm always like this when I have too much wine. Can't judge distance wurf a damn."

Mindy examined Joe's stain. "We've got to get this cleaned."

Joe grinned. "Not to worry, I brought a spare." He winked at Jazz. "But I've only got one spare, so watch yourself."

"Ha! Ha!" Jazz laughed so loud Mindy pulled back. "I will, I will! But I best put my jacket somewhere safe 'cause *I* don' have no spare."

Joe's laughter mixed with hers as they entered the house.

"YOU JUST sensed something, didn't you?" Julie stage whispered, looking down at Ben.

Ben looked over at her, somewhat rattled.

He'd taken a seat on the upper deck to watch Jazz and her booty. When Julie spoke to him, he was still reeling at the sound of Jazz's laughter, so much like his presumed dead wife's overly loud laugh when she was liquored up.

"The goddess in the machine?" Julie said, urging him on as she sat facing him. Ben frowned, his heated senses still on the flexing Butt crack in the red silk dress.

"Yeah," he mumbled. "goddesses. Three of them. A three-headed goddess."

Boy-Butt-Girl started talking excitedly while he nodded, not listening as he considered the axiom that behind every obsession lies an *archetype*, the word archetypal therapists used for the gods or goddesses reflected in ancient myths. Then he reflected on what it was about Jake's lady friend that had affected him so. She looked and sounded like his wife who'd disappeared thirty years ago, long before Jazz was born. She'd been a top tier international tournament wrestler who'd attracted the attention of wealthy men worldwide who gave her large sums of money in exchange for kinky sexual favors. She had several regulars, mostly on the Eastern Seaboard and the Middle East.

Ben was respected in his profession for his insights into abnormal sexual complexes. His book on pathological sexual obsessions had got her attention. She came to him as a patient, after having been violated to the point where she felt befouled beyond relief. It was difficult for her to keep regular appointments because she often had to hop on a plane with little or no notice for dates with clients, who were the kind of men she could not say no to. A pentagon general and a Saudi prince were the most demanding of her time. They were also the kinkiest and the most generous. They'd never threatened her, because she'd never said no to them. She came to Ben, as she put it in her inquiry letter, "To learn the fine points of the use of role play to entice archetypes to see through the extreme things that happen to me, to find their hidden meanings in the Underworld."

At first he suspected English was not her native language. When they met in her hotel suite, he found a strikingly beautiful, athletic Black woman whose efforts at hiding her Southern Black accent were less effective face-to-face. Then she went silent. They stared at each other for some time, until she asked in a throaty intense whisper, "Show me the Underworld," which led to their first explosive ritual-rape encounter. He'd never experienced anything like it before. Neither had she, or so she claimed after having spent a good fifteen minutes writhing on the floor after falling off the bed during an incredibly loud and long orgasm. She'd convinced herself, and him as well, that he had a magic touch that released her entrapping sexual tension.

They impulsively got married in Italy during an around-the-world luxury cruise. The years he'd spent with her had been the happiest of his life. Then she disappeared.

He hired detectives to find her, but she was gone without a trace. The money in her accounts untouched, most of which he would spend trying to find out what had happened to her. His world collapsed. He knew he would never recover from his loss.

"Are you listening to me?" Julie demanded in a determined voice. "I said I'm ready to drop my act, whatever that means. So, what are you trying to get at?"

"Are you really Ollie's daughter?" Ben replied. "By blood?" he added.

Julie's face went through a series of changes, from surprise to irritation to frustration. "He says he's my dad, but we don't look anything alike. He said he found me in a basket on his doorstep with a note saying I was his. He kept the basket and the note. It was signed, Flora. She'd been a patient of his." She paused. "He said they'd had sex only one time, then she disappeared. He didn't go looking for her until after he saw me on his doorstep. That's how he found out she was dead."

"Okay." This should be interesting, Ben thought. Even *if* it's just an act.

"I'm not making this stuff up," Julie said, defensively. "That's what he told me!"

"Oh, I'm sure he did just that," Ben said as he took a packet of vials from a pocket and pulled out a purple one. He twisted it opened and held it out for her to sniff.

She backed away. "My god! What the hell is that god awful smell?"

"That's just what it is," Ben said as he replaced the stopper then put it back in the packet. "It's just that. A god awful smell to match your god awful act."

"It's not an act!" Julie sputtered, obviously offended as she stomped off in a huff.

"Thirty years ago," Ben muttered as he watched Julie's retreating boy butt.

As he turned away to ogle the visible crack in Jazz's flexing Big Butt, he realized he was *now* in the midst of a stream of time in an archetypal field. It was his grasp of such things that had drawn his beloved wife to him. It was his reason for being here now, on the thirtieth anniversary of her disappearance. His reason for tempting the fates. The time was right.

WORTHINGHAM glanced at Marcia with a curious icy light, pale blue and depthless, like a creature that could see in the dark. She smiled nervously as she approached.

"Mr. Worthingham?" *It'll be all right, if he sees me as innocent and vulnerable.* "I was wondering what you'd think about putting a porn actress in a Riley T. horror film?" Worthingham's eyes blazed coldly, a warning of indestructible certainty. Then he laughed a laugh with absolutely no humor in it while Marcia crumpled behind her mask, into a state of overwhelming hopelessness. She'd said the wrong thing, and now nothing she could say would be of the slightest interest to him. She'd never felt so naked.

Worthingham smiled a smile that was not a smile, nor like any smile she'd ever seen before. Then Shannen smiled back at him.

A HAND gingerly grazed Jake's shoulder.

Thinking he'd inadvertently brushed against someone, he turned to look. An elegantly dressed woman in her late thirties, her hair pulled neatly into a tight bun, smiled at him. There was a tension about her, in her face, in the taut muscles along her narrow jaw, and in her hands, twisted together at her belt line.

"Janus?" said Jake. "Janus Terror. I almost didn't recognize you. You look so different."

"Yes, yes, I know, but I may be needed in the orgy scene so I have to dress the part. Got to look like I come from money. Officially, I was only suppose to cast this sucker, but," she lowered her voice, "let me tell you, I sure as hell did *not* cast these bowsers. Mindy gave the usual spiel, you know, must have glamorous types who'll fuck for free. She should consider herself lucky to find lookers who'll work cheap. But then, her investors said they'd send over their swing buddies. I don't know these idiots so what am I suppose to think, right? Tell you what, I sure didn't think *this* would be their idea of sexy. I'll probably end up being a port-a-pussy because the assholes didn't come through."

"Now, Janus," Joaquin grinned. "You'd make a great port-a-pussy and you know it."

She smiled self-consciously. "She'd be in a hell of a jam if all she had was old cows. I'm no spring chicken myself, but I'm a damn sight better than any of them."

"Absolutely no contest." Joaquin chuckled. "Why don't you give Jake a peek at what you got on underneath? You're going to love this, bro."

Janus mumbled, "Well, I don't know."

"Check it." Joaquin reached over to loosen then pulled her dress down to her waist, exposing a black leather bra with circular holes in the middle of each cup barely covering her breasts. "Check out how the leather accentuates her humongous nipples, drawing attention to what really counts." He pulled the dress all the way down then pointed at circular openings in her leather panties, front and back. "Am I right or what?"

"What's the going rate for port-a-pussies nowadays?" asked Jake.

"Nothing, for me," she said, pulling her dress back up. "I wouldn't be able to sleep at night if I compromised my professional standing as a sex therapist by taking money for sex, like I was a prostitute or something. Sex therapists are under enough suspicion as it is, so I have to be careful how I get my image out there." She looked around. "The guys, though, sure are butt ugly. I'm not crazy about going at it with any of them. They're not the best thing that's ever happened to me, that's for sure."

"Come on, girl," said Joaquin. "You're hot and you know it."

"Sometimes I think maybe I'd get away with it. I'm too old to be a major star, but any kind of work's nothing to sneeze at. Puts food on the table."

Jake chuckled. "Who do you think are more butt ugly? The men or the women?"

"Oh, the men, for sure, they're gross. The women may be old and out of shape, but the guys! Ugh! They're regurgitory with all the personality of a bucket of warm spit."

"What about Lars?" said Jake, with a grimace. *A bucket of warm spit.*

"Oh, please! That guy's strictly loony tunes. Most transies are so screwy it isn't even funny, but he's crazier'n a bed bug. As far as I'm concerned he's a walking AIDS epidemic. By the way, I hear you're doing something. I hope you'll consider using my services. You know, locations, casting, the usual. I'm willing to, um, do sex scenes as part of the deal. You know, if you need an older woman. You usually don't, do you? Use older women, I mean."

"I have," said Jake. "Usually not."

"Well, I could be an extra body, or whatever. And there are lots of guys hanging around the sex institute who'd do it for nothing that are a damn sight better looking than any of these guys, that's for sure. Of course, they might not be able to get it up. There are so many goofballs out there who think they're god's gift to women, but when it comes right down to it they can't deliver. Are you and Jazz doing a scene?"

"Not unless she's paid. She's pissed about being passed over for the lead."

"Yeah, well, she never was in the running for that. Mindy needed a name so Shannen had it in the bag. Then Will put up half the budget on the condition Moira got the part."

"Worthingham, eh? How do you know him?"

She considered how to answer. "I can't go into detail since he's a client, but he hired me as an escort to a swing party where I happened to introduce him to Mindy."

"Oh, guys, I hate to say this but I have to go," Joaquin said, glancing over at Julie who was gesturing impatiently outside the sliding glass door. "Looks like something's about to happen." He hurried off.

Janus lowered her voice to a conspiratorial whisper. "It's about time they got this show on the road. Let me tell you, I wasn't crazy about talking Moira into doing this."

"She didn't want to do it?" said Jake.

"Hell, he didn't even tell her it was a fuck film, which is strictly out to lunch. This is top secret, so don't tell anybody. He kicked in an extra two grand for her to do it. You know, cash, no deferral. The others would have a shit fit if they found out."

"Who the fuck are you?" slurred Jazz, sloshing wine from her glass onto the floor.

"What?" Janus said, startled.

"I saaaaaaaaaaaid, who the fuck are you?" said Jazz, her nostrils flaring. "Oh, Janus! You look diff'rent. Don't mind me, I'm just fucking wif you." She finished off her wine then glared at the empty glass. "Everybody's axing me to get naked for this damn thing. Not me. I'm not just some *body*." She made a sweeping gesture with her glass. "I'm an actress, a le-gi-ti-mate actress. I've done dinner theater in Florida wif Burt Reynolds. I've done A.C.T. I got me a portfolio and everything, yes! Ha! One thing's for damn sure, I'm not doin' no damn fuck film for nothing. No sir, not this girl. Now if they needs a Black girl, yes I'm Black, can't do nothing about that, thank you very much, then we be talking."

"Hey, Jazz!" Joe hollered. "Come on down and watch us tape."

"I'll be right wif you, sweetheart," she purred, her eyes half shut. "Gots to go. My *good* lookin' *young* white boy requires my assistance. But first, where's the damn red wine?"

"There's some left on the buffet table," said Janus.

"Fine." She made an exaggerated bow then straightened up with a stagger. She left snickering with more of her butt exposed.

"She's half-mast and seven sheets to the wind," said Janus. "She'll end up between the sheets before all's said and done."

"No," said Jake. "I won't let that happen unless they meet her terms. But I doubt I'll have to bother. She can take care of herself."

"Worthingham's coming this way," said Janus. "You should get to know him. He might help you with your project, you know, since you've done so much for Mindy."

"All I've done is tell her why she's going to lose money."

"I was wondering," Worthingham said to Janus as he approached. "If it bothers you that Mindy expects you to do a sex scene when she won't do one herself?"

"Oh, no, she's a public school teacher, for Christ's sake. If one of her students or a parent or another teacher recognized her—" she stopped, suspecting he was toying with her. "Will, have you met Jake Zakheim, the director?"

He shifted his eyes slightly to Jake. "Zakheim?" His grin crinkled the skin around his blue eyes. "Funny, you don't look Jewish."

"That's because I'm not." He fidgeted with a bottle cap, annoyed by his clipped, loud voice and the heavy smell of mint and cologne. "Zakheim's my *nom de porn.*"

"*Nom de porn?*" The grin went away. "Why Jewish?"

"It was an ex-partner's idea, since most distributors are Jewish and neither of us were. He figured our films would be taken more seriously with a Jewish name on them. Anyway, no one uses real names. I know a Jewish director who uses an Italian name, an Irishman with a Spanish name, and a tiny Jewish princess who makes male gay films and passes herself off as a large Black man. And I have other names, like Petant Troudecul or Fritz Geminer for gay flicks, and Viva La Femme for lesbian features." The bottle cap fell from his hand. Jake hesitated then bent down to pick it up.

Worthingham turned his smile off then shifted his eyes away.

2

An Expensive Lady

Changing light and shifting wind added to Julie's concerns over light-ing and sound distortions so typical of low budget schlock. Then, too, there were the actors—Joe booming as if he were on stage and Moira mumbling. Only Shannen kept a consistent, realistic volume.

"What say, Min, we make this one a take?" said Joaquin. "Tape's cheap."

"I'm ready," said Shannen.

"Ditto," said Joe. "Let's do it." Then, noticing Moira's weak smile, he asked her, "You okay? Nervous? Don't be. Piece of cake."

Julie aimed the boom microphone. "We have lots of wind distor-tion here, Joaq."

"No way we're gonna get perfect sound," said Joaquin. "Do the best you can and we'll filter it out later."

Julie muttered, "Pretty freaking rinky dink."

"We don't have time," said Joaquin. "We're going to have to live with it."

"Action!" yelled Mindy.

Shannen looked around anxiously. "I can't do this! I thought I could, but I can't."

"Oh, Jenn, chill out," Moira said in the exaggerated fashion of an amateur. "I mean, you don't *have* to do anything, you know."

WORTHINGHAM joined Jake on the deck looking down on the action in the backyard. "What do you think of Moira?" he whispered.

Jake muttered, "A bit stiff." He didn't like her black velvet blouse fringed by white taffeta either. Made her look like a French maid.

"With ta-ta's like hers, you're talking about acting? Or did I misinterpret what you meant by stiff?"

Jake frowned, not looking at him.

"You scouting for talent? I know a cute little teenybopper with a bodacious rack of hooters who's looking for work."/

Bodacious? Jake bit his lower lip.

"Don't know if she can act, but she sure as hell can make a dead man hard." He stared at Jake. "She's a college student. Sharp as a tack. Great personality."

"Maybe I can help," said Jake, keeping his eye on the action below.

"You have a card?"

Jake pulled a card out of a shirt pocket. "That's my porn card," he said, as if he had others of better quality, which he didn't.

Worthingham took the card into his beefy, manicured hands and examined it, then put it into an Italian wallet smelling of new leather.

"I feel so out of place," Shannen sighed. "I've got nothing in common with these people."

"Don't take things so personal," said Joe, stroking her cheek. "Imagine we're in a church in a strange town. What you think of the congregation doesn't matter since we're all reflections of the Almighty. By suspending judgment and uniting with strangers we expose everything we are to the Light. Without shame or secrets, we acknowledge our connection with everyone and, thereby, the Almighty. Time has been suspended. We shall never grow old or die. Like monsters and gods, nothing restrains or inhibits us."

"Say what?" mumbled Jazz, stumbling up to Jake. "What kind of shit is that?"

"Shhh!" shushed Jake. "They're taping."

"Well, shut my mowf," she mumbled, sticking a cigarette in it.

Shannen screwed up her face and said, "The Almighty?"

"We have become ...," Moira stumbled, "sacred and obsessive? Um, through sex we, um, get to God?"

"Sh-he-it," Jazz scowled under her breath. "They hired that White bitch 'stead of me? Goes to show what being White'll do for you." She made a crazy little laugh.

"Who's your friend?" Worthingham said to Jake.

"She's my thrill, Jasmyn Esad," Jake whispered. "How would you describe our relationship, Miss Esad?"

"Too close for comfort," she snarled, her nostrils flaring.

"What was once men and women, um," Moira mumbled, focusing on Joe as he mouthed her lines, "has become ejaculation, orgasm and, um. A fixed idea? Ultimately we're all children of God. From ourselves, to others, to God?"

"As god plays with the time of the surface world," Joe boomed, like an evangelist, "so should the inner divine man play with the revealed wonders of God in this world to open the Divine Wisdom in all creatures. The Divine Melody comes not from a choir of angels but from the transformation of this bodily life into joyful play."

"Excuse me?" snorted Jazz. "Who the fuck wro' that crap? You, Jake?" She chuckled. "That's right. That shit stinks so bad, you had to've wrote it."

"Shhhhhh!" Jake shushed.

"SHE-HE-IT!" replied Jazz.

"Bart, right about now I feel like I'm knee deep in something," said Shannen.

"Ha! Ha! Ha! Ha!" Jazz broke into loud laughter. "That's right! You tell that shit head a thing or two!"

"Cut!" yelled Mindy, irritated.

"Ha! Ha! Ha!" laughed Joe.

Mindy turned to Joaquin. "What do you think, Jack?" she asked.

"Looked great. Let's go in for close-ups so we can mike for better sound."

"Here comes my pretty, little, White boy," said Jazz, watching Joe leaping up the stairs. "Can't get enough of me. Like white on rice."

"Well, I don't think he's worfy of you," said Jake.

"Wor-*thy*," she said, darkly. "The *word's* worthy."

"Has he axed you to go into a betroom wif him?" asked Jake.

"No, he has not *asked* me to any *bed*room *with* him. It's not that kind of party. We're just friends, that's all. He's a very nice boy." She frowned. "Am I too drunk? Am I talking shit?"

"Talking shit?" said Jake. "You? Na. Never."

"Jazz!" yelled Joe on his way up, vaguely noticing Ben leaning against the wall behind Jake and Jazz. "You took my cigarettes. Can I have one?"

"Ha! Ha! Sure." She stuck her cigarette back in her mouth then reached into her cleavage for the pack.

BEN had been following Jazz. When he heard *Esad,* he stepped out on the deck, trying to remember where he'd heard the name *Esad* before.

"Esad?" said Worthingham. "What kind of name is that? African?"

"That's my pro-fess-ion-al name," she said with a smirk.

"Does it mean something in African?" Worthingham persisted.

"It means something, but you gonna have to find that out your own self."

"Is Jasmyn also a professional name?"

Professional name? Jasmyn Esad. That's it! Ben realized. The lady wrestler. Billed herself as an Ethiopian princess. He'd gone to see her fight a biker dyke because the photo of her on a flyer promoting the fight reminded him of his presumed dead wife who'd been a pro-wrestler. Esad had ended up going too far in dishing out insults at the start of the match, calling her biker dyke opponent a fat, stupid, white bitch. Took a severe beating for it. The fight had to be stopped. Very interesting, indeed.

"My mama named me after some White boy she had a crush on, Jason something-or-other. Myself, I prefer Latinos. They gots lots of fire. Frankly, I don't know why I'm wif this old White fart. Must be crazy. Ha!"

Jake grinned. "You're named after a White boy?"

"Now, don't you laugh at my mama!" said Jazz.

"I look forward to seeing more of you," Worthingham winked.

Jazz gestured with her cigarette, brushing it against his jacket. "I'll haf you know I'm a *le-gi-ti-mate* actress. If you wants to see me naked, I don't come cheap."

"I'm sure you are an expensive lady," he said, brushing off his sleeve, "and no doubt worth every penny." He glanced at Dr. Ben then back at Jake. "We'll talk later."

"That man's evil," Jazz sneered after he left.

"What?" said Jake.

"He gave me the Evil Eye. Now don't tell me you didn't notice."

"What's this?" Jake grimaced. "Voodoo shit again?"

"Don't mock what you don't understand."

"Like what? His eyes are sunken. He probably looks like he's giving the evil eye all the time. What makes you so sure he's evil, other than he's a fucking lawyer?"

"I know. I know about these things. Trust me."

"Yeah, right," said Jake, noticing Ben off to the side, apparently listening in.

"He is weird," said Joe, agreeing with Jazz. "By the way, what does Esad mean?"

"Huh?" said Jazz. "Oh, that's just a joke 'tween Jake and me. Stands for Eat Shit And Die. Means we're fucking wif him, that's all. I don' want the motherfucker to know who I am. Gimme another cigarette." She took the pack from Joe.

"Jake, it's good to see you again," said Joe. "I thought you quit the business."

"More or less," he said, self-conscious with Ben listening in. "I got married."

"Say no more. It's tough finding a woman in the biz who won't eventually go jealous on you."

"Well, that's not why I got out. I never intended porn to be my life's work so I had to quit sooner or later. Anyway, I was tired of getting fucked over."

"You know, I've been in the biz for going on six years and haven't had any trouble to speak of," said Joe. "Oh, sure, piddling shit'll hit the fan every now and then but nothing like what I'd have to put up with on some dumb fuck job in the real world. No offense, but you may have brought it on yourself."

"That's what I keep tellin' him! If you think shit's gonna happen, then it will. Fact!"

"Well, there's a world of difference between being an actor as opposed to a producer-director," said Jake. "I've no problem with the actual making of a movie, it's the before and after that's hell. Especially the after."

"Yeah, I know what you mean. You can't just do the job, get paid and go home. But no matter what business you're in, if you're in charge, headaches are part of the deal."

"That's right!" said Jazz. "You should listen to this boy."

"Have you ever known somebody who brought you nothing but trouble?" asked Jake. "You know, like, if he or she introduced you to somebody, that person would be trouble. If she did you a favor, it'd cost you more than it was worth. No matter what that person did, it *always* brought trouble."

"Yeah," Joe nodded. "Matter of fact I have."

"What are you getting at?" asked Jazz, suspicious.

"That's the way it's been with me and porn. Seems like whenever I get involved in it, I'm punished for my efforts. Makes me mindful of the Law of Life's Highway. If everything's coming at you, you're in the wrong lane."

"Fuck," said Jazz. "What a cop-out. You get in trouble 'cause you fuck up, simple as that. You just plain fuck up. You get what you deserve, end of story."

"Does that mean the rumor going around about you stirring up more trouble is bogus?"

"Depends on if I'm shown real money," Jake said, wondering if Ben had followed Jazz out onto the deck. "If I'm to be a whore, I don't want to be a two-bit whore."

"Ooooh, a whore, are we?" laughed Joe. "The way I see it, porn's a big wonderful party. Sure I enjoy a challenge now and then but when you get right down to it, I love to fuck and for me porn's fucking hog heaven."

"That's right!" said Jazz. "When shove comes to push your problem's ne-ga-tive thinking. You always thinking you gonna get screwed, so it happens. It's all your own damn fault, nobody else's. The troof hurts, don' it?"

"The key word here is whore," said Joe. "You think of yourself as a whore. Not that we don't have them in the biz; but if a working girl's in it for the money, she can make more elsewhere. If fun's not part of the picture and you're only in it for the bucks, that's when you're a two-bit whore."

"Thank you!" said Jazz. "And you be the worst kind of whore 'cause any whore wurf her salt ain't in it just for no damn money. No sir. It's the adventure, the drama — the control, not just money. Your problem's you're too damn negative and all you think about all the damn time is your damn precious money."

"Hey, hey." Jake held up his palm. "I'm afraid I got my metawhores mixed."

"Metawhores?" Joe laughed.

"Money's not the most important thing to me, never has been." Jake glanced at Ben who, having realized he'd been spotted, had moved in closer. "A project has to stimulate me in other ways, be it fun, ambition, whatever. *But* when I see the realities behind the fantasies, bucks become important. Money's real, fun and ambition are fantasies."

"Joe!" yelled Joaquin. "Get your ugly butt down here. We need you for a take."

"Got to go." Joe dropped his cigarette into Jake's half empty bottle on the railing then bounded down the stairs.

"I'm bored." Jazz said as she stuffed the cigarette pack down the front of her dress. "Let's go somewhere for a smoke. I don' need to listen to that crap."

"Let me get another beer then let's go out on the front porch," said Jake. "Can't stand the acting, eh?"

"Huh? Shit, none of them can act wurf a damn, but I'm a Christian and that script's blas-a-me. I don' need to hear that shit. Who the fuck Mindy think she is?"

"A pornographic priestess," said Jake.

"She is that, indeed," said Ben. "That shit you think stinks so bad comes from Jacob Boehme, the primary source of Protestant mystical theology, early 16th century."

"Whatchoo talking about?" Jazz snapped, annoyed.

"The script paraphrases him, as well as Christian and Jewish Gnostics. The Jewish version stems from the Kabala, wherein the true god is a sexual being. The Gnostics believed the world we see was created by an evil, or at least an iniquitous god."

"*Iniqui*-what?" said Jazz.

"Utterly harmful. Wrong and immoral, resulting in great injustice or unfairness. Behind this god stands the true God, the discovery of whom is every Gnostic's goal. In every human there's a small spark of the divine, and it's the task of every Gnostic to reunite his spark. To free their sparks of the divine, Gnostics *must* violate social rules. The best way to do that is through sex."

"Shit, I was a prostitute doing all kinds of sex, violating all kinds of rules, and I sure the fuck didn't see no divine sparks."

"That's because you weren't aware of what you were doing."

"I knew exactly what I was doing!!! I fucking knew that *and* the why for!!"

"Uh, Jazz," said Jake. "Let's go have that smoke."

"GIMME some red wine," Jazz growled. "That little weasel's been following me around talking all kinds of stupid shit, like how he likes big butts and wants to jump my bones." She stopped herself from adding that he'd offered her three thousand dollars if she'd let him do whatever he wanted with her butt for two hours. She'd turned him down, thinking he might give her more, but also to give her time to think about it.

Jake opened the cooler on the floor and took out a Guinness, then offered it to her.

"That stuff is *nasty*," she scowled. "You wanna make me sick or somethin'?" She shoved the cooler's contents around. "Ah! This'll do. Dos X, Mex'can beer."

"The double cross," said Jake.

Jazz lost her balance as she straighten up, staggering against an elegantly dressed fiftyish Danish woman whose drink spilled on her dress.

"Oh, I am so very sorry," said the Dane. "I hope I didn't ruin your so nice dress."

Jazz looked at the thick red liquid in her glass. "What's that?"

"Vodka and tomato juice," said the Dane.

"A Bloody Mary!" said Jazz. "Where kin I get me one of those?"

"My son, Lars, is mixing drinks in the master bedroom. Tell him I sent you. My name's Karin."

"Lars? I like that name. Where is this betroom?"

Jake took hold of her arm. "Let's go out front for that smoke."

"I wanna get me a Bloody Mary first," she protested.

"First, outside, let's talk." He guided her toward the door.

"What's so damn important?"

"Jake! Jake!" Janus yelled, hurrying after them. "You're not leaving, are you?"

"What's this?" Jake looked at her leather underwear and knee-high lace-up boots.

Janus smiled sheepishly. "I thought I better start getting people in the mood before they got it in their heads to leave. We desperately need younger bodies, and we're about ready for the group scene. Could you stay at least through the beginning of the orgy?"

"Don't worry," he said. "We're just going out for a smoke."

"Oh." She looked uneasy. "Good. Then I'll see you?"

"I wouldn't leave without saying good-bye."

Janus smiled nervously and turned back.

"If I were her, I'd keep that bony ass covered," Jazz said, eyeing the large opening in her leather panties.

Jake opened the front door and scanned the area to determine whether the shrubs offered a sufficient screen from curious neighbors. A White man and a Black woman seen together in Benicia, a conservative backwater, might draw unwanted attention.

Satisfied, he sat on the steps.

"Uh-uh, I will not sit on no dirty porch and fuck up my dress. No sir, not this girl."

He reached up. "Give me a cig."

She made a face and handed him the pack.

"You want to leave?" he said, taking out a cigarette.

"Gif me my damn cigarettes!" She grabbed the pack and a couple of cigarettes fell out into a rosebush. "Damn! Look what you made me do!" A thorn caught her dress when she reached into the bush. "Damn! No, I don' wanna leave just yet. I need to make me some money, period."

"They make you an offer?"

"No, just a $200 deferral, might as well be nothing. I'd never see any of it, that's for damn sure. She expects me to fuck in front of these sorry ass ol' white folks for the fun of it. I don't think so." She snickered. "You see how they be checking on my booty?"

"You like the attention don't you, little girl?"

"Yeah," she said in a light happy voice. "I do. They all acting like they be so interested in what I'm saying when all they're really doing is lusting after my black ass." She frowned. "Too bad they all be so damn old. Who'd want to watch them fuck? Who they kidding?" She took a swig of double cross beer. "They all must be fuckin' bored to def with their white bread American lives, thinking their pathetic selves glamorous being in a porno film, ha!"

"The two leading ladies have nice butts," Jake said softly to encourage her to lower her voice.

"Shit," she scowled. "What the fuck you talkin' 'bout? Those tiny, pale things? You gots to be kiddin'."

"Hey, hey," said Jake, holding up his hands. "Your butt beats the competition, which is better than having no competition?"

"There is *no* damn competition," she snarled.

AS FAR BACK as he could remember, Ben had fantasized another life. At eleven, while practicing singing and playing instruments, he fantasized a life as a child blues performer who was admired and respected and praised by adults for his soulful songs. In his teenage daydreams, he was a teen heartthrob sensation who toured with a Black back-up band so he could get to know their lead female singer, a tall, beautiful Black woman with a big smile and a Big Butt. She would eventually become his Lady. This did not go over well with White America, and radio stations stopped playing his music. His duets with his Lady were the centerpiece in their shows. Their love and chemistry stirred up both envy and anger. Occasionally he'd have to perform with a battered face, which helped solidify his credentials as a genius of rhythm and blues. He and his Lady were inseparable and their mixed race audiences came to love her, too.

His fantasies stopped when he met his wife, then started up again some years after her disappearance, when he resumed composing music. This time around, he imagined his missing wife as his Lady, that they'd managed to magically return in teenage bodies with all the wisdom they'd gathered over time.

In his original fantasies, as a boy and a teen, sex had been very much a part of it. In the return to a youthful version, he very much wanted to include sexual fantasies, but found he couldn't. Not with her, nor with anyone. He could only imagine merging into the hidden depths of their music performances. In the earlier versions, his Lady had followed his lead, expecting him to be her guide. Then, after the disaster on Riley's last film, his Lady had merged with him, to save him. He found himself listening to her, following her lead as if She were a goddess, his guide to the Underworld. Being vulnerable, he could not resist this fantasy. It was a dangerous thing to do, because he was incapable of discerning what he'd energetically merged with.

"Okay!" Julie snapped at Ben. Then, adjusting her tone, she went on, "I'm not Olli's daughter by blood. I'm here at his directive to annoy and distract you, to draw the attention of the goddesses to you. The long and short of it is to entice you into a stream of time. To do that, I have to be mysterious. It'd work better if you had no idea of what I'm up to."

Ben nodded. "Okay. Stream of time." Then he paused when he saw Jake and Jazz entering the living room. Noticing Jake's distracted grin and how he was handling himself he knew Jake was vulnerable.

"Do what you have to do," he said to Julie as he stood up.

"Take off your damn hat! I'm *not* being seen wif you if you keep that damn thing on," Jazz said as she walked away before he took it off.

Jake placed his cap on a shelf behind a couch on which a wizened gent lay atop a hefty fifty-something woman with his hand up her dress. She winked up at Jake.

"Still the fool, tangled up in the affairs of anima women and their labyrinthine riddles," said Dr. Ben as he approached Jake from behind.

Jake turned, his brow furrowed. "Better than chasing after them acting like a fool."

"Ah, well, the key word there is *acting*." Ben rocked his head side to side "I enjoy annoying anima women in social situations. Throws them off their game. Nothing they can say or do makes an impression. I just keep right on annoying them."

"Well, it makes you look like a nut job, doc." Jake frowned. Something smelled sickeningly sweet.

"I don't care what these people think. As far as the ladies go, any anima-possessed woman worth her salt knows her worshippers are fools, clowns if you will. My over the top behavior calls their attention to the absurdity of taking themselves seriously. And you're not exactly above playing the fool fucking with people either, by the way."

"Okay. Well, thanks for the heads up," said Jake as he turned away to leave.

"Remember our little talk from what, fifteen years ago?" Ben held up a pointer finger, then started moving it slowly, in circles. "You came to my clinic to discuss my investing in a project of yours. We ended up talking about other things. Like your anima, ambivalence, and your being sexually assaulted in the army."

"Wait a minute! What the hell?" He'd never mentioned that to anyone, other than shrinks and a chaplain. If he told Ben, of all people, he definitely would have remembered that. He motioned him toward an empty hallway. "We never discussed any such thing."

"Well, as I recall, we were talking about your previous work," Ben said, "and I mentioned how I much I liked the gang bang rape scene in your army stockade film, and—"

"Okay, okay, okay, maybe you did," said Jake, smelling something vaguely familiar, smoky and ammonia-like. "But I didn't say anything about *my* being raped."

"Well, I *do* beg to differ. You mentioned feeling *conflicted* and very horny after your discharge from the stockade. Said you got into porn to work out sex issues. *Especially* those that cropped up in the army."

"I didn't say *especially* anything cropping up from the army!"

"My specialty is sexual aberrance, *especially* those that break laws. I can easily spot a victim, as well as a predator. When I saw your film, I *knew* whoever made it had been raped. You wrote it, directed it and edited it. Let's say your film told me. It told me other things as well. Like you did it to seek relief, to take away the shame. But it didn't." He clasped his hands together, chin level. "Want to know why?"

Jake tried to appear calm. He remembered attempting to bond with him, as a potential investor, by talking shop. Psychology had been a major interest of his since high school. At some point, though, he'd sensed an ulterior motive behind Ben's probing. He was raising money for a hetero film but Ben kept harping on about re-visiting male rape in a gay film, and taking it to a whole other level. Rape, as the ticket to the Underworld.

"You told me how depressed and spaced you felt when you got into porn. Or, as you so elegantly put it, *probing the dark world.* You said you felt as if you'd sold your soul to the devil and were afraid you could never come back or obtain the perspective necessary to live. You did it because you wanted to confront various uglies to gain depth and understanding, but feared you'd get lost and gain nothing."

Dr. Ben was quoting him! That Ben could remember, after all these years, not just what he said, but how he said it, shocked him. It also brought back the memory of the overwhelming feelings of fear and loathing he had had at the beginning of his porn career. His friends from the stockade came out crazy and suicidal, and his civilian friends considered him to be just like them. He had to find a way to deal with his shame and degradation. Porn offered a different perspective. The people in the business experienced the things he feared as fun, not as shameful or degrading.

"You were right to doubt yourself because pornography *is* a repository for dangerous knowledge," said Ben. "Dangerous, because what brings on the self-transcendence, the seeing through to the depths visionaries seek, can result in self-destruction for ordinary people. And that, my friend, is what you're afraid of. Self-destruction. That, and that you may be ordinary."

He recalled Ben's strange intensity during their discussion of the rape scene, how he'd felt as if he were being seduced. Or worse, hypnotized. Because, in some strange way, he was tempted, which was probably the real reason why he'd ended the interview.

"You hold back because you complicate things with moral issues, and concern over hurting yourself or others. Where you must go, you have to knowingly break rules to bounce freely off the sexual energy of others, *if* you are to *see through* to the depths."

He remembered Ben saying something about pushing limits in a gay film, since he was too inhibited to do so in a hetero film.

"I'm more into balance and harmony."

Ben considered this. "The Nirvana complex. Avoid the work of psychic reality by escape into spiritual salvation. The cure is not to get rid of, or to give up. The Buddha's last words were *decay is inherent to all composite things—work your salvation with diligence.* Meaning: work with decay."

"All right, everybody!" Mindy shouted, changing the tape. "We need a few minutes' worth of dancing before the next sequence." She punched in a hip hop number. "We're behind schedule so just go for it."

Jake excused himself when he spotted Jazz, who rolled her eyes at him as if to say, "Don't make me wish you weren't here." He resigned himself to a few basic moves while she glided, gracefully interweaving through the dancers, arms waving sinuously above her head to the nasty driving beat. Jake considered her one of the clumsiest women he had ever known, yet she could dance on air; whereas he couldn't dance to save his soul.

She stuck a finger in her mouth, and the other dancers cheered. She tossed Jake a *check out the goofy White folks* smirk.

Scanning the slack-fleshed faces drawn into smiles of delight, Jake realized he didn't care what they thought of his dancing. This somehow freed him to do whatever he pleased. The absurdity of it all inspired him to play a fool mesmerized by a femme fatale.

Jazz banged her booty against him, looking irritated. And he turned away, as if from the temptations of her undulating ass.

"Yeah! Okay! Push it, babe!" Ben yelled. "P-p-p-push it! Push it real good!" The throbbing music: "*Give it up, gonna ssuh-ssuh-ssuh-suck yo ass-ss-ss-ssss.*"

Jazz arched her back, so that when they watched each other's sorry, shriveled white asses they'd remember the Butt-That-Got-Away.

"Gonna ride you like the wind!" Ben yelled bucking his hips. "Oh, baby, Ba-By!!"

Jake dropped to his knees and stared awestruck at her swaying derriere as it came closer and closer until it buffeted his face. Jazz thrust her semi-bare butt forward and everyone yelled and clapped as Jake felt her butt muscles tighten on his face. She threw her head back, arms straight out, bending backward, every muscle in her body quivering.

Her audience kept on cheering after the song ended.

"Hey, guys that was fucking great," said Joaquin as he put the camera back on the tripod. "It'll make the movie. You missed your calling, Jake. You're a natural comedian."

"Wai' a da, mi-nu'!" said Jazz, covering her mouth. "You shot that wifout my permission? Now I *am* going to be paid for *that*!"

"That wasn't a sex scene, Jazz," said Jake, rising up.

"I'm just fucking wif you," she mumbled.

"You have to do a sex scene after that dance," Joaquin nudged Jake. "Come on, Jake, you horn dog, you could use a little pork pie."

Jazz showed them a soft contact lens on her palm. "I gotta get me a wet cloth or somethin'. Your stupid dance distracted me and I caught my lens on a fingernail."

"Really?" said Jake. "On your fingernail?"

"I put it in my mowf to keep it wet then everybody started making nasty sounds and you got all stoop-id."

Jake shook his head in disbelief. "You put it in your mouth?"

"You can't let 'em dry out," she explained. "I stuck it on the roof of my mowf. I took it out 'cause it makes me talk funny. I hope they got some saline solution somewhere."

"Ask make-up," said Joaquin.

"Where's that?" asked Jazz.

"In the bedroom wif the mixed drinks," said Jake.

"Drinks?" She perked up. "Oh, yeah. Excuse me, gentlemen. I've got business to attend to." She dashed off, passing by Moira who was gazing at Jake with a placid smile.

"Let's rewind and have a look," said Joaquin.

"Yeah, sure," Jake said, noticing Moira watching him as if she were considering approaching them.

"Can you imagine catching a soft lens in your *eye* on a *fingernail*," Joaquin said as he pushed rewind. "Only Jazz could pull something like that off." They both laughed.

"Excuse me," said Moira. "I'm sorry. Am I interrupting something?"

"Uh, no, no," Jake stammered as he turned to face her. "No problem."

"You're Jake Zakheim, right?"

"Now and then," he said with a foolish grin. Her confused look prompted him to add, "Yes. Yes, I am."

"Um, this may sound silly but the first, um, porno I ever saw was one of yours."

Jake's grin faded. "That must have been strange. I remember the first hard core film I saw. It struck me as, uh, very..."

"Scary?" she giggled.

"Yeah," said Jake. "Uh could you elaborate on that? What do you mean by scary?"

"Oh." She averted her eyes and rocked her head back and forth a few times until her sparkle returned. "There was this one scene, okay, where a guy sticks his, um," she giggled, "his cock, um, in this lady's bum." She giggled again. "And, um, he shoved it like way up in there, and it's like really, really big and fat and long and everything. Then this other lady, she like pulls it out and, um," she crinkled her face, "you could see like way up inside her. Her bum hole was like this, um, like a big gaping hole. Scary."

"I remember that shot," said Joaquin. "That was Storey Welles, known in the biz as Stovepipe Wells because her asshole did that. See, stovepipe's what that kind of shot's called in the industry."

Moira grimaced. "*Then* the lady who like took it out, puts *it* like in her mouth and sucks on it without cleaning it or anything and, um. Like you could see it was, um, dirty."

"Now that's called Southern love," said Joaquin. "Coined back in the seventies when somebody noticed southern belles liked sucking on dicks fresh out of assholes."

"I had no idea people did things like that," Moira tittered, then whispered, "much less, you know, like on film, like for all the world to see."

Joaquin laughed. "You have to admit, bro, we've done some sick shit in our day."

Jake tossed him an annoyed look, then to Moira, "You didn't like the film, then?"

"Oh, it was disgusting! I had my eyes closed through most of it." She giggled.

Jake cleared his throat. "How old were you when you saw it."

"Twelve," she said, proudly.

"Twelve! That's way too young to see something like that."

Moira looked surprised, then thoughtful. "I don't think so. Sex isn't so scary if you don't hide it. Besides, it's better to learn about sex that way then, you know, like be a virgin and not know what to do. Sex would be really scary then." She giggled. "I've seen all your movies. They're cool. A great way to learn about, um, ... being *dirty*."

Jake smiled vacantly. He did *not* know what to say to that.

"I found it!" said Joaquin. "Check it out."

They watched Jazz's hand advancing on the monitor in slow motion, fingers bent, across her face to her eye. The two men groaned when her eyes squeezed shut, then laughed at her double take, squinting at her hand. When she stuck her finger in her mouth, they roared with laughter. Their laughter carried across the dining room, through the open glass doors to the deck where it hooked onto Shannen's curiosity.

"What's so funny?" Moira asked, squinting at the monitor.

"Nothing," Jake said, suppressing his laughter. "It's an in-joke."

Shannen approached, wearing a purple silk robe.

"How are you, Jake?" she said, cocking her head to one side with a look of concern. "I heard about Cedar. You all right?"

"I'll survive," Jake said, surprised by this unexpected recognition of his love for his ex, that she thought his love mattered. Her face said, *Poor Jake.*

"Didn't she do anything to try to hold the relationship together?"

"Her idea of trying was to allow me to try," he said with a slight quaver. Shannen shook her head, *What a shame.*

Then he said something he'd imagined saying to his ex-wife. "It reminded me of a line from an old song. *I got a feeling, that you been stealing, all of the love I thought I'd been giving to you.*" Shannen gave him a strange look.

"Believe me, bro, you're better off without that witch," said Joaquin. "She could learn a thing or two from a couple of whores I overheard talking about what makes a good whore. One of them said, and I quote: A good whore is one who can take a man for everything he has yet leave him feeling he got a good deal. Wives don't care how you feel, bro. If they do, it's that you feel screwed blue and tattooed when they leave."

"Okay, people!" Mindy shouted. "Time for Shannen's dance of the seven veils. Form a big circle. The camera's God, and God's interest is in the tease, so keep any touchy-feely brief. Shannen will mime the dance and the music will be added later. We need ambient sound so go ahead and talk, but keep it down. We don't want to hear what you're actually saying. I want *all* of you to look as if you want to eat her up."

"No prob-lemo!" yelled Ben.

"I miss anything?" Jazz said, holding a Bloody Mary in her hand.

"Na," said Jake. "Shannen's gonna dance."

Shannen slid off her robe, her veiled body evoking appreciative murmurs.

"Dance? Hrmmmmph. If they want dancing, they should've hired me. They gots to pay me something now 'cause I tore my lens and that's gonna cost me money I don't have." She flicked her wrist, spilling some of her drink. "If they ain't payin' me nothing, I wanna leave right now. I can only see through one eye as it is."

"Come on, Jazz. They're about to start shooting."

"And you'll be saying the same thing an hour from now."

"I hope not," said Joe as he approached her from behind. "I've built up quite a load these past three days. If I don't pop soon I'm gonna burst. Mindy said I could bone you in the orgy scene if I disguise myself. What'd ya say?"

"You'll haf to ax the old fart about that," said Jazz.

"What's this? You guys monogamous or something? Jake, you just got divorced and you got yourself into another monogamous relationship? Ha! Ha! Ha!"

"I'm divorced, too," Jazz said frostily. "That's no reason not to be monogamous."

"Would you three mind sitting in front of the couch?" Mindy said, gesturing at a couch with the oldest extras on it.

"Come on, Jake," said Joe, as they repositioned themselves by the couch. "You don't expect me to believe you never played around the entire time you were married."

"I considered it, yeah."

He managed to suppress any such thoughts by respecting the Fourth Wall, an invisible barrier separating those behind the camera from those in front. Respecting that wall, he believed, separated the pro from the sleaze ball. Playing around with actresses was a trap guaranteed to suck you into the seedy side of the skin trade. The only loophole Jake allowed was when an actor failed to perform and a stunt cock was not available. He closed even that one after he met Cedar.

"Why do that to yourself? There's nothing wrong with having a good time?"

"With a porno bimbo?" hissed Jazz. "Pleeeease. Only a low life'd betray his wife for a porn star. If that hurts, I don't care, but that's the way I feel about it."

"Penile assertive behavior costs you one way or another," Jake stage whispered.

"All right, everybody," yelled Mindy. "Action!"

"Hey, go for the burn, bro," whispered Joe. "Nothing in life's free, and nothing's worth paying for like good, hot sex."

"Rolling," said Joaquin as he followed Shannen with the camera.

"If you're always concerned about what might happen, then chances are something will," said Joe. "Same thing with relationships. We bring our worst nightmares onto ourselves."

Jazz snarled, "If he fucks some bimbo, you're damn straight it'll bring on his worse nightmare."

Shannen affected a slinky way of moving into the center of the circle, shaking her hips in a belly dancer's motion while watching the anticipation building up in her admirers. Fans flocked to strip joints around the world to see her, to have their picture taken with a pornographic goddess. She once told Jake, while watching him intently, being the only naked person in a crowd of admirers sometimes gave her a spontaneous orgasm. She'd looked at him as if his reaction to what she'd just said was in some way important.

Shannen pursed her lips, reddening them, then brushed Jake with a veil. He retreated behind a foolish grin as she removed a veil from her chest and dropped it over his head. When he removed the scarf he found himself faced with a close view of her tits and the scattered blue veins on the creamy surface just under the skin, and a little crimson stain where her round breasts met and the violet shadow began. Her bust seemed bigger, firmer than he remembered. In fact, her entire body had better definition.

She shimmied away, crooking her arms, moving her fingers and shoulders.

"Why didn't you cop a feel?" asked Joe.

"With an avenging angel by my side? Why didn't you?"

"I've fucked her in so many films it isn't funny. Besides she's not my archetype."

Ben grabbed at the veil around Shannen's groin. She allowed him to take it, then moved deftly away.

"What a geek," Jake muttered.

"He's got bucks and connections up the ying yang," said Joe. "Half the budget's courtesy of psychiatrists from his clinic."

Shannon granted a gracious smile to a misshapen obese man of indeterminate age and an elderly podiatrist with pale slack skin and an open sore on his bare skull. Worried their window of opportunity was about to close, they both reached for a tit.

Shannen moved away, tossing a playful vampish look Jake's way.

Her seductiveness seemed to him a deception. He remembered the final hours of his last porn film. Two a.m., with a bloody sore in the crack of her ass from her cheeks being pulled apart too forcefully, and her mouth numb from futile attempts at reviving her partner, he told her he appreciated her professionalism under such trying conditions. She said she was enjoying herself, which he found hard to believe considering how everyone else wanted the damn scene over and done with so they could go home. She asked him if he'd step in as stunt cock. He said he could not, out of respect for his wife. That was when he first noticed the strange look Shannen sometimes gave him. It didn't seem sexual, but something about it made him want to fuck her. He left to slip off his wedding band in private, but by the time he returned her partner had miraculously rallied.

Shannen returned to bend over Jake, sweat glistening on her pale swaying breasts, smooth silken orbs close enough to smell. Fresh peppermint. *No Fourth Wall, I'm an actor,* he thought as he buried his face in undulating flesh, absorbing her warm, sweet milky aroma, her moist skin against his cheeks.

She dropped the final veil then danced away naked, to her inner music. A dance across time to be watched in darkness by strangers to some other music.

"Wipe that shit eating grin offa your damn face," Jazz muttered while maintaining an *isn't-this-fun* smile for the camera.

"Cut!" yelled Mindy. "All right everybody, we're behind schedule so let's get at it. Do your thing. We'll shoot whatever's interesting."

"All right! It's about time!" Joe said to Jazz. "I want to do you."

"I'd love to, baby," she purred, "but they ain't talked real money yet. When they do, I'll give you nooky you'll never forget."

"I'll see what I can do."

"You like to eat pussy?" asked Jazz.

"I moist certainly do," Joe winked, and walked off.

"Remember that white bread blonde bitch we saw earlier?" Jazz said to Jake. "They offered her four hundred dollars and she walked out on them. Damn straight I expect them to make me an offer, and it's gonna cost 'em for making me wait so damn long."

"What if they axe you to do it wif Dr. Ben? Maybe he'd foot the bill."

She frowned. "To tell the troof, I don' wanna do it with nobody, not even with that pretty White boy. All I want is for them to ask me. I wanna do like the White bitch did. Bicker, tell 'em all the shit I will and will not do, make a bunch of dumb ass demands and then, after they agree to everything, I up and walk out. Yep, that's what I want to do."

"Come on, Jazz. That's unprofessional. Why do something like that?"

"Un-pro-fess-ion-al! You callin' me unprofessional? Listen, baby, I *am* professional. All these losers are unprofessional. I am *the* professional here. That's right, you heard me. I haf the training, I haf paid my dues, I haf worked on stage and I haf rave reviews to prove it. I *am* the professional here and you best believe it. They'll pay *un*-professional pretty little White girls but not the *pro*-fessional beautiful Black girl and that ain't right. I don' care what you say, that just ain't right."

"Keep it down, will you," said Jake.

"I will not shut up! You said your piece and I listened politely but when I wanna say sumpin, you can't be bothered. You just don' wanna hear the troof, that's all. The troof hurts, don' it?"

"Say what you want, just keep it down," Jake whispered.

"That's right, Mr. White Is Right. Not only do you *not* want to take the time to hear what the Black girl's got to say, you don' want nobody else to either!"

"You've no idea how hard it is to talk to you. If you want to motivate people with insults, be my guest. No doubt you understand White folk better than I ever will."

As he turned away in exasperation, he spotted Janus across the room looking undecided as to whether to approach them.

"Look, I'm not stoop-id," she said lowering her voice. "I wouldn't' talk to them like that but you make me so damn mad wif that holier-than-thou shit you always dogging me wif. Always telling me what the fuck to do, like I'm stoop-id. Always lecturing, never listening. So that's it. End of story."

THIS SHOT will make the movie! Joaquin thought as he assessed angles from under the glass table. Sex with food, his favorite fantasy. From the table's point of view. *Brilliant!*

"You're the one who's uptight about wasting time, Joaquin Spanamaker," Julie said, squatting next to him. "It's a bitch to light and definitely not worth the time."

"Oh, it's worth it, alright," he said, aiming a light at Shannen's backside. "What'd I tell you? Looks great!"

"Looks scrunched," said Julie.

"Okay, okay," said Joaquin. "That's good, too. It's real."

"Sundae anyone?" said Mindy, brandishing a jar of maraschino cherries and a can of whipped cream.

"I will," Karin the Dane said, taking the whipped cream. "I know what she likes, yes?" She aimed the can at Shannen's pink tuft, caressing its nozzle with her fingertips until it spurt a stream of whipped cream onto her pubes. The spectators laughed then applauded when Mindy placed a cherry on top of the whipped cream.

"Oh, I like," Dr. Ben moaned. "I like it like that!"

"You're missing important stuff up here, Jack," said Julie.

"I can see everything from between her legs," Joaquin grunted. "Looks absolutely surreal. I should win an Oscar for this shot."

"Yeah, an Oscar Mayer Wiener up your ass. You've got more than anyone in their right mind would ever want to see from that angle."

"All right, all right." He moved out from under the table. "That was hot, though. You're going to love it, trust me. You're gonna eat your words, guaranteed."

"Sure I will," muttered Julie.

"The hot fudge is ready!" the podiatrist announced. "Let me know if it's too hot for you." He poured some on Shannen's left tit and she winced. "Too hot?"

"I want to eat your pussy," said Karin. "I want to make intimacy with you."

"Oh, chocolate nipples!" cooed a woman in her fifties with bright red-dyed hair.

The podiatrist smeared fudge over Shannen's thighs and calves, working his bony fingers down to her feet as he bent down to suck her chocolate toes.

Julie then noticed a fly on the sore in his scalp. *Joaquin would like that,* she thought, tapping him. *It's real.*

"Looks great, guys," said Joaquin, ignoring Julie's tap.

Shannen writhed as the center of attention in a glorious play land. The world a carousel, an amusement park of spinning lights and loving noises. She imagined herself in a Riley Theirault movie as a naughty Catholic schoolgirl at the mercy of trolls, twisted spirits of the unspeakable. Being devoured by admirers! *How delicious! What vile fun!*

Karin gripped the cherry stem with her lipstick-stained teeth and sucked the cherry off the mound and chewed it, the stem sticking out between her lips. Then she extended her tongue, seeking slick flesh, and buried her face in the whipped cream.

"Please be careful how you move, you guys," said Julie, shooing the fly away from the podiatrist's sore. "The sound's reverberating."

"Let me see the action," Joaquin said to Karin.

"What?" she said, confused. "You cannot see?"

"Angle your head to the side so I can see what you're doing. And pull the lips apart. Show me plenty of pink."

The podiatrist poured more fudge on Shannen's thigh as the fly returned to his sore. "Ohhhh!" Shannen stiffened. The fudge too hot.

"You like that, don't you?" Joaquin said, zooming in for an extreme close-up of Karin's long pointed tongue circling Shannen's glistening, protruding clit.

Jake, Janus and Jazz entered the kitchen together. Jazz glanced at the action, snorted then left, as Jake and Janus approached the table.

"Hot fudge sundae, anyone?" Ben said as he took the pot of fudge from the podiatrist, then poured it on Shannen's slit. "And I mean *hot!*"

"Ahhhh!" Shannen flinched, her eyes wide open. Fudge running over her groin, blending in with the whipped cream, turning it a lighter brown under the multitude of hands smearing it all over her. Lars, the pre-op, moved into her field of vision, daubing at her lips with the fudged sticky tips of his long fingers.

"Looks fucking great, guys!" Joaquin said while Shannen unbuttoned Lars' shirt to fondle her/his breasts.

Jake jumped, startled by a hand on his ass.

"We should be doing something, eh?" Janus whispered as she removed her hand from his butt to guide his to her moist lipped patch in the circle of her leather panties, while Ben slipped his fudge fingers between her thighs to her patch from behind.

Jake jerked his hands away and left the table. Ben's antics and the sight of Karin's sticky face kissing Shannen bothered him. After all was said and done, he was still just an Oregon country boy at heart.

"Excellent!" said Joaquin. "Show me lots of tongue. Oh, Shannen, baby, you kno-oow what we like."

"Must you talk while you're shooting, Joaquin?" said Julie.

"Trust me, it's cool. Shannen, would you suck on Lars's titties, please."

Worthingham was leaning against the kitchen counter. He signaled Jake over. "Aren't you going to join in on the fun?"

"No," Jake answered. "What about you?"

He shook his head. "I'm a watcher." He took a swig from his flask. "Don't take this the wrong way but your flicks, they're okay for what they are, but you could do with less artsy and a lot more fartsy."

And you are all fart and no arse, thought Jake.

"Audiences shouldn't have to put up with bullshit when alls they want is sex, lots of dirty sex. I understand the couples thing, stuff guys can show women. But women today like smut, same as the guys. They may pretend to be sensitive, I don't know what the fuck for. Probably think it turns guys on. First time, maybe show them a pretentious piece of crap. But after you fuck 'em, alls they want to watch is dirty dirt dirt."

"Yeah, you're right," said Jake. Always agree with a drunk, that way they never know what you're thinking.

Worthingham took another sip, suspecting he was being humored. "Seriously, though, that teenybopper I told you about, she's down on her luck and desperate enough to walk the streets, if you know what I mean. She's a good kid. Too damn proud to accept help from anybody. Has to support herself. I don't want her back on the streets. It's not safe. I hope you can find her some work."

"I'll see what I can do," said Jake. Worthingham's earnest act reminded Jake of his father's drunken sentiments. "You ought to check with Janus, too."

"I don't trust her, she's a flake," he slurred, his eyes pricked with suspicion. "Mindy said I could trust you."

"Oh, there you are," said Jazz. "Can't find my damn jacket. I think the blonde bitch stole it."

"You remember where you put it?" said Jake.

"Yeah, I remember," she growled. "Ain't there. Can't afford to lose it, don't belong to me." Then she added as she turned away, "Gonna axe Mindy."

"Okay. Then let's leave as soon as you find it," Jake said as she left in a huff. Worthingham placed a hand on Jake's shoulder. "Seriously. Take care of the little girl for me. Watch over her. She's worth it, believe me."

"What's her name?" Jake asked, wanting him to remove his hand.
"Robin."
"Robin?" Jake looked surprised.
"Robin Byrd," Worthingham said, suspicious. "You know her?"
Jake chuckled, "No, I don't believe I've had the pleasure."

PART TWO

Past and Present Future Games

There was a time when meadow, grove, and stream,
the earth, and every common sight,
To me did seem
Appareled in celestial light,
The glory and the freshness of a dream.

— William Wordsworth

3

Drowned Rainbow

June 1971

Tennessee Valley, Karmichog Farm

S hafts of late-morning sunlight slanting through the east wall broke the barn's cavernous interior into a patchwork of dazzling light and cool darkness. A gentle breeze blew through the slats, stirring the scent of dry alfalfa as Raphael reached out from the darkness into the light for the razor strop dangling off a square rail driven into a wall joist. He took a long, thin knife off the wall behind the workbench then turned toward the waterwheel behind the forge. The chirps of a single cricket inside the barn caught his attention. He paused to listen to how its chirps seemed to punctuate the subdued whir of the insects outside where his daughter was at play.

LITTLE KATIE licked the dust off a rock then held it up to a slash of sunlight to watch the wet spot as it receded. Then, hooking her legs on the pigpen's top rail, she leaned over into the pen giggling, upside down; the sun filtering through the twig roof filling the air with sunbeams and singing sounds, swelling around her as the pigs gathered round, snorting and sniffing for handouts. Big Mamma came closest, raising her snout.

"No!" Katie yelled, pulling herself up. "Go way!" The pigs grunted. "Rock not food." She tossed it at them and scrunched up her face. "You want mommy?" she said in a sad voice. "She gone. Back for my birfday." She held up three fingers. "This many. Now!" She raised a forth finger. "This many. Back!" The pigs snuffled. "Don't understand?" She looked for Snort's familiar black markings among the pigs.

Snort was tame. Uncle Riley taught her how to tame him. Gave her a watch to show how to visit Snort same time every day. Said tell him nice things, like he's a smart, pretty piggy. Give him food, then sit real quiet. Don't make noise. Be still! If Snort go away, don't follow. Stay put 'til watch hands are on top. Come back every day and sit closer each time.

One day as she approached, Snort stared at her. He scary! The black patch around his eye sometimes make him look mean. She sat down anyway and stared back. After a long time he made a sigh sounding like words strung together, then lowered his head. Didn't go away. Stayed 'til watch hands said time gone. When she got up, he looked at her so she would know he was tame, and they would watch out for each other. He was Special Angel to her, and she to him. She wanted to shout with joy, but didn't.

Uncle Riley said this was Special Time. Angels must be quiet in Special Time. "Snort!" she yelled. "Where you, Snort!"

A faint breeze stirred the air, bringing a heated compost of underground smells from a dark watery hole swarming with flies by the barn. Katie climbed off the fence then went to the Fly Hole. Gobs of pale, clay-slimy, worm-like flesh covered with what looked like clumps of puffy rice. "Guts," she whispered.

Daddy says people full of guts, but grownups were always trying to trick her into believing things that weren't true. She wouldn't let him trick her into believing in guts, because then she'd grow guts, and that would make her grow up. She did not want to be a grown-up.

Flies, crazed by the hot stink of guts, circled the clumps of writhing rice, writhing as if alive. Maggots. Baby flies.

"Daddy!" Little Katie yelled.

THE WATER in the scalding barrel hanging from an iron tripod over the fire pit began to boil as Raphael slung a pulley attached to a short length of chain over the limb of a tulip tree outside the lean-to. He took a piece of iron, consisting of two long curved spikes like the horns of a bull, joined by a loop in the middle, then moved behind the pig to grab his rear trotters.

"Daddy! Daddy!" Katie yelled as she ran toward him.

Snort grunted anxiously and Raphael straightened up. "Pipe down, Katie." He did not want her to be part of what was about to happen. "You're scaring Snort."

Katie held up her arms with childish trust as he knelt down, the air around him steaming with the stink of freshly dropped dung and crushed alfalfa.

Then she noticed the chain looped around the pulley.

"Snort angel," she muttered, stepping back. "Joseph say can't eat angels."

"Snort, an angel?" her father chortled, his face transformed by a lop-sided, foolish grin. The grin quickly faded into a puzzled frown when he realized her mutters meant her ghost had talked to her. Either that, or she had not believed him when he said Joseph had gone along with her mother and her ghosts Playfaire and Tarwater when he took them to the sanitarium. His bruised fingers gently touched her shoulder.

"Ghosts are liars, Katie," he said. "They lie for the sheer pleasure of it. They don't even care if you believe them."

"Mommy love Snort!" she yelled impatiently. Grown-ups never understood anything unless you explained it, and she didn't know how to do that. "You wait 'til mommy BACK!" Mommy knew how.

Raphael had found her mother's ghosts intriguing, at first. Unlike most ghosts who were simple mindless wanderers around the scenes of their past lives (mindless because they had no memory), Playfaire and Tarwater had memory, which made them capable of so much more than malicious mischief. Such ghosts looked for ways to attach themselves to people's energy and give them strange urges. Like to spontaneously stab themselves, or to jump off a cliff. Or worse. Tarwater was especially bad. He had to commit Victoria after Tarwater made fifty-five needles appear out of thin air in her heel.

"Joseph say you hurt Snort, he hurt you!" Katie yelled with the stran-gled voice she employed when Joseph was speaking through her

The breeze suddenly died.

Raphael blinked. Victoria had relayed a similar threat from Tarwater to discourage him from having her committed. He must not allow Katie to think her ghosts could threaten him as well. "Ghosts can't touch me."

"Joseph make fall down!" she yelled. "Boom!!!"

A raucous cry of a crow came from the loft. Something must have startled it, he thought as he looked up. The crow raised its black wings in the air; then, with a rattling of quills and stabbing motions of his head, took three side steps along the ledge of the loft.

"Look, I know you love Snort, but he's a pig," he said, his voice growing faint, "and pigs are our business. I can't afford to spare one every time you form an attachment."

"No! No!" she yelled with the full force certainty of a three-year-old. "Snort angel!"

"Well, if that's true there's no way I can harm him since people can only kill things with guts. You see, angels don't have guts." Raphael remembered how when he was small his father had bullied him into watching him kill and butcher his pet rabbit, how he'd let himself sink into the absolute solitude of an evil dream where no one could follow him. He'd hated his father for what he'd done, yet in some strange way he was also proud he had done it. He was being made into a man. Beads of sweat stood out on his forehead as he searched his daughter's face for his own lost expression.

He grabbed hold of the rope.

"You better go, Katie," he grunted. "In case Snort's not an angel."

A lizard emerged from behind the bales of alfalfa. Raising and lowering his tiny dragonhead, he flicked out his tongue then turned his unblinking eyes in Katie's direction.

Katie focused her thoughts on the dust motes, dancing like tiny angels in the sunlight, willing them to stop daddy.

"Go! Leave!" Raphael yelled, something in him rebelling against what he was about to do. "Now!"

Katie yelled back, "No! No! No! You wait for mommy!"

The buzzard scurried across a bale and caught the lone cricket.

Without further thought, Raphael jerked the rope. The curved spike ends thrust between bone and tendon behind the hocks. He stuck the hook into the loop and hoisted a screaming Snort up into the air, his head moving from side to side.

"NO!" Katie yelled as the pigs outside joined in, all screaming like people in terror.

Raphael no longer had normal thoughts, only something like images of feelings that struck and passed as he secured the rope's end to a trimmed branch. Then, like a dancer, he went down on one knee beside the pig and slid the knife through his throat just behind the angle of the jaw. With a quick motion of his forearm, he pushed the blade forward, severing the jugular, the windpipe and both carotid arteries in one flawless motion.

Snort's eyes opened wide as he jerked and bled, making a noise in the wide shallow pan like cow's milk in an empty bucket at the morning milking.

After a while the blood merely ran. As the pig lost control of his bladder and rectal muscles, it dribbled. Then, except for the dead monotonous buzz of flies, silence.

The crow, animated by Katie's anxiety, watched her with dinosaur eyes under bluish lids as she curled her fingers into the sticky familiar warmth of her palms.

Raphael stretched his mouth, showing the roots of his teeth, as he lowered the pig's body into the boiling water. He kept Snort in the water a while then plucked the bristles on his hocks with an old pair of pliers. Satisfied the bristles were loose, he pulled Snort out of the barrel and scraped the hair off with a flat bladed two-handed scraper.

When her father put the knife on Snort's belly, Katie wanted to scream at him not to hurt Snort. But she couldn't move.

A squishy ripping sound. He used a pair of heavy hedge clippers to split the sternum to gain access to his heart and lungs.

"You see, guts," he said as he tied off the esophagus just above the collarbone and the intestine just above the anus. "Snort's not an angel," he said, not looking at her as he cut the ties to let the whole stinking mess drop onto a plastic tarp.

Katie stiffened, thinking if she didn't move Snort would be all right. The guts could be put back and make alive again.

"This is Snort's tummy." He poked, his fingers damp and twitching as he slit it open, and stuff came out. "That's what he ate today."

She felt as if her father had created the guts with words, talking them into existence with the magic of his voice.

"Guts turn food into poop. Anything that poops has guts. Guts are what make us organic beings. They're also our weak point. Make us grow old and die," Raphael said, his face soft and sagging. "Angels are different. They're like a pure light that can't be defiled by filth of any kind. They don't make stinky poo like organic beings. They make a dark liquid light that gives off a warm glow instead of stink. Angel poo's never sticky or smelly. That's because they don't have germs. Germs are what make things stink."

The crow opened his thick blue beak and cawed, then put his head on one side to observe the effect of this.

The longer Katie looked, the more she felt she was to blame for what had happened, as if Snort's death was an evil thought that sprung out of her head, and watching it made her part of it. Then a big fly settled on the guts and scratched, undisturbed in its wrinkles.

Snort, so still. She knew then he would not get better. That he got guts because he got big. Angels not supposed to grow up.

"I'm an angel," she mumbled. She would never grow guts.

The crow put his great wings up over his head, flailing dark feathered shadows across the barn. He opened his beak, showing a black pointed, snaky tongue, and began a series of harsh, grating cries. Then Big Fly jumped off the guts and came at her.

Katie screamed and ran off, afraid if Big Fly touched her she would grow guts. She ran along the narrow strip of shade cast by the long wall of the barn, the trees shrieking loud in her ears with bird grunts and insect crackle, her arms in front of her face to avoid snagging spider webs in her hair.

She stumbled into a seam of green light, then Big Fly landed on her shoulder. "Go way!" she yelled, waving her hands. "I squash you!"

Big Fly flew off, and she watched to make sure he stayed gone.

A breeze came to life, breathing faintly through the brush, carrying the scent of decayed vegetation and rancid mud up from the roadside ditch. Flies gathering around the cowflop drying at the edge of the dark ditch. Brown water stretching to a brown shore, dead insects floating like tea leaves on the surface of a dirty mirror. Katie looked down the embankment at the stagnant water leaking beneath smooth boulders around an oilcan bleeding rainbows into the weeds. The little striped and hairy bruises of an oil slick.

"Drowned rainbow," little Katie whispered.

4

Black Dancers

An old boot jammed on top of a post marked the track that led off the half-graded road to the ridge overlooking Sandoval's place. After nineteen miles of jolting ruts and windless heat, Spear was relieved to see the boot pointed in, signaling somebody would be at home. As he slowed to downshift, a sudden gust enveloped his truck in gritty dust and the burnt-cloth stink of exhaust fumes. The wind followed him up the ridge then shifted near the crest, clearing away enough dust to make the caves in the distant red sandstone cliffs clearly visible.

Haskie Sam, the maternal uncle of Spear's uncle Sandoval, had advised against building a hogan so close to caves where witches were said to incest and kill their relatives. Near the hogan site itself was a blow-hole known to attract restless spirits, and under the sloping overhangs in the surrounding canyons were the rock houses of the enemy dead said to be inhabited by ghosts that took a peculiar delight in infecting the living with ghost sickness.

"Only a witch could like such country," Haskie Sam had warned Spear when Sandoval built his hogan there. "Stay clear of witches. They are like spirits and ghosts. They go after anyone who wanders into their territory."

Spear slowed to a stop beside an outcrop of volcanic basalt rising at the ridge's high point like four gigantic arthritic fingers. He looked down at the buildings, using his left hand as a shield against the sunlight reflecting off the corrugated sheet metal roof of a plank and tarpaper lean-to. He spotted a small red convertible under the brush arbor next to the stone hogan where he had expected to find Sandoval's battered pick-up.

He eased his truck off the track onto the steep winding trail that led downward through rabbit brush and gray mesquite to Sandoval's place. Near the base of the mesa, where the trail straightened, a bird suddenly fell dead from the sky directly in front, jolting him into a state of alertness. He slowed the truck to a crawl, looking for anything that deviated from the harmony of the expected. Four summers ago when he spent a night there alone, a vague feeling of something unknown prowling outside had so unnerved him he'd made a vow never to be down there alone again, day or night.

The rusted corpse of a school bus and a cannibalized flatbed truck mounted on cinder blocks flanked a new Montgomery Ward storage shed. The thistle in the insulating layer of dirt on the hogan's roof gave it a scruffy, unshaven look. The pole corral had too many poles missing for it to be useful. The only thing that did not belong was the low clearance convertible with California plates.

Spear pulled up under the gnarled limbs of a one-seed juniper, a polite forty yards from the hogan. Navajo custom required visitors to wait long enough before approaching a host's hogan for the ghosts that followed travelers to grow impatient and wander off, and to allow the host time to get in harmony with the idea of a visit. Whoever might be inside would let him know when they were ready to receive him.

The noonday heat radiated off the ground, causing the light to shimmer. He inhaled the familiar aroma of wilted leaves and dust. A hot, dry wind suddenly blew out of the southwest, spawning a gray-white dust devil that danced off toward the olive tree where his uncle draped his shirts and jeans to dry. Nothing was on the tree.

Spear was then instantly aware that, except for dry cottonwood leaves, nothing was on the ground. No broken furniture, no boxes, no barrels, no litter, no pots hanging under the brush shelter. His uncle had always kept the exterior of his site indistinguishable from those of his distant neighbors who left things outside to make room inside.

The front door then swung open and a short, white woman with long, braided blonde hair stepped out onto the makeshift porch. Her fringed buckskin jacket, Indian jewelry and beaded headband made him think *Hollywood Hiawatha*. She appeared to be around his age, twenty-three. She made the traditional circular Navajo welcoming wave.

His first thought was she must be one of the strange white women Haskie Sam had warned him about, that Sandoval had instructed in the sacred ways. Spear had never met nor seen one of them before; nonetheless, he found it hard to believe Sandoval would have approved of an apprentice wearing such an offensive outfit on the reservation.

Spear tucked his travel-rumpled, blue flannel shirt into his pants then climbed out of his truck. He walked with an easy grace across the hard-packed earth, the turkey feather jutting from the silver-and-turquoise band of his black felt hat stirring in the breeze. His long torso, narrow pelvis and massive shoulders were typical Athapaskan, but his long face and wide mouth was somewhat softened by a Pueblo blood mixture. His most remarkable feature was his eyes, golden like the sacred pollen. A Hopi coed once said they made him look like a *powaqa*. A two-heart, someone with the soul of an animal and the soul of a human. In other words, a witch.

A breeze riffled through Hollywood's hair. Her eyes, almost closed, watching him as she slowly moved her head until her left eye cast a reflection of the sun. *Burning Eyes*, Spear noted. She had the look of one who saw visions.

"*Yaa' eh t'eeh*," Burning Eyes said, handling the Navajo glottal sounds perfectly. She gave him a strange placid smile as he stepped onto the porch. He noticed a pouch shaped like a miniature jaguar strapped to her waist.

"*Ya-tah-hey*," he said. She smelled of sunshine and sage, odors that attract good, and her eyes had a pleasing shine, but the dimple on the left side of her face gave her grin a definite cockiness. He had seen similar looks on the faces of Anglo coeds in Native American studies at the university, the look that asked whether he was really any different from the Anglo boys they grew up with. He could think of only one white woman he had ever considered a friend. The rest had just brought trouble.

"You must be Yellow Wind," she said in a raspy but utterly feminine voice.

His dark face turned a shade darker. Sandoval, his key clan uncle, his "Little Father" whose responsibility it was to instruct him in the knowledge taught by the Holy People, had secretly given him that name, whispering it through the mask at the Yeibichi ceremonial when he changed from boy to man. It was the only name that counted. All others were circumstantial. No one but those closest to him would know this name; otherwise its power would be diluted, watered down.

A war name had power and was not to be voiced in a warrior's presence, except to summon power. Undue repetition would leave the warrior unable to rely on it. The name could even turn against him.

She licked her lips then caught the lower lip between her teeth. A plank on the porch made a long, loud groan as she shifted her weight.

"What would you have me call you?" she said, looking him in the eye.

The Anglo habit of searching for nonverbal signals on another's face made him uncomfortable. Such behavior among the People was considered an invasion of privacy. He kept his face blank, to send no signals.

"Call me Dugai." He said, giving his reservation name in a sonorous voice, noticing right away the tone wasn't right. Impatient, stiff.

I screwed up, he thought, feeling disgusted with himself.

"What a magnificent display of temper," she said with a knowing smile at his breach of Navajo manners. "Now I see why your White classmates called you Shakes-Spear." Her body shook from suppressed laughter, rattling the bone and hoof pendants on her clothing. Spear had a sudden and strange thought, like those that come just before falling asleep, of Changing Bear Maiden, the Holy Girl also known as Maiden-Whose-Clothes-Rattle, the cruel and ruthless virgin mother who bound man to the Wheel of Time, to beginnings, decay and death.

"Sun Elk left me here to bring you to him." She pointed Navajo fashion by shifting her lips in her car's direction. "We'll take my car. It's more comfortable than it looks."

Spear masked his alarm with a dispassionate look, determined not to expose himself again. He would behave like a Navajo. He would endure.

Sun Elk, according to Haskie Sam, was the name the Hopi sorcerer Sawkatewa gave Sandoval for use in what Haskie Sam considered evil business, such as instructing crazy white women in the sacred ways.

"Witches hate being talked about," Haskie Sam said when Spear asked why he had never heard anyone use that name. "They hate having their evil business being discussed. People do not speak the name of a witch because he might come. They don't want him to come. If they talk of a witch it is only with people they know, never with a relative of a witch because he may also be a witch." After a long pause, he added in a cracked, weary voice, "Or become one."

KATIE SLIPPED a cold thumb into her mouth. Everything was getting cold. The tent flap wouldn't zip shut, the zipper stuck again. She hated the cold. It made her feel exposed, vulnerable, especially without Blankee, her blanket.

Eleven years ago on this mountain, she emerged from the warmth of her mother's womb into the cool light of a dying sun. Uncle Riley said his sister hated being pregnant. She felt the growth inside her was eating a hole into her life and its alien movements in her swollen belly reminded her of a monster she saw burst out of a woman's gut in a movie. He even overheard her chanting "you must die" to the life growing inside her.

Katie rummaged through the filthy clothing stuffed in Riley's grimy dufflebag looking for something to keep her warm. She found an old field jacket with a tattered lining and sniffed at it. Like everything else in his pack, it smelled dirty.

Riley liked stinky things. He left a cooler full of guts in the sun all day on the set of *The Spawn of the Stinking Dead,* a film he was directing. When he asked her to open the lid, the stench was so bad awful she threw up. He couldn't stop laughing.

When he calmed down, he said, "All civilized behavior is a lie. A lie that shrivels when faced with organic truths like stinking guts. What so-called civilized folk call cleanliness is, in reality, a deadly sterility."

"Deadly sterility," Katie muttered, grasping at the leaking words. "But how can you stand that *gaayuck* stink?"

He replied, waving his large hands like a magician, "Because strong odors alter the mask of appearance into a *magical* reflection of our own blood-smeared birth. *Magic* is the taste of cooked blood, the clinging, carnal, milky taste of organic life. Cleanliness is a sterile attempt to hide ourselves from ourselves, from our decomposing stench. Cleanliness is a subterfuge."

"Sub-ter-fuge," she whispered, memorizing the word to look up later.

The dictionary said: "An evasion; an artifice used to escape censure or the force of an argument, to justify opinions, conduct, etc." Like her mom's complaining about the substitution of water buckets for toilet paper at the open pit privies when what really bothered her was people could see her making poo. Flies were what riled Katie, especially after a huge horsefly took a bloody bite off her butt.

"Some birthday," she muttered as she worked herself into the smelly jacket.

Hearing a thin flutter of leaves in the branches overhead as she crawled out of the tent, she looked up at the sun straining through the trees, collapsing toward twilight.

"*When it getsss darrrk, it will beee verrry co-ld,*" her ghost Joseph whispered from up in a tree, blending in with the leaves. "*Rrraphael and Victorrria are veRRRyyy cooo-ld.*" She hated when he played games with his voice. It meant he was up to no good. She ignored him whenever he did that.

Her father disliked ghosts. He was always telling her not to listen to them.

"Ghosts lie," Raphael said. "So they can't be your friend. A friend who lies to you is, at best, an imaginary friend."

Lies or not, Joseph had protected her from her mother's evil thoughts when she was in her womb. Soothing her with a rhythm of music. An uninterrupted flow of sounds like high and low pitched voices accompanied by something like a deep bass drum.

The odor of pig entrails came to her like smoke from the leaves in his shimmering tree. Joseph made that smell when she'd done something dirty wrong. A memory surfaced of when she was two years old, crying, diapers full of sticky, and grandpa Seabolt covering her mouth to stifle her screams, smothering her melodious child within, a soft musical echo flapping like the wings of an angel as Joseph melted into her throat to stop her cries taking her to a hiding place where she sealed herself off with a vow never to cry again. A vow she would keep until her sixth birthday.

Why was Joseph numbing her with such terrible memories?

"He's trying to make me feel something horrible has happened," she muttered, pushing the tip of a finger at the center of her forehead. "Trying to burn it into my mind." She scanned the horizon. "Everything will be all right when the rainbow comes."

"*It frrrrooooze last night,*" Joseph said as he glided down from the tree, his presence hovering over her like a hummingbird.

"*It will be much cooolllderrrr toniiight.*"

"Where's that stupid rainbow," she muttered, slipping her thumb into her mouth. This would be her second night alone with Riley. Her mother never allowed that before.

According to family legend, she was born at sunset under a triple rainbow during the annual pagan gathering. Some god there told her father they had to observe her birthday every year at the gathering until a rainbow failed to appear. A rainbow had always shown up on her birthday, but not this year, which also happened to be the first time the festival had returned to this mountain since her birth. Her father said they had to wait for a rainbow before celebrating it. The next morning, she said she wanted to go to Riley's camp, a two-hour hike up the mountain.

"It's crowded and cold up there, Katie," her mother said. "You hate the cold, and crowds upset you. Remember last year, when those boys teased you about your eyes?"

She defiantly brushed aside the veil of blonde hair she sometimes used to obscure her slightly crossed left eye. "Nobody bothers me when I'm with Riley."

"You've been isolated on the farm for far too long," Victoria said. "You're not used to being around so many people. When you can show us you can handle yourself around strangers, then we'll see."

"That's stupid! How am I ever gonna learn anything hanging around with you guys? I'm eleven years old now. I'm not a baby anymore."

"That's all well and good, dear, but you're staying with us," Victoria said, shoving a roll of forbidden toilet paper into her pack.

Toilet paper! Katie rolled her eyes then stomped out of the tent. "March back here right this minute, young lady!" Victoria yelled.

"You sound like your mother," said Raphael. "Let her go." Victoria glowered at him then went after her daughter.

"You think you're so damn cute, don't you," she growled, grabbing hold of her. "You think you're so cute you can do anything you damn well please. Well, I've got news for you, young lady. You've got another think coming because you're not cute. You're ugly! You hear me! Ugly!" Katie started crying. "You should see yourself. You have no idea just how ugly you are right now. Eleven years old and you cry at anything, just like a baby. When you behave like this, you *are* ugly. And you wonder why we don't let you go off by yourself. When are you ever going to grow up?"

"Never!" she screamed. Tearing herself loose, she ran up the track and did not look back until she reached the crest of the hill. When she did, she saw her mother standing on the same spot, her face buried in her hands.

"*RRRED RRRAINBO-O-W,*" Joseph whispered, pulling her back to witness a red rainbow emerging from the eerie rose glow of the sunset flooding the eroded peaks.

Katie jerked her thumb out of her mouth. "Oh, no," she gasped, slipping her thumb back into her warm, wet mouth. Not a good omen.

BLACK SHADOWS sharply outlined the dying sun's reds and pinks against the broken cliffs as the red Fiat convertible crossed over an irrigation drain on a rattling plank bridge. Burning Eyes pulled over a few yards beyond the drain levee and flicked off the engine. Spear listened to the ticking of the cooling engine and the distant sound of diesels moving on the old cracked asphalt of U.S. 666 out of Cortez.

She shook her head slightly, sniffed the air, then she said, "Sun Elk's up on Big Sheep Mountain. The spirits inhabiting that place are especially dangerous at night. We will wait here during the crack between the worlds for a sign it is safe to go up there."

Spear watched the tops of the evening thunderheads gradually change from a luminescent pink to a deep glowing red that streaked a purple afterglow across the desert.

The hours of the predators' hunting cycle were about to begin.

"A pagan festival was held up on Big Sheep eleven years ago," she said softly. "This was before Sandoval became Sun Elk. He went up there to find and stop a Navajo Wolf, who had incested and killed his relatives, from spreading ghost sickness among the pagans. He failed to find the Wolf in time to prevent him from infecting a pregnant woman. The pagans, and the mother and child, *and* the Wolf, have all returned to Big Sheep.

Sun Elk has been up there for some time, before the pagans arrived, to acquaint himself with the designs of the Powers there. This morning, he sensed you were coming, and he sent me down to wait for you."

She chuckled. "The pagans, for the most part, are wearing costumes and behaving in ways out of harmony with the Powers of this place. As strange as my costume may seem to you, it is in harmony for what we must do with the restive spirits of Big Sheep. Sun Elk designed it himself. He had an old blind wise woman put it together. Everything on it has a purpose."

She paused, then added, "Disharmonies that restore harmony."

A hummingbird suddenly swooped down and hovered over the hood of the car. Spear watched it, thinking of how the Aztecs regarded hummingbirds as the spirits of dead warriors rejoicing in time without end, no longer remembering the affairs of the day or the affairs of the night, basking eternally in the warmth of the sun, drunk with joy, their mouths full of sweetness, having returned without memory, knowledge or desire, to a perfect, final paradise of warmth and milky bliss. Suckling babes once more. The bird zoomed away, pausing briefly above Burning

Eyes' soft pale hair. Then he remembered the Navajo ceremonial name for the hummingbird. Maiden-Who-Goes-About-Rattling.

"My war name is Changing Bear," whispered the Maiden-Whose-Clothes-Rattle, her steel blue eyes burning with a mute emotion that felt like a weight on his chest.

STRANGLED ECHOES of drumbeats reverberated around the mountainside, punching holes in the night air as the darkening sky gradually filled with strange stars, and an oily cloud covered the moon. Katie shivered. The sky here was cold and hostile, unlike the soft, warm protecting darkness of her Tennessee valley home. Her first night on the high mountain she'd spent huddled in a grimy sleeping bag trying to keep warm until Riley staggered up to the tent, his steamy breath reeking of cigarettes and bourbon.

"Every star is a god," he said, looking up at the stars. "The empty space around them is a devil. The heavens represent the way the starlight of consciousness is balanced and ultimately devoured by an abyss of darkness. The star gods shine only as long as it takes the demonic light-swallower lurking behind them to develop an appetite. Then the dragon of darkness devours the light."

She gathered up the sleeping bag, and went outside to spread it out on the hammock while Riley drawled on and on. After she got into the bag and pulled it up over her head, Riley stopped talking. He needed to see her in order to talk to her. After awhile he went into the tent, passed out, and promptly, began to snore. Loudly.

She lay awake, suspended in the hammock for most of the night with Joseph hovering overhead in the branches, waiting. Without her security blanket, it'd be easy for him to slip into her head once she fell asleep. To keep him out, she focused her attention on the moon's gradual emergence from behind an oily cloud, watching as it grew larger and larger like an immense disk of ice, until it filled her skull with cold.

Her second night, she intended to sleep by the warmth of a fire. To do that, she'd have to find her way through the dark mass of trees between her and the bonfires.

The darkness flashed with yellow then flashed again, internal lightning illuminating a black cloud. Now, out of sight of her tent, a hauntingly sad owl cry came from a blue-black tree towering above her like a witch wrapped in darkness. She slipped her thumb into her mouth and bit down on it. A sharp noise to her left, like two rocks being struck against each other startled her and her thumb popped out of her mouth. She almost walked into the smirking skull of a tree, its dead branches reaching like finger bones into the heavy sky. As she strained to see in the blackness, she heard a series of soft noises like rocks being struck gently, rubbing together. The foliage in front of her began to pulsate, flowing like black skirts blowing in the wind. But there was no wind.

Then a yellow-blue glimmer swelled in the sky, stuttering like a fluorescent tube, lighting up the ugly clouds enough to enable her to see the vague silhouette of a man carrying a dead animal standing fifteen yards away, almost merged with the bushes.

"Joseph?" she whispered, her thumb cold from being wet. The figure had a slight chartreuse glow. *What have I gone and done?* she gasped. *An inorganic being? Must be careful. Inorganic beings can project themselves wherever they want.*

Ripples ran through the muscles of her abdomen when something flickered in the periphery of her vision. Then a sudden rustling behind startled her into abruptly turning around causing her to stumble noisily into the shrubs, gashing the heel of her left foot.

A clicking sound like the smacking of lips came from a dark mass that then lurched at her. She screamed, her fright so out of proportion she lost her balance and fell backwards. Unable to breathe, she opened her mouth gasping for air, her ears buzzing.

The foul smelling entity made hollow, rhythmic, smacking sounds with its lips as she struggled to resist its eerie insistence pulling at her. Then, just as she felt herself dissolving into a seizure, a sudden jolt stopped her shaking and she could breathe again.

Someone had splashed bourbon on her face. Awesomely calm, everything was clear. The noise was laughter. The foul smell, bourbon and cigarettes.

"Angel fall down, go boom?" slurred Uncle Riley. "You look like somebody just knocked a turd out of you eight foot long."

She decided she would ignore him. No matter what.

THUNDER RUMBLED faintly, far to the northeast, as Changing Bear turned off the dirt road onto a meadow full of vehicles. She parked alongside an old church bus with a bumper decal exhorting people to BEWARE OF GOD! Its Bethel Island Church logo had been altered to read Brothel Island Church, and the phone number changed to 666-6969.

Bear signaled Spear to grab a bedroll, then started off in the direction of a bonfire. A flash of lightning illuminated the cluster of people gathered around the fire. The explosion of thunder that followed set off a racketing barrage of echoes cannonading from the canyon cliffs. A prepubescent girl emerged from the cluster then, pursued by the wind, she ran with the easy grace of a child who has not yet forgotten how to race her shadow. The sky lit up again, revealing a large trampoline and the ragged basalt shape of the rock formation facing the girl as she stopped to remove her clothing.

"Welcome, Spirits!" she yelled as she climbed up on the trampoline. Extending her arms, bouncing as high as she could, she cried out, "Blessed be!" to the Rolling Thunder.

Her behavior puzzled Spear, who thought Whites saw lightning as the wrath of God, a kind of divine punishment for trying to make one's self divine. To the Navajo, lightning and thunder were considered to be predominantly evil, shattering forces that spread disease and mischief. Either way, only a witch would welcome such forces.

The drum patterns seemed to reflect off the cliffs, like the wavering firelight reflecting off the faces of the people gathered around the fire and the bare back of what Spear thought to be a girl child who was moving sensually to the drums. The child turned around and looked him directly in the eye, as if she knew he'd been watching her.

She had fully developed breasts.

He froze, momentarily disorientated by the strange look she was giving him. Changing Bear hissed. Spear turned toward her. She was standing twenty feet away in a muddy stream that spread out over the flat sand separating the meadow from the entrance to a narrow canyon. The dim yellow light of the moon tinged the top of the sheer cliffs. She beckoned him to follow her to the side that was in total darkness. A light breeze suddenly shifted down canyon, carrying the faintly acrid smell of ozone released by the electrical charge. He inhaled the high-country smells, the air cold in his nostrils.

"This canyon's inhabited by a friendly water spirit," Changing Bear yelled to announce their presence to the spirit. The whistling call of a whippoorwill sounded far down the canyon; then, except for muffled drumbeats, it was eerily silent and still. "Let our voices wash over this place like a black flood," she yelled. "Allow the water spirit, who abides here, to dive into our feelings and be carried along with us. Outside this canyon powerful spirits surge like a gnawing flood, pulling men, dirty with lies and greed, into their flow. Let us seek shelter from their storm with the water spirit who lives here."

A rasping hoot touched off a dull pattern of echoes in the canyon, awakening in Spear a primeval, trapped-animal fright. Ghosts sometimes took the form of owls when they moved in the darkness. He was feeling something he hadn't felt since boyhood, not so much fear of the dark as of the ghosts that inhabit it.

"With visible breath I am walking," Changing Bear sang softly, a white cloud wafting from her mouth. "A voice I am sending as I walk. In a sacred manner I am walking. With visible tracks I am walking. In a sacred manner I walk."

The existence of witches and ghosts was not something Spear questioned as a boy. He remembered the terror he felt on losing a flint arrow point while collecting holy things for his medicine bundle on Dzilidushzhinih Peaks, home of Talking God. The loss of a sacred item under such circumstances could only result in misfortune, perhaps even death. He had searched until darkness set in, and with it came the Dark Wind that turned men from harmony and beauty to chaos and sickness. In the surrounding blackness he had felt the evil chill that seduced men into becoming witches, that drove them to madness, and compelled them to spread sickness.

"Witches come like the tide when there's a moon," Changing Bear whispered. "Tonight, the moonlight will rain upon us, Yellow Wind."

"A war name should not be repeated uselessly," Spear said pointedly. His dark voice panicked an owl and it flapped past them, trailing its chittering quick-quick-quick call before vanishing in the shadows. "Call me Spear."

"This is war talk in a place of power, do not talk so plainly," she whispered. "I cannot use your White name here." She studied him for a moment then, giggling softly, spread her bedroll out on a soft bed of fir needles and aspen leaves.

Spear lay down in the cold, dead silence. With the roundness of Earth Surface World beneath him, he looked up at Yikaisdahi, the Milky Way, the great fluorescent sweep of footprints left by spirits on their pathway across the sky. There, the pattern of Pleiades, the constellation that revealed Monster Slayer's heroic odyssey among the evil things born from the self-abuse of women maddened with desire. As forces that could not be brought under dependable control, stars were feared by the Navajo.

Looking out into the universe through the thin, high altitude air that made the stars shine with such incredible silent brightness filled him with the same unbearable awe that had inspired him to ask his uncle how to talk to the Holy People.

"There are no volunteers in the spirit world," Sandoval had said. "The Spirit selects who will learn its ways. It's not up to you, or to me. The Spirit is the player, we are the pawns. We cannot move without an appropriate sign." In the meantime, he'd advised Spear to study the ways of the White man until he understood their world. Only then could he properly make the decision he must ultimately make.

"The White way is about money and its power. The Navajo way is to walk in beauty. You must understand what these things mean before you can chose between them."

A SHADOWY FIGURE leaped out of the darkness at the outer edge of the fire circle and landed in a squatting position behind Katie. Alarm flickered across her face when she saw a wolf's head pushed back on a big man's forehead, its snout pointing upward, the forepaws and pelt draped across his shoulders hanging limply down the front of his black shirt. One side of the man's face was fiery in the wavering firelight, the other black. His fiery eye was so bright it looked as if it would burst with blood. She held her breath, silently cursing Riley for leaving her alone with these weird people.

Then she recognized him, and her face went blank. Riley was wearing a dead animal pelt. Playing monster.

Acknowledging weirdness only encouraged him to do more. Riley huffed and puffed to the beat for a while, then dropped something on her lap.

"Blankee!" Katie cried out, gathering up her security blanket. Riley barked out a laugh at her reaction to the intimate stickiness of the blood on it. Her alarm changed to anger when she remembered what her mother said on the set of *The Stinking Dead*.

"Some people get close to you only to hurt you," Victoria had said in a voice so low she had to concentrate in order to hear her. "Remember. Ignore everything when he's being weird. No matter what Riley says or does, ignore everything."

"How can I ignore yucky stuff?" Katie had said. Sometimes figuring out what her mother said was like doing arithmetic.

"If you focus on anything he says or does, you lose control. Ignore *every*thing."

A burning log collapsed, and the fire flared in an explosion of sparks. The drums stopped. A hunchbacked dwarf, a feather hanging from a braid of his frizzy hair, approached the fire and placed a large jar of water on the ground. He opened a pouch attached to a belt of heavy silver conchas around his waist, then sprinkled a powder from it on his palm. Raising the hand up one side of his body, then down the other, he brought the powder up to his face and inspected it, breathing some of it in. Then he flung the rest on the fire. The fire jumped!

Realizing what was about to happen, Riley slipped off the wolf pelt, the firelight highlighting the strings of fur on the wolf's head as he did so.

"Alil!" the dwarf yelled, scooping up a fistful of dirt. "Run your fingers through your Mother's dirt! Feel it, settle your eyes on it, inhale the air that moves across it, touch it with your mind." A drum started beating softly. "All living things on the surface world spring from Mother's dirt. Her dirt is sacred!" He spilled the water on the ground, adding the ashy smell of mud to the boiled root stink of dirt, food, sweat and blood.

"Holy shit," Riley laughed. "Who does the piss-ant think he is, Water Sprinkler?"

Katie frowned. She didn't like when he talked dirty.

The dwarf raised a muddy hand. "Her dirt and water pass through us that we may live." He rose slowly as if stretching against an enveloping force, his arms, trunk and head trembling as though an intermittent electric current were going through them. "When the water of life departs us, we return to Mother as the dirt we have always been." His clean hand waved up and out with an elegant motion. The muddy hand repeated the pattern, in and down; both hands alternating in a wavering, hypnotic, slow movement, fingers quivering, streaking lines of mud across his face and torso.

"He's making stripes," Riley said, nudging Katie. "Evil Spirits are afraid of stripes."

"We are dirt!" the dwarf yelled, the drum pattern quickening, people clapping to the rhythmic shuffle of his moccasins. "Accept your primitive side! Keep what we really are constantly in mind." He thrust his pelvis forward obscenely. Someone laughed.

Riley moved up close to Katie's ear, his hot breath whispering, "Black Dancer."

Feeling a wave of heat from his body, like a vapor of blood in the air, she tittered, "Ah, ha. Black Dancer." *Ignore everything,* she reminded herself.

"A sacred clown, a Navajo ceremonial figure reflecting the paradise of children before they learn of good and evil, purity and filth." He moved his lips close to her cold ears, the heat of his breath whispering, "In their initiation ritual, sacred clowns eat shit."

Katie crinkled her nose. "They do not!"

"Oh, but they do, Sunshine. They break every rule. Black Dancers mix shit in with the mud they smear on themselves."

"That's stupid!" Katie frowned, whispering. "You're making that up!"

"Sometimes, during sacred ceremonies, they grab people, strip them naked, then cover them with poo."

"Blaah!!" Katie stuck out her tongue, contemptuously. *Ignore everything!*

"Gods aren't interested in punishment or obedience. To hell with the *do what I say and nobody gets hurt* load of religious crap. The gods could give a rat's ass what you do so long as you don't blunder across significant boundaries. If you do, then you got their attention, and you're in deep doo doo. They don't have to do a thing, just having a god hanging around is enough to drive most people crazy. And they won't go away until boundaries are restored. Smearing filth on yourself is a way of doing that, since balance is restored and maintained by calling on opposing forces."

A barefoot Indian around Katie's age wearing only a loincloth plopped himself down in the mud, his glittering eyes staring at her as he smeared mud on himself.

Katie gasped, "Earth poo."

Riley laughed. "Earth poo! Got that straight."

"Ah, ha, straight," she giggled. "People are poo."

"Don't you know!"

"Poople."

"You got it!"

"Earth poople," she giggled.

"The Navahos sometimes threw their children to the Black Dancers, the ones that are weak in body and mind, but not actually sick. Makes them stronger."

"Stronger poople," said Katie.

"Mud loosens the hold evil spirits have on them."

The mud-smeared boy stood up and began to mimic the dwarf's pelvic thrusts while the dwarf watched him with the relentless, pitiless neutrality of the gods.

"The gods allow sacred clowns to scoff at the sacred. They watch the clowns like they watch the misfortunes of life, seeing in their antics the secret face of the world."

Poo Boy then glanced at Riley then shrieked, his body arching in the middle as though moved by a direct force. Convulsions rippled through him from head to toe until he faltered and fell to his knees. The drums gradually died away, leaving only the hypnotic sounds of a single pot drum and the tinkle of the bells on the dwarf's legs as they moved in the intricate, mincing, dragging steps of spirit dancers. Poo Boy then slumped forward, his forehead sinking in the mud, his arms in front to protect his eyes. Jerking convulsively, he rolled onto his left side, his body crumpling into a contorted position.

"Monster's got him," Katie muttered.

"The sacred doesn't see the sordid effects of punishment," Riley said. "It responds only to the hidden spirit of language and gesture. Meaningless nonsense is precisely what has meaning to the gods."

"Meaningless nonsense," Katie mumbled. *Ignore everything.*

"Whatever people think they mean in the time and space world is meaningless to the gods because people haven't a clue as to the absolute meaning of words. It escapes them, like an offering, a sacrifice."

"Sac-ri-fice," she whispered, watching Poo Boy lying there stiff on his right side, his back to her. Hands between his legs. *Ignore everything.*

"Words don't represent what we see." The firelight reddened Riley's face, boring empty holes in his eyes. "They represent what we can't see."

Katie got up to approach Poo Boy, his face dappled by the fire, his hair alight. "Is he dead?" she muttered, looking around, thinking no one else seemed to be aware of him.

Riley handed her a stick. She noticed the wolf head and pelt folded under his left arm. She waited for the dwarf to face away, then prodded Poo Boy with the stick.

He twitched, and she muttered, "Poo," then dropped the stick.

THE FAINT SOUND of flapping wings fading into the stillness prompted Spear to jerk upright. He sat stock-still, staring across the canyon, listening. Something primitive in his mind signaled danger, telling him he'd forgotten something. What was it?

He shifted his eyes slowly down canyon, examining every shape under the flat, yellow moonlight, then examined every shadow. The moon had risen halfway up the sky, flooding the west wall of the canyon with pale light. A burrowing owl gliding slowly down the moonlit side of the canyon floor brought back memories of boyhood nightmares of the angry Chindi of the dead that filled the sky over the Big Reservation. He thought of the Chindi's odd, angry deerskin masks, their great beaks clacking, and the round, empty eye sockets, proof that they were dead. Ghosts. Embodying only those things in the dead's nature that were weak and evil.

A cool breeze created a thousand little wind sounds among the ponderosas and Spear felt himself drifting back out through time and space, uneasily on the margin of sleep.

A rainbow somehow appeared bright against the night sky. Above the rainbow, something towered with a blue face and a tall white forehead, holding a great wand edged with obsidian. The figure moved in close and breathed his breath, taking the wind of his life as it left his nostrils. Then, vaguely, through a veil of hopeless dread, Spear remembered what he must not forget. *Never allow a witch to touch you.*

THE DWARF returned with a thick wool blanket, chanting into the cold air as he gently covered Poo Boy:

From the pond in the white valley, the young man doubts it.
The god takes up his sacrifices, with that he now heals.
From the pools in the green meadow, the young woman doubts it.
He takes up his sacrifice, with that he now heals.
With that your kindred thank you.

5

Witch's Brew

July 1978

The sun rose like a tide of light, gradually stripping the shadows from the makeshift camp kitchen. An ant crawling on the congealed blood on Katie's security blanket bit her, waking her to the sour waves of garbage smells, wood smoke, dogs and the rancid-yam smell of latrines. The stench reminded her of the disgusting, fly-infested shit holes.

"Every year it's the same damn thing," Riley said three days ago when she came up to his camp. "You and your mom are too damned tight-assed to get the lead out at the gathering, then start acting like you got turds stuck in crossways. The world will look a damn sight better if you marched your butt up to a shitter and took a nice healthy dump."

A nearby stream snuffled like a pack of hogs. Katie glanced over at Poo Boy asleep under a blanket near the fire's dying yellow vapor. With dry mud caked all over him, he looked like death warmed over. . She picked a hand mirror up off a nearby stump to examine her messy hair, sunburned nose, and the dirty whitish lines of soot around her mouth and eyes.

A gleam in her left eye caught her attention as the mirror darkened. A pair of violent eyes formed behind the gleam, and a round shape suddenly locked onto her, preventing her from turning away when the violet spots of intense light engulfed her amidst the din of a multitude of insects. Everything gradually came back into focus.

Joseph's Rasputin-like image glared out at her. Dressed in black, a bad sign. She felt his raspy whisper forming in her throat. *"They're not coming. They're dead because of youuu."* It took a monumental effort on her part to turn the mirror around.

She found a constellation of stars hovering on the mirror's back-side, shimmering in a blue round mass.

"YOU MUST DIE!" a cracked voice snapped to her left.

"Tarwater," Katie whimpered. Horrible things happened when her mother's ghosts spoke to her. Behind her, a growl. She gasped, then turned to look. A dog, chewing fleas out of its scarred hindquarters. And Poo Boy, now awake, picking at blister scabs of dead skin on his elbow.

An incredible wave of physical sadness suddenly gripped her chest, her diaphragm and stomach seeming to push up into her chest cavity. She dropped the mirror and pressed her forehead against the bark of a tree stump, waiting for her anguish and pain to reach the level where it would dissolve into a vague thought about something that might have been but actually had not. Then she would be *else*. Somewhere *else*. Somebody *else*.

And the only life left in her would be a thin warmth of sadness.

"DUGAI!" Changing Bear whispered forcefully.

Spear opened his eyes. He saw two slightly diffused bright spots in the thin cirrus clouds above her, one to the left of the sun, the other to the right.

"Sun dogs," said Changing Bear. "I've been waiting for such a sign to begin this day aligned with power." She glanced at his belt buckle, a sand-cast silver replica of Rainbow Man curved around the symbol of Father Sun. "Fix the image in your mind of familiar things you have with you. You'll need them as props to protect you, to bring you back."

Spear then noticed what had at first looked like birthmarks on her heels. On closer inspection, he saw they were tattoos of fanged faces. An Aztec design. Looking back at her face, he saw her teeth had a glistening red sheen. His muscles tensed with a flood of adrenaline as he struggled to recall the significance the seductive power a woman's reddened teeth and mouth in motion held in the Aztec world of eaters and the eaten. Teeth cosmetically reddened with cochineal were iden-tified with the sexually dissolute, with prostitutes. Aztec men, who controlled their own mouths, found a woman's freely moving mouth strangely erotic. Misted with drifting veils of erotic associations, an energetically chewing mouth was a sign of engulfment, extinction and death. A prostitute's lips and tongue in uninhibited movement, red-dened teeth clacking, was a vision of freely indulged oral pleasure. Dangerous and powerfully enticing.

"Let beauty walk before us," her lips and tongue addressed the sun. "Let beauty walk behind us. Let beauty walk all around us." She opened her medicine pouch, took out a pinch of pollen and offered it to the moving air. "In beauty it is finished," she said in a quiet, unhur-ried way, her gaze lingering. Then she looked at him.

There was a gleam in her calm eyes, as if she were about to let him in on a secret. A gust of wind moved a loose strand of blonde hair across her bottomless blue eyes, as if to remind him this was a white woman. A potentially dangerous white woman.

SUBVERT THE DOMINANT PARADIGM was painted across an old VW Camper where a pretty girl and a wiry boy held signs asking passersby to *Dose Us, Please*.

"Spare some green energy, sister?" Wiry Boy held his hand out to Changing Bear.

"Welcome home, brother," said a Scrawny Man with a haunted but kindly face. He had noticed Spear's interest in the fourteen-year-old girl standing in the middle of the dirt road, her face buried in her hands. "Her name's Willow, in case you run into somebody looking for her. Says she saw an E.T. cutting up a couple of bodies last night." He offered his hand to Changing Bear. "They call me Dr. Shitter." She shook her head, and he lowered his hand. "I'm in charge of digging the shitters and taking care of the brothers and sisters on bad trips. Any strange shit goin' down, I get whiff of it sooner than later."

"Did anyone else see the bodies?" Changing Bear asked.

"Don't know, didn't ask. With all the crazy rumors floating around, I don't pay no never mind to that kind of talk less I see it myself. There's a weird kid, a little older than her, calls himself Kosmo Lars, says he's from a planet of hermaphrodites. His ship's up there scoping us, checking out the vibes. Plans on taking all the good boys and girls to a better place. He, or somebody like him, probably's just fucking with her head."

The bright, glittering spray of a Celtic harp caught Spear's atten-tion. Off to the side of the road were four fresh-faced young women flanking the harpist, a burly biker with big-haired female vampires tattooed on his biceps that shimmied as he played a rippling cadenza, a stream of sounds cascading through its gorges. Then he began to sing in a pure tenor that soared ever up with the high grace-notes, his voice floating for a time until it ceased, the strings echoing, and re-echoing, like wild voices in a glen.

The image reminded Spear of Kokopelli, the fertility god of the Ancient Ones, a mischievous humpbacked flutist who mesmerized women with music. He then thought of the Fire Dance and the silly obscenities of Water Sprinkler, Kokopelli's Navajo equivalent, remembering how the smiles on the faces of women and children tempered with surprise and fear when the god approached too close. Showing that underneath their amusement was the shock that anyone, even a god, dared to ridicule sacred things.

The sound of a heavy motor and the noise of wheels crunching over a stony surface interrupted his reverie. A vapory shimmer of heat rose from the metal hoods of a police car and ambulance as they idled pass, leaving a trail of fruity, sourly luscious gasoline fumes and engine noises.

"Sun Elk was right," Changing Bear said in a hushed nervous tone. "The people behind this event are blind to the forces inhabiting this place. Otherwise they wouldn't have lured these people here. It's foolish to approach such forces with blind trust and little to no understanding."

Spear had an odd sensation of his eyes being fixed on the movement of her lips and on her reddened teeth as much as his ears were on the sound of her words. As if he needed to hold onto every word she said to anchor himself.

"Power must be met with power, or you will get a cauldron of seething excitement, instincts, opposites, mixed together, attracted and repelled at the same time. No fusion. A chaos that can easily turn into a horrible mixture of sensuality and cruelty." Her lips parted in the fierce smile like an act of love performed in darkness. "Witches' brew."

Spear instantly recalled the story of the essentially good Changing Bear Maiden, how she became evil when her power intermingled during sex with that of Coyote who, lacking control, was evil. From her came the Endurance Chant, called Prostitution Way by some anthropologists, which sought to dissipate the evil results of uncontrolled lust as well as undo the effects of any kind of recklessness. Since all secrets, even those of sorcery were divulged during the sex act, it also dealt with the dangers and illness caused by trying to keep a secret during sex. And for those exposed to witchcraft, the chant turned the evil around and directed it back against the witch who started it.

"Elvis loves you, brother," said a short middle-aged Australian in a t-shirt urging everyone to GET IN TOUCH WITH YOUR INNER ELVIS.

Spear then noticed a sign by a footpath. All of the paths branching off the fire road had some kind of sign naming the "tribe" inhabiting the area. This one said SHITTER. The wind, tugging at a note attached to the sign, spread the rotten-sweet latrine stink like the smoke smell of burnt toast. The note said: "*Please cover your shit, otherwise dogs will eat it and get sick,*" signed Starfeather.

Spear glanced across the road at a banner suspended between two trees. The banner said, ELVIS DIED FOR YOUR SINS.

"Elvis loves you!" yelled an Elvis Worker, so all could hear the good news.

"No In-dun tribe is represented here," Changing Bear said, using the Navajo pronunciation. "They can't understand the White Eyes' frivolous approach to sacred things. Sun Elk says if the white man could put rainbows in zoos, he'd do it."

Spear looked around. "Tourists."

"You're right," she laughed. "A tourist trap." Her clothes rattled as she made a sweeping motion with her hands. "Step right up, folks! Let Mother Earth and her Forces entertain you!" A sudden strong gust of wind jolted them, and she turned in its direction.

"Hear me, four quarters of the world, a relative I am," she said with fierce concentration. "Give me strength to walk upon the earth, a relative to all that is! Give me the eyes to see and the strength to understand that I may be like you. With your power only, can I face the winds. Great Spirit, my Grandfather, all over the earth the faces of living things are alike. With tenderness have these come up out of the ground. Look upon these faces of children without number that they may face the winds and walk the good road to the day of quiet."

The wind died down.

She shivered as if splashed by cold water, and gestured for Spear to come closer.

"A spirit's been following us for some time now," she whispered. "Don't say anything if you can help it." Then she added in a casual voice,

"The powers here know me, they're used to my voice," and continued walking as if nothing had happened.

They came upon a dirt track that went off the main track down an incline to a large clearing. A hummingbird shaped sign hung from a withered branch of a broken tree. A shadow darkened the broken tree as a cloud drifted, blocking off the sun.

"An evil omen." She pointed at the mangled tree with her chin. "Anyone conscious of the forces of nature can see that."

Spear then spotted the ambulance and police car in the camp below. A cop was examining the blackened hands and feet of the naked bodies of a man and woman.

A breeze set up a distant murmuring in the ridge top spruce, bringing up through the brush a faint smell he instantly recognized as the yellow smell of death and decaying flesh.

"The wind of life has left them," Changing Bear cautioned in Navajo, using the long, ugly guttural sound signifying the moment of the movement life inside a person's personality ceased and the disharmonies that had tormented it escaped through the nostrils to haunt the night. Trembling with irrational nervousness, Spear approached the camp.

Wind had drifted a little dirt against the man's outstretched hand, lying palm up. The blackness was dried blood. The skin from the palms and fingers, the heel pads, the balls of the feet, the under tips of the toes, and the glands of the man's penis had been sliced away. Witches made corpse powder from skin with the whorls of the soul stamped on it and used it to infect people with the Ghost Sickness.

The cop examined the red strings and fat of a clawed-open wound on the back of the woman's neck. "What do you make of this," he said to a medic. "Part of her neck's been gouged out. Same thing on the male."

A sickish chemical smell came from the tent, the stench of disinfectant producing the choking stink of shit-house ammonia. Spear fought a wave of nausea as he considered what their reaction would be if he told them witches took the small bones from where the neck joined the skull, dried and pulverized them to be used to spread corpse sickness.

"Like I said, dudes," a sinewy blonde male bystander said. "The E.T.'s did it."

"The gaseous birdlike things, right?" said the medic, trying to keep a straight face.

"Now why would creatures from outer space do something like this to us earthlings?"

"Their vibes weren't right," said Bystander. "Too slow, too weak. You have to be fast to survive. The quick and the dead."

Changing Bear had stayed where he left her up the track. When he saw how strangely pale she was, he realized he no longer had the ability to get a reliable focus on his thoughts, or on what he was doing, and he knew whatever their presence had triggered was about to begin.

SPEAR HAD NO IDEA how much time had passed when they reached the crossroads. A boom box was blasting *Riders on the Storm* for a tribe called the Doors of Perception who were dancing around a weathered portrait of Jim Morrison under the moving shadow of a Cooper's hawk swinging in the sky above.

"A cyclical being," Changing Bear whispered, pointing with her chin at an eleven-year-old girl clutching a filthy blanket, limping toward the crossroads. "If she speaks to us, it will be a proper omen and we will be obliged to do as she says."

Katie glanced at Spear as she limped by, her eyes the color of sky and clouds with mad, birdlike flutters of panic surfacing here and there on her dirty face.

"She has the Ghost Sickness," Changing Bear said uneasily. "It is good she did not speak to us." Noticing how Spear watched the child as she walked away, she hesitated. "She does have rather striking eyes. An unusually beautiful child, horribly soiled. And, she glanced at you in a way that said more than words could. They may be omens. If so, she will return." She then gestured up at a ridge alongside the mountain. "Sun Elk is up there."

They forded a stream and climbed the opposite bank into a clutter of fallen logs left by an old forest burn. The slope rose sharply, choked by brush and tumbled boulders. Spear stepped silently over ropes of blackened human feces among the stones, keeping well behind her.

SANDOVAL/Sun Elk was sitting on a sheepskin in a natural enclosure in the rim rock, his legs crossed, eyes closed, his body blackened with ceremonial ashes. Four prayer sticks were laid out in a basket on an altar of sand to inform the gods they were expected, and to warn persons not concerned to stay away.

"*Huu tu tu, huu tu tu.*" He sang the sound of night birds to summon the spirits to attend to the affair at hand. Then, his voice rising, "*Ohohoho, hehehe heya haya,*" the sound of the spirits answering in a language known only to the gods.

A large image of Kokopelli playing his flute on top of the yin/yang symbol, bent so far forward his flute almost touched the symbol, was painted on Sandoval's teepee.

Haskie Sam never reconciled with such odd mixtures of mysticism and Pan-Indian nationalism, especially the adapting of ceremonies to accommodate those who preferred the warmer months over the traditional season when the thunder sleeps. The Holy People taught that certain ceremonials must not be held until the snakes were in the ground, when the ground was frozen. Disrupting such rules reversed the sacred flow that restored people to the peaceful harmony that enabled them to walk in beauty, leading instead to madness and chaos. A shaman's knowledge, weakened by error, would ultimately destroy the shaman himself. Sandoval, though, compared Haskie Sam's attitudes to those of Christian fundamentalists who can't see the metaphors in the scriptures. *Hozho*, the basic concept of the Navajo, he said, allowed for adjusting ceremonial systems, like the adjusting of anything else, to keep in harmony with the inevitable.

Sandoval rose to his feet. "You expended much breath to get here," he said with a solemn side-glance.

The peculiar greeting evoked in Spear the strange sensation that comes when the real takes an unexpected shift to the unreal. He was seeing his uncle for the first time as Sun Elk. "I wish not to trouble you, my father," said Spear.

"Everything you do today counts," said Sun Elk. "Your mind, it must be right. It must be free of wrong thoughts. Free of anger."

Sun Elk entered the tepee, leaving them outside, and began a chant to waken the spirit in a Holy One's mask from its cosmic sleep. He put on the serrated, pink flint of Reared-in-the-Earth, who originated from Monster Slayer's buried afterbirth, then emerged from the tepee with Monster Slayer's mask. Time had darkened the leather thongs lacing up the sides and formed patterns of tiny cracks in the paint covering the sacred deerskin. Sun Elk jutted his chin and twisted his lips in a silent command not to say anything.

"The *nahualli* is here," he whispered, pointing his chin in the direction of a group of medium sized boulders a hundred yards to the left; tilting his head, as if to listen.

Spear scanned the area around the boulders for anything unusual, a shadow, a strange formation of rocks, a small animal, an insect, anything. The *nahualli*, as he recalled, was either an Aztec term for the transformed energy of a witch, or something to do with direct contact with the sacred powers.

"Fix your gaze on the *nahualli*," he said with an eerie rhythm, his words muffled, like soft coughing. "All thoughts, and words; they must be washed away."

Spear then heard a sputtering sound and turned toward it. A hummingbird stopped inches from his face and hovered there, looking straight at him, giving the strange sensation of a fast-twittering voice telling him something. Then the bird was gone.

Sun Elk tilted the feathered crest of the mask slightly and put it on, then took a rattle in his right hand and a pair of elaborately painted, feathered prayer sticks in his left. He crossed their shafts in an X, and raised the prayer plumes high, inviting the spirits of Reared-in-the-Earth and Monster Slayer, guardians of Big Sheep Mountain, to enter him.

"Be careful not to look at things directly," Changing Bear whispered, gently pushing Spear's arm to encourage him to look at the boulders again. He could feel her close to him He could smell her cochineal-scented breath.

The distant sound of a branch cracking followed by the flapping of bird wings startled him. A massive wave of energy rippled overhead and the boulders seemed to darken. The light became opaque, as if the sun had set.

"Let me hold your hand," Changing Bear murmured, carefully taking hold of his hand. Before he could respond to her touch, Monster Slayer let out a formidable scream, a yell so loud Spear felt the back of his neck swell and his entire body flush with an intensely pleasurable anguish. Then a sudden jolt on his arm pulled him inward like a sleeve being pulled inside out, leaving him wide open, devastated as everything closed in, beating on him, filling him with irrational animal fright as he fell spinning, full speed down a tunnel.

All he could see were cloudlike formations, dark masses, clusters of sparks and beams of light. No longer able to sense where his body was or whether his eyes were open or shut, he found his way into a clear place in the center of his panic from where he could see Changing Bear's eyes. They were not human eyes. A soft rustle moved toward him, like a snake slithering over small dry leaves. He experienced the nausea of an overdose of adrenaline and tried to get up, but his muscles had no strength.

"Don't focus on sound," said a voice drifting soundlessly like the wings of a butterfly. "There is no land, no air, no water. You're floating in a time that has nothing to do with the time in the smoking mirror of organic life. Listen to the whispers of the *nahualli*."

His eyes crossed and he saw strange figures kneeling over him, the left eye image of Monster Slayer superimposed on the right eye image of Changing Bear, and an iridescent being standing between the merged figures.

"Don't cross your eyes." Monster Slayer tapped him on top of his head.

Something on either side gripped him, lifting, his head jerking, bobbing back and forth, then limp. He saw tufts of weeds passing underneath. Then a sharp hummingbird's beak tore his chest open and its beak turned into light. Spirits, suspended in dewdrops, reflected in the shiny eyes of a jaguar. The dazzling radiance of a little girl's eyes filled with dancing birds.

"Don't come unglued, *nlyci lysoi*." Monster Slayer tapped him on his head again. He became a yellow mist in the glow of an enormous mass of undulating light that somehow whispered clumps of information, units of feeling full of the innuendoes associated with thinking, but they weren't thoughts. They were certainties, as if he were witnessing the organization of the world. A glare, superimposed on the normal world, created two separate worlds, and he moved between them, pulled in two directions, going away, coming to, all at the same time. A sudden series of sounds then came at him through a long tube.

"Blink!" Monster Slayer said forcefully in his right ear. "Stop indulging, blink!" The tube shortened and the sounds became recognizable. First as noises, then as loud words, and finally as words being yelled in his ears.

"Push your belly down," Changing Bear hissed in his ear. "Push your belly down!"

Her words acting like pliers, twisting and molding his feelings, so he knew to push his diaphragm down by gasping in air. The waving swell of his diaphragm then matched the swell of the earth below until there was no him, no complication of him. Only a luminous outline filled with liquid.

"Pull yourself together," said Monster Slayer. "You are an organic being, slide through that feeling and walk."

Their voices seemed to possess the power to separate him from the whisperings that were pulling him. Feeling his body relax, he found himself suddenly conscious of familiar things passing under his dragging feet. Clumps of dirt, small rocks, dry leaves. The ground then turned into a watery mutter, swelling into the sound of tumbling boulders sending icy water gushing into his boots. The numbing cold drove the air from his lungs.

"It's a pity you're so heavy," Monster Slayer said as he maneuvered him onto a sand bar created by luminous tissues of gravel that lay exposed between the rocks and the water. "You hook too easily on bewilderment." He scanned the surroundings with his ears. "The Forces that guide us brought you here for a purpose. You must be ready, like a hunter who hunts whatever presents itself to him."

Changing Bear examined Spear's eyes. Only then did he notice the raven beak secured to a juniper stick with yucca and buckskin thongs in her right hand. He wondered if she had poked him with this symbol of contempt.

"*This is the end, my friend,*" he heard the dead Door singing out from a distant boom box. "*My only friend, the end.*"

"We will now go to a tree where we will wait in silence for the Power that summoned us here to reveal Its designs," Monster Slayer said.

KATIE STOOD SUSPENDED inside a bubble. The mutterings of the people swarming around her parents' tent were like hymns to her solitude and silence. Clutching at her security blanket, she tried to make out the faces in the body bags without breaking the transparent membrane separating her from the noise and activity. Someone bumped her, rupturing the magic bubble, engulfing her in a sudden wall of insect howl when she saw a big fly land in the corner of the dead man's mouth.

A cop waved the fly away as he zipped the bag up over her father's face. When he glanced over at her, he saw a girl with a filthy blanket trembling against her dirty face. He'd never seen such a serious expression on a child before.

"You know these people?" he asked.

Katie swallowed a mouthful of silence when she realized the cop had bagged her parents like so much garbage. What had once been her parents reminded her of the scene in *The Spawn of the Stinking Dead,* the one where they hacked the screeching spawns to bits. She stood there staring at the stinking dead while the birds lolloping in nearby branches began making loud cranking cries.

Then a Big Fly landed on the cop's sweaty face.

"You're hurt," the cop said, noticing the blood on her left heel.

"Leave me alone!" she screeched with sick, defiant eyes.

"It's okay, sweetheart. I won't hurt you," he said, brushing the fly away.

She screamed, "No! No!" and limped as fast as she could away from the fly.

"Wait!" yelled the cop. "Come back!"

The burly biker/harpist then stepped in front of the cop, blocking him.

A buzz bruised the air behind her as Katie, feeling heavy like an animal shot with a tranquilizer dart, the light bleeding from her eyes, weaved through a maze of bizarre strangers. A naked prophet with a flowing beard. A towering, painted Negro in pantaloons, an updraft of wind turning his sleeves into beating wings. A disheveled man in a crochet and appliqué jacket covered with doll heads and photos of Elvis.

"All the children are insane!" she heard the dead Door screaming from a boom box.

CHANGING BEAR tensely whispered to Spear, "The cyclical being returns. Once you've crossed a certain threshold it is the nature of the gods to put a blueprint in front of you. Children are messengers of the gods. Watch everything she does."

The buzz grew louder. Katie turned, expecting to see a fly but saw a hummingbird instead, zooming directly at her. As she veered aside, she tripped and fell on a creosote bush howling with insects, the bush pulling at her hair, ripping her flesh.

A middle-aged man with a medallion strapped to his forehead approached her. Paper peels of skin had burst on his nose, leaving hot patches, his face black with soot and dirt, his hair matted in a sickly black red sheen Spear thought was blood.

"Death's disruptive residue has drawn a vulture," Monster Slayer said to Spear. "The little bird pointed this child out to you. Placed her in your charge. From this point on you can no longer afford to be careless with power or it will turn against the both of you."

The Bloody Man grabbed hold of Katie's wrists and jerked her up, the bush ripping at her clothing and flesh. She screamed until she tore herself free of him, then jerked at her blanket until it ripped loose, and stumbled back, banging her head on a tree. Dazed, she staggered, staring blankly at the long weeds hanging in hanks from the crooks of branches like witches' scalps, until she collapsed and lay still at the base of the tree, whimpering like the newborn young of an animal calling out for those who loved her.

Changing Bear quickly went to her, sprinkling ashes on the Blood Man and the bush she had fallen on. She then placed the fingers of her left hand on the crown of Katie's head and whispered in her ear.

Monster Slayer said to Spear, "This child, she can't possibly grasp what Changing Bear is telling her. Or remember what she was told. But there is a part of her that will understand. And remember everything."

As if waking from a dream, Katie suddenly became aware of the swarms of flies buzzing around peoples' filthy feet and scabby ankles. A deeply wrinkled old woman with wild hair and a scrawny youth wearing a long Dr. Seuss hat approached her.

"Go away! Leave me alone!" she yelled at them.

"She's the dead couple's kid," Long Hat said in a high-pitched nasal voice.

"Oh, my," said the old woman, stepping back. "The poor child."

Monster Slayer handed the prayersticks to Spear. "Brush her back," he said. "Death is stalking her. Do not indulge your solemn nature."

After a brief glance at the sacred markings representing lightning and rainbows on the Thunder prayersticks, Spear went directly to Katie and brushed them across her back.

"Don't touch me!" Katie squawked, turning around with a frantic flicker in her eyes, like a bird inside her head wanting to get out. Her pupils had shrunk to a point, the ragged line rimming the large speckled blue irises accentuating the clarity of the surrounding whiteness.

The first time Spear saw blue eyes, they seemed odd to him. He thought their owner must be blind.

Katie absently brushed her hair over her left eye, the reflex of a bruised spirit. He wondered what her frightened eyes were seeing. When her troubled face took on a serene expression, time seemed to slow down to a stop. He heard her say "I'm an angel" in a soft voice so full of grace and compassion it startled him, filling him with a sense of awe.

"You've been energetically injured," he whispered respectfully. "You need help. My uncle, he's a medicine man."

The Angel watched the young Indian's kind eyes; his skin, the color of smoke, giving off a strange coolness with a faint scent of earth. She followed the movement of his chin, pointing at his masked uncle. The frightened child in her screamed. Her eyes, now like two wounds, drawing his attention to her bloody cuts and bruises.

"GET AWAY FROM HER!" boomed a deep voice.

When she heard his voice, Katie immediately calmed down. She glanced at the large gnarled toes protruding out of an old pair of sandals then up at Riley's towering six foot seven muscular body, his wavy shoulder length hair, his close-cropped beard.

"Poor little match girl fall down, go boom?" Riley muttered as he squatted down. "Quite a performance. Pity I didn't catch it on film. The living dead and the fallen angel."

She nestled into his familiar odors of cigarettes and bourbon. "Mommy and daddy," she cried, sobbing so hard she gagged, then cried more because of the gagging.

He touched fingers to her lips. "Sssssh, Angelica, I know," he whispered, gently stroking the crown of her head. "Everything's going to be all right, Sweet Face."

"But they're ... d-d-dead!" she gasped, choking on her vulnerability. Angelica was her weakest personality, the one least able to defend herself. Riley had called on her to deal with the death of her parents. She was afraid to know why.

"Yes, they are," he whispered, his large hands brushing the ashes off her hair. "But let's put a lid on the sackcloth and ashes bit for now, okay?"

"But it's my fault!" she sobbed. "If we'd stayed like they wanted us to, they wouldn't be dead! Joseph said they died because of me."

"Remember when you got into your dad's stash of angel dust because Joseph said it'd turn you into an angel? If I'd found you any later than I did, you'd be dead."

"Wasn't Joseph," she whispered.

"What?"

"Tarwater made us do it."

Riley stiffened. None of her personalities had ever mentioned her mother's ghosts having spoken to them before. "Why did you say Joseph put you up to it?"

"Cause he didn't stop me," she gasped, trying to keep from crying.

His face twitched while he considered this, then he asked, "Has either Tarwater or Playfaire spoken to you the last few days? Anything? Anything at all?"

Sensing the tension in his voice, she lied. "No." Though it was not really a lie because Tarwater talked to Katie, not to her. Then she remembered, *Ignore Everything.*

"If your mother's ghosts come to you, do *not* acknowledge or allow them access of any kind. If you do, now that your mother's dead, they'll attach themselves to you. You don't want that. They are the ones responsible for your parents' death."

"I could've screamed or done something to save them," she sobbed.

"No," he whispered as if telling a secret. "It happened too quickly. Your being there would've made no difference." He tilted her chin up and looked her in the eye as he considered whether to tell her more. "That's not quite true, Face. The difference it would have made … is… the man who killed your parents, he would have killed you, too. He was looking for you when I killed him."

Her wide-eyed, open-mouthed face stopped him. He lowered his voice and spoke gently. "He's the one who infected you and your mother with the Ghost Sickness that brought on your premature birth. The Wolf costume I had on last night, he wore it when he infected you both, and again when he killed your parents. I took it from him after I killed him. I don't know why I put it on. I knew I shouldn't have, but I did anyway because I wanted to … know its evil. To experience its power. I burned it after I left you, and got rid of his body. Took me all night."

"He made the ghosts?" Angelica whispered.

"I saw him throwing some kind of powder on your mother when she was trying to relieve herself. A big Indian there at the time said it was Corpse Powder, that it was used to infect people with Ghost Sickness. He told me this man was a Navajo Wolf, that he'd come to find and kill before he could infect anyone." Riley hesitated, watching her troubled face for some time before adding, "The parts of their bodies the Wolf took from them are the ingredients from which Corpse Powder is made."

MONSTER SLAYER beckoned Spear with a subtle movement of his head. "Now is the time to brush the child again, behind her left shoulder blade, as you state your intent to follow the Spirit's command. We are in the presence of power. Fear, confusion, feelings of unworthiness, none of that matters now. Power will find a way if you state your intent without reservation. Hold back nothing or power will turn against you and her vision of this life will be short. Her identity with divinity will blind her to the forces that guide us and she will be torn to pieces in the world of opposites."

Spear had a vague, undefined feeling that time was running out, and something unnatural and evil was afoot.

"Be careful of this man, *nltci ltsoi*," said Monster Slayer. "He's been somehow damaged beyond fear into an erratic and treacherous animal."

Spear spoke in Navajo as he approached. "*Aligned with the Spirit's command, holding back nothing! My will protects this child!*" he yelled, brushing her with the prayersticks.

"What the fuck you think you're doing?" Riley yelled.

"Powerful medicine," he said in English, brushing her again.

Riley shoved the sticks aside. "Beat it, Tonto!"

"*Yil tsa xockali!*" yelled Monster Slayer.

Riley turned toward Monster Slayer. Suddenly remembering the big Indian at Katie's birth, he realized the Indian behind this mask was the one who'd cautioned him of the powers behind masks. He backed off. Slowly at first, maintaining eye contact for a comfortable distance before turning his back to him and walking off, carrying Angelica.

"Changing Bear, she will place a prayerstick under a tree at the south and in a branch of a pine at the west where the gods must see them," said Monster Slayer. "Sun Elk, he will place one in the east and one in the north." He pointed at the pinion tree Katie had bumped her head on. "You will sit, facing that tree, until Sandoval comes for you."

"SOME MOVIE, eh?" Riley said to the face nestling against his shoulder as he carried her. "The Unknown is out there watching us, and we have no idea what will happen next. The only thing we know for certain is the world will never be the same. You know the difference between fear and excitement, Face? What do you think it is?"

Angelica mumbled, her thumb in her mouth.

"They're the same thing. Just a matter of degree, that's all. Fear is excitement out of control. So when things gets to be a bit too much, to get back on an even keel what you do is roll with it, roll with the fear. Unless, of course, you enjoy being scared shitless."

She squirmed, wishing one of the others would take her place. "Hurts."

"Yeah, hurts so good. That's how you know you're alive. In frenzy lies a hot little kernel of satisfaction. Gets you attention. And you do so love attention."

She closed her eyes and contorted her face, wishing harder.

"Yeah, yeah, I know kids are treated like mushrooms. They're kept in the dark and every so often someone dumps shit on them."

She choked on a sob, realizing she was afraid.

"C'mon, roll with it. Ever hear of gallows humor? That's when things are as bad as they can be. The righteous are fixin' to tear you apart and the only choice you got left is how to spend your last moments. Making light of the whole damn thing is the easiest way to enjoy the situation. When someone gives you the evil eye, give 'em the cold eye. The illusion of looking unconcerned is magical, Angelica. Anyway, we need to keep our wits about us the next couple days. Later when things cool down a bit, we can go to a secluded beach in Baja and scream, curse god, do whatever it takes to get it out of our system. You with me on this? You understand what I'm saying?"

"Sounds good," she sniffed because she had not understood a word he said. *Ignore everything.*

"If you aren't one pathetic looking angel," he laughed. "You got blood, sweat and tears, not to mention snot, dirt and sticky shit all over your face. Know what I'd do if I were an animal?" She shook her head. Then he licked at blood on her forehead.

Disgusted by the smell of his whiskey lips, she jerked her thumb out of her mouth and yelled, "Riley!" When he tried to lick at her eyeballs, she scrunched her eyes shut and pushed at his face. "Riley! Stop!" she screamed.

"Am I on an owie?" he said, re-positioning his hands.

She grimaced at the blood and filth smeared on his face and lips. "Ew! Gross!"

SANDOVAL signaled Spear not to speak when he returned, then sat down facing him.

There were many things Spear wanted to ask, but Sandoval seldom allowed him to ask questions about the Spirit. He said to think one could understand such things by asking questions was foolish. Questions were a routine that made concentrating on what was said difficult. Smarter to simply let people talk. You learn more with the ears than with the tongue.

"Women, they weave the web of life," Sandoval began. "They're the first instructors of all tribes. That I might learn the White Way, the Spirit sent four young white women as my instructors. The first two came when I was young. The third, Dr. De Stefano, you know from the university. Changing Bear, she is the fourth." Sandoval closed his eyes.

Spear appreciated the silence. He needed the time to adjust to the idea the only white woman he'd ever considered as a friend, Dr. De Stefano, was among those Haskie Sam referred to as Sandoval's crazy white women.

Sandoval spoke with his eyes shut. "These women, they came to me filled with a directionless urgency they resisted disciplining or channeling in any conscious direction. They had fallen under the spell of their unbridled drives, from which they found release only through emotional battles. Their indiscriminate, devouring feminine natures had to be transformed into something more disciplined and creative, so they could recognize and show the proper respect for their inner world. If not, they would have soon been pulled into the womb of death." He opened his eyes. "It was the design of the Spirit that I claim my knowledge of the White Way by unraveling the webs spun by these Spider Women."

"I have observed the ways of white women, as you said I should," said Spear. "But I have learned little, and understand nothing about them."

Sandoval shook with the laughter that rises from the belly. "Whites, they confuse you because there is much spirit sickness among them. They act as if they have no family." He signaled Spear to remain silent. "Eleven years ago, when the pagans held their first festival here, Pinto Pasquaanti and I came to this mountain with Old Woman Gray Rocks. Gray Rocks, she was concerned about the evils the intrusion of the pagans might unleash in this place of power. She asked the wind what was required to restore harmony. The wind told her to paint lightning on my legs, corn on my breast and back, rainbows on my shoulders, and Rainbow Man on my chest." He outlined an arch from nipple to nipple with his thumb. It was bad luck to point at a rainbow with anything other than a thumb. "She did these things here, under this tree. When she finished, three rainbows, they formed in the sky." He gestured with his thumb in the direction the child had fallen.

"Pinto, he addressed himself to the pagans. Came as a mudhead, the Zuni sacred clown. The idiotic, deformed, insane fruit of incest. Covered himself with pink clay, wore the mudhead mask. You know it. Distorts the shape of the head. Hairless, many knobs. Tiny-rimmed eyes, puckered mouth. He did a crazy dance, to remind the pagans that compared to what the Creator wanted us to be, all men are clowns. He intended to make them laugh at themselves, but a pregnant white woman, she thought he was a demon. Got hysterical. Went into labor. Gray Rocks, she tried to calm her. The baby's father, he spoke to us in the manner one speaks to the Holy People. Asked what we wanted. The wind told Gray Rocks to bury the child's Twilight Cord to the west. Grey Rocks, she told the father the mountain demanded the umbilical cord as payment. We buried her cord at the roots of this tree here, to tie the child to the mountain, to draw her back to the spot where she was born when the Spirit was ready to reveal its designs. The Navaho Wolf, he knew this. He knew this child must return."

Sandoval stopped for a moment, then spoke slowly, weighing what he would say and how much he would say. "In the beginning, in the small and the great darkness, life is not something. It just is. Beginnings are not exact. They are darkness drawn to a minute point of non-darkness. Silence gathered into a small sound. It is in endings that light comes into focus, and the sound of creation rises in the silence. Endings are less shadowy than beginnings because consciousness has shaped them. Yet they, too, are not exact. For each end has in it the seeds of a new and unfamiliar beginning. Endings are completions of a cycle." He looked at Spear thoughtfully.

"That child is the seed of a cycle. She will be your instructor. You must try to restore her rhythm of growth when her walk through time brings her to you again." He allowed the silence to take over, giving Spear time to frame a response. Spear simply nodded. "When she comes, the webs she spins may seem impenetrable. Go into their darkness and follow the restless longing upward. Let no small thing stay forgotten and unhonored. And remember, seek the formless mover at the center of the speaking movement."

RILEY HAD CAREFULLY positioned Angelica face down on his pungent sleeping bag in his tent, then he foraged amongst the clutter for a bottle of hydrogen peroxide.

"This is going to hurt you more than it'll hurt me," he said as he opened the bottle.

"What're they going to do with—YOW!" Katie squealed through clenched teeth when he poured peroxide on her left heel. "W-w-what's gonna happen to them!"

"What does it matter, they're dead?" he said as he pulled her shirt up and worked her pants down. "If you must know there'll be an autopsy to determine the cause of death." He poured peroxide on a large cotton ball then dabbed at her scratches and cuts.

"YOWWWWW!"

"Would you rather I lick it? That's what animals would do."

"NO-OOO!!!!" she squealed, bracing herself as he applied the damp ball to the scratches on her back. "What's an autopsy?"

"They take out everything, blood, guts, everything," he said, dampening her forehead.

"Guts," she moaned, shutting her eyes tight to keep out a trickle of peroxide.

He took hold of her jaw to dab at a dirty cut. "Like gutting a pig."

His words fell on her like stones into a reflecting pool, turning mirror images into shattered confusion. "I feel sick," she mouthed through his sour fingers.

"They'll cut their stomachs open to analyze its contents. They'll do the same with their lungs, livers, hearts, brains, what have you. Slice 'em up, looking for evidence."

An intense glare of light reflected off him, his glowing eyes seeming like malignant reflections of swirling reddish lights. She gasped, a scream flapping in her throat, but she heard nothing as swirling lights pulled her into an interminable darkness.

"Look for the hot little kernel of satisfaction, Angelica!" he yelled. "Look for it!!!" Then something ripped inside her and she could no longer hold the muscles of her mid-section tense. Solid stench slid out of the spawn of the stinking dead. All fall down.

PART THREE

The Labyrinth

Sometimes we are devils unto ourselves
when we will tempt the frailty of our powers,
presuming on their changeful potency.

— William Shakespeare (*Troilus and Cressida*)

6

Devil's Decoy

May 1990

San Francisco

A child choked on the heavy light spilling like a luminous fluid from all her bodily openings, encasing her in a shroud of greenish gold light. *An-gel-ica!* the liquid voices gurgled, condemning her, filling her ears with a roar of bubbles in the rustling darkness of the hot, oppressive cave. Trying to cry out, she gulped in the darkness. Her body stupid with heaviness. Unable to make a move or make a sound as the nauseous pressure in her stomach swelled, spreading like shame.

"You must die!" the disembodied voices droned, anticipating her surrender as they engulfed her into their dark folds. She swallowed again and again, feeling herself letting go, submitting to the glow flowing out of her, its light soothing her nervous stomach.

Then nothing mattered anymore. Everything was over.

ANGELICA awoke with a jolt. She glared at the foppish stuffed frog in a pink frock lying on a pillow next to her. She swatted it, raising a puff of baby powder. A-frog Hitler, her dream protector, had failed to divert a childhood nightmare.

A slight buzz in her ears stopped her from swatting Hitler a second time.

The Others wanted her gone. She was their weakest link. Feeling her weakness, she lay back down on her pillow and pulled Hitler up over her eyes, sticking a thumb in her mouth, clenching it with a suck. They wanted her gone. Everyone did. Except for Dr. Ben. And Uncle

Riley, who'd done frightful things to her. The buzz got louder. "What if I died right now?" she whispered with her thumb still in her mouth.

She imagined the police report.

May 5, 1990. Body of a twenty-two-year-old white female found in fetal position with a thumb in her mouth and a frog on her face.

The buzz suddenly grew louder, vibrating inside her head, forcing her to fling Hitler off her face. The enveloping darkness had taken on ethereal iridescence. She glanced up to where Joseph sometimes hovered like translucent eyes in the ceiling.

"Joseph?" she whispered, imitating her ghost's raspy voice.

A grunt to her left! A tingling chill flushed her face and she bit down on her thumb. The sound reminded her of the funny snorts her father used to make for his purring pig routine to comfort her after a bad dream. She jerked her thumb out of her mouth. Daddy disapproved of her thumb sucking. Then she heard muffled footsteps, like the sweet tentative steps her father used to make when he came to tuck her in.

"*Katie?*" she heard him whisper.

"Daddy!" she cried, bolting upright, fully expecting to be transported through time to find her father at the edge of her bed smiling at her, not as a ghost, but as she remembered him. His voice had been so clear, so vivid, she was shocked when she found herself alone in her room. All alone, with no one to protect her.

She closed her eyes, and there he was. Not as a childhood memory, but as a clear vision of what he had actually been like. She scrutinized the incredible detail of his face, especially his sad eyes she had somehow forgotten over time.

"Something bad's going to happen," she whispered.

A foghorn moaned in the distance. It sounded like a tuba, adding a comedic-tragic feel to the fog. Catherine glanced at her watch. Ten past nine. Riley was late.

A squawk from a seagull prompted her to remember a t-shirt Riley used to wear to annoy her grandfather, Reverend Seabolt, with a seagull on it soaring over the words: *If you love somebody, set them free. If they don't come back, hunt them down and kill them.* The most holy revered Reverend had never loved her. He could hardly stand to look at her, believing as he did she was possessed by demons.

Riley, though, if he'd ever loved anyone, it was her. She'd found comfort in that, even after having heard someone say he was a terrible enemy, but as a friend he could be much worse. She knew he regarded her as neither an enemy nor a friend. She was much more important to him than either of those.

Suddenly her stomach contracted as if something were pulling her down from the middle of her body. The pain in her gut had an abstract edge to it, like a memory of pain and not so much as the pain itself. The air felt moist and antiseptically cold against her face.

"*How are you?*" whispered a tight raspy voice.

"I'm fine, Joseph." She disliked Joseph's questions, not so much because he already knew the answers, as he was always looking for whatever she deprived him of by being less than truthful. He liked when she asked him questions, even though he knew what her questions would be before she asked them. He used to visit her only in mirrors and bathrooms, or when she closed her eyes; but he'd taken to popping up wherever and whenever he pleased after she'd asked a medium if she could summon Hitler's ghost.

Joseph said he could speak for Hitler since they were both suicides. "*What did you do to your hair?*" An odd question for Joseph to ask.

The hair along her forehead hung in loose ringlets; and the top, parted down the middle, was pulled into a tight bun in back. Loose and tight. "Nothing."

She closed her eyes to see if he would be there. He was. Dressed in white, just like her. Not good. She did *not* want him around her today. She needed her wits about her. The part of her known as Angelica woke up far too early and could not go back to sleep, which would make it easier for Joseph to distract her into slipping into Angelica when she was with Riley. That would be disastrous.

A sudden squall from a flock of gulls startled her. *An omen!* She found it hard to calm down enough to grasp at its meaning. A warning? Probably. Definitely!

A black Cadillac limousine emerged from the fog then slowed to a stop.

BEN KEPT HIMSELF HIDDEN behind dark sunglasses while the limousine made its way through the dense morning fog. Peter, their investor, an Arab in his late-twenties, had greeted him when he got in the limo. Booth, a tall somewhat obese middle-aged man dressed in black, said nothing due to his taking Ben's wearing dark glasses in the fog as a signal to leave him be. After positioning himself facing Peter and Booth, he waited for the limo to pull out into the fog before he turned away to stare out the window.

His failure to stabilize during the disastrous final hours of Riley's splatter film last year was something he chose to keep from others, in hopes the damage done would weaken enough over time for him to overcome it. Until then, he'd do what he could to keep up appearances by spending at least a few hours a week in his clinic.

Then Oliver Jodorowski came to him with a proposition.

Ollie and his father, Andre, had helped the eleven-year-old Ben deal with his having been raped. Ollie, three years older than Ben, had also been raped at age eleven, then again some months later by three drifters who had tortured and mutilated him.

Ollie's father came to the hospital after the police brought him in. He'd put off mentioning Ollie's mother, intending to wait until Ollie asked about her before telling him she'd killed herself. Ollie didn't ask, and Andre began to wonder why. When he finally decided to tell him, Ollie said he knew. He'd felt her death as it happened.

OLLIE'S TRAUMAS had been far more severe than Ben's, especially considering everyone knew about it. Ben did not want *anyone*, especially his parents, to know what happened. He did not want anybody looking at him the way they'd looked at Ollie after word got out of what his kidnappers did to him.

He was afraid his skittish mother would kill herself, like Ollie's did.

Going with Ollie to see Andre was difficult for Ben, because Andre was the psychiatrist who'd put his father, Irving, in the nut house. Ben did not want anyone, especially his parents, to know he needed help too. Andre, who was rendering his services free of charge, had assured Ben he would not send him to the nut house, nor would he, under any circumstance, break a confidence.

Ben eventually relaxed, until some months later when Andre drew his attention to the interlocking links between masturbation, rape and the underworld.

Ben's shocked feverish face told Andre all he needed to know.

Andre had been instrumental in influencing Ollie and Ben's decision to become psychiatrists. He was a Freudian who dealt with, among other things, complexes related to gods and goddesses. Ollie and Ben both chose Carl Jung and James Hillman for their spins on relationships with archetypes, Ollie focusing on archetypal fields of events. Ben centered on sexual pathologies, a result of personal traumas that made him prone to restive fevers with an itch he couldn't scratch. Rape, as the entrance to the underworld.

BEN WAS SURPRISED when Ollie contacted him after hearing what had happened on the final shooting day of Riley's chaotic splatter film last year. He'd called to let him know that Mindy, a mutual acquaintance, was making a porn film that could serve as an archetypal counterweight to Riley's disastrous splatter film. Mindy's eros versus Riley's chaos. For it to work, Ben had to play the irritant factor within the dynamics of her project, which was purposefully constructed to tempt the fates. Together, Oliver and Mindy had managed to convince Ben that, if he played his part through to the end, he'd have an opportunity to reboot the balance of his mind.

WILL HAD TRIED to lure Ben to his special place several times before. This time he managed to, after the shoot was done, because the special place was adjacent to the swing party house where Mindy's movie was being shot. Will owned both buildings, and used his status as a benevolent landlord to check out Mindy's swinger parties for women attractive or young enough to tweak his interest. Bartering with what he referred to as *these life forms* for the use of their bodies in his special place excited him.

The special place was a large room in the center of a much larger basement. He'd made an effort at keeping it from smelling like a basement, but the thick carpets and peculiar wallpaper lent a turbid atmosphere to the place, so much so Ben felt as if his vision was blurring as they descended into the dimly lit basement. He noticed several dark rooms along the wall facing the stairs that appeared to be cells. Will pushed a button on a keypad and the exterior of his special place lit up, enabling Ben to confirm the dark rooms were cells. When Will pushed another button, the steel reinforced door of the special place clicked open. Its interior lights went on when he pulled the door open.

The interior of Will's special place was much larger than Ben expected. Well over two thousand square feet, the center of which was hidden behind Arabian Carpets suspended from the ceiling. The room itself was cluttered with cameras, film equipment, trunks, folding chairs, boxes of various sizes, and cages large enough for one or more humans. The bondage and discipline paraphernalia and sex toys made

Ben uncomfortable, as did the mixture of strange odors he could not identify. Will pushed yet another button, and the hanging carpets began to slowly roll up, gradually exposing a pale, unconscious, naked young girl sprawled out on her back, on an autopsy table, her hips somewhat wider in contrast to a much thinner waist. A miniature hour-glass figure. Ben had never seen anything like it before.

Julie disappeared from the set before the shoot was done, without letting anyone know where she was going. Here she was! Unconscious, looking pale enough to be... a flash of panic jolted Ben when he saw the smirk on Will's face.

"She's quite beautiful naked, is she not?" Will slurred in a heavily nuanced voice. Ben said nothing.

WILL AND RILEY became friends in the summer of 1938. They'd managed to stay friends over the years because Riley helped clean-up the aftermath of Will's having gutted his uncle Franz, who'd sexually abused both of them when they were kids. Franz had bled out by the time Riley got to Franz's hunting cabin to help dispose of his remains, a result of Will's having sliced off his uncle's genitals to pickle them in a jar to keep as a souvenir. This blood sacrifice had intertwined Will's and Riley's lives on an archetypal level.

Earlier that same summer, Riley had tempted the Fates in a field of events linked to Ben. Riley was the first boy molested by Franz, Ben the last. Both boys had bolted on the same day from what they thought was a she-devil in a park, leaving Ollie behind to face the consequences. Only Ollie understood this was Hecate, Queen of the Underworld and protector of women, but it was years before Ben grasped the implications. All of which eventually resulted in Ollie's efforts to lure Ben into Mindy's project in 1990.

Will was a few years older than Ben, and a good two feet taller, with a loud intimidating voice. Ben wanted nothing to do with Will or Riley. Nonetheless, over the years, the Fates kept linking them together. It was in hopes of ending their connection that Ben agreed to work on Mindy's project.

The sight of Julie's naked body shocked Ben. Whatever Will had done to Oliver's daughter was sheer madness. If Will was afraid of anyone, he should be of Ollie.

"Check her out. Give her a sniff," Will giggled, snorted. "You know you want to."

Ben found himself biting down on his lower lip, like a frightened boy.

"Well, then," Will said in a breathless voice as he turned her over on her belly. "Let me show you something that will absolutely blow your mind. A fine firm compact bubble butt, wouldn't you say? Just barely wide enough for an hour glass figure. Quite unique, I'd say."

Beautiful, Ben thought. Like tropical flowers or exquisite jewels. Judging from the sheer beauty of her mound, Ben had expected her holes to be exquisite as well. But what he'd felt when he touched her was shock, as if he'd touched a high voltage wire.

Will sniffed at her. "Wooo! You're going to love this," he giggled-snorted as he pulled back from her. "Go on. Take a sniff. Trust me, you'll be glad you did."

"She's Oliver's daughter," Ben said in a loud whisper. "You've got to be crazy to mess with her. Ollie will know."

Will made a condescending snort. "She isn't his daughter. He raised her. He did do that. But she isn't his blood. If he is watching us, and you're right he most likely is, he'll neither interfere nor punish us. He will leave all of that up to the Fates."

Feeling as if he'd been hypnotized, Ben found himself bending toward her. Then it struck him. This was the altered state Ollie had promised. The opportunity for him to—to what? Restore? Balance? Yes! To his mind. He needed to allow his mind to shift, to let in whatever needed to be let in. He thought of Ollie, who'd cultivated a reputation for being something of a magician. One capable of becoming an invisible observer who could only be seen in mirrors. And not even then, should he so choose. Anyone touched by Ollie when he was invisible would have gotten a shock, like the one he had when Will spread Julie open. Ollie did it to let him know he was there. Having realized this, Ben sensed Ollie was watching him sniffing her. That was when he realized he actually was sniffing her. He had no idea when he'd started, nor for how long he'd been doing so. He felt as if he'd fallen asleep, dreaming of his fingers digging into her. Only when he dreamed he was pulling them out, did it occur to him her body felt cold to his touch. He panicked as he reached to feel her pulse. No pulse! She was not in her body. If this were a dream, it was a lucid one. Like the lull between delirium and psychosis. His ears started buzzing with the silence of the Underworld when he realized he had no idea of what he was doing.

He was in a dreamlike realm of darkness and silence. Everything, unstable. In flux. Suddenly he became aware of what he was seeing. Two wide open holes. The most dazzling glorious shades of pink. Beautiful beyond belief. More so than he could ever have imagined. He couldn't stop sniffing, his eyes shutter blinking on their own accord as he breathed in beautiful cool scents of some deep sensual sweetness, rendering him incapable of grasping the reality of what he was doing. His mind afire, lost in a magnificent world of odors and taste. Out of control, he closed his eyes and lowered his nose to breathe her in. Blessed with bucolic visions and pristine images of giggling nymphs.

When he pulled her eyelids up, he found himself staring into two lustrous pools of darkness. A view into an oceanic abyss. He could remember nothing after that.

WHAT HE DIDN'T KNOW was Will had taped everything Ben had done to Julie's unconscious body. A few days later, he came to Ben's home to show him an edited version of what he'd done. Ben was too shocked to say or do anything as he saw himself turn into a slurping, drooling monster. Sucking her toes, grunting like a pig. Slobbering as he licked. Unable to control himself, like Pan with his nymphs.

A grunting, groping ogre devouring a Sleeping Beauty. Mouth! Ears! Nose! Digging into her, shouting "Finger licking good!"

He could not remember doing any of this, and saw nothing of what he thought he remembered doing. When he saw himself licking her eyeballs, he yelled, "SHUT IT OFF!" over and over, and kept on even after Will had shut it off. He stopped shouting only after Will handed him a photo of Julie tied up. Naked. In a cage.

Ben heard himself roaring, "DID YOU KILL HER!!!" over and over while Will looked on, snickering. Until Ben lost his voice. Then Will sprayed him with something that knocked him out. When he regained consciousness, Will was gone.

He'd left the video cassette behind, and the cage photograph.

Ben stared at the photo of Julie looking dead, his heart thumping so hard he could hear it. "Oh, my God! I hope she's not dead," he whispered as tears formed in his eyes.

In ways he could not quite grasp, he knew a part of him loved that so-very-much-alive-impossible girl. "I'm sorry for what I've done. So sorry. Please, don't be dead," he gently whispered to the photo, remembering the sweet scent of her spiked red hair as he felt himself sinking into a darkness devoid of light and sound, collapsing in on itself.

WORTHINGHAM claimed he'd always paid the women or girls he used. Tying naked women up (the younger the better) and taking pictures of them in a cage was what rocked his world. But with Julie, sensing she'd refuse him no matter how much he offered her, he took a different tack. One of his clients had introduced him to something he referred to as a vapor, capable of rendering a target instantly unconscious for at least two to three hours. It also rendered them incapable of recalling anything that had happened up to an hour *before* their being vaped, making it difficult for them to know who or what had knocked them out. Or, of what may have transpired while they were unconscious.

Ben, though, had *always* paid for sex with only conscious, consenting adults. He would not have it any other way, not even with his missing wife, who'd found it rather disturbing on their honeymoon. Although she'd been accustomed to being paid for sex for most of her life, she did not want her husband to pay for it. They compromised by opening a joint account consisting only of the money he'd given her after having sex. She'd made it quite clear she had no intention of spending any of it, and she didn't.

He'd financed his search to find out what had happened to her from this account.

After having done what he did to Julie on the thirtieth anniversary of his wife's disappearance, when he was most vulnerable, he remembered why he thought she might still be alive. The day she disappeared, she'd called him a monster when she handed him photographs of him raping a young woman in a sleazy motel room. He reminded her that was how they'd met. They'd both approached him *as a client* to ask him to take them to the Underworld. Seeing how upset she was, he promised to change his ways. He'd stop paying her for sex, he'd never again take any one else to the Underworld, or have sex with a client, or anyone else other than her. She'd listened in silence, not saying a word even after he was finished. She left in silence. Taking nothing with her. And never returned.

He hired a detective to find the detective she'd hired, to ask him to join forces to find out what had happened to his wife. Twenty years later, he figured she either didn't want to be found, or she was dead. He wanted to know which. The detective she'd hired said she didn't want to be found. The detective he'd hired said she'd disappeared in Saudi Arabia under suspicious circumstances, and was never heard from again. Ben chose to believe she was alive. That she had found the peace she could never have had with him.

THEN BEN spotted Katie, dressed in white, leaning against a fence in the fog. "There, that's Katie," he said as he took off his sunglasses. "Let's wait and see what she does."

Booth said, "She looks skittish. Are you sure it's a good idea to mess with her? We don't want to scare her off."

"I know her. I was her therapist. Just watch what she does."

"She's beautiful," Peter said out loud, as if to himself. "Absolutely radiant. I can see why Riley calls her an angel." He moved to open the door.

"No!" Ben reached over to stop him. "Wait for her to come to us."

Catherine watched the handsome young Arab in a silk Hawaiian shirt and baggy white pants step out of the limo, leaving the door ajar.

Peter stared at her as if she had an invisible barrier that drew him to her while holding him back. Her eyes, exquisite blue jewels embedded on glistening clear white orbs, captivated him. He felt a strange urge to lick them. Her soft lips parted, shifting his attention to her wet, evenly milky teeth, then a cascade of crystalline laughter shattered his spell.

"The gull of it all!" Catherine said, pointing at the fresh splotches of seagull poop on the limousine's roof.

"Catherine Seabolt?" Peter stammered, mystified by her laughter and girlish voice.

His nervousness emboldened her. "You must be Riley's investor," she said, making a show of checking him out. "Peter Hakim, right?"

"Yes, right. Pleased to meet you. Sorry, I'm a bit, uh, I didn't expect you to be—"

Catherine giggled. "Riley brings out the monster in people, doesn't he?"

"Monster?" He looked worried. "Uh, no. If anything, he thinks you're an angel?"

She signaled him to come closer, and positioned her lips by his ear. "Where angels tread, monsters follow." She felt him freeze, her hot voice resonating in him. "They attract devils, so keep the angel talk to yourself." She glanced at the limo. "Why black?"

"Black? Oh, the limo's not mine. Belongs to John."

She noticed the Fat Man watching her through the open door. "John?"

"The production designer. Also, Riley's understudy. He'd finish the film if Riley was to, you know…"

"Really? His *under-study*?" she giggled, nervously. "The big guy there?"

"Yes," he said, inhaling her crushed flower scent as she moved past him, watching her white sweatpants riding up between her butt cheeks when she leaned into the limo.

She shot a glance of disapproval at Dr. Ben, then turned to the Fat Man with an amused grin on her face. "How do, stranger?" she said to him with a Tennessee lilt.

"John Wilkes Booth," the Fat Man said with a soft Georgia accent, gesturing for her to come sit next to him.

"John Wilkes?" she grinned, as she entered the limo. "For real?"

"Descended from an illegitimate child. My daddy was right proud of that."

"Right proud." She nodded at Booth. Then, noticing Ben seemed to be amused by something behind her, she glanced back and caught Peter gawking at her backside.

"Where's Riley?" she snapped as if he'd done something utterly incomprehensible. "He's supposed to be with you."

"The motel." Peter blushed. "We're picking him up on the way. It's close, not far."

She quickly reconsidered going with them. First, there was the problem of Joseph and Angelica. She could ill afford having either one around today. Then, the omen. A warning. Thirdly, Riley was supposed to be with them; and he sends Ben in his stead, knowing full well how Ben's smelly mind games upset her. Mostly, though, she didn't like how goofy nervous she felt. In spite of all that, Peter's boyish embarrassment somehow reassured her. Thinking she could work with that, she got in and sat beside Booth.

Peter re-positioned himself next to Ben, facing her.

"Let's go, Christian," Booth said to the driver.

She tittered and the three men all turned to stare at her as they drove off in silence.

"So, John, why a black limo?" she said with an unaccented professional voice.

"I like black," Booth said, pushing his black wire rimmed glasses up on his nose. "Gives it a touch of European elegance."

"Euro-peon el-e-glance," she said, reverting to a Tennessee accent. Then silence as she considered making a comment about how black made her think of it as a hearse.

"Hell-o, Katie," said Ben, gazing at her chest. "Long time no see."

She leaned forward, placing her elbows on her knees. "Oh, you're not going to do your talking to my tits routine today, are you now, doc?" Ben immediately locked onto her eyes and she found herself feeling considerably more uncomfortable with eye contact. "And, don't call me Katie. My name's Catherine, with a C."

Ben lowered his eyes back on her chest. "Catherine is it now? I haven't seen you since that mess you made on Riley's last picture." His eyes moved back up to lock on hers. "Aren't you in the least bit concerned he might scare the crap out of you again?"

"Okay, more weirdness," she shrugged, turning away to look out the window. Ben liked to play mind games, planting image-feelings in people's heads. Riley was especially susceptible to them.

She turned to Peter to ask, "What's the good doctor's involvement in all this?"

"Ben thinks Riley's lost it, and there's no getting *it* back," Peter said, looking anxious. "I've never worked with Riley before, but from what I've heard he's always been rather loopy as a director."

"That's his MO, alright," Ben said, addressing her tits while mimicking her Southern accent. "But you ain't seen hide nor hair of him in a coon's age, Katie." Then, grabbing her with his eyes, he shifted into his professional voice. "He got into crack after you abandoned him, and he's managed to twist himself completely outside the loop."

"Yawl fixin' to tell me, what kind of loopy loop that is, doc?" she said, feeling less vulnerable hiding behind a backcountry twang. "Once again, my name's Catherine."

"You want me to tell you?" he said as he lowered his eyes to her tits. "Well, let's compromise. I'll call you Catie with a C. So Catie, it just so happens to be one of those things you have to see for yourself." He looked up, grabbing her with his eyes as he asked, "If I were to tell you that you have a beautiful body, would you hold it against me?"

Catherine squinted, pressing her lips together in a frown, smelling patchouli. "Are you going to be on set, doc?" Smells were among his bag of tricks. Little spray vials.

"You betcha, Tender Tits. My job is to keep his fires under control."

"Yeah, I'm sure you no doubt will," she muttered, feeling violated, *a feeling he no doubt intended to implant.* She didn't like it, but she knew from experience, feeling through Ben's image and odor implants often worked more effectively than mentally processing his more to-the-point monologues. *Feeling through* generated both the experience and the image of Eros and Chaos being set up. Or, so he claimed.

"It's important you grasp the situation," Peter interjected, worried by her frown.

"I think I do," she said. "You all feel things are getting out of hand in pre-production. You'd like to fire him but you need his name for a distribution deal. Riley says he can keep it together if I worked the project with him. Will got *him* to commit, if he got me, it'd be on con-dition I'd have the power to fire *him* if I deemed it necessary, without *your* losing the right to use *his* name on either this project or the next. Riley agreed, providing if he were fired, he'd be paid in full and that I'd work both projects, to represent his interests. That about it?" Peter winced as he nodded. "What do you think, John Wilkes?" she said, circling a finger around her temple. "Has he looped the loop?"

"I'm an ex-vice cop," Booth said, scrutinizing her eyes for signs of madness. "I've seen all kinds of crazy. I'd say he's lost his moorings."

"His moorings," she mumbled, tensing. *I'm a mooring. A major mooring.*

"Not your usual make-up job, eh?" said Ben. "Hope it's not too weird for you."

"Well, boys," she said with what she hoped would pass for being amused. "Don't really matter much one way or t'other. What's a little weirdness? That's life and, what the hey, it might even be fun." Then, sud-denly, it struck her, Ben *was* warning her against Riley repeating what had happened the last time. A direction Spear expected Riley to go, as did she. And Ben no doubt knew that. He was warning her there was more to it?

"Yeah," Peter ventured cautiously. "But if it's more than a mind fuck and he really is crazy, we need to know. There's more to this than just my investment to protect."

Feeling the tension in the air, she exhaled through puckered lips. "I know," she said in her gentlest voice. "If worst comes to worst I will fire him and take the heat for it."

Peter nodded, satisfied by her word.

Ben looked her in the eye. "Did the Chief say anything about Riley's behavior?"

"The Chief?" She made a wry face.

"Your guru, the Injun. Douglas."

"Yeah, I know who you meant. No," she lied, trying to pay attention for the hidden meanings behind the annoyances he was planting. "I didn't ask. He didn't say"

"He didn't?" He looked doubtful. "The woo woo said nothing? Not even the title of the splatter movie?"

"Well, no, he didn't. But I have a sneaking suspicion you're about to."

"*Devil's Decoy,*" he said, looking at her tits. "Pure splatter, only worse than his usual. Much worse." He looked up into her eyes. "Much like Riley."

"Ooooh! Sounds scary," she giggled like a school girl. *Is he warning me away?*

"That's his motel up ahead," Booth said as the limo slowed to pull to the curb opposite a multi-level structure with rooms opening on exterior walkways.

"Room sixty-eight," said Peter. "Sixth floor."

"You expect me to go up there and fetch him?" she said.

"Yeah." Peter looked worried. "He made a point of that. As a sign of respect, you come to him. You know, as a friend. He wants a private conversation first."

"Nervous, darlin'?" said Ben. "Thinking this may be more than a mere mind fuck? Feels that way, doesn't it? Maybe a bit out of your league? Too much for you to handle?"

She crossed her arms over her chest, with a fixed smile on her face, something Ben would have commented on if this were a therapy session. This, however, was a very different kind of game. Checking her out while making her check herself out, while they both tried to determine if she were, in fact, out of her league.

"So, you want to know his twisty loop?" Ben leaned forward, looking her directly in the eye. "He's seeking redemption and considers you, his Angel, as the only one whose voluntary submission could break his spell of madness. But, I doubt whether an angel's purity is special enough to survive that kind of submission. What do you think?"

"Angel's purity?" she giggled, knowing better than to answer his question. *He was warning her.* "Redemption?" *About what? Not to go to him now?* "Spell of madness?" *Or, was it a set up?* "We seem to have made a transition from horror films to fairy tales."

She reached over to open the car door, brushing Peter's knee with her fingertips while mouthing the word *monster* as she did so. Peter focused on her butt as she got out.

"Maybe this time he'll go easy on you and just scare your pants off," Ben shouted.

"I wouldn't be so sure of who his intended victim is if I were you," she said as she turned around and leaned back in. "Could be Spear and I are in cahoots with him. Maybe I'm a witch just waiting for the right moment to put a hex on you." She gestured to the sky with both hands. "May the frozen lavatory waste from a passing jet crash through the roof and flatten you." She laughed a tight little laugh as she watched the three men.

Peter laughed self-consciously. Booth rubbed his chin.

"Or," Ben said, looking her directly in the eye. "You could just go on up there and, should you ascertain he's unfit tell him flat out he is just that. Then fire the son of a bitch."

His suggestion shocked her, and she was acutely aware they'd seen weakness and confusion on her face. She put on a mischievous grin, then addressed Booth and Peter.

"Remember, boys. Just because you take something seriously doesn't mean it's not a game." She winked then started to turn away. Ben stopped her with a wave of his hand.

"Seriously. If he fucks around with you, fire his ass," said Ben. "Game over."

She sensed he was addressing her link to Angelica, her weakest personality, something he used to do when he was her therapist. He'd always been overprotective of Angelica. Why would he want to put Angelica in a position like this?

She hardened her face, focusing on Peter. "Are you on board with this, Peter?"

"If you think he's crazy," Peter said, nervously. "You know, whenever, if you decide he's crazy? It's up to you."

"Of course he's crazy. Always has been. That's why people like his movies."

"No, no. You know," said Peter, then whispered, "Disemboweling someone crazy."

Disemboweling someone crazy? Alarmed, she turned to Booth for his input.

"I want his job, and the use of his name," said Booth with a shrug.

"I say, fire him. I'd put off doing Decoy, maybe not even do it. We'd do the erotic feature first."

"Don't give him an inch," Ben said in the softer voice he used with Angelica.

Ben and Riley both had a knack for speaking through the Seabolts to Angelica. Angelica was the one part of her that she and the Seabolts did not want to relate to these two. Then a chill, a strange mixture of awe and dread, worked its way through her, and suddenly it was quite clear Ben actually wanted *Angelica*, the child woman, to fire Riley. Why? She needed to think this through; but she felt Ben watching her, so she shifted her attention to Booth and Peter. Is this what they really wanted? To fire Riley? Game over.

"Games are never over with Riley, Doc," she said, looking back at Ben.

"If *you* fired him," Ben told Angelica, "the game would be over."

Then it occurred to her, maybe Angelica firing him would actually have a stronger impact on Riley than if any of the others did. Well, except, maybe, for Angel.

"Well, boys," she said. "Here goes nothing." Then she walked away.

"That's got to be the most exquisite woman I've ever seen," Peter muttered, watching her butt walking away,

"Well, that went well," Booth said to Ben, ironically. "Do you think she'll do it?"

"Oh, yeah. Eventually, she'll get around to it," Ben said, then added to see if Peter was paying attention to anything other than her butt, "Unless Riley kills her first."

"There's something almost hypnotic about her laugh," Peter said, still watching her butt as it got smaller and smaller in the distance.

"You're hypnotized, alright," Ben snorted. "Hypnotized by her bubble butt."

"Riley says she's a virgin?" Peter said as she disappeared on the stairwell.

"Yeah, and a rocket scientist to boot," said Ben.

"I've done some checking up on her," said Booth. "There's something to the scientist bit." "She's studying for a degree in particle physics. Her father got her interested in it. All in all, she is more functional than I expected. I was down South when her grandpa accused Riley of killing her parents. Some folks down there still believe he butchered

Katie in a snuff film then turned her into a zombie."

"Her parents were murdered?" said Peter.

"Officially they OD'd on cocaine," said Ben. "What made folks suspicious was their bodies had been ritually mutilated postmortem."

"What's a snuff film?" said Peter.

"That's a film where someone is murdered for real," said Ben. "Riley supposedly shot one in South America."

"He didn't, though, right?" asked Peter.

"Well, who knows," Ben shrugged. "Maybe Sweet Buns is a zombie."

"I can see why he calls her an angel," Peter said. "Her eyes are like jewels. And her mouth. In the old country, they say you can tell what a woman's cunt is like from her mouth. If so, she has a spectacular mound. A beautiful flesh flower."

"Yeah, and Little Orphan Fanny's shit don't stink, either," said Ben. "Bet you think it comes out the poop shoot gift wrapped with little pink ribbons."

Booth chuckled. "Swear to god, you two are nuttier than she is."

"You know, the sweetest kittens have the sharpest claws." Ben made claws with his hands. "By the way, she shaves her flesh flower."

"And how would you know that?" said Peter testily.

"Trust me, angels don't have pubes."

"Devil or angel," Booth laughed. "Lighten up, it's just pussy. Let it go."

THE DREAMER found the Young Woman sitting on a white bed in an empty foggy white room. He sensed in her a terrible fear. She was in love and, being in love, could no longer protect herself from the secret longings of her beloved. The Dreamer tried to console her, but found himself incapable of uttering sounds. He attempted to direct the thought to her that her beloved loved her too much to hurt her.

The Young Woman seemed to understand what he was trying to do and in a clump of energetic feeling communicated to him love had deprived her of self-control. She had no choice but to trust him, even though he could do anything he wanted with her. It would be so easy for him to betray her trust without intending to.

She seemed to falter, as if she were about to faint. A boundless wave of affection overwhelmed the Dreamer.

"I couldn't take the pain," he felt her say. *"Not from him."* She looked at him, pleading. *"He has to understand! I have no control!"*

He felt the pull of her fear, and he desperately wanted to reassure her, but a membrane of energy he could not pierce separated them. There was nothing he could do.

Then he felt her cry out, *"The pain will kill me!"*

JAKE AWOKE WITH A JOLT, surfacing through the dream's terrible desperation into the world of daily affairs. Before he was fully awake, he sensed some kind of message had stuck to him. He tried to grab and assemble what he could of the dream to get at the hidden feeling, the message. He'd wanted to comfort the dream woman, to tell her he'd never betray her. Who was she? She felt so familiar. Not that it mattered. He was not her lover, so anything he did ultimately did not matter. Her emotions felt so alive, so real. What did they mean? Residue of his love for his ex-wife? Losing control of the trust given to loved ones?

"Geez," he moaned, lying in his rumpled bed as if he had been thrown there. He maneuvered onto his hands and knees, "Ahhhhhrg!" arching his back.

The image of his hair in the smudged headboard mirror, awry in bunches of standing hackles, caught his eye. What happened to the vibrant, still boyish face of a year ago? *Forty-three.* He liked to think he looked thirty. Good muscle definition, firm butt. He used to wonder what it would be like to look in a mirror and realize he was no longer young. He used to think he'd feel relieved, no longer having to concern himself about it.

But he was not prepared for this feeling of … What?

He looked around the room. So many things to do. Cluttered dresser, messy closet, clothing on the floor. The "X" would no doubt feel vindicated if she saw what had become of their bedroom. As if she would give a damn.

He pulled his underwear off. Dropped it on the floor, then grabbed the phone and carried it into the bathroom where he turned on the shower. A sad face in the mirror stared back at him, its sadness pulling at him as his image faded into a fog.

Then the phone rang. He turned the shower off and picked up the receiver.

"Hello," he said. Silence. "Hello?" Faint breathing.

"Hi." A girlish voice. "Where are you? Right now."

"Uh." He hesitated. The voice sounded familiar. "The bathroom."

"Oh," her voice quavered. "Are you naked?"

"Well, I was about to get in the shower." Heavy, expectant silence.

"Are you alone?" she asked him.

"Yes." He sat down, on the toilet. Could Jazz have put someone up to this, to test him? "And who might you be?"

"Kali," she said playfully.

"I don't know a Kali." The voice sounded like a child's.

"I'm a friend of Lili's."

"I don't know a Lili either." He listened to her breathing, wondering what she was thinking.

"If I were there with you," the voice trembled, "what would you do to me?"

"Right now?" He did like her cute voice. "Well, I am naked."

"Ye-es!" she gasped. "I'm naked, too." Silence. "Do you like big tits?"

He considered playing along, to draw her out. "Are yours big?"

Phone sex made him uncomfortable. Maybe there was something to its being anonymous. More imagination.

"Ye-sss! I'm playing with my nipples. Tell me what you'd do to my big tits if I were there with you right now."

"Ooooh," he said, trying to sound sexy. "I'd suck on 'em."

"Oh!" That was easy.

"Squeeze 'em. Uh, pinch the nipples."

"Oh! Oh!" Too easy.

"Then I'd bury my face between them and push 'em together."

"Yeees!" She moaned, and waited for him to continue.

He felt forced, uncomfortable and guilty because now he had to find a way to stop it. But he had to say something so he said, "What'd you like to do to me?"

"I got your cock in my hand. Can you feel it?"

To be polite he said, "Yes."

"I'm licking the tip of your hot, hard cock." She sounded certain he was hard. "You like that?"

He shouldn't have said yes. Should have stopped it. Should stop it now.

"Are you hard?"

He hesitated. Stop now! He glanced down at his limp dick. "Yes."

"Are you holding it?"

"Yes." He wiggled it. Why was he doing this?

"Mmmmmmmm! I'm swallowing it all the way, rubbing it against the roof of my mouth. So hard, soooo very hard. Can you feel it?"

"Yes." He started to get an erection. Imagine that.

"You wanna put it between my big tits?"

"Love to." He'd rather put it somewhere else.

"I'm rubbing the tip of your hard cock against my hard nipples, oh!" She waited for his response. "You want to eat my pussy?"

"Yes."

"Tell me."

Unnerved, Jake stalled by breathing heavily, wanting to stop now but unsure of how to do it. "It's a sweet pussy," he moaned tentatively.

"I'm so wet!" she cried. "Can you feel it?"

"Oh, yes," he said. "I'm rubbing my face in it. Your pussy juice is all over my face. I'm sticking my tongue up into your sweet cunt."

"Oh! Yeeeessss!"

The instant feedback started to arouse him. "I'm spreading your lips, lapping your love button with the tip of my tongue."

"Oh! I'm so wet!"

"Sucking your sweet juicy lips into my mouth."

"Ohhh! Your fingers!"

"Shoving my fingers way up inside your steaming slit." He sounded aggressive to himself, almost violent. "My hand, drenched in your delicious juices."

"Oh! Oh! The hand! The whole hand!" she cried out.

"My hand," he grunted self-consciously, having had no experience in fisting, "Is sliding right up into you, into you, all — the — way — in!!! to you!!"

"Oh!" she squealed.

"I'm licking the edge of your sweet pink, rubbing my nose in it." He listened for approval in the timbre of her breathing. "Oohhhh, I want to fuck you!"

"Ohhh, yeeees!" she wailed.

"I want to fuck you bad! I want my cock inside you. I want to feel it hot and sloppy, sliding in and out! You like that?"

"Oh, yes! Oh, tell me! Tell me I'm a slut!"

He never liked calling women names during sex, but decided to give it a try anyway. "You want it, don't you, you slut?"

"Oh, yes! I want it! I do want it!"

Her enthusiasm freed him. "Say, it, slut!" he said with rare conviction. "Say you want me to fuck you!"

"Oh, yes! I do! I want you to fuck me!"

"Well, that's what I'm going to do. I'm going to fuck your brains out."

"Oh, yes! Do it! Please, do it to me! Tell me! Tell me!"

Now he felt obligated to bring her to orgasm so he breathed noisily to give the impression of being lost in his own fantasy getting himself off. He hoped she'd take the cue and do the same, but there was only silence on her end.

"My cock's plunging into you. Sliiiiding into you! Deeeeep, deep, deeper! You feel it, don't you, slut?"

"Oh, yes! Oh, yes! Oh, please! Harder! Make it harder!"

"You want it harder, you whore? Is that what you want?"

"Oh, yes! Make me! Make me!"

Make her? He didn't like the sound of that. "I'm thrrrrrusting into you, deep into you! My hard cock slamming Into You! Ramming you! Ramming into you!"

"Ahhhhhh!"

"Faster and faster." He breathed louder. "In, out, In, Out!" He let go of his limp dick. "Hard! Ramming into your hot juicy hole! I want to feel you come!"

"Oh, YES!!!"

"Come for me, you little whore!" he said, anxiously wanting to get it over with.

"Yes! Yes! Yes! Tell me! Tell me!"

"Come For Me! I'm squeezing you tight! Thrusting my Shaft deep INTO YOU, again and again! Come for me! You luscious, slut whore!"

"No, yes! Oh! Oh! Yessss!!"

"I want to feel your hot quivering orgasm. I want to hear you scream as I explode into you, shooting off deep into you! Come for me, slut, come for me!"

"Ohhhhh! Tell me! Tell me! Please! Please, tell me!"

"Oh, baby, I'm close." This is too fucking much, he thought. "I want you to come with me." Come or forget about it, for Christ's sake. "It's building, it's Building! Oh! I'm going to explode! Getting close! Thrusting! Thru-st! Thrust! THRUST! into you, Slut! Into you, into YOU! no, No! No, no, no, no! YES! Ohhh, sweet Jeeeeeesus! God I'm coming! Coming, come with me. Come with me! more, more! Deep into you! Ooh! OH!" You better not expect an encore, he thought as he reduced the intensity of his breathing. Her silence during his fake orgasm annoyed him. Here she'd been all hot and bothered over nothing yet for the grand finale, the silent treatment.

"Did you come?" she whispered.

Oh, brother, he thought, really? "Yes." Maybe he overdid it. "You?"

"No." Little girl disappointed voice.

Fuck it. He waited for her to say something. Silence. "You still horny?"

"Yes."

"I'd like to do you for real." He heard her breathing.

"Would you like that?"

"I don't know," she whispered.

He decided to try talking her into meeting, even though it was highly unlikely she'd show. "I like your voice."

"You do?" Her voice, pleased. "Why?"

"Well, it's sweet, cute." He used his most soft, seductive voice. "I'd like to see you. If we met, you know, you could leave whenever you felt like it, no questions asked."

"If we got together, I'd want to fuck. I'd want you to fuck my brains out. I'd want you to be an animal!"

"Well, yeah, that, too. Whatever you want to do."

"I don't know."

"Are you of age?"

"Yes, of course! Do I sound like a kid to you?"

"Well, then what's the problem?"

"It's certainly not my age! But, you know, I don't know you. It's kinda crazy."

"Yeah. What a turn on." He sensed she was going to agree to meet. Showing up, though, that would be another matter.

"We could meet in a public place and if things don't feel right, you turn around and go home."

No response. "What'd ya say?"

Silence. "All right."

"That's great!

"When?"

"Now."

"Now? You must be real horny."

"Oh, yes! You?"

"Oh, sure! But I have a business appointment in the City at noon."

"Um, I live in the City. Maybe we could meet there?"

"Yeah, okay. Is there someplace that's convenient for you, say around three?"

"How about the corner of Sixth and Market?"

"Sixth and Market?" he said, surprised. "That's kind of a rough area."

"Ohhh," she said, excited. "Then don't keep me waiting."

"All right. Uh, how will I know you?"

"Let me surprise you," she said suggestively.

"Okay, I'll be at the southwest corner at three in a black Toyota pick-up with a white camper shell, and I'll be wearing a wide-brimmed desert hat."

"Ooooooo, a trucker. I like that."

Even though he was not sure if he wanted her to show, he did want to encourage her. "I can't wait to see you in the flesh," he whispered.

She was silent for a moment. "You might be disappointed."

"No, no, I wouldn't." At least he hoped he wouldn't. "Why would I be disappointed?"

A heavy silence. "We all have our secrets."

Oh, no, he thought.

"What we like and what we don't. You might not like me."

"Hey, I'm more interested in the inhabitant of a body than the body, and you sound like an inhabitant I'd like to know." He listened carefully and heard a click, as if she had carefully hung up the phone. "Hello?"

"I'll see you at three, Sixth and Market," she said.

"And I'll be looking forward to it," he said, softly. "Do you have an extension. I thought I heard a click?"

"I didn't hear anything. Bye-eee," she whispered.

"See you." He lowered the receiver.

What kind of woman starts her day with an obscene phone call?

Rrrrring! Oh, brother. He picked up the phone. "Hello."

"Hello?" A nervous voice. "My name is Robin? Mr. Worthingham said I should call you? He said you might have some movie work for me?"

"Yeah, X-rated movies," he said. "You know what that means?"

"Sure, I guess so. I have sex, right? I mean it's not like I haven't seen them before."

"You're okay with that?"

"Sure, why not? Sounds like it'd be fun," she laughed nervously. "But how much do I get paid?"

"Depends on who you work for, what you do, what you look like, how much time's involved. Could be as low as fifty bucks or as high as five hundred."

"That sounds great!"

"You're new so you probably won't get more than three hundred."

"That's fine, too."

"You consider yourself pretty good looking?"

"You want me to describe myself? Hmmm, let me see, well, I've got big tits. I'm, well, I want to be the sexiest star ever."

"You want to be a star?'"

"Yeah!"

"Okay, then. When would you like to get together?"

"As soon as possible."

"Tonight?" Jake remembered the arrangement with the obscene caller. "Say about eight?" If the caller showed, he should be done with her by then.

A PRESSURE entered the back of Catherine's skull, stopping her in the middle of the concrete stairwell. Her sense of where she was and how she got there was fading fast.

Barely sensing herself stepping on stairs, she stopped and stood still.

"A blaa-ack hole is sucking your liii-ife into it, biiit by biit," a raspy voice whispered, then made a sound like a sharp whistle that turned into a tight laugh and shifted over into her mouth to say, "The su-un's comii-ing out. Coo-old and we-eak."

A sharp current surged through her when she realized Joseph was using her voice! He was trying to possess her! She grabbed hold of something cold, a railing, and shut her eyes. He wasn't there, but she felt his face pressing against hers.

To keep him out, she kept her eyes shut tight and held her breath. "Spear triii-icked you," her mouth whispered. "He's sub-terrr-fuge. He's drrr-aining Angel."

A sound like a splash of water prompted her to open her eyes. The shadows on the floor shimmered. An uneasy feeling expanded in the pit of her stomach. What if Joseph was telling the truth? She lowered herself onto a step and cowered against the railings.

What if Spear was in league with Riley? That would be the cruelest cut of all.

"Heee's control-ling you with liiies. Yourrr pow-err maasks fool no one, not even youuu."

To stop his talking, she stuck her thumb in her mouth, locking her index finger on her nose.

"You'rrr geeet-ting dirrr-ty." Her tongue moved, her thumb distorting the sound, then her mouth chomped down. She jerked her thumb out with a gasp of pain.

"Ri-leeey wil-ll see a weak, dirr-ty angel. I can pro-oo-tect you, Angell-lica." Angelica trembled as she mumbled in a child's voice, "Everything's over."

Then she heard something like the flapping of wings overhead and jumped to her feet. "You all right, child?" said an old Black woman in a white uniform.

"I'm fine," she stammered to a grandmotherly face standing over her four steps up.

"What's the matter, honey? You don't look fine."

She slowed her breathing. "I'm afraid, I, uh—, I mean—" She glanced up the stairs at a large cart with cleaning materials and a bin full of towels, wondering how long she had been observing her? The old woman stepped down closer to her.

"Of what, child? What are you afraid of? Where are your parents?"

"Huh?"

"You have a place to stay?"

"I ... Look, I'll be twenty-three in July. I'm not a runaway."

"Twenty-three," the old woman repeated, sounding doubtful.

She felt like a child trying to sound older as she said, "I'm not crazy, I'm not on drugs. I'm just upset, that's all. I haven't had much sleep."

"It's okay, baby, you're a long ways from home," she said, responding to her southern accent. "Let it out." She lightly placed a hand on her shoulder. "A good cry can work wonders."

Thinking the old woman might have been sent by the Spirit, she tossed back her head and said the first thing that came to mind. "My parents are dead. I live alone."

The old woman took a moment to decide whether to believe her, or not. "I'm sorry, child. Is that why you're afraid."

"I came here to see my uncle."

"What room is he in?"

"Sixty-eight."

The old woman pulled back. "I knows that man. He's been doing all manner of filthy disgusting things in there."

"How do you know that?"

"I cleans the rooms. Been cleaning rooms most my life. When I goes in a room I can tell exactly what sort of person been there. What that man do to you?"

Angelica winced. "Nothing. He just likes grossing people out."

"I'll bet he does."

"It's not like that," she said, her mind racing. "He makes scary movies. He acts a bit crazy when he's working, but he's really not that way all the time."

"And you're afraid on account of him? Listen to me, child, decent folks don't scare children so bad they stay scared when they be all growed up. He's the kind what if he's feeling bad he gots to make others feel that way, too."

"When I was little," she said, feeling like a child, "he was the only adult who took an interest in me. The only one who really liked me for me."

"Stuff and nonsense, child. Sometimes sensitive children be like that. They be thinking nobody loves them no matter what their people do, then they go run off with some fool who don't give a damn about them, thinking he loves them."

"My parents didn't love me. They were ashamed of me."

"You're a beautiful sensitive child. Any parent would love such a one."

"They made fun of me because I was a scaredy cat and cried too much. Like the time my dad got stoned and talked to me in a strange voice and I got scared and cried *Daddy be yourself!* and everybody laughed. They were ashamed of me! They'd rather any of their friends' kids been theirs. I'm goofy looking and—"

"Excuse me? You're what? What on earth you talking about?"

"I'm cross-eyed."

"Let me see." The old woman looked in her eyes.

"The left one," she said, pointing.

"Honey, I wouldn't have noticed if you hadn't pointed it out. You have the prettiest eyes I've ever seen, and that's the god's honest truth."

"But all the kids made fun of my eyes!"

"Honey, children, god bless 'em, be like that. They be jealous and they make fun of what they jealous of. You was probably the prettiest, and that's why they picked on you."

She winced as Angelica averted her eyes, shifting to Angie, a Seabolt. Angie felt stunned, everything around her glaring, including sounds. She felt no more fit to be there than had Angelica. Then the earnest look on the cleaning lady's face caught her attention.

"When you be in pain, you gots to laugh or you gots to cry. I learned a long time ago laughing's best, but if you can't do that, then go ahead and have yourself a good cry."

Angie looked surprised. Spear said laughter was the best defense in the face of the unknown. He also said never indulge in self-pity in the presence of power. Catherine and Angie had both been guilty of that. Self-pity was their link to Angelica.

Catherine pulled herself through Angie then, dropping her Tennessee accent, said, "How's my make-up? Is it smeared?"

"Of course, child. You been crying."

"Have you got something I could clean up with? I don't want him to see me like this."

"Help yourself to the towels in the bin."

She went to the bin, grabbed a towel, then rubbed her eyes. "Do I look all right?"

The old woman took the towel. "Stay away from that crazy man," she said. "If you gots to go, go another day. Not today."

When she tried to consider whether the omens meant she should take her advice, she slipped back into Angie. "Why? You don't think I'd survive?"

"Survive?" The old woman drew back. "You thinks he's gonna kill you, child? He gots you that scared? We all have crosses to bear, honey, but I sure wouldn't want to be in your shoes."

"I didn't mean it like that! I meant, like can I hold my own." Angie wanted to shift away to Catherine, but she knew if she tried she'd probably revert to Angelica.

"Hold your own?" She made a face. "What kind of talk is that?"

"That he won't overpower me mentally or spiritually. A friend of mine says I had to find the strength to stand up to him. He taught me ways to do that."

"What sort of ways?" the old woman asked, skeptical.

"Ways of moving, attitudes. Various things."

"You don't need any of that. The kind of strength you need comes from a higher power. Ask Jesus. He'll show you the way."

Angie froze into the moment. "Thanks for your help," she said, coolly. "I'm going to get this over with. Excuse me, please." She walked past her then jogged up the stairs.

On the sixth floor landing she paused to look for the limo. It was gone! *This IS a set up!* She grabbed hold of the railing then leaned forward, desperately looking around.

What to do! A sign! There ought to be a sign!

Not that I'd know what it meant," she mumbled. Then a wind suddenly struck her, blowing a piece of paper into her hair. She frantically tried to brush it off while particles of dirt swirled off the floor up into her face with an eerie hollow whistle.

"Power! What do I do? What! What! What!" she exclaimed as the wind whirled around her. Spinning in the direction of the wind, she clenched her teeth as she chanted, "Don't indulge! Don't! Don't!" She stopped when she saw the old woman looking up at her from the landing below. The old woman shook her head, and the wind stopped.

Without hesitation, Angie shifted to Catherine who then went directly to room sixty-eight and knocked. She inhaled the cool air, and knocked again, loudly.

JAKE HAD NO TIME to search for a downtown parking space so he headed directly for the homeless mission, an area avoided by meter maids and motorists during feeding hours. There were no cars on the block when he arrived. His would be the only one.

Two young men sharing a bottle of screw top wine watched him park. He feigned looking through his satchel for something while he considered whether his truck would be safe. He decided it would be, so long as he didn't draw attention. He got out and put a coin in the meter to give the impression he'd be back soon, rather than from concern over a ticket. A young woman sitting in a doorway glanced over at him, her dark hair uncombed, her dumb eyes wandering, looking worried, trying to look bored.

Being judgmental of street people felt wrong, having been homeless himself, most memorably in Europe and Africa, to avoid Viet Nam. He remembered the hassles of trying to find places to stash his rucksack, or to get out of the rain, the heat, the cold, or just to sleep. And being dirty, wanting to wash himself; or at least his socks. He hated the feel of dirty socks. He did not want to think about how it ended. The stockade.

Dr. Ben had stirred up long buried memories. He used to be haunted by shameful, painful memories of Sergeant Sarno, a marine the army brought in to discipline prisoners, sticking his foul mouth in his face yelling, spraying spittle as he dared him to make a move. If his hands were to rise above his waist it would be considered assault, then the guards could gang up on him. One of them simply said he saw his hand start to rise, then Sarno smashed the back of his skull against the shower wall. The guards stripped him naked while he lay stunned, face down, bleeding on the tiles. Sarno then twisted his nuts. They all laughed while he screamed, then laughed even louder when Sarno positioned him on his knees, bare butt up, while Sarno worked two fingers up into him, ordering him to poop them out. Then someone kicked him in the gut.

What happened after that he chose not to remember.

When they were done with him, they propped him up under a freezing shower while the guards scrubbed him with a floor brush to stop the bruising so he'd have nothing to show the shrink or chaplain. Then they forced him to sign a waiver requesting his discharge to be changed from an honorable to an undesirable. Some months later, after his discharge, he was alienated and more than willing to do things he'd never have otherwise considered. Eventually he met Hasib and his porn career began.

A reflection of the painful expression on his face in a store window caught his eye. What would the teenage soldier think of this haunted face of a forty-three-year-old version of himself rushing to a meeting at a strip joint in a blazer, stone pants and desert hat, concerned over parking amongst the downtrodden?

THE SIGN on the theater door said *closed*. He pounded on the glass door.

Omar came to the door and opened it. "We are closed, Jake."

"I have an appointment with Hasib," said Jake, pleased that Omar addressed him by name. He usually behaved as if he did not know who he was. "Why are you closed?"

"It's Monday. Monday's not good. We open at one." Omar let him in. "I'll let Hasib know you're here." Omar then went behind the counter to pick up the phone.

Jake scanned the posters in the lobby. Coming in June! HANNAH HOOTERS, JENNIFER CANTALOPEZ and World Famous Porn Star SHANNEN BARDO. Next Week: Don't miss The Black Bombshell BOOTY HILL!! An Ass To Die For! Now Playing, by special engagement, International Sensation DIXIE BELLES!

A young woman in a sheer negligee stepped out of the dressing room. Her skin was unusually pale, her face askew, eyes glazed. Jake thought he recognized her. *What's her name?* Sensitive, intelligent. Has problems with abusive lovers. Said she wanted to die young and in disgrace. He'd tried to help her, but she was addicted to the burnout.

"Hey, Willow!" She gave him a startled look, and ducked back into the dressing room. "Isn't that Willow Stanfield?" Jake asked Omar. "Stage name Melody D'Amour."

Omar shrugged, as if to say he couldn't be bothered with remembering strippers' names. "You know the way. The door should be open, but take the key just in case."

"Thanks," Jake said, taking the key.

Bins of swinger magazines lined the top of the stairs. Video box cover photos of naked women covered every square inch of wall space along the wide staircase. Just inside the open basement door was a poster of a garishly made-up, pucker-lipped, obese woman in a string bikini. Outside Hasib's office was another poster of five, firm femme fannies on motorcycles. Inside the office, autographed photos of headliners and large monthly calendar sheets with play dates covered the walls.

Hasib, as usual, was on the phone. Hasib Hakim, fifty-eight, tanned from a recent visit to his clubs in Hawaii, gestured for Jake to sit. A young Arab woman in tight jeans watched Jake without interest as he sank into a low couch opposite the desk.

Hasib hung up then spoke to her in Arabic. She attempted to argue but he silenced her with a wave of his hand. "I don't have time today," he said in English. "But I'll talk to her before her shift tomorrow."

She kissed him on the lips then said something in Arabic.

Hasib laughed then said, "Chantal, this is Jake Zakheim, the famous director."

Chantal shrugged, not bothering to look.

"How'd that shoot by what's her name turn out?" said Hasib.

"Well, I doubt anybody's gonna get rich off it," said Jake.

"Not good, huh?" said Hasib. "Sorry to hear that."

"Not commercial, not even by my standards. She has only two attractive women in the entire feature. Who's gonna sit through a pretentious fuck flick with only two hot honeys in it? I never tried to foist anything like that off on you, did I?"

"No, you didn't," said Hasib. "But, as far as pretentious goes, that's another story."

"Yeah, well, I didn't know much of anything when I started working for you. I was a kid testing limits. But that's the past. I have no illusions or agenda now, other than to give the public what it wants and to make money doing it."

Hasib knew Jake's divorce meant he needed money. He also knew, even in hard times basic character rarely changes. One way or another, Jake would do something foolish, otherwise there'd be strength in his eyes instead of the quiet desperation American men got at mid-life. Hasib suspected he wanted to be turned down.

"Got to go, Hasibi," said Chantal.

"Come along, join us for lunch," said Hasib. She shook her head no. "Okay, then I'll see you tonight."

Abdul came in as Chantal left. He glanced at Jake's wrinkled pants, athletic shoes and desert hat. *A desert hat in the city?* He saw Jake as an arrogant American peasant, so easy to cheat it was like taking candy from a baby. If he ever figured out he'd been had, he'd whine like a woman, then all you had to do was slip him some line of shit and he'd bend over and let you do him again. The fool deserves to be cheated.

"Good to see you again, Abdul," said Jake. "It's been awhile."

Abdul ignored him. Hasib, in Arabic, told Abdul to be courteous since the three of them were having lunch together. Abdul said he lost his appetite. Jake picked up a newspaper and thumbed through it. Abdul mimicked him, then made a reference to the unshaven legs and armpits of Jake's first wife. Hasib held up his palm and told him not to insult this woman. Pinching Abdul's cheek with his thumb and forefinger, Hasib said he saw how he watched Jake's ass, then released his cheek and gave him a playful slap. Abdul protested, saying he bought the gay movie house only because Hasib told him to. Hasib winked. Abdul accused him of fucking Jake, why else would he keep him around? Hasib laughed and said not to let that stop him. Abdul said his dick was so big it'd ruin the hole for him. Hasib laughed and stood up. Abdul asked if he had ever fucked Jake.

Hasib slapped Abdul on the wallet in his back pocket. "Right where he likes it."

"COME HERE, BITCH!" a disheveled middle-aged man bellowed at a young Asian woman outside a restaurant. "I said come here, slope!"

"Hey!" Hasib yelled, walking between Jake and Abdul.

"Come the fuck here, you slant-eyed yellow slut!" He reached for her. Eyes averted, she pulled away and slipped into a restaurant. "I hate you, gook! I hate all of you!" he yelled, looking around. "You're all scum! You should all die deaths as disgusting as you are!" He glared at Hasib. "And I especially hate you, camel jockey! I hate all you worthless desert jackals!" Then he swaggered off shouting curses.

"Nice guy," Hasib muttered, watching him as he turned a corner in the direction of the mission where Jake's truck was parked.

They entered a Greek take-out restaurant, a long narrow room with a counter and cooking facilities in front and a few tables in back.

Hasib and Jake placed orders, Abdul did not.

"The most successful film you ever did for me was *Anal Probe*," Hasib said as they settled in at a table. "You should do a sequel."

"Funny you should mention that one," said Jake. "One of the two leading ladies in Mindy's project said it was the first porno she'd ever seen."

"There, you see. It's a classic. There'll always be a market for it because people love anal movies and there's never enough product to meet the demand."

Anal Probe consisted mostly of silent anal loops. All he did was shoot sound tie-ins to utilize the old footage. A hack job.

"Actually my most successful film was *Blondes On Blondes*. Also the most expensive *and* the most story intensive. Look, if we go cheap we end up low-balling it with all the other crap out there. A quality piece with wider market potential is a better deal in the long run."

Abdul, a small man with a weak chin, large nose and no shoulders or ass, watched Jake mangle a paper napkin with his beautiful but neglected hands. His body was wasted on him, he thought. A fool with no idea of its worth.

"You listening to this, Abdul?" said Hasib. "Didn't he say he'd listen to me on how to make money. Is this listening? Forget about it."

"Of course, I'll do whatever you think is best," Jake interjected.

"I don't want to risk the kind of money you're talking about. It's not worth it. Who needs the headaches of a major production. You know what I'm talking about. Those things attract trouble."

True enough. His big movie brought in a lot of cash, but after the exhibiters and distributor took their cut, litigation absorbed most of what was left.

"Look, I'm not proposing anything large scale. I've learned a great deal over the years on how to minimize hassle. I just don't want to be a bottom feeder."

Hasib took out his worry beads and moved the beads between his fingers. "You should get some beads, Jake." Jake put aside the mangled napkin.

"I don't intend to start something I can't pull off. I can't afford to fuck around and I sure as hell don't want trouble. Just think about it, will you?"

"Yeah, sure, I'll think about it. What do you think, Abdul?"

"I wouldn't give him the sweat off my balls if he were dying of thirst," Abdul said in Arabic.

"In English," said Hasib.

"You know how distributors are, Hasib. They have to screw somebody every day to feel good about themselves. Jake's the sort of asshole they love to fuck."

Hasib's frown made Jake wince.

"I understand all that," Jake said, rocking back on his chair. "I won't give them a chance. Strictly COD."

"Don't worry about it," said Hasib. "I'll take care of it. Just give me something that doesn't cost much. Get new girls, ones you can bargain with. Guys you can get for nothing. Use my clubs for locations, and forget about the story. Nobody cares, believe me. Project some old loops on the screen, right there you have most of the show. For the rest, have some people fucking in the audience. But give me more breathing and dirty talk this time, you never do enough of that. As far as acting goes, forget about it. I'd rather you watched for pimples on the girls' butts. And no hemorrhoids. If you're too bashful to check, Abdul will do it for you." He gave Abdul a playful slap. "Jake did a film with a girl with an enormous hemorrhoid at three o'clock. Filled the screen with it for what? Five minutes, swear to god."

The owner brought them their food and asked Hasib, in Greek, to speak lower.

"Guess who's coming to town next week," said Hasib.

"Booty Hill. Now there's an ass to die for," said Jake.

"Great slogan, right? You remember something like that. I've been talking to her about doing a video to promote her act. You have a way with Black girls, maybe you'd have more luck."

"Getting Black women on film is a major pain in the ass," Jake said, his spirits sinking. "They'd rather sell it on the street. They're more concerned about family seeing them than White girls are. A White girl can tell her mama *isn't me* and she might believe her. But a Black girl's mom, forget about it. Finding one willing to take it up the butt doesn't make it any easier, especially with the AIDS thing."

"Doesn't matter, believe me," Hasib said, scooping up tabouli with lettuce leaf. "Spread their cheeks, play with their assholes, use fingers, tongues, dildos, whatever, doesn't matter. There's plenty of ass fucking in the loops."

"How much of a budget we talking about?" asked Jake. Hasib shrugged. "How much you need?"

He suspected Hasib wanted a budget like when he was a novice so he decided to lowball it. He could always try to raise it up later.

"Have to be at least four grand," he said, regretting it immediately. No way he'd make enough out of that budget to be worth his while. What a pathetic swan song.

"Four grand?" said Hasib. "Why so high?"

Jake put his hand to his forehead, wanting to kill the deal right there and then. But he needed at least the illusion of a pending deal while seeking investors for a quality project. No need for them to know his ace in the hole was a cheap butt fuck compilation.

Hasib worked his worry beads, waiting for his response.

"There are too many variables. Any unexpected expense would wipe out my incentive. Four grand is possible, maybe. But anything less, I don't think so."

Hasib returned the beads to his pocket. "Put together a budget. Break it down, how much for you, how much for the crew, actors, what have you, then bring it to me and we'll see what we can work out."

"Okay," said Jake, without enthusiasm.

Abdul shook his head then excused himself and left.

Hasib asked Jake to drive him to the bank. "I didn't want to ask in front of Abdul," he said outside, "but are you still seeing, what's her name, the Black girl?"

"Jasmyn. Yeah, I see her but we're just friends at the moment. I guess you could call it that. She's much too dangerous to be lovers with."

"Why's that?"

"She has a compulsion to punish anyone who fails to live up to her expectations, and she's particularly vicious with her lovers."

"What're you doing for sex then?"

Jake held up his hand. "Mother Superior and the four sisters."

Hasib laughed then said, "Where's your car?"

"Across from the mission."

Hasib made a clicking sound with his mouth as they turned the corner. He usually carried thousands of dollars in cash on him, but as king of the Tenderloin no one touched him. Shopkeepers, schizophrenics, everyone knew and respected him; but a newcomer, not knowing who he was, might try something.

No one was outside the mission or on the side of the street where Jake's truck was. A parking ticket was on his windshield. He'd never seen anyone ever get a ticket there, ever. And now, out of the blue, he got one. A bad sign.

Hasib took the ticket off the window. "Let me take care of that for you."

"Thanks," said Jake. In that moment, without knowing why, he knew *Anal Probe II* would never happen.

CATHERINE STARED at the motel door, thinking of what Ben said to their investor about Riley being crazy. He even outright urged her to fire him, something he wouldn't have done unless he considered Riley dangerous. If so, why hadn't Spear warned her?

The door suddenly swung open.

She looked up wide-eyed at Riley, towering over her in a loosely tied robe, exposing more than she'd want to see. She pressed her lips together.

"Katie?" he said, checking out her hairdo. "Is that you?"

"Riley?" she tittered, scanning his hair, eyebrows, beard and chest hairs, all now more salt than pepper. "Is *that* you?" He looked much older than when last she saw him.

He opened his arms. "I'd recognize your girlish giggle anywhere." She placed her hand over her heart when he pulled her into an embrace.

"Good to see you again, Face." His breath had the sweet-sour reek of bourbon, cigarettes and coffee. "I remember the first time I heard you laugh, Pudding. I was changing your diapers at the time."

She pinched her nose shut, her face twisting into a grimace. "What's that smell? Smells like piss."

Her pinching her nose awakened a memory of him chasing her around the barn when she was two and a half. He was playing Pepe le Pew, the amorous French cartoon skunk, calling out after the giggling child, "OH, HO! she plays hard to get, zees one. I like zat in a woMAN."

Little Katie stopped running then arched her back and slapped her butt.

"You like zat, poo poo head," she giggled.

He looked at her, somewhat taken aback. "Oh! Zee little beauty, she tempts me."

"I poo poo you," she squealed, running off.

"But you are so beau-TI-ful," he protested, coming after her. "I want you, only you, my little chocolate cabbage."

Glancing back, she tripped and he swooped her up in his arms, muttering, "Mmm, mmm, mmm," with puckered lips. Little Katie crinkled her nose, then pinched her nostrils shut with her thumb and forefingers. "You're poo poo," she giggled. "You stink."

"What *is* that smell?" Catherine sniffed the air. "Crack?"

"Na. Crack has a clean litter smell, like eucalyptus."

She slipped her parka off, revealing a t-shirt with a cartoon of a youth looking up at the stars, blissfully unaware he was about to step off a precipice into a den of wolves leaping in anticipation of tearing him apart. The caption: A romantic enters the world.

"That's good," said Riley. "I like that."

"Is that how you see me?" she said with a crooked smile. "An innocent, blind to her fate, about to be torn apart by wolves."

"The fate of all innocents, Angel Face, *is* to draw the attention of wolves," he said, noticing a smudge on her left eyelid. "Speaking of witch, is your Wolf still celibate?" he asked, knowing full well calling Spear a wolf, as in Navajo Wolf or witch, annoyed her.

"I'm still a virgin," she said with a frown. "If that's what you're getting at."

"Yeah? As far as you know," he said as he gathered the damp sheets balled up on the floor, tossing them into a corner, "And about as independent as a hog on ice."

Catherine frowned when she heard the shower go on. "Who's that? Your script girl?" Referring to Riley's penchant to hire script girls based on their perverse proclivities.

"No. A victim." He sat down at the foot of the bed on a pile of blankets that looked like the carcass of a large animal. "We will disembowel her in the first film."

Alarmed, yet relieved they were not alone, she made a sound like a laugh. "The more things change," she said as she sat down on the bed, "the more they stay the same."

"No, not quite. Nothing is what it seems, and that has to change. The little tart's Worthingham's niece. An orphan, like yourself. Long story short, she's the Devil's Decoy in the movie as well as in real life." Then he whispered, "She's trying to lure me into a trap. Not to worry, though. You know how I enjoy flipping things around."

"What are you getting at, Riley?" she said, gesturing for him to come out with it.

"Have you ever considered how no one knows what he or she smells like? A smell is invisible, yet it tells you everything a person has ever thought or done." He waited to see the effect his words had on her. She blinked. "I've gotten so far up the shit end of the scare biz, I can't escape the smell. The time is ripe for me to go."

Her eyes seemed pierced by a shifting light of bafflement and curiosity. He knew she had to be intrigued by what he'd said.

"You want to abort the deal?" she whispered.

"Abort? You mean quit?" He stared at her, as if disappointed. "Na. Where's the fun in that? They'd like that just fine since they bought my name not me, which as far as I'm concerned ain't worth a crap right now. You know the second project is porn, right? Peter and Booth call it erotica, but it's hard core porn."

She didn't know it was hard core, but she did not want him to know that. Another thing Spear failed to mention.

"One thing's for sure, Sunshine, porn's for real. In horror the action's fake, but porn's the real deal. So, if they're both bad in the grand scheme of things, which do you suppose is worse? Fake blood and guts, or real cum and twats?" Without waiting for an answer, he shifted to a confidential whisper. "I don't know how or when it happened, but I've become so corrupt I'm capable of anything." Then he winked. "Hello, Angel-ica."

Catherine furrowed her brow, puzzled by his wink, until she realized her thumb was in her mouth. Angelica was listening in, and her reaction must have been more intense than hers. That meant she was now where she didn't want to be. She was in flux.

Catherine casually slipped the thumb away from her mouth.

"When you left," he said, using the soft voice he used with children, "I thought you were behaving like an oversensitive twit. But it was *the* crucial moment for us to get out. Not the way I had in mind, mind you, but you were right, I should have done it then."

She attempted a soothing tone. "Why don't you just bail now. Get it over with?"

He shushed her. "I must disengage properly, Pudding. Otherwise the dizziness of irremediable horror will suck me right back in again. Have you ever heard of Hypatia?"

"Hypatia?" she smiled involuntarily. "The porn star?"

"No," he laughed. "She had the finest scientific and philosophic mind of her times, the late 300's and early 400's. You would've liked her, you have a lot in common. Like you, she was beautiful. She had a sweet voice, and she regarded math and astronomy as a way to reach a state of mind where the structure of the universe as we know it dissolves, putting her in touch with its creative source. Sounds a lot like your goal in particle physics, am I right?" She nodded slowly. "She called this direct merging with the One, First-Born Divine. For her, wisdom was not enough to get there. The necessary insight was a kind of purity on the fringes of knowledge that recognizes only beauty. The unclean cannot handle that kind of purity, so she and her disciples had to be spiritually beautiful. They brought about the necessary spiritual alteration through a kind of self-control called sophrosyne."

"Sophrosyne," she said, her eyes dreamy, as if she had been reminded of something long forgotten.

Riley adjusted his tone, making it softer, slower. "It requires one to observe decency and restraint in all situations. And she set the highest standard for herself. Chastity became her most famous virtue. She was a virgin her entire life."

"You want to touch what is pure," Catherine said in her soft Angel voice, the one that made anything she said, even utter nonsense, sound profound.

Riley was surprised Angel had appeared here and now, because he felt too unclean for Her to address him directly. He shifted to as respectful a tone he was capable of when he addressed Her. "Like Hypatia, you've been obsessed with purity, ever since you took that angel dust when you were six. But, as I've said many times before, purity's a subterfuge since it can't exist without filth, no more than beauty can without ugliness. They define each other. So why, pray tell, can't the unclean handle that which is pure?"

"Purity in beauty is a nuance, a shade of meaning, a complex of feeling, subtlety of perception," said Angel. "There are no words or mental category for it. Nuances exist in the fractal spaces between categories of thought or, as you said, the fringes of knowledge. Words and thoughts are impurities because they're categorical or organizationally closed. They rapidly simplify and flatten whatever they touch."

Riley stared at her, uncertain of how to respond to that. It reminded him of what she wrote out for him, when she was thirteen, to explain her interest in quantum physics. "To contemplate illusion conception. The perception of objects or events with no existence in reality is to organize visual impressions. Visual images, hallucination." At first he thought she was talking about gods or ghosts, but then he decided her meaning, if there was one, was hidden from adults.

"Are you saying it's some kind of violation of quantum physics?" he ventured.

"It's not that simple. Subatomic particles have no objective existence. That means you can't assume they have an existence apart from their interactions with an observer. At subatomic levels the laws of physics don't specify what must happen as ordinary laws of physics do, they specify what cannot happen."

Her father once said her genius was unbalanced by a muddled mysticism inherited from her mother that drove her to want to know more than any human, much less a ten-year-old child, was supposed to know. The key to understanding her babble, he said, lay in grasping that making sense was not important to her. *Resonance* was all that mattered.

"Everything causes everything else," Angel said softly, "to the extent everything is everything else. Your concern here lies with strangeness, involving the interaction of strong and weak forces."

"Okay, then, if purity's contaminated by the touch of the unclean, purity and beauty must be the weak force and filth and ugliness the strong."

"The strong force binds, the weak force decays," she said, her eyes searching his eyes to see if he knew that. "The idea is to hold on to the vibrating force that binds us together as a conglomeration of energy fields."

"Precisely, yes, and if you hold on long enough it'll shake off the impurities," he said while her eyes continued to work him over. "The interaction between the weak and the strong forces." Her look suggested she'd sensed an anxiety in him over losing his edge, his memory, his strength. "Strangeness," he said as if to remind her. He had the sinking feeling that, like Dr. Ben, the Angel in her doubted his depth, his intelligence.

"You can't touch anything without changing it," she said. "Like touching a baby."

He hesitated, not sure what to make of that.

"What Hypatia meant was to approach purity you must do so with grace," she said, "or it will elude your grasp."

"Right," he said, relieved Angel had identified with Hypatia, which was what he wanted. "That's consistent with her explanation for keeping the mysteries from the masses. She said the masses can never understand the mysteries of the cosmos. Should they try, the Divine would lose its meaning and the knowledge would be abused."

The shower stopped, leaving only the sound of the blower in the bathroom.

"My name's not Riley, it's Cyril. Granny Rose named me after St. Cyril. I was born on his day on the saint's calendar. Are you familiar with him?"

No response. He waited, suspecting Angel had left.

"He was the patriarch of Alexandria, sort of like a pope, and he used his position to incite fanatics against what he considered enemies of divine truth, specifically Jews, Pagans and intellectuals. His main opponent was Orestes, the governor of Egypt, whose opposition Cyril blamed on Hypatia. Cyril said she was a witch, that she'd corrupted Orestes. I'm telling you this because I'm the reincarnation of one of Cyril's fanatics. A monk known to history as Peter the Reader."

She slipped her thumb back in her mouth, locking a finger over the end of her nose. He knew then Angel had withdrawn, and Angelica had taken her place. *Why her?*

"I was the leader of a band of fanatics who pulled Hypatia off her chariot," he said, searching for Angel in Angelica's eyes. "We stripped her naked, then dragged her through the streets to the main cathedral where we gouged the flesh off her body with seashells."

"Oh, god," she moaned, her eyes rolling up into her head.

"Above the altar was an immense painting of Christ, our loving master, watching us with a mysterious smile as her screams echoed across the vaulted ceilings. After we'd finished tearing her apart, we scattered her flesh and guts around the city, then burned her bones in the marketplace." He noticed Angelica flickering out in her eyes. "Your coloring don't look so good. Are you going to have a fit?"

Her eyelids fluttered. She got that scared look again, hunching her shoulders, giving them and her head a little shake, the signature of Aura, her seizure-related personality.

"You know how it is with those who worship the forces of destruction. We believed we serve the greater good, in this case fulfilling God's will by killing a witch. But we were fools. It was just politics. We committed a grisly evil out of ignorance, no getting around that. Not even after sixteen hundred years. That's why I'm stuck making horror films as some sort of penance. Fooling myself while I sink back into the muck."

"Please, stop," the wavering Aura whispered.

"Hey, no problem. I don't want Satan's Lure in there to hear any of this, so hang on 'til she comes out. *Decoy* is not my signature nice girls gone bad flick. This one sprang from Worthingham's twisted imagination." He leaned in close. "It's about a monster who disembowels virgins. You see, Peter the Reader disemboweled the virgin in the church."

She covered her ears, another Aura-like gesture.

"Had to. Couldn't stand her eerie shrieks. Wail after wail while they skinned her. Her ear-piercing screech when they gouged out her eyes." Ashen, Aura pressed her hands to her midsection. "All around her waves of monks tore at her flesh, shouting, pushing and crushing in on us. Blood everywhere! I couldn't take it! They were tearing *YOU* apart and you wouldn't stop screaming!"

"Ahhh!" she cried, her eyes shooting open.

He stared into them as he said, "So I sliced your gut open, worked my hands in, grabbed hold of your rectum with one, your vagina with the other and ripped the screaming life out of you!"

"Uhhhhh!" She gasped as if the air had been sucked out of her, and collapsed on her side, her legs curling up into a fetal position. She stopped breathing, her eyes vacant.

"Gotcha!" His voice remote, metallic as if it were coming through a loudspeaker. "Don't fight it, Face. Your body needs fright. It likes it." The face behind the loudspeaker voice looked as if it were submerged in a tank of water. "Can you hear me?" he whispered while he watched her eyes dilate and she gasped for air. "Better prepare you in case you mess yourself." He went to a suitcase and took out a few towels.

She felt a cool sensation spreading slowly down her lower body as Riley pulled down her pants. An old card with an image of an angel on it fell from her pocket. Riley picked it up and sang "She had an angel in her pocket" as he leaned the angel up against the telephone where it could watch over her.

"You are a fragment of Hypatia's soul spark," Riley said, jostling her head while placing a towel under it. "The purity of the virgin's soul." She felt his actions as a series of abrupt jolts, with intermittent blurry, shimmering faces hovering over her. "The monsters couldn't scrape or burn away her soul spark, but we did manage to fragment it."

Her drool dampened his hands when she opened her mouth.

The loudspeaker voice had caught her attention, his low drawl tugging and burring at the back of her eyes until his face lost its radiance and became solid.

"I remember watching your eyes when you were born, to see your first reactions to this world. There was such incredible awe in them. Such depth, such beauty. And purity. Unbelievable purity. I understood then the meaning of Hypatia's words 'First Born Divine.' I saw the Divine in you. I loved to get close to you when you were a baby. So I could breathe your air as it came out." He slowly inhaled. "Sweetened by your life-force."

She became aware of sounds flowing out of her, rising up from deep inside like bubbles, and bursting on the surface. There was something monotonous about its rhythm.

"Hmmm, your whimpers are sweet, not at all like screaming demons," he whispered into her open mouth, watching the flickering in her eyes as he did so. "Don't fight the monster, Face. It'll piss it off and it will have to punish you until you see what it wants you to see." Then he exhaled the shameful smells of bourbon and cigarettes up into her nose as he whispered, "The monster loves you."

She gasped, trying to breathe, her ears bursting with a peculiar pressure, like a leg that has fallen asleep. Then her eyes went out of focus. Everything ceased to move. Still-life. Like a painting. "Uhhhhhhhh!" she grunted as a mixture of banana cake and green tea flowed out over Riley's hands onto her jacket and the towel under her. She coughed then spewed forth again. He sniffed at the vomit on his hands, then licked it off.

She felt herself spinning. Her left eye felt as if it were protruding outward while her right eye contracted, whirling inward. Something snapped forward, then she felt herself grabbing hold of Riley's head before her hands had actually reached it.

"You are a ghoul!" she heard herself howl, then she let go. Alarmed that some part of her had demobilized him by grabbing something inside him.

"Hello, Josephine," Riley said when he regained his voice. "Nice of you to join us. Are you going to stick around this time, or is this another one of your hit and run jobs?"

"I won't let you mind fuck me," Catherine snapped, aware Riley hadn't grasped Josephine had left the moment she let go of him.

He stood up then moved from the bed to a chair facing her.

"Sorry, Face, but I had to be sure you had a piece of Hypatia in you."

"Give it a rest, Riley," she said, having trouble stabilizing her shaky voice. "You … play with people's heads to … test … stupid … shhh-hit … and… d-d-don't give a damn who you hurt. I'm not going to let you sucker punch me again."

"Do you realize how few people *really* care to know what's out there? Most can't even imagine why anyone would want to know, much less that it's possible. You and I, though, we test limits because we have to. We have to want to know, and we know things no one else does because we understand it's all about direct personal contact with what's out there. That knowledge has been part of us since Hypatia's time. Even before."

Struggling with trembling hands to pull her pants up, she muttered, "Riley … I don't want to hear it."

"Hypatia's failure to grasp the manner of the nightmare she was being pulled into, and her grisly death, folded her into recurring patterns. But, things are coming around this time in a way where we have a shot at getting the Boost we need to shift dimensions." He raised an eyebrow. "The Wolf, he's Orestes. And Worthingham is St. Cyril."

"Let me get this straight. You're saying Spear and Will think I'm Hypatia?"

"Doesn't matter what they think. The underlying pattern is all that matters. Your Wolf probably thinks the Great Spirit pointed you out because of something I said."

"What was that?" She rubbed her left eye. "What did you say!"

"What did I say? I mentioned the circumstances of your birth. You know, how your mom was whacked out on LSD at the time, and how a Navajo Wolf killed your parents when you were eleven. Your Wolf found all of that very interesting."

"You told Spear that! Why? How could you dare to tell anyone that!!"

"It was at a party, months before you two met. I was drunk and you'd been driving me nuts all day over it. Then Ben called to tell me about a party some Indian students at U. C. Berkley were putting on for a Navajo cinematographer. He said he'd seen some of his work and considered him perfect for what I was looking for. I didn't want to be bothered with it right then, being drunk and all, but when he mentioned the students thought he was a brujo, that hooked me. I wanted to know more, but I was too drunk to remember a brujo can snatch your soul."

"What are you talking about? What's a burro?"

"A sorcerer. Navajo Wolf."

"Riley!" she said, impatiently.

He studied her. "You expect me to believe you don't know he's a sorcerer?"

"If he is, so what? Half my dad's friends were sorcerers, burros, wolves, witches, warlocks, wizards, whatever. It's no big deal."

"I don't mean wishful thinking neo-Pagan crap. He's the genuine article. He knows how to exploit a tenuous grasp of reality, and he never gives a seeker an even break."

She looked away, and noticed her angel card on the nightstand.

"You don't get it, do you? You're damaged goods. You can't possibly survive in his world. He can suck your soul right out of you, like oysters in a shell."

She turned her back to him to retrieve her angel card.

"Look, we're stuck in a dangerous spiral. You're young, and no doubt think you have all the time in the world, but listen to me. We have to break loose from that ancient pattern. Together we must become part of the chaos and resonate with it so we can reflect a different kind of order. Everything depends on how we play off the original elements. Orestes disappeared from history after Hypatia's murder, while Cyril triumphed over his enemies. He was even made a saint. I was his ignorant instrument then. But this time, I'm with you. Together, we have our best shot out of this hell hole."

Then the toilet flushed.

"Riley, you've got to stop doing crack," she said as she shoved the angel card back in her pocket. The bathroom door suddenly flung open and Moira sprang into the room naked, her hair wrapped in a towel. The startled Catherine stared at her huge, hanging tits.

"Hey, Asslick," Moira said to Riley. "I have a little something here for you."

Then she closed her eyes halfway as she scrutinized Catherine, smelling her vomit. "Hi-eee," she cooed, scanning her disarrayed clothing.

Catherine turned to Riley and opened her mouth to say something, then she froze. Riley watched expectantly as Angelica's childish energy flickered into her face.

"Uncle Riley. You're unfit," said Angelica. "You're fired! Game over."

7

Definitely X

May 1990

San Francisco Bay Area

Jake stopped on the corner of Sixth and Market and looked around. Plenty of women on the street, several alone. None of them looking his way. He did not consider himself promiscuous. Fondling the privates of a stranger, an obscene phone caller whose body and mind could be seriously diseased for all he knew, was not something he would have imagined himself willing to do. Yet here he was, in the low life district waiting for an anonymous obscene phone caller. A plain woman glanced at him as she walked by.

What if she were the caller? The idea stirred something perverse in him, and that bothered him. What was he doing? Flirting with disaster? *Is this being jaded?*

"Hi, Jake," said a young woman standing outside the passenger window.

The girl from Mindy's shoot. The attorney's niece. What was her name? Then it occurred to him that the caller might not approach if she saw him with another woman.

"What brings you downtown?" he said, hoping to get rid of her quick.

"You don't look happy to see me," she pouted.

"I'm just surprised to see you down here," he stammered. "You alone?"

"What do you think?" she grinned. "Waiting for someone?"

"Well, yeah."

"Really? Who? An actress?"

"No, a dangerous liaison. And you?"

"*Moi?*" she giggled. "Why I came to see you, of course."

"What?" he said, dumbfounded. Only then did he recognize the voice.

"You should see your face," she giggled again. "You look like you were expecting a Hunk of Burning Love and got the Blind Date From Hell instead."

"I…," he mumbled, unlocking the passenger side door. "Get in."

"You're not going to change your mind, are you?" she said, getting in. "I was worried you might. I'm horny. Are you?"

"Yeah," he said. "I haven't gotten any lately."

"Ooooo! I thought you and that Black girl were an item."

"It's a long story and I'd much rather hear yours. You do this often?"

"No." She smiled seductively. "I woke up ver-ry horny and I had to do something about it like right away, so I decided to call someone. I picked you."

He glanced at the traffic. "Why me?" he asked, getting hard.

"I thought you'd be good at it. I was right."

She must think I'm a sleaze. "Where do you live? Want to go to your place?"

"No, let's go to yours."

He found it hard to concentrate. "You didn't intend for me to find out it was you when you called then?"

"Oh, no, never. That sort of thing screws up the fantasy. You were clever, though. You got me all hot and bothered, then wouldn't let me come. And you knew exactly when to stop so I'd have to spend all day thinking of you fucking my brains out. Is that what you're going to do to me, Jake? Are you going to fuck my brains out?"

He drove onto the Bay Bridge thinking the sweet young thing had no idea he wasn't the sleaze ball she thought he was. She put her hand on the bulge in his pants.

He flinched. "You had me at a disadvantage," he said quickly to cover the flinch. "You knew who I was but I didn't know who you were."

"Guys shouldn't know." She unzipped his pants. "Otherwise they power trip." She grinned as she unzipped his pants to take out his stiff cock. "Let's get kinky."

Kinky? "What you got in mind?"

She squeezed his cock. "What do *you* have in mind?"

He glanced at her lascivious grin, then back at the traffic. "Well, I don't know. Way I figure, whoever makes the suggestion calls the tune. What do you like?"

"I want *you* to get kinky, Jake. I want you to do to me the most vile disgusting things you can imagine. Tell me, Ja-a-ake!" she said with a guttural slur of the *ake*. "Don't think I didn't notice you watching me. You wanted me. Come on, be as nasty as you want to be. Whadaya wanna do to me, Jaaake."

"Well, I was, uh, just admiring you. I wasn't thinking anything kinky."

"Oh, I know you were thinking something filthy. You can tell me. I want you to. After I saw your movie when I was a kid, I fantasized about the dis-gus-ting things the people who made it would do to me if they had the chance. I didn't have much by way of tits then but I knew my butt was bootylicious. Tell me."

"I'm a professional. I was making a movie. Didn't you feel anything like that when you did your sex scene?"

"Oh, no! I was turned on. I'll bet you were, too."

Evidently she didn't know that he left before her sex scene.

"Tell me what you want." She looked up, her lips against his shaft.

The bridge, cars, everything seemed like an illusion in the heat of sexual urgency. *What* did *he want?* "I want you naked. I want to feel my cock inside you." "Mmmmmmm," she purred, her lips on his balls. "But what do you really really want? Don't be bashful, be kinky."

"Well, I don't know what you think is kinky."

Pouting, she looked at him. "I'm just a kid. What do I know? You know, though. I want you to do something kinky, nasty."

"Okay, I'll do whatever comes to mind. You tell me if it's kinky enough for you."

She licked the tip of his cock and gazed at his face. She liked listening to his slow slightly nasal twang. There was something filthy about it, something hidden.

He knew what she wanted, he just didn't want to do it with her, and he didn't know why. Her desire was pulling him in, but something else was turning him off.

Strange what desire makes foolish people do.

Jake pulled into his driveway. The neglected flowers, trees and bushes on his front yard were all suffering in varying degrees from insects and disease.

"Very nice," Moira said looking at San Francisco in the distance. "Love the view." He got out of the truck.

She made no move to get out, so he went around to open her door. "Madam," he said thinking she expected it of him because of the age difference.

She gave him an ironic smile, then giggled at the awkward way he locked the door and slammed it shut after she got out. *Quirky artist type*, she thought.

The moment they were inside his musty house she pulled him to her and eagerly forced his lips and mouth open with her tongue. Astonished by the vigor of her hungry tongue darting from side to side in his mouth while he tried to position his under hers, he managed to work his tongue up over hers.

Excited by this, she pulled back and slipped out of her blouse, looking him in the eye, as if challenging him to fondle the huge tits imprisoned in her bra.

He experienced a moment of confusion until he recalled how *long* passionate looks followed by sexual abandon used to be considered hip. He could never quite get the feel for exactly when to end the stare. Then she grabbed at his butt and squeezed. The hunger in the pressure of her fingers caused him to hesitate for what felt like a moment too long before he reached to unclasp her bra.

"Ah!" she cried.

The size of her tits and the enormous aureola around her thick long nipples surprised him. The sweet little girl face and voice had absolutely obscene tits. He would have no problem manhandling these hooters.

"Oh, you're so rough," she moaned as he sucked. "Call me a slut!"

He froze a moment, then muttered, "Slut."

While she probed his ear with her tongue, her breath harsh with heat as she whispered, "Tell me."

He hesitated again, wondering what she wanted. *Ah, sub-titles.* "My face on your tits, your hard nipple's in my mouth. Feel that?"

"Oh, yyyyyesss!"

"My teeth," he gnawed. "You like?"

"I do! Oh, yes!" She grabbed hold of his head. "Hurt me!"

Hurt. He had not expected that. "Feel this?" He rubbed at her cunt through her panties.

"Ah!" she whimpered. "Yesssss!"

"You like my hand on your puss, don't you, bitch?"

"No, not bitch!" she gasped, eyes closed squeezing his shoulders as his hand slid into her panties.

"Okay, you filthy slut!" He shoved a finger into her. *God Almighty!* This was the *juiciest* cunt he'd ever felt. *Sloppy as hell and stinks to high heaven.*

"Ohhhh!" she cried. "Yessss!"

"You like that, you little whore?"

"Yes! Oh, yes! I do!" He slapped her ass.

"Oh, yeSSSS!"

Likes spanking. He grabbed a fistful of hair.

"Ahhhh!" she gasped as he pulled her head back. Then he gently released her.

"Let's go to the bedroom," he said with a boyish grin.

Moira squinted and smirked. He looked like a poor little boy in need of a mommy. The image made her laugh. When he joined in with an uncertain chuckle, she gave him a look of disbelief. His look of concern, like *she* was the crazy one, struck her as hilarious and she laughed loudly, turning away with tears in her eyes. Concerned, Jake placed a hand on her shoulder. Seeing the change, the slippage in his face, like he wanted to help, she tipped her face back in triumph and broke into convulsions of hysterical laughter.

THE YOUNG WOMAN standing in Jake's doorway nervously cocked her studded leather cap to one side. "We had an appointment, right?"

Jake opened the door wider. "Yes, of course. Come in."

She waved at an old Cadillac blocking the driveway, her reddish brown hair flouncing across the shoulder pads of a multi-zippered leather jacket. The car sped off as she swaggered into the house.

He felt something familiar in her mixture of vulnerability and bravado, as if she were a secret niece he knew nothing about, illegitimate maybe, or adopted out. If she were family, he would not be part of bringing her into the porn labyrinth. But she wasn't family. She was a teen street hooker, effectively already in the skin trade.

"Nice place," she said, admiring the view of San Francisco sparkling across the bay from his living room. The early eighties artwork and furniture reminded her of her parents. Then she noticed Jake's somber expression. "Look, Robin's my street name," she said, fidgeting. *Old guys always seemed to pass judgment on her without giving her a chance.* "My ID says Tracy. You can call me that, okay?"

"I'm sorry for staring. I was admiring your face. It's very expressive."

"Um, well, thank you, I guess. Yours, too." She winced, looking away. *What a stupid thing to say!*

"Have you done any acting?"

"Acting? You mean like in a movie? No, but I can put on an act and fool everybody. Does that count?" She grimaced. *No! No! Of course not, dummy!*

"What about modeling?"

"Not professional, no. I'm in the no-experience-necessary category. Is that going to be a problem?"

"No. Looks are what counts. You could be brain dead as far as most producers are concerned."

"So, I look good enough?" she said with a tentative smile.

Surprised, he said, "Yeah, of course. You're box cover material. You could be a star."

Her face brightened. "Really?" Then faded. "Please, tell me the truth. You *really* think I could be a star?"

"Yes, absolutely. You have the look, and you have expressive eyes. Eyes are the most important tool an actor has."

She looked doubtful. "When can I start work? I need to make money right away."

"I don't know. I'll have to call around. Could be a week or so."

"Oh," she pouted. "I'm broke, I got to come up with some cash like right away."

"I could get you a job tomorrow as a dancer."

"Dancing!" She shook her head emphatically. "No way!"

"Why's that?" he said, surprised by her vehemence. "It's safer than the streets and you'd make more money than from videos. Fact is, some dancers do porn like celebrities do talk shows, more for self-promotion than for the bucks."

"I can't dance."

Jake shrugged. "Neither can I. I used to feel like everybody was laughing at me in school dance classes."

"Yeah, me, too."

"But the kind of dancing we're talking about, the audience could give a flying fuck how good you are as long as you look good."

"I'd care," she said. "I'd feel awful if I weren't the best dancer, even if no one else in the whole world cared."

"Okay, I appreciate that. Tell you what, let's see if we can find a way around it."

"No. There isn't any."

"I'm not talking a real way. I'm talking acting. Pretend like you're a movie character who's afraid to dance."

"No, no, no, no, no!"

Fascinated, Jake said, "You never dance?"

"Never."

"Not even when no one else is around?"

She hated when adults tried to trick her. "Sometimes," she pouted. *He better not use it against her.*

"Did you like it?"

"It's not the same! It's not the same thing!"

"Now, hon, stay with me, don't get ahead. Did you like the way it felt?"

"Yes, but it's not the same!"

"I understand, believe me I do. I do aerobics every day by myself and it feels great, but I'm sure if someone peeked in on me they'd laugh."

Tracy laughed.

"If you dance as bad as I do then forget about it, you're hopeless. But I bet your classmates teased you because they picked up on your vulnerability. You probably can dance and just don't know it."

"No, I can't! Besides, you can't know that, you can't!"

"It's my job to know these things. You have grace and rhythm. I see it in the way you move. If you co-operate, I'll prove it to you."

"But I don't want to!"

"An actress has to be willing to be something she's not because that's what's expected of her."

"I don't wanna be an actress either! I just wanna make some money quick."

"All right, then, let's compromise. Producers usually want to see you with your clothes off. I'm a producer, I ask you to undress but there happens to be music playing in the background."

"I'd rather suck the producer's dick."

Jake frowned. "No, don't ever do that. Don't let yourself be taken advantage of. If you give yourself away, no one'll respect you. You could be a star, you want them to want you and to pay big bucks for the privilege."

"All the same, I can't dance."

"Okay, then consider this. There's just you and me here, kid, and you're the best dancer in the joint. I won't laugh or make fun of you." He went over to close the drapes. "When I turn the music on, sensually take off your clothes."

She thought of how annoyed he was going to be when he realized she was wasting his time, as if a pale kid jerking around like a spaz could possibly be erotic. She avoided eye contact as she unbuckled her belt. Anyway, there was no way she could dance to *that* music. It was at least ten years old. Old people stuff. Her tight jeans resisted her efforts to pull them down and he was staring at her like she was a moron.

"No! No!" she cried, sinking dramatically to her knees. "I can't! I can't!"

Jake placed a hand on her shoulder. "It's all right, you don't have to. Let me help you up." He guided her to her feet. "Sit over here on the couch."

Sniffling, she started to adjust her pants.

"Don't bother," he said. "I still have to see you naked." She sat on the couch. "Go ahead, take them off."

She untied her shoes and kicked them away. "Need a hanky?" he asked.

She shook her head and worked her way out of her jeans.

"Hold it. I want you to take your clothes off as if you're being watched. Be seductive."

"Not with the music on. Please."

"Oh, sure." He turned off the music.

She took off her leather jacket, tossed it on the couch then pulled her shirt up over her head.

"Slow down," he said as she reached for the clasp of her bra. "I'm watching you. Arouse me, be seductive."

"I can't!" she pouted. *This is so stupid. Who needs this artistic crap.*

"Try it," said Jake. "Sloooow. Seductive. Turn me on."

"It'd be easier if you did it."

"What do you mean? You've undressed in front of men before, haven't you?"

"No. Guys always do it for me."

He covered his mouth and looked away. Something was wrong. He wondered whether she'd be able to perform on film.

"You've seen porn before, right?" he asked.

"Sure," she frowned. *He must think I'm like a total geek.* "Lots of it. I like porn."

"Can you do the sort of things people do in those videos with strangers standing around watching?"

"Oh, yeah. Sure!"

"Fucking? Sucking?"

"I've got no problem with any of that. Just don't ask me to dance, okay?"

Jake undid the clasp of her bra and her large pointed breasts with exquisite, subtle brown nipples sprang free.

"Wow!" he gasped.

"Thank you, but they're not mine. That is, of course they're mine, what I meant was I had them made a few months ago."

"Really?" If she were older it would have occurred to him such perfectly sculpted tits had to be fake. "I need to get an idea of how you're likely to perform on a shoot. Porn's not like any kind of sex you know. You're told who you are and what to do. In regular sex, or sex with a trick, you have some control over what goes on. I want you to pretend we're doing a video and I'm the director and I've told you to lie down on the couch and play with yourself."

"Huh?"

"Masturbate. It's got to look real so do it like you normally would."

"But I don't masturbate."

"Really? Never?"

"That's right. Never."

"But you've seen films where women do it, right? Just do like they do."

"No," she whined. "I've never done that before and I'd look dumb. Look, put me with a guy and I'll be fine, I've done that."

He reminded himself of the Fourth Wall. No sleaze. Touching a model during an interview would be sleazy. But this was not exactly an ordinary professional situation.

"All right," he said. "I'll touch you and you respond. This is an act, right? Not real. Pretend to be aroused."

"Okay," she shrugged.

"Good." He fondled her breasts, attempting to detect the implants. "Amazing, they don't feel fake. I don't see any scars. How'd they do it."

"There." She pointed to a scar in her armpit. "It wasn't supposed to leave such a big scar but I fucked up."

"How's that?"

"I wasn't supposed to expose them to sunlight for a few days and I did. I wanted them bigger, too. These are too small."

"Are you kidding?" he said to her nipples. "If they were any bigger you'd look like a freak. They're proportioned just right for your body." She smelled of some small sweetness, like that of a single crushed flower. "Do you wear perfume or use a bath oil?"

"No. I wouldn't waste money on that stuff."

Her natural body odor, he thought as he sat on the couch. *Tropical flowers.* He turned her around and pulled down her panties and stared at her butt for awhile. Then, like a sculptor ascertaining its exact contours, he cupped her cheeks. Feeling its firmness, its roundness, disregarding the surrounding curves as if her cheeks were a fragment of a statue he had unearthed from which the rest of the body was missing.

"Am I supposed to be doing something?" she said.

"You're supposed to react."

"I'm sorry. I guess I'm nervous."

"You're right." He pulled back from temptation. "I'm pushing you too far too fast."

"But I know I can do this," she said, worried. "Can't you put me to work anyway?"

"The only work I can get you right away would be as a dancer, otherwise I won't know anything until I've made a few calls. Frankly, though, I think you should stay out of the skin trade altogether."

"Look, I'm tired of being broke. I worked in a donut shop and did without a lot of stuff and still had to ask my boyfriend for help. I decided a month ago I'd rather suck dick than live like that any longer, even though it meant I had to leave my boyfriend."

She paused, then added, "And I loved him."

"Maybe you should go back to him."

"No, I've made up my mind this is what I'm going to do. I want to make a lot of money."

"Tell you what, join me for lunch tomorrow and I'll introduce you to someone who can help."

"I guess I can do that," she said, thinking. "Um, could you pick me up at school after my 10 o'clock."

"All right, sure. Go ahead and get dressed."

"Oh, thanks." She stood up. "I can do that. Guys always take your clothes off but they never put them back on."

"I'll do it for you, if you like."

"No, I can do it faster. What time is it?"

"Nine forty-five."

"Damn!" she muttered. "Could you give me a ride to San Pablo Avenue? I'm suppose to meet someone there at nine thirty."

AFRICAN JAZZ-rock-calypso fusion blasting out into the street and the long line outside the club surprised Ben even more than the twenty-dollar cover for Jazz's new band. The people behind him were crowding him into the people inside, shoving him into the wall-to-wall throb of the beat. The ten performers on the stage were all playing an instrument, except for the lead singer and a woman dancing in place beside him. Ben wouldn't have recognized Jazz if he hadn't known she was in the band. Her colorful African clothing, pillbox hat and toothy grin made her look like someone else. Then her lusty voice took over, belting out, prompting the dancers to dance like puppets attached to the beat, their mouths moving, their voices drowned out in a room filled with electronic thumping beats. The music increased in intensity and the crowd went wild with their shouts, screaming and stomping, louder and louder, until they could be heard and felt over the beat.

Then the music stopped. The male vocalist said with a Nigerian accent, "Thank you! Thank you! We take a break. Return soon." The dancers cheered as they walked off.

Ben then spotted a boyish looking girl who resembled Julie accepting a drink from a young stud. A dead ringer. "Could it be?" he whispered with a thrill of hope. She had the reddish spiked hair, boyish mannerism, and was dressed like Julie, minus the crucifix.

Then he saw Joaquin standing nearby. "Oh, my god!" he gasped. Julie is alive!!!!!!

"*My god, my god, my god!*" he kept muttering as he felt an immense weight lifting off him. He could breathe again. He so very much did not want her to be dead. The way he'd felt, when he thought she was, he would have willingly given up his own life that she might keep hers. What struck him most at the time was he absolutely knew, if it were possible, he would do it. He was so *ashamed* of what he'd done to her.

Then he spotted Will at the bar, raising his drink to toast him, a big drunken grin on his face. His mood darkened. He'd been messing with him, making him believe she was dead! Ben glared at Will, breathing through clenched teeth. This was the sort of combination of events and madness so typical of those that tempted the Fates. Having realized this prompted him to hold off approaching Will, until he had cooled down.

"Jazz looked great up there, didn't she?" Joaquin said as he approached Julie. When Julie turned to face him, she noticed Ben glaring at Will by the bar.

"What are *they* doing here?" she snapped.

"I invited them. Be cool. They have serious connections. Big time."

"I don't care what they got, they creep me out. Especially that *fuck-face lawyer!*"

Joaquin frowned at her. "Be nice."

Julie's eyes flashed at him. "The fuck!!! You *know* why, Joa, Joaq Spannamaker!" Then everything defocused as she felt herself slipping out of this Stream of Time.

THINGS GOT OUT OF CONTROL after Jazz and Jake left Mindy's shoot. Will said something that upset Julie who then stormed off, heading downstairs to the backyard where she plopped down in a lounge chair under the deck and closed her eyes trying to calm herself down. It was dark when she re-opened them. She felt incredibly groggy with a throbbing headache, strange acidic tastes in her mouth and sour scents in her nostrils.

A hissing propane lantern on a nearby table drew Julie's attention to Janus Terror, who appeared to be asleep in a lawn chair next to her. As if on cue, Janus opened her eyes, then promptly sat up straight when she realized Julie was awake.

"Good, you're alive," Janus said, looking relieved. "I thought for sure you were dead when he brought you out. You sure looked it, but you had a slight pulse, so I fig—-"

"*DEAD!*" Julie heard herself exclaim. "What the fuck! Dead?"

"You don't remember?" Janus whispered, looking surprised. "Will paid you extra to let him drug you unconscious before he put you in the cage—"

"He DRUGGED me!! And put me in a *CAGE!!*" Julie yelled, cutting her off.

"Everybody has to strip down naked before he ties them up," Janus mumbled, gesturing for her not to yell again. "*Then* he puts them in the cage. He won't take any pictures until they're in the cage."

"He TIED me up! And took PICTURES of me! NAKED!" Julie sputtered.

"The models don't have to be drugged, but there's a good-sized bonus for those that do," Janus whispered. "His contacts in Japan will fork out a lot more for photos of unconscious, caged naked, healthy-looking pretty girls. Even more if they look like they're freshly dead. And you did. Which means you've hit the Jackpot! At least 100K in royalties, guaranteed." She paused. "That's how I met Will. When I was young and fresh-faced, I was his guinea pig back when he was, you know.... experimenting with knock-out drugs. Looking for ways to make me look healthy yet dead." She paused again.

"Uh. Where was I? Oh, uh. Yeah." Janus handed Julie a packet of documents and a thick envelope marked fifteen thousand dollars. "Uh, that's an advance against future royalties. Like I said, at least 100K. You were convincing, let me tell you. Yeah, uh." She paused, trying to focus. "I thought you were, uh, dead for sure. Or dying. Let me tell you, I was sweating bullets. You're gonna get a lot more than —"

"Oh, god," Julie muttered as she thumbed through the documents, seeing what appeared to be her signatures. "I don't remember reading or signing any of this."

"Not remembering is one of the possible side effects of the drugs he gave you—"

"Drugs!" Julie snapped at Will's guinea pig. "Plural?"

"It's rare, but you're not the first model to black out from his cocktails. If you're worried if he, you know, had sex with you, don't be. He's impotent. Couldn't do anything even if wanted to. Diabetes. Can't get it up."

"Yeah, but he can still play doctor," Julie muttered, giving her a look that matched her tone of voice, insinuating she thought something was seriously wrong with her.

"His Japanese customers regard what he does as art. That's why they pay him so much." She paused, as if trying to remember something. "Oh, yeah. He told me he'd like to do more with you. Conscious or unconscious, your choice." Janus handed her a card with a phone number on it. "He's open to negotiation."

Julie was then aware she'd been slipping in and out of memory streams of time, where the past and future are fluid, connected by a present. Being born aware of the stream made her capable of sensing waves of the past and future, to the point where she could shift events in whatever present she was in. Oliver said her shifting abilities had been compromised by the drugs Will gave her. He insisted she hadn't lost her abilities, so much as the strength of her link to a part of her Dreaming Body that was essential for sensing and shifting the flow at the right moment.

Then she felt herself re-surfacing as she heard Joaquin whispering, "Play it cool, Jules. Fuck-face will get his, trust me on this." Then he said more loudly, "Jazz's band's great. She should quit her day job."

"Yeah, right," she heard herself say as she felt herself disconnecting from her Dreaming Body. "I knew a guy in a hot band who thought it'd last forever. Inside of a year, he was broke and had to go live with his dumb ass parents in fucking Texas."

"Julie," Joaquin muttered, with a look of aggravated impatience.

"I wasn't being negative! Just realistic. It's a fucking pipe dream."

"And you're still just a kid," Joaquin said in a low voice. "You don't know shit about the arts or why people make the sacrifices they do."

"*I* don't know about *art* and *sacrifice*? The only real thing she's got going for her is her job. Someone in the band will fuck with her, and she'll blow it. You know she will."

"Man, you've been bitching or dogging me about one damn thing after another since Mindy's project, and I'm sick of it. What the fuck's gotten into you?"

Julie opened her mouth to reply, but stopped herself short. She'd told him, and only him, that Will had drugged her. But she'd gone no further than that because she'd felt herself losing power by having said that much. Oliver confirmed what she suspected, that the more people who knew about had what happened, the more compromised her situation would be. He'd also confirmed something else she'd suspected.

Oliver's Dreaming Body had witnessed everything, including what Dr. Ben had done to her. He told her she could use her power over them more effectively if they didn't know what she knew. He also urged her to re-learn how to stabilize herself while slipping in and out of Time Streams by seeking ways to recognize her Dreaming Body.

When she felt herself slipping out of time again, she realized she'd somehow lost control in the Stream. All she could do now was to observe whatever presented itself.

Sometime later, when she slipped back into the bar, Joaquin was still talking. She could not understand what he was saying, but she heard herself say, "Those two, Fuck Face and Dr Ben, something about them makes me angry when they look at me."

Joaquin raised his eyebrows, then started talking while she felt herself slipping back out into the Stream. For a brief moment, before she disappeared, she was aware of Joaquin talking to her image, unaware of her absence. She'd felt as if she'd fallen asleep and was in a dream. Then she snapped back into the noisy bar in time to hear Joaquin say,

"I'm going backstage to pay my respects to Jazz while she's on break. Shouldn't be too long before they go back on. Will you be okay?"

She heard a voice that felt like hers, but did not sound like her, say, "Yes."

Then Oliver's face appeared before her, and she realized things were getting seriously out of her control. It was not unusual for her to sense Oliver's presence in the Time Stream, but seeing him face to face like this meant she was in serious danger.

Then Oliver grabbed her with his eyes, and she felt herself relax as she held on, until she re-surfaced in the bar and found herself listening to Ben. He seemed to be somehow aware of her confused state as he gently guided her toward the bar. She understood every word he said, but found it difficult to remember them once heard. It was something about the child goddess Artemis attempting to merge with her.

Then Ben handed her a sweet, sticky drink that tasted good, telling her it was important that she drink it down, quick.

"Where's Jasmine's boyfriend?" Will asked Julie when Ben brought her up to the bar.

"You'd think he'd at least put in an appearance on her opening night?"

Julie stared at him, blankly, as she heard herself mumble, "Why are guys so stupid when it comes to women?" *Feeling… Outside of Time … Where everything is nonsense.*

"Devil's bargain, my dear." Will raised his glass, toasting her. "People never seem to learn you *can't* placate the devil, or women."

"What he's getting at," said Ben, chuckling, "is some women are devils and some men seek redemption through them. Most women, though, are stupid and most men expect redemption to come through rescuing women. Or, from a woman rescuing them. So you see, one way or another, men seek redemption through women. That's why they're so stupid when it comes to women."

Will took Ben aside, watching Julie as he said, "She's disorientated from a drug I had someone slip into her drink to disrupt any memory traces she might have related to what we did to her. She should be fine in a day or two."

Ben glared his displeasure, hoping the drink he gave her would counteract it.

"YOU CAN'T go in there," a large black man said, blocking the backstage door.

"I'm a friend of Jazz," said Joaquin. "She invited me."

"Who?"

"Jasmine," said Joaquin. "The singer."

"Jamayla, you mean Jamayla. Hold on." He opened the steel door and yelled, "Jamayla! There's some old white dude says he knows you."

Jazz laughed. "Old man? Yeah, let his sorry ass in."

Joaquin entered the large, fluorescent-lit room. The musicians inside, talking among themselves, ignored him.

Jazz limped toward him. "Got a cigarette?" she said.

"You shouldn't smoke when you're singing," said Joaquin.

"Just shut up and just give me a damn cigarette. Gives my voice character."

Joaquin handed her a cigarette. "You haven't replaced your contacts yet?" he asked, noticing her squint.

She shook her head. "No, can't afford to. I got an ol' pair of glasses but I can't wear them on stage, wouldn't do." She looked around. "But I can't find where I put the damn things. Hope nobody sat on 'em."

"What do they look like?"

"Glasses!" she snapped. "They look like damn glasses!"

"Are they wire frames or what?"

"Any damn glasses you see will be mine! Now where did I put 'em? I hope they didn't get lost 'cause I can't do my day job without no glasses."

"Here they are," said Joaquin, spotting them on a windowsill.

"Good, good." She put the large plastic-framed glasses on.

"What's wrong with your foot?" He looked at her big toe wrapped in gauze.

She laughed. "You're not gonna believe this but I had a fungus growing on my big toe. I went to the doctor and he told me they haf to pull the toe nail off."

Joaquin winced. "Ohhhhh!"

"I told them no fucking way 'cause I had this gig and he says he has to take care of it right there and then 'cause he can't see me again for a long time. So he has some doctors or interns or whatever hold me down while he pulls on my nail. I put up one hell of a fight and did I ever yell. They were upset wif me big time."

"How is it?"

"Hurts damnit, and I have to go on stage wif this damn thing. You have to be barefoot for this kind of music. Then, as if I didn't have troubles enough, I washed clothes today and when I went back to the launder mat all my panties been stole. Nothing else, just my damn panties. What kinda low life do a thing like that? Now I don't have no underwear."

"I like your costume. You look sexy in African clothes."

"Oh, really?" she snarled. "Is that surprising to you? I'm Af-ri-can so why shouldn't I look sexy in African clothes?"

"You're wrong about the lead male being better than you. You have it all over him, girl. They don't need any left-handed motive for picking you. You're good, for real."

"Thank you," she sighed. "I enjoy being on stage again, but I'm gonna be so tired tomorrow at work." She snorted. "Should've behaved myself last night. Wonder why Jake's not here." She noticed the other musicians leaving the room.

"I better be getting ready. You staying for the whole show?"

"You bet your sweet booty," said Joaquin.

"Good, 'cause I need somebody to party wif."

"What about the day job?"

"Hey, ol' man, I'm young, I can make it through another day," she said. "I gots to get high, I'm feelin' too low, and I can't go in that house alone. I sure can't go with anyone in the band. No sir, I'm not that stup-id."

"Uh, I've got to work, too. And I'm old."

"You like eating on my pussy?"

"Yeah, you know me. I love two kinds of crack. The kind you smoke and the kind between your legs."

"Shit, you crazy," she snorted. "For that you can lick my booty."

Joaquin thought for a moment, then suggested, "I think we should leave right now, instead of god knows how many hours later. You need sleep, not staying out all night then going to work in the morning. Come up with some story about your foot, or whatever. If you have to, bargain for only one more set, then leave."

"I can't do that. It's opening night."

"Yes you can, they need you. The audience will miss you, but it'll work itself out."

JAKE SCANNED the dance floor. The dancers, sliding together with sex on their faces, moving with eyes closed. Then he saw Julie sitting at the bar next to Worthingham, licking the sticky inside of her glass, getting it all.

"Mr. Zakheim," Will said as he gestured for him to join them. "What did you think of my girl?"

"A bit inhibited," said Jake, surprised to find him here with a very drunk Julie.

"Inhibited?" His laugh crinkled the skin around his icy blue eyes. "You're talking about a girl who sucks off Ragheads for twenty bucks a pop and thinks she's struck oil. She's anything but inhibited."

"She hasn't been on the streets long," said Jake, watching Julie's glazed eyes. He doubted she even knew he was there. He would have to make sure she got home safely.

"She tell you that?" asked Worthingham.

Jake shrugged. "Who are we to talk. We've all sold ourselves in one way or another."

"Have I offended you? There's nothing to be offended about. *All* women have a price. Like your friend, the singing stockbroker. Where is she? Not up on the stage."

Jake frowned, shaking his head. Then he noticed Julie was flushing pale.

"Esad, she left with a trick. Opening night and she leaves with a trick."

"What do you mean a trick?"

"I don't feel so good," Julie mumbled as she wobbled up off her seat.

"Like I said," said Worthingham. "Some old guy likes what he sees, flashes a wad of cash and off they go. I don't want Tracy to turn out to be like that, like trash. She's too proud. I'm teaching her what I know but, my god, she is such a little liar."

'Uhh!" Julie moaned as she stumbled up against Will, vomiting all over him. Jake grabbed hold of her before she could collapse on the floor.

Then Ben suddenly appeared to help him steady her on her feet.

"Could you help me get her to my car so I can take her home?" Ben asked Jake. Jake hesitated, wondering whose home he intended to take her to.

"Jazz left with Joaquin," Ben said in a low voice as they guided Julie out. "Their band manager came out to tell the audience her foot was infected and she needed medical attention. She did a couple of numbers, then she left with Joaquin a half hour ago."

When they got to his Lexus, Ben added, sensing Jake's apprehension as they worked her into his car, "I put something in her drink to make her throw up after I saw Will slip something into a drink he had someone give her. I felt it best to get it out of her system sooner than later." He paused, then, "Listen to me. I owe her. She's safe with me."

"And you just happened to have an antidote on you," Jake said, suspiciously.

"Yes, always. I can't even begin to tell you how many times I've had to use them."

TRAFFIC was at a standstill. Jake cursed himself for not allowing enough time. Tracy was unlikely to wait patiently, and Hasib, not at all. Any chance of their connecting with Hasib depended on finding the college parking lot fast. He did, but he did not see Tracy among the students. There was only one white woman there, a blonde. She approached, dressed in a black leather jacket and cap.

"Where the fuck you been?" said Tracy, opening the passenger door.

"Sorry," he said. "There was a traffic jam and I had to take side streets. What happened to your hair?"

"What do you think?" she snapped, getting in. "I dyed it."

"Why'd you do that?" he asked.

"Why?" she scoffed as he drove off. "Because if I'm going to be a star, I should look like one. I wanted to get it styled, too, but I couldn't afford that. I hate the idea of making a movie and not looking right."

"Good news," he said, restraining from saying he preferred her natural look. "There's an amateur taping the day after tomorrow. Doesn't pay much, though."

"What does that mean, amateur?"

"That's the low end of the industry. Suppose to look like it's done by your neighbors. You know, like regular people, no stars. The pay's low. Fifty bucks."

"That's okay," she said in a less irritable tone. "I mean, it's my first video. I need the experience."

"Yeah, but we should get together beforehand to prep so you don't freeze on set."

"Aren't you going to be there?" she said, worried.

Surprised, he glanced at her. She was staring straight ahead. "I could be, if you like."

"What do I do? What part do I play?"

"It's a group scene with a bunch of guys and another woman."

She stiffened. "A bunch of guys? How many? What kind of guys?"

"Hard to say. Non-professionals, whoever Janus digs up."

"Oh," she mumbled. "I don't want any Black guys."

"All right."

"It's not that I'm prejudiced or anything, but I was raped by a Black guy once and I don't like them."

"No problem."

"And no girls. I don't do anything with girls."

"Okay, but you should try to overcome that since girl-girl scenes are a staple and you'll lose a lot of work."

"I don't care. I won't do it."

"Fine, but why not? You don't have to like it to do it, you know."

"I'm not going to lick anybody's cunt. That's—" She stuck out her tongue. "Yeeech!"

"What about a girl licking yours?"

"No! I don't want them to touch me. It's weird."

"What's the difference if it's a guy or a gal who eats your pussy?"

"Look, I don't like it when a guy does it either but I'll let him because he's a guy, but a girl's different. They know how disgusting it is. It's like really weird, you know."

"You don't like it when a guy eats you?"

"That's right, it's gross," she frowned. "It's dirty."

"No, it's not. Your pussy's sweet. Lots of people would love to lick it. Anyway, most women love having their pussies licked."

"Fine, but I *don't!* Look, if a guy has to eat my cunt he can, but don't let a woman touch me, okay? Am I understood here?"

"Gotcha. So when would be a good time for us to get together to prepare?"

"What does that mean, prepare? What do I gotta do? How long?"

"Figure a couple of hours, maybe less. You need practice taking directions."

"Oh," she mumbled. "I got a lot of studying to do and I have a class tonight. Would tomorrow afternoon be all right?"

"Sure, that'd be fine."

Jake stopped at the bridge toll booth, paid the toll.

"I should tell you what to expect when you meet Hasib," he said as they drove off.

"Would you mind if we didn't talk?"

"Na." *Oh, brother. Now what?* "Silence can be golden."

"My parents were always talking at me in the car and I hated it. I'd rather watch the scenery, you know."

"Yeah, scenery's more enjoyable without conversation."

"You mind?" she said, irritated.

Difficult as it was, he managed to suppress even the urge to curse traffic.

JAKE SCANNED the meters as they approached the homeless shelter. Every car had a meter violation but no tickets. He chose a space near an old woman asleep on a tattered sleeping bag. Tracy got out and went to the parking meter.

"Wait," said Jake. "Meter maids rarely work this block."

"Doesn't matter. Look." She held out a handful of slugs. "My boyfriend gave me a bunch of these so it doesn't cost us a thing. Cool, huh?"

"We'll be gone longer than the time on the meter."

"Maybe not." She put in a slug.

"Don't tell Hasib you won't dance," said Jake, watching an old man checking them out from across the street. "I realize you have no intention of working there but I want you to play along and observe everything without pre-judging or jumping to conclusions. Take in the atmosphere, the audience, everything, and we'll talk about it later when you've had time to absorb it. You understand what I'm saying?"

"Yeah. No big deal. Like a field trip or something."

"Right. You're an intelligent woman. You should make an informed decision before becoming part of the industry. I don't want you thinking years from now you were somehow tricked into it."

"Look, this is nothing," she said, impatient. "If I don't do this, then I'm back on the streets. I invested in these tits to make money." Tracy made a face at the mammoth breasts on the posters in the theater lobby. "These people work here?"

"They're headliners," said Jake. "Look at the dates under the posters. This one's today's headliner."

"Dixie Belles. What a stupid name. And Booty Hill, an ass to die for. That's sick."

"Let's go," he said, taking hold of her arm.

"I don't think I can go through with this," she groaned.

"Just do it and think about it later. Observe and absorb. Think of it as Tracy's Fun House adventure. Nothing bad's going to happen. It's like watching a play."

She looked at him as if he had said something incredibly stupid.

Omar glanced up from counting money inside the ticket booth. "You here for Hasib, Jake?"

"Yeah," said Jake. "Let him know I'm here. Please."

A dancer stepped out from the dressing room into the hallway to their right. The tiny dancer looked as if she had had a cruel night and was resigned to having many more.

Tracy furrowed her brow and stared at the haggard woman's stretch marks and sagging tits. "She's a dancer?" she whispered. "Who'd want to watch *her*?"

"You'd be surprised how good these girls look on stage," he said, watching her eyes. He used to watch Cedar's eyes to gauge whether she felt he was lecturing her. If she did, she'd tune out like she did with her father, the professor. "A plain woman can come across incredibly sexy if she handles herself right. When a guy's turned on, everything looks different and he's capable of doing anything, like sticking his tongue up a complete stranger's butthole."

"Oh, that's gross!" Tracy stuck out her tongue. "On an empty stomach! I think I'm going to spew."

"When did you eat last?"

"Not since yesterday afternoon," she said. "I don't think I can handle this. Could we get something to eat?"

"Sure, but we have to see Hasib first."

"Oh!" she whined.

"Hasib says go on down," said Omar, hanging up the phone. "The door is unlocked."

Tracy lingered on the stairs, scrutinizing the enormous tits on video jackets lining the wall. Jake waited by the black basement door and pushed it open when she approached. She glared at the obese woman in the bikini poster and made a gesture of throwing up.

"It's meant to be funny," said Jake.

"How can you tell? It's bllllah!"

"Well, look at her lipstick, the way it's formed in the middle of her lips, like a kiss. Her incredibly long lashes. The exaggerated sexy pose. It's too outrageous to be taken seriously."

"Okay," she shrugged. "If you say so."

Hasib was on the phone when they entered the office. Willow, a dancer Jake knew, sat facing Hasib. His son Peter, also on the phone, was at a desk to his left.

Hasib hung up then gestured toward the couch. "I'll be with you in a second, Jake. Why don't you and your friend sit down." Then to Willow, he said, "So, sweetheart, exactly what is it you want me to do?"

"I don't know," said Willow in a childish voice, averting her eyes. "I thought maybe your friends, or—"

"That's why we have rules," said Hasib. "This isn't the first time something like this has happened."

"I know, I know. But what can I do?"

"Park your car further away and have someone walk you to and from the theater."

"How do I get somebody to do that?"

"Omar will give you the dancers' schedule. Make arrangements with one of them." He gave her a sympathetic look. "Don't worry about it, sweetheart. He'll give up if he can't get at you."

Willow stood up and left without acknowledging Jake.

"What happened?" Jake said after she left.

"She was stupid enough to go out with some nut who thinks he's in love with her," said Hasib. "He's been vandalizing her car because she doesn't want to see him again."

"Does that happen a lot?" asked Tracy.

"No, no." Hasib shook his head. "The customers keep their distance as long as the girls do what we tell them. Normally I'd fire a girl who dated a customer, I don't care who she is, but I can't in this case. It's too sad." He frowned, then he smiled at Tracy. "So you're interested in being a dancer?"

"She's considering it," said Jake.

Hasib glanced at his watch. "Dixie's on in a minute. Why don't you go up and see how a pro does it. Afterwards, we'll have lunch."

"Sounds fine to me," said Jake.

"I'm starving now!" she said, annoyed. "Couldn't we eat and watch her later?"

"It's only an extra fifteen minutes. I'd like to hear what you think of her."

"Fine," said Jake, taking Tracy's hand. "We'll meet in the lobby after her set."

Peter Haikim hung up the phone. "Oh, dad, I won't be here when you get back."

"You were out of the office all last week, Peter. It wouldn't hurt to put in a full day now and then." Hasib winked at Jake. "He fancies himself a movie producer nowadays."

"I DON'T LIKE THIS," said Tracy. "I want to leave, get something to eat, and not come back. I definitely don't want to watch anybody named Dixie Belles."

"Relax," said Jake. "I didn't say you had to like it. We're here, so let's complete Tracy's Fun House Adventure."

"This is not an adventure."

"Adventures aren't comfortable. They're challenges and often downright unpleasant ones at that. It's only later in memory they're adventures."

"I do not want to remember this! I want to eat something and forget all about it."

"You're here to observe, so get over the attitude problem. We'll discuss your feelings and thoughts later."

Frowning, she followed him through red double swinging doors into darkness. Dixie was on stage, wearing a red Southern Belle dress, illuminated by red lights that flashed on and off to the Rolling Stones's *Sympathy for the Devil*.

"Let's get out of here!" she whispered loudly. "I can't see a thing."

"Wait a minute," said Jake. "Your eyes will adjust."

"Ohhh!" she moaned.

Dixie removed her dress then pranced around the stage in red underwear, her immense cleavage held in place by a corset.

When his eyes adjusted, Jake pointed out the lap dancers. "See the girls on the guys' laps?" he whispered. "That's how they make most of their money. The guys tip them to move around on their laps. Some guys come that way, even though they're not allowed to touch the girls on illegal spots."

"That's dumb," muttered Tracy. "I didn't spend all that money on my tits so nobody could touch them."

"There's an empty row. Let's sit over there."

Dixie raised an enormous tit up to her mouth to suck its nipple.

Squirming, Tracy said, "I don't need to watch this."

"Think of it as a scary movie," said Jake.

Dixie removed her corset, spreading out her pendulous orbs. A man in front tossed a bill up on stage, prompting Dixie to lean over to pummel him with her breasts while the audience cheered her on.

"Oh!" Tracy groaned, covering her eyes.

Dixie then turned her butt in Tracy's direction, her thin G-string leaving little to the imagination as she spread her cheeks and pussy lips. Then she pulled the G-string aside to insert fingers in both orifices.

"I'm gonna be sick," Tracy hissed. "What's she gonna do next? Let everyone sniff her fingers?"

Dixie then lay down on her back, pulling her knees down to her chest, spreading her privates wide open for all to see.

"I've had enough!" Tracy said, getting up. "Let's go!"

ANGELICA GRABBED hold of the railing to brace herself for the ferry's impact against the tires hanging off the Angel Island pier. A figure on shore, standing in the shadow of a kiosk, caught her eye. There was something menacing in his stance, in the tilt of his broad brimmed hat, in the way his hands rested on his hips, legs apart.

She slipped a thumb in her mouth to calm herself as she tried to make out his face.

Could it be Spear? Why would he be wearing a hat like that? Probably not him.

A drop dripped from nose to knuckle, reminding her she needed to get some tissues before disembarking. She grabbed her backpack then headed for the ladies room, a damp metal cubicle covered with battered layers of paint.

After locking herself in, she started the struggle with her tight pants. She'd put off peeing to the last minute due to the ordeal of prying them down then back up again.

Her reflection in the mottled mirror above the grimy steel sink caught her eye. She slipped her thumb back in her mouth, biting down on her thumbnail as she examined her face, turning red from the cool bay breeze.

"You know what you did?" snarled a shape, forming in the mirror.

Her thumb popped out of her mouth, like a cork yanked out of a bottle. Then she faced away to the paper towel dispenser, on which someone had scrawled OFF THE NUTSACKS! She tore off a couple of sheets to blow her nose.

*"You must suuf-f-f-ferr for what you did. Speearr will fin—ish you.
He's suub-terr-fuge,"* Joseph said, using her mouth to voice it.

ANGELICA made it on shore without spotting Spear. She hoped he
wouldn't show so she could go back on the ferry. Riley's mind-fuck had
disorientated her. She'd felt herself unraveling on her way over, not sure
of who she was, nor of what she'd done. She did not want Spear to see
her like this. He would disapprove of her bringing A-frog Hitler along.

She slipped off her backpack, and opened it for Hitler to witness
what happens to those who failed her. Then she took out the Bad Angel
card, the one that failed to protect her from Riley. She muttered "Bad
angel," as she tore off the tip off a wing. Possessed by a constricted
pleasure, she watched Hitler as she tore off the other wing, ripping
them to pieces. "You don't deserve to be an angel. I'm taking his wings
away, bit by bit. He'll never be an angel again, because I'm scattering
the pieces."

She threw the pieces up in the air, into a breeze that carried them
out toward the Bay. Biting her lower lip, she then held the wing-
less angel over a lighter, its flame blackening his face. Then a strange
shadow merged with her shadow. She froze. The shadow of the man
in the broad brimmed hat! She turned around, slowly.

"What are you doing?" said Spear.

She pouted. *Disguised himself so he could spy on me!* No wonder she'd
felt compelled to snoop, which was how she found his passport with
what she assumed was his real name. Dugai Bistie, age thirty-four. The
age of her father when he died.

"The angel, he betrayed me!" she said with a sick look of defiance.

He looked her full in the eye with cold detachment, his eyes ruthless
over his friendly smile, a combination that made her heart race. There
was something utterly inhuman in his wild amber eyes, peering into her
from a face with such a finely chiseled nose and delicate high cheek-
bones. She looked back at him. Wide-eyed. Her thumb in her mouth.
Her fist in her face. Then his knuckles tapped her on the top of her head.

"Riley made me get sick! So I fired him!" she blurted out, feeling
foolish, unable to stop the flow of words. "I wouldn't have come at all
but I had to let you know we are okay." She glanced over at the ferry.
"I have to go back. I can't spend the night."

He made a clucking sound. "You fired Riley," he said, his voice neu-
tral, masking his surprise. She nodded, glaring back up at him. His

appointment was with the Seabolts, not with their weakest link. He watched her face, waiting for a Seabolt to take over while he circled around her, noticing the tight fit of her jeans. None of the Seabolts wore tight jeans, which means she must have maintained some control at the beginning. He had to take her to count. "Something valuable's been taken from you, Angelica."

"Valuable?" she tittered. "I got sick on my shirt and had to leave it with Riley's lady friend, if that's what you mean. She lent me her sweater so she could clean it." She saw him glance at Hitler in her backpack. His silence disturbed her. "Was that wrong?" she asked in an attempt to draw his attention away from Hitler.

"Let's go." He nodded in the direction of the kiosk. "You must be ready by twilight." He picked up her pack then walked off.

"Ready by twilight?" She hesitated. "But I have to go back!" she yelled after him. "I-I-I had a seizure." He stopped, and turned to look at her.

"You will regain your strength here, tonight," he said, his soft voice pulling at her. "There's no time to waste." He walked off toward a tower of lockers.

She tried to decide what to do. "Look, I'm not well," she moaned, wobbling after him. "Could we maybe do this some other time, please?"

"Accept your condition and see it as it is. A challenge," he said, not looking at her as they walked. "Neither a blessing nor a curse. It's simply a challenge."

His voice soothed her. Sometimes when he talked she did not listen so much to his words as to something safe in his voice that made her feel as if she understood.

"Never allow an obsessive to take things that belong to you," he said, still not looking at her. "Especially something personal like soiled clothing. It can be used against you. If she returns your shirt, you must burn it."

"Why?" she pouted. *He always talks at Angelica like she's stupid.*

He stopped by the lockers and looked at her. "Moira focuses a very dangerous part of herself on the things she takes or gives. In a manner of speaking, your shirt's been cursed with her concerns." He held out his hand. "Give me her sweater."

"But I need it. It gets cold as hell on the Bay at night."

"You can't take anything belonging to someone else to a power spot," he said with a touch of impatience.

"But I'm sick," she whined, sensing a part of her self struggling to overcome her resistance.

"It's draining you. You will feel better without it."

Her cap fell to the pavement as she pulled the sweater over her head. When she knelt down to pick up her cap, she noticed she did feel better.

Spear tossed the sweater into a trashcan, then put Hitler and her pack in a locker. She looked up at Spear. His eyes now had the soothing compassionate shine that always made her feel he was her friend. Although she still felt foolish, she sensed something had changed. Somehow he had fully accepted her presence.

"All she got was some barf on a shirt," she blurted out. "It's nothing. Just waste."

"You should be more careful with how you dispose of your wastes."

AS THEY WALKED, Spear's thoughts were on Sandoval and what Haskie Sam said about Sandoval's dealings with crazy white women. Now, here he was, taking a crazy white woman to a sacred power spot. Sandoval regarded turning an out-of-balance white woman's self-destructive energy into creative energy an ultimate challenge. Such women were gifts, he said, because you cannot seek them. The Spirit must present them. That way you know you will be given the signs you need to fulfill the task. There are always signs when dealing with the powers that guide. Follow them, he said. As long as you don't become infected by the women's madness, you will know what to do.

When they reached a crossroads, Angelica suddenly bolted, then stopped directly in front of him. Her blue eyes, framed by a blue patterned watchman cap and royal blue scoop-roll neck tunic against the blue bay, peered into his yellow eyes, as if they were a mirror.

Looking directly into another's eyes was a traditional Navajo way of suggesting disbelief, but he sensed the fierce eyes boring into his were looking for something specific. Something withheld. They weren't ordinary eyes. They were those of Josephine, a dark fragment of Katie, who'd never before manifested herself through Angelica.

A bluish hummingbird buzzed up to Josephine's left shoulder and hovered there. She turned away to glare at the bird until it zoomed away.

When she turned back to Spear, it was with Angelica's child-woman insecurity. Sensing the heat of his thoughts, she scanned the area behind her in search of whatever he was reacting to. Finding nothing, she glanced at him in shifts while he waited for her to say something. Then she said with an accusative squint,

"Why won't you tell me anything personal about yourself?"

A loud explosion, like a sonic boom, distracted him. She now stared directly at him, something Angelica would never do unless she caught him off guard, which she had. He masked his feelings with an impassive expression while he considered the signs.

Josephine popping in to see what he was up to did not surprise him, but her reverting to Angelica after the bird left did. Angelica was being unusually persistent. His first encounter with Catherine/Katie, when she was eleven, was with a flash of Josephine followed by Angel, her most integrated self, the one that understood everything by seeing things as they are. But Angelica, a shattered child personality that ignored everything by constructing realities as she saw fit, quickly jumped in. Nine years had passed before they would meet again. She had grown into an adult with eight personalities, of which only Angel and Josephine remembered their first encounter. Angel rarely stayed around for more than a few minutes. Josephine occasionally popped in to check him out, but she never spoke to him again. He dealt primarily with a cluster of five personalities that passed as moods of a merging personality he addressed as Seabolt. That Angelica had managed to usurp the Seabolts' appointment, and had resisted their and his attempts to shoo her away meant, one way or another, he had to take her into account.

"We're concerned with things more important than who I am and what it is I do. If you thought you knew who I was, you'd expect me to behave like that person, and try to tie me down with your thoughts." Her look of disappointment prompted him to add, "You and I, though. We have something personal in common."

She smiled, pleased with the change in his tone.

"There is a tradition of giving hallucinogens to newborns, to aid them in acquiring a guardian spirit. Both of our parents beckoned the Spirit in that way at our births. My mother, she knew what she was doing, whereas yours did not. We are both products of their intent, regardless of their understanding of it. There are consequences, though. One being the manner in which the Spirit manifests."

"Consequences," she whispered, thoughtfully.

"Your sense of self was collapsing when our paths crossed eleven years ago. It was the Spirit's command that I intervene." He waited for her to make the connection to their first meeting. She did not. "I must follow the indications of the Spirit, whether I want to or not. That's a consequence. Whereas my teachers have been impeccable, yours tend towards arrogance, ambivalence and aberrance."

"Aberrance," she tittered, as a soft breeze ruffled her golden hair.

Then he remembered his uncle's words, when she was eleven. "*She doesn't understand what's being said, yet some part of her understands everything.*"

THE LIGHT IN THE LOBBY momentarily stunned Tracy when they emerged from the dark theater. "God, that was disgusting," she said, fumbling for a cigarette in her jacket. "There's no way I'm going to do that."

"You've seen porno, right?" Jake said, accepting a cigarette to kill time until Hasib joined them. "That's no more disgusting than what you see in a porn film."

"I told you I've seen porn before. Gol, you must think I'm like a total wanker."

"If I do it's because you overreact to certain things. If you find that disgusting, you've chosen the wrong field."

"Look, I've seen porn films, okay? That doesn't mean I gotta like looking at girl stuff, especially an old cow like that sticking her finger in her butt. I mean, if that were Hasib up there, would you wanna watch him stick a finger up his ass?"

Jake laughed. "Okay, I see your point. But old? My guess is she's mid to late twenties. That's not old."

"For a woman, that is old," she said, authoritatively. "I got it all over her. I'm younger and prettier, and the only reason guys like her is her tits are bigger than mine. Oh, I wish that stupid doctor'd done what I told him!"

"Tracy, your tits would sag like hers if they were that big. Trust me, more guys are turned on by firm pointed titties than sagging monstrosities any day of the week."

"No, they're not! If I were on stage with her, they'd watch her not me, and they'd throw all their money at her because of her tits. She's probably real stupid, too, but she can afford to be stupid because of her tits."

"What kind of crap is this? You sound like an envious bimbo, kid."

"Don't call me kid!" she snapped. "And I'm not envious! Why should I envy a stupid old ugly sow who thinks she's so hot because she has big tits. It's not fair that's all."

"If all she's got going for her is tits, you'd be the star because you've also got beauty, presence, talent and brains."

"I wouldn't need any of that if that damn doctor'd given me what I asked for!"

"Damn it, Tracy." *Could she really be that stupid?* "They say an ounce of image is worth a pound of performance and, trust me, you have the better image. Your tits are perfect. Any bigger and you'd be a freak like her. Can't you see she's a deformed freak? Sure men like tits but very few are *that* fixated on them. Yours are at the edge where they are pleasing to people with tit fetishes and to everybody else, too."

"What do you know?" she muttered, scornfully. "On the street, you're worth a lot more with tits like that, a lot more."

Jake shook his head. Like Cedar. Pointless to argue.

"Let's get out of here before I faint from hunger."

"No. I don't want Hasib to come up here expecting to take us to lunch and not be here. That's not a good impression for you to make."

"I don't care if I make a good impression or not because there is no way I'm gonna work here."

"Always leave a good impression with powerful people whether you intend to work for them or not," he said. "You got to start showing me you're serious."

"I'm not gonna be a star! No one's gonna put me on a box cover. They want stupid cows like Dixie Belles!"

"Come on! No, they don't. I'm a pro and I know star material when I see it. Women with tits like that don't become stars. I can't think of any big names with tits bigger than yours. Can you?"

"I, I don't know," she mumbled. "I don't know their stupid names. Look at the box covers on the wall!"

"Yes, and look at the posters of coming acts. This theater emphasizes hooters because of the clientele they cater to and they put up boxes featuring their headliners, but that doesn't mean they're big porn stars. Stars appeal to big audiences, these girls are specialty acts. Which would you prefer, a bigger audience or bigger tits?"

Tracy frowned.

"Hey, good lookin'," said Hasib, accompanied by a plain looking woman with no make-up. He took his hand from her shoulder and signaled Jake to accompany him to the other side of the lobby. "Your friend looks upset. Something the matter?"

"Well, you know how it is with women, they're all X-rated, what with two X chromosomes to our one. And she's definitely X."

Hasib made a face. "Seriously, what's her problem?"

"She's just cranky because she's hungry. You know kids."

Hasib sucked on his teeth and shook his head. "Zip up your pants."

"She's nice," said Jake, fidgeting with his fly. "Really."

Tracy glumly followed the three old people into the bright sunlight. A car pulled in front of the theater and the driver got out. Hasib opened the passenger front door for his guest and Jake opened the back door for Tracy. Hasib got into the driver's seat.

"Amanda, this is Jake and, I'm sorry, but I didn't get your name."

"Tracy," said Tracy, coolly.

"Right," said Hasib, friendly. "Tracy and Jake, this is my good friend, Amanda."

"I am pleased to make your acquaintance." Amanda offered her hand to Jake. He placed a kiss on her fingers. Tracy looked away in disgust.

"Amanda and I were discussing terms," said Hasib. "If there's anything you want to know about this profession, ask this little lady. She knows everybody and everything. A real pro."

"Oh, Herbie!" Amanda put her hand on his shoulder. "You make it sound like I've been at this forever. It's only been two years."

"Is that all?" said Hasib, surprised. "Two years? In just two years you can force me to pay you $10,000 a week?"

"Don't listen to him, honey," she said to Tracy. "You can command that in less than a year if you have a good act. You're lucky to be working for Herbie because he's the kindest, most generous boss you'll find in the industry, bar none."

"Ah!" Hasib laughed. "I'd better change right now or that reputation will be the ruin of me."

"No, it won't, silly man," said Amanda. "It's good for business. Everybody wants to work for you."

"Because I pay too much."

"No, because they like you. Now where are we going to lunch?"

"Something special for a special lady," said Hasib. He glanced back at Tracy. "Make that two special ladies. The Opera House Cafe."

"Oh, my, Herbie!" Amanda gushed. "You remembered!"

"How could I forget."

Tracy rolled her eyes and stared out the window.

An hour before dawn, Jake had awoken from a dream in which he tasted Tracy's flavors. A strange desire had lingered on afterwards like a low-grade fever. After all her nonsense, desire should be the furthest thing from his mind, but it wasn't.

He could not forget her sweet tropical scent.

SPEAR POINTED up the hill with his chin. "We leave the path here."

Angelica bounded effortlessly up the hillside, moving in front, climbing as if she knew the way, rocking her head from side to side, her arms swinging wildly front to back with playful flicks of her wrists. She glanced back to see if she could catch him eyeing her butt. He wasn't. Disappointed, she said, "Have you ever heard of Hypatia?"

"Yes."

"Oh." She blinked and pondered this. "Really?"

"Gnosticism, theurgy, Hermetics and that period in history interests me."

"Oh," she muttered, adding a kind of wiggly looseness below her knees to the end of her footfalls. "Riley said Will's the reincarnation of the guy that had her killed."

"Hmmm. When St. Cyril died, a contemporary church historian said, although his death made those who survived him joyful, it did grieve the dead. He feared the dead might find his presence too troublesome and send him back to us. Perhaps they have."

"He said you were the governor of Egypt. Some guy named Orestes."

A heavy flapping of wings overhead distracted him. A murder of crows flying toward a clearing, swarming over the eucalyptuses, cawing as if something had frightened them. Spear tapped her on top of her head with his knuckles.

"Be as quiet and motionless as possible, until the crows calm down."

He carefully took off his hat then placed it on a boulder while the crows landed in the trees. Then he leaned against a tree, touching it only with his shoulder blades and the back of his head. He signaled her to do the same.

She positioned herself against a tree a few feet to his left.

The crows gradually stopped cawing, until there was total silence.

In the distance, she heard the cries of gulls and the dull rumble of a plane, but in the clearing itself there were no sounds. Not of insects, nor birds, nor wind. Nothing but silence, and the crows watching in unnerving stillness. She glanced at Spear, frightened.

He signaled her with his eyes to look down. His feet were slightly apart. "The antidote is the earth," he whispered. "She is alive and understands every feeling. She will soothe you, and cure your pains."

She rearranged her feet.

"Riley, he activates patterns in people to ignite a cluster of activity around what I call a core. He does this to isolate the core. So he can locate it. Align himself with it."

"Core." She furrowed her brow.

"Many cultures call cores gods. I prefer to label them with something impersonal, since they are impersonal forces."

"Ah ha, strange attractors."

"You can call them that. They are the organizational forces in nature, around which consciousness and events gather. Like energy fields, extending across time and space to effect the flow of events. Seeing them as forces of nature, rather than as gods or demons, exerts less of a pull toward morbid ritualistic subterfuge."

"Subter-fuge," Angelica gasped.

He closed his eyes. She was about to say something when she noticed his eyeballs move, giving her the strange feeling he was watching her through closed eyelids. Then his eyes opened. "When an attractor's activated, extraordinary things happen. People and events, they are pulled into the patterns of meaning dictated by whatever attractor's been triggered. An ordinary man can be pulled into an archetypal field without realizing anything out of the ordinary has happened to him. But if he got too close to the core, he'd get such an incredible jolt there'd be no doubt something's up. Depending on how aligned or balanced he is with the attractor's intent, he could be either shattered or empowered."

She gave him a fierce look. "He said some part of me is Hypatia."

Spear was quiet for some time as he considered this. Riley must have met Angel, hence the Hypatia fantasy. He might also be aware of Angelica's bipolar connection to Angel, hence her involvement in the field of events. But her inability to stay centered concerned him. She must be capable of rallying her entire attention when necessary, but her attraction to ghost whispers and scattered detachment bothered him. The only way it would work would be for Angel to step in at the crucial moment. Then he realized the connection, how it worked when they first met, and why Angelica was here now. He knew, too, what Riley was up to.

"If Hypatia were a complex in an unresolved field of events, and Riley was part of it, his game would be to tempt the Fates," he said. "A fool's form of theurgy."

"Theurgy? What's that?"

He looked up at the crows. "When a core, attractor, god or whatever you chose to call a divine agency, is activated by mortals to direct the flow of human events, that's theurgy." He looked back at her. "Neo-Platonists who recognized the phenomenon, dedicated themselves to finding ways of enticing specific divine agencies to intervene in human affairs for the purpose of working miracles. Hypatia's knowledge of theurgy was given as a justification for murder. Christians regarded theurgy as sorcery. Witchcraft."

"Oh," she mumbled, looking down at her feet. "Riley says I'm like a fragment of her. They tore her to pieces."

He picked up his hat. "You're too suggestible, and take yourself too seriously, perfect conditions for being grabbed by the fixations that accompany attractors."

"Grabbed?" She moved away from her tree. "What does that mean?"

He regarded her critically, doubting Angelica could grasp the enormity of the theurgy Riley was up to. "Tell me everything that happened before, during and after your meeting with him."

TRACY STIFFENED when they entered a high-ceiling cafe with a classical decor and waiters in tuxedos. The headwaiter greeted Hasib and his guests.

"Could you excuse me," she said, feeling out of place in her leather jacket and tight jeans. "I need to use the bathroom."

"Certainly," said Hasib. "It's down the hall."

The hall was a wide corridor with glorious plants, elegant classical sculptures and marvelous carvings on the ladies room door at the end of the hallway. She felt the disdain of the waiter as she walked briskly toward the bathroom.

The waiter showed the old people to a table by a window.

"She's very young," said Hasib, after the waiter left. "Did you check her ID?"

"Yeah. She has a California ID, a social security card and a college picture ID."

"I mean did you check them?" asked Hasib.

"Well, uh, no. Her IDs were good enough for the plastic surgeon who did her tits."

"Pornographers are held to a higher standard than doctors," said Hasib. "You better check her ID with the DMV and get a copy of her birth certificate."

"She's actually nice, you know. She's just in a bad mood."

"I don't think she'll work out," said Hasib. "Too nervous."

"Oh, I agree. She needs some experience before she does stage work. Too green."

Hasib shrugged. "No personality."

"Well, she's shy but she's smart. She's taking tough subjects like statistics and chemistry, doing more than full time, and she's at the top of her class."

"You believe her?"

"Well, yeah. I picked her up on campus and I've seen her textbooks. And, uh, the College of Alameda doesn't have the highest academic standards, so it wouldn't take a genius to be at the top of it. She's no bimbo."

Hasib leaned back and frowned.

"What?" Jake said, disturbed by his disapproval.

Hasib shook his head and said, "That's disrespectful."

Jake glanced at Amanda who looked bewildered. "Bimbo?"

Hasib stared at him with a look of contempt.

"I'm sorry," he said, flustered. "I didn't mean any offense."

"Are you infatuated with her?" said Hasib.

"Well, I, uh, like her."

"I wouldn't fuck her if I were you. She's trouble."

"Give her a chance. Talk to her, draw her out. She's all right."

"She seems perfectly sweet to me," said Amanda. "I'd fuck her myself if I were him."

Amused, Hasib said, "You like little girls and old men?"

"Little girls smell better," she purred. "But old men are better fucks."

Hasib laughed, "Don't get any ideas, Jake."

"Ah, here she comes." Jake waved to Tracy across the room but failed to catch her eye. Noticing a look of panic, he stood up. "Excuse me."

Tracy was relieved when she saw him approach. "Thank god you didn't leave me. I don't have enough money to get home."

"What a funny thing to think. We wouldn't leave you."

"I'm not doing what you want," she said, upset. "I'm not what they want. I don't belong here. Could we please just leave."

"No. You're hungry, let's eat, be sociable, then we go."

"I don't want to eat! I lost my appetite. I want out of here."

"You lost your appetite? You were starving a moment ago."

"When I'm not hungry, I don't eat. Period. Let's leave."

"Sweetheart, you're going to be hungry later. Please try to eat something. We'll talk about it later."

"I don't want to talk about it later, and don't call me sweetheart like that old pimp called the whore in his office."

"You don't have any money and it's a free lunch. Take it. It's an adventure, it'll all make sense later, trust me."

"All right," she groaned. "I'll sit through this but I'm not going to eat anything."

"Fine, but please try to lighten up a bit."

"Our lady returns," said Hasib, looking interested. "Jake says you're in college. How long have you been at it?"

"Just started this spring," she said, sitting down. "I had to work for awhile to make money so I could go."

"How did you two meet?" asked Amanda. Tracy gave Amanda an unfriendly look.

"We met at the Fog City Diner where she worked," Jake said. "I flirted with her, one thing led to another and I told her she could make money doing porn."

"What'd you think of that?" Hasib asked Tracy.

"Sounded cool, I guess," she answered, lifelessly. "I mean, I need the money and it sounds pretty glamorous, so why not?"

"What did you think of my dance?" asked Amanda.

"Huh?"

"Herbie told me you and Jake watched my dance."

"That was you?" said Tracy.

"Yeah, uh-huh," said Amanda. "You don't recognize me?" Tracy stared. "So what'd you think?"

"I don't think I could do it," stammered Tracy.

"Why not?"

"I don't think they'd like me," muttered Tracy, sarcastically.

Amanda laughed. "Honey, they'd love you. You're sweet."

The waiter bowed. "Excuse me. Are you ready with your orders?"

Amanda ordered. Hasib asked Tracy what she would like.

Tracy frowned and said nonchalantly, "Nothing for me, thank you."

"Oh, surely you want something," said Hasib. "You were hungry awhile ago."

"I'm on a diet. I should stick to it."

"A diet," laughed Amanda. "You need to loose weight? Ha! Ha! I should need to lose so much weight."

"You should eat something," said Hasib. "A salad perhaps?"

"Nothing," she said, avoiding eye contact. "I'm on a diet."

"I'll order a mixed platter. Perhaps you'll bring yourself to nibble something from it."

"Suit yourself." No Arab pimp and his big boob bitch could tell her what to do. She'd show them.

AN EERIE heavy stillness hung over the clearing. The field was surrounded by a natural corral of boulders camouflaged by thick bushes and what appeared to Angelica as a shallow grave, freshly scooped out of the soft dirt at the center point, with two backpacks resting on a tarp outside it.

"This is the power spot," Spear said. "We will spend the night here."

"Spend the night?" She stared at the grave. "What about the campground?"

"You've been weakened by a power intrusion. You must spend the night buried in that trench to regain your strength."

"Buried!" She shivered. "I'll freeze."

"No. You won't." He drew a line in the ground as he said, "Feel the silence. The area, it's imbued with power." He beckoned her to cross the line. "The earth, it will give you the necessary boost to recover what was taken from you. It will rearrange your feelings so you can make important decisions."

"What are you doing?" she said, trembling.

"Do not indulge in the presence of power," he said sternly as he stepped over the line. "The Spirit's been kind to you, but don't try its patience, here of all places. You were given several warnings, yet chose to remain a prisoner of your fears. You knew the Spirit sent the cleaning lady to warn you, yet you chose to ignore her out of childish fear of Christians. Aberrance exists in all disciplines. It's a fact of life, especially yours. Christians do not hold the franchise on stupidity, believe me."

"But she told me to ask Christ for help," she protested, alarmed at how he would know these things, as if he were there, somehow watching.

"Christ is a manifestation of the Spirit. You must not judge Him by the madness of his followers. The old woman's purpose was to steer you away from doing battle on Riley's turf. I told you, *you* must choose the battleground. What amazes me is the Spirit sent the wind to fortify you against the consequences of your stupidity, as if you were a warrior whose mind wouldn't be twisted by its power."

"What?" she cried, scanning the area, looking for a way out.

"Look at ME, Angelica! It's a matter of your survival. *You* must now decide whether to enter this place of power."

"I can't do that," she whined.

"Yes, *you* can." He beckoned her to cross the line. "*You*, no one else. *You* decide. You, and you alone, fired Riley. *Your* decisions now have power."

"How do you know these things. You weren't there! Were you?"

"This is a power spot. I have stepped over into it. It shows me what I need to know. It fortifies me. It will do the same for you if you do as I say. You must do it now."

She gasped, her face rippling with an incredible mixture of terror, panic, pain, curiosity, seriousness and excitement. Then she stepped over the line.

"Please, don't hurt me," she whimpered.

"Don't indulge," he whispered through his teeth as he took her hand in his. "Power turns on weakness. Get hold of yourself."

Then he jerked her arm with such force she lost her balance.

As she fell forward a blow on her shoulder knocked all the air out of her lungs and a string of liquid from her mouth and nose. She broke her fall with her right arm, then felt herself being pinned down by a pressing on her neck. Unable to breathe and overwhelmed by panic, she would have vomited from the pressure in her stomach if he weren't holding her mouth shut. Then, she sank into a darkness punctuated by tiny pinpoints of light darting in and out of her head like glowworms in the night.

WHEN JULIE SPOKE to him, Ben was in his bed, unsure if he were asleep or awake. Or, if he'd slept at all. He was in trouble, he could tell from the way she looked at him. The worst kind of trouble. The Julie looking at him wasn't the Julie he'd tucked into his Presumed Dead Wife's room. He'd tried his best not to see what he was seeing, but the image of a naked nine-year-old Artemis with her bow and arrows and the rage in her eyes, all directed at him could not be blinked away.

He could not get his mind to function. He was in Her thrall. Artemis slays without mercy anyone who so much as glimpses Her naked body. He desperately tried to wish away what he'd done to activate Her.

When he saw Artemis change into a fully dressed Julie, he realized he was looking at her like a deer caught in the headlights. And that she knew all his secrets.

Then he found himself telling Artemis Jake's secrets. It was her demand.

8

Stuck on Stupid

"You've reached Jake and Coyote Blue Productions," said the machine. "You know what to do. Beep!"

"Jake, you there?" Moira said through the machine. "Something weird happened and I don't know what to do. Could you *please* call me as soon as you get up?"

Jake picked up the phone. "Hold on," he yawned. "Don't say anything until the machine shuts off."

"I'm sorry to call so early," she said after it shut off. "But I had to talk to somebody."

"It's okay. I had to get up anyway."

"I'm so glad you're there. Some weirdo called me about my being in Mindy's movie."

"Who? Someone from the orgy scene?"

She considered this. "Don't think so. His voice wasn't anything like anybody there. It's quite distinctive."

"Well, maybe he knows someone who was there."

"Jake!" she said, frustrated. "I don't know anybody who behaves like that. I have no idea who the hell the jerk is!"

"All right, take it easy. Did he say what he wanted?"

"No! All he did was go off on how awful it was a nice girl like me could desecrate herself, like my body was a fucking temple or something. Desecrate? Oh, please. I thought he was joking. When I realized he wasn't I got like really mad and told him he was stuck on stupid, and like he should shop that shit around before putting it in my face. Then he called me a mother-from-hell and said he'd tell my parents."

"Mother from hell?" said Jake, incredulous.

"Like how does he know I have a kid? Nobody knows that except family."

"Maybe he doesn't. Just a figure of speech, like motherfucker."

"I'm sure," she said, impatient.

"Could be a mind fuck. You know, some jerk's been watching you from a distance and this is his way of getting intimate with you."

"He sounded like some sort of religious freak."

"Whatever he is, don't give him what he wants. No reaction of any kind. No anger, fear, contempt. Nothing, nada. *Any* response establishes a link he can feed on."

"No response! How can you *not* respond to some jerk who's threatening you?"

"Because he's less likely to act without the validation of a response. When he calls, disconnect."

"What if he tells my parents? They'd be furious."

"What can he say? They know about the porn anyway, right?"

"No, of course not."

Jake hesitated. "Uh, well. Then, deny it. Trust me, parents would rather believe their daughters than some anonymous caller."

Moira breathed quietly for a minute then whispered, "If I were there with you, what would you like me to do?"

"Well, I could use some help pulling weeds."

"I'm horny," she moaned. "Tell me something kinky and I'll leave you alone."

"The only kinky thing I can think of right now is what that asshole's doing to you."

"You're spoiling it! Why are you doing this?"

"Yeah, well, I'm not sure what you mean by kinky."

"Nasty, dirty, filthy, trashy, hot!" she said, exasperated.

"Could you be more specific?"

"Excuse me? Like it's gotta come from you. *You* gotta tell *me*! I know there's something. Let me in, I want to know."

"Maybe if you gave me a hint I'd come up with something. What nasty, disgusting, vile thing would you like to do to me?"

"That's not fair! I asked you first."

"Look, I think phone sex is kinky, okay? If you want something kinkier than that, you have to clue me in on what that might be. What would you like to do to me if you could do anything you liked."

"I'd take you shopping for a new wardrobe."

Jake laughed. "That's too kinky for me."

"You have something in mind and just won't tell me. I want to know. What do you think about when you masturbate?"

"What!"

"I want to watch you masturbate."

"Jesus," he muttered.

"Tell me what you fantasize about when you jerk off?"

"That's private."

"That's private," Moira mimicked. "Jake, Prince of Porn, is inhibited. You're holding back. You don't trust me, do you?"

Jake had never discussed his fantasies with anyone. He might have once with Cedar, had she been interested.

"Don't you trust me? You can trust me. I'm discreet. Let me in. Talk to me, Jake."

"I was betrayed by someone I loved and trusted who turned out to be so self-absorbed she hadn't a clue of who I was, and didn't much care to either. Experiences like that make me extremely cautious."

"Why are you making things so complicated? You can trust me, it's as simple as that. If it doesn't work out, it doesn't work out. I'm not out looking for trouble. I trust you. You can trust me."

"Trust is serious business. I'd rather die than go through anything like that again."

"Hello? Anybody home? What are *you* talking about? I'm talking mutually satisfying pleasure here, not marriage."

"Okay, okay. Before I can trust you, I need to be sure you understand the rules of engagement and can stick to them."

"I understand trust. I know all about keeping things hush hush. I just want to watch you jerk off. That's my kinky thing."

"That wouldn't be a turn on for me."

"You were jacking off on the phone, right? You liked that, didn't you?"

"I wasn't totally into it," he said. "I didn't come."

After a heavy silence, she said, "Well, if that doesn't say it all."

"I was uncomfortable because I didn't know who you were," he said, defensively. "I couldn't help wondering whether someone had put you up to it for a cheap thrill."

"I'd never be part of something like that," she snapped. "That's not my *thrill*."

CATHERINE DRIFTED slowly into consciousness, the cold pinching at her face as she opened her eyes. Staring into the fog, not knowing who or where she was, as if that part of her were still asleep somewhere far away. She gradually became aware of the odors of damp leaves and moist earth. Then someone moved into her field of vision.

"Katie?" Spear whispered, his fingertips gently touching her head.

She grinned back up at him. His kind eyes filled her with a sense of the world being in balance. The tranquility, the exquisite quiet, moved her to joyous tears.

"Incredible waterworks," Spear smiled as he took the bandanna off his forehead. "Now I understand the expression bathed in tears."

She sniffed and giggled. "I can see your breath."

"Shhhhh." He wiped her tears with the bandanna. "You're not solid yet."

She tried to sit up. *She was naked, and encased in a mound of dirt!* The shock of this surged through her with such force she thought she would faint.

"Shhhh, don't indulge," he whispered, soothing the top of her head as if she were Angelica. "You must leave this place peacefully. You spent the night buried in power. The Earth Spirit was gentle with you. You must now show the proper respect for what you have received."

"I don't remember a thing," she stammered nasally. "How did I get here?"

"Blow into this." He positioned the bandanna under her nostrils. She grimaced. "Go ahead, you'll feel better." She blew. He gestured for her to be thorough. She blew again. "There's a story from Hypatia's time about a student who thought he was in love with her. He approached her on the street and raised his robe to show how much she pleased him. Hypatia, she pulled her menstrual rags out from under her robe."

Spear showed her the snot on his bandanna. "She said, *This is the source of your longings. The beauty you worship is an illusion.* Then she threw her bloody rags at him. Her intent was to shock him into realizing beauty cannot be identified with concrete objects."

"Wouldn't work on Riley," she tittered. "He would've liked that just fine."

"Hypatia, she believed beautiful bodies to be but images, shadows. Anyone who clung to them as reality, they were destined to sink into darkness. To consort only with shadows. To identify beauty with concrete objects like bodies, it distracts from the deeper meaning of beauty. But in the end, images and shadows. They were her undoing."

"How?" she whispered, noticing her head was pillowed by her rolled up clothing.

"The Christians of her era were obsessed with the corruption of the flesh. They killed one another over disagreements on such issues as whether Christ passed through the Virgin's genitals during birth, or if He had biological functions. Flesh was believed to be so corrupting that coming in contact with it would corrupt even a god. The reverence and fear Christians experienced in the face of Divine Truth distorted their understanding of it by forcing them to discard anything that didn't conform to their expectations. The resulting ignorance undermined their strength. It led to obsessions with what they believed and, finally, to a morbidity that required the sacrifice of enemies to their God."

"Morbidity," she whispered.

"The story I told you about the rags, it was a popular spin of what actually happened. The student, he knew his feelings were inappropriate. He tried to control them. But he could not. So he confessed his love. To shock him out of his fever, Hypatia showed him her menstrual rags. The shock enabled him to grasp the secondariness of the world of objects. Things that are beautiful in one aspect, ugly in another. In that moment, he realized the true value of self-control. He was able to tear himself away from the illusionary nature of the world. To replace assumption with true recognition."

He picked up his bandanna. "There are those who believe an object soiled by the corrupted reality of an organic angel has power. Had she understood the nature of the morbid obsessions being projected onto her, a beautiful, independent virgin, she could have foreseen the danger of fantasies about the corrupted reality inside the facade of her beauty." He put his bandanna back in a pocket. "The people who killed her, they did so because they believed her to be a witch who corrupted minds."

"Were you the student she showed the rags to?"

He ran his tongue over his teeth while he considered whether to remind her Navajos did not believe in reincarnation as understood by Whites. However, since he had long since ceased being a traditional Navajo, he signaled her to be silent as he began disassembling the mound constructed around her body. It consisted of forked branches, stuck in the dirt, serving as supports for long sticks covered with small branches, leaves and layers of dirt. When he finished, he pulled a poncho from his pack and spread it out.

Then he saw Angelica looking up at him.

"I'm cold," Angelica said shivering, hugging herself as she squatted on the poncho. Spear handed her a red, woolen, cowl-neck head warmer. "Why red?" she grumbled, her teeth chattering. He touched her lips, indicating silence, then handed her a rose-hued sweater and underwear and socks. He then carefully scattered the sticks, branches and leaves, then scooped the dirt taken from the trench back in. After covering it with debris, the area looked as if nothing had touched it.

"Thank the Earth for its boost, Angelica," he said to her firmly.

"Don't look at me like that," she shuddered. "Are you angry with me?"

"You must learn to show the proper respect, or you will be trapped by obsessions, and die a brutal death. Thank the Earth for its boost."

"Alright, already." She cleared her throat. "Thank you, Earth, for the boost."

"Louder. With power. With respect."

She knelt. Placing her palms on the soft soil as she bowed her head to the ground. "THANK YOU, EARTH, FOR THE BOOST!" she said.

Satisfied, Spear folded the poncho then put it in his pack.

A BIG HOLE was punched through the front door of Tracy's third floor apartment. Jake peered from the outside walkway through a curtain-less window into the kitchen and dining area, both lacking furniture. A makeshift wall of cardboard boxes separated the living room from the dining area. The lock on the sliding glass window was broken.

He slid the window open. "Tracy! It's me, Jake!" he yelled.

"Wait a minute!" Tracy answered from somewhere inside.

She emerged from a bedroom to the right of the kitchen a moment later. "Sorry, I'm on the phone," she said, opening the door, dressed in a denim skirt with a frilly white blouse. "Come in. I'll be off in a minute."

"No problem," Jake said as she dashed back to her room.

A bathroom, to his right. No toilet paper. Warped floor. Soap residue in a broken soap dish. Cheap fiberglass shower. No shower curtain. No towels.

He entered her bedroom and looked around while she talked on the phone. Her bed, a lawn chaise lounge with a sleeping bag, no pillow.

Her desk, a folding card table and a lawn chair. On the table, a small cassette player, a few cassettes, textbooks, notebook, pen. An open UPS box, an invoice listing its contents. One hundred condoms. Under the table, a box of magazines. On top, a bondage and discipline magazine; cover photo, woman in a leather mask with a hole only for her mouth. He rummaged through the magazines, stopping at a comic concerning the sexual escapades of high school girls. The cartoon heroine on the cover saying, "I'm over eighteen. Honest."

Tracy hung up the phone. "Sorry. This guy I know is in trouble. I helped him out last night when he needed a place to hide out and my roommate threw a fit this morning. That was him telling me he found a motel room."

"Trouble?" he said. "What kind of trouble?"

"Oh, it's not his fault. The cops think he stole a car, but he didn't. This other guy stole it and didn't tell him it was hot. So this guy got caught and blamed it all on Eric, my friend. Anyway, so the cops are looking for him."

Jake frowned.

"Look, he's a nice guy. I mean, he's been there for me when I needed help, or he would've if he could. Anyway, I like to help people out."

"Well, there's never a shortage of people who need help. Hope you learn how to handle that before you become a star or you'll burn out fast."

"I'm not going to be a star and I wish you wouldn't say that. I need to make money fast, that's all." She looked worried. "Is that thing still on for tomorrow?"

"Yeah."

"Oh, good!" she said, relieved. "Will I be getting cash? I mean, it's a weekend and I don't think I can get a check cashed. I have to buy food."

"Don't worry, it's cash. That's the only way I'd let you work. We'll know your potential after tomorrow, but I'm sure you'll do just fine."

"Yeah, right. I can't act and I'll screw up for sure. Besides I got a dorky face and my voice is real dumb."

"Listen to me. As a director I can sense acting potential, and you have it. With a bit of experience, you'll put the current crop of stars to shame because your face has a unique beauty that projects nuance better than the generic beauties can ever hope to do."

"I can't do it. I don't know why you think I can, but I can't imagine myself acting. I'll look stupid and people will laugh."

"No, they won't. You are your own worst critic."

She glared at him, wondering how he had cued in on her fantasy of being a star, the most desired woman in the world.

"Acting isn't your problem. Sexual response is. So lesson number one, porn is a separate reality. You're a character in a story and everyone around you is doing their job. You could be having the mother of all orgasms and the people on the set might be reading newspapers or sleeping. It's not like any other kind of sex. It's a performance. There is money involved, but it's not in any way related to prostitution."

Tracy unwrapped a stick of gum. "Want some?" she said, tossing the wrapper into a paper bag serving as a trash can.

"No, thanks. Stop me if you have questions."

"Oh, I will."

"So, where was I? Okay, some performers enjoy porn sex because of the lack of responsibility and emotional ties. It's acting, whereas prostitution is more real, personal."

"Okay, so what're we going to do?"

"We need to address the insecurities you've shown in past situations."

"Yeah, like they were pretty weird situations."

"That's how you look at it, but those weird situations are normal in Porno World. Think about it. You were upset over someone having bigger tits."

"Come on, you're a guy! You wouldn't understand. I mean, how'd you feel if some guy had a bigger dick than you, okay?"

"Good point. If I were a novice and didn't know better, I'd think people were comparing and judging, and if I were the jealous type I'd get jealous. I'm not saying your reaction is abnormal."

Tracy sighed impatiently.

"However, a pro is used to those things and wouldn't waste energy on them. In any case, you're more likely to be the object of jealousy than to have cause to be jealous."

"Good! I hope so."

"No, you don't. Jealous people will talk about you like you did about Dixie. Who needs that? It's better to accept one another and not waste time on jealous bullshit."

"I wasn't jealous! It's insulting to suggest I could be jealous of someone like that!"

"Hey, kiddo, that's a typical jealous response. Watch your attitudes because if you don't, they'll sabotage you. You listening?"

"Yeah, I'm listening," she pouted.

"First, let's work on response. You respond the way I tell you to, not any old way but the way I tell you to. Got it?"

She nodded.

"Okay, I'm going to touch you." He put a hand on her shoulder and she looked at it. "I'll move my hand from here to your tits. Follow my hand with your eyes and the moment I touch your tits, close your eyes and give me a sexy smile. Got it?"

She shrugged and fixed her attention on his hand.

He watched her face as his hand moved from her shoulder down her polyester blouse to fondle her breasts. She closed her eyes and grinned.

"Now I'm going to remove your blouse," he said, unbuttoning it. "Act like you're getting turned on."

She opened her eyes. "What do you mean, turned on? What do I do?"

"Do like in the movies. Move a bit, a little heavy breathing, moan, lick your lips."

"That's stupid! I wouldn't do that."

"Maybe not, but in Porno World you do. Think of it as a job where you have to act stupid when you're diddled."

She frowned, closed her eyes and waited.

He opened her blouse then gently caressed her silky nipples with his fingers while pushing his nose against her smooth, warm skin, inhaling her crushed flower scent. He remembered what she said about how she'd rather suck a producer's cock, and that he wanted her. But her lack of response put him off, both professionally and personally.

"This isn't working. Let's try something else. Open my fly and take out my cock. This is the part you don't have a problem with, right? Remember, it's an *act,* and you follow directions. You okay with this?" She gave him a conspiratorial grin then nodded. "Start with your hands on my shoulder. Now move them down my body to my crotch."

She moved her hands directly to his crotch.

"No, no, you're not being seductive. Do it slowly. Turn me on."

Tracy moved her hands awkwardly down his chest to his crotch, unzipped his pants then extracted his rigid cock and proceeded to fellate it with a skill far exceeding his expectations. The intensity of his desire grew as the Fourth Wall faded away.

He guided her to her feet then kissed her full on the lips. She pulled away.

"What's wrong?" he asked.

"I don't kiss."

"What?"

"I don't like kissing, never have. I don't let anybody kiss me, especially with tongues. It's so gross."

"Sweetheart, people kiss all the time in the movies. You'll have to get over that."

"No, they don't! I've seen them where nobody kisses. No kissing, okay?"

He shrugged. "Okay, fine. Lie on your back. I'll kiss your pussy instead."

"Do I have to? I mean I'll do it on film, but do I have to now?"

"Lie down."

Pouting, she complied.

He knelt, reached under her skirt and pulled off her panties.

"You dyed your pussy hair, too," he said, surprised.

"Yeah, I think the wrong color pubes look so phony."

"I've never seen that done before."

He spread her legs.

"Oh!" She closed her legs. "My pussy's so gross."

"Say what?"

"The lips are too long. When I stand they just sort of hang there. That's so gross. I can't be a star with an ugly pussy."

"I think the wings of your sex are lovely," he said, spreading them.

"Wings, ugh," she grumbled. "Makes me sound like Dumbo, the flying elephant."

"Cunt lips aren't the only thing a guy notices. Yours are mounted on a lovely mound, a sweet, glistening pink." He moved in close. "Ah, what a fine fresh scent it has."

"It smells!" she cried, attempting to close her legs.

"Yeah," he said, holding her legs apart. "It smells nice."

"Now I know you're lying! It doesn't smell nice at all. It doesn't!"

"Okay, let's do something different. I'm going to slip my cock into you. I want you to close your eyes and visualize we are one. Stay still, not moving, feeling each other's energy. I feel you, while you concentrate on the connection of my being inside you."

"This is like a ritual or something, right?"

"Yeah. Yes, it is."

"That's cool."

Jake held her close as he pressed his cock against her. With a low, entranced rhythm he entered her body, invading her, the little passageway closing tightly around him, swallowing his essence within her. Eyes closed, he focused on this elongation of his being in which his blood had concentrated, lying in the voluptuous darkness of her, filling her womb. Sensing the feel of silk in every opening of her body.

Tracy imagined herself captive, forbidden to move, in a dungeon with an open furnace. Eerie music, diabolical noises. A rod buried deep inside her. The restraining demon pulling her closer still, thrusting his knobbed dagger into her again and again, until he pulled it out and placed it against her belly.

"Geez, Louise!" Jake cried out as his seed shot out on to her. "Oh, my God!"

Definitely weird, she thought as his body convulsed, shaking like a seizure.

"You still want me there with you tomorrow?" Jake asked as they dressed.

Tracy stiffened and said, "I thought you were going to be. I don't want to be alone with a bunch of people I don't know."

"Yeah, I thought as much. Look, I'm a director, writer, producer, editor, all those people you don't see on camera, but I thought since this is your first scene and you're uncomfortable, perhaps I should do the scene with you."

She smiled, relieved. "That'd be great. I was nervous about who I might have to work with."

"I'll tell Janus you'll only work with me. If you want someone else, just let me know."

"Yeah, that's fine. It makes me feel a lot better."

"Good. Something bothers me, though. It felt to me like you haven't had much sexual experience. I don't understand how you could work the streets and be so inhibited."

"I'm not inhibited!"

"How is that? You won't strip, or kiss. Don't want women to touch you, don't masturbate, don't want your pussy licked. Think assholes are gross, afraid to dance."

"So I can't dance," she pouted. "That doesn't make me inhibited. Besides, I've fucked nearly fifty guys, so I'm not exactly inexperienced either."

"It must be hard for you on the streets."

"Yeah, it's hard, real hard, because I had to give up my boyfriend. He loved me and I loved him, but I was tired of being poor. We never had any money and I knew I could get it on the streets. It's easy, most guys pop in a couple of minutes and I get $25."

"So you don't fuck, then?" he said, thinking that could explain why she was good at cock sucking and little else.

"No, well, unless a guy wanted me to stay the night. Then I'd use a condom. That's why I got that box of condoms on my desk. If you buy a bunch of them they only cost like a quarter a piece, including shipping."

"There's a hundred of them in there. You must have planned on staying at it awhile."

"Sure, why not? I mean, like what else can I do to make a living? I was getting $4.50 an hour at the cafe. On the streets, I get $25 for just a few minutes work, tax free."

"It's dangerous with all the sleaze balls out there, and it's degrading."

"Four dollars and fifty cents an hour is degrading! I'd rather suck some stupid Iranian's dick for a few minutes for twenty-five bucks than have to take his shit all day on some dumb ass job for twenty-five bucks, which is all it'd end up being after deductions."

"Yeah. I did clerical work for minimum wage before I got into porn. Once I got a taste of easier money, I couldn't imagine putting up with the hassles of low-paying jobs. I told myself I was learning a craft, that after I got enough experience I'd quit and go legit."

"Are you saying you're ashamed of being a pornographer?" she said, surprised. "Why? There's nothing wrong with it. Why would you be ashamed?"

"Well," he shrugged. "It's cheap, exploitative garbage and I'm capable of better."

"I like it," she said, perplexed. "I haven't seen your stuff but Wormyham says it's classy, so you should be proud. I love porn, especially the trashy stuff."

"I've done my share of trash, believe me. But that's the right attitude for a porn star. Myself, I never intended to be a force in the industry."

"If you don't like it and everything, why are you helping me?"

"I intend to do one last project because I need the money. Speaking of which, why won't you accept help from your parents?"

She frowned. "I don't want my parents to know where I am. I don't want anything to do with them."

"Why?"

She breathed heavily. "When I was twelve, they put me in an institution for anorexia and kept me locked up there for a year and a half. When I got out, I ran away. There's no way I'm giving them a chance to put me away again."

"You ran way?" he said, surprised. "You mean, you never went back?"

"Yeah, and I never will."

"How'd you get by?"

"I stayed with some friends for awhile and eventually came out here."

"When was that?"

"Um, six years ago."

"Six years? How'd you survive underage for six years?"

"I had boyfriends, if that's what you mean, but I didn't sell it until a few months ago."

"How did you pay for the tit job?"

"It was a necessary business expense so somebody lent me the money. I figured nobody'd want me if I didn't have big tits. I got to pay the money back which is why I have to get work right away."

"Your boyfriends liked you when you didn't have big tits, didn't they?"

She laughed. "My boyfriend Tom wanted to ask me out for a long time before he got up the nerve. He was so happy when I said yes. He said he didn't think he stood a chance with a girl like me."

"And that was without big tits. You're beautiful, and most guys are intimidated by beautiful women which is why they don't get asked out often."

"He doesn't count, he's a loser! Besides I'm sure he'd prefer a girl with big tits but settled for me because I'm better than nothing."

"Oh no, you're wrong. I don't give a rat's ass about your tits. I like you because of you, not because of how you look."

"Me?" she smirked. "What do you know about me?"

"I'm drawn to you by abstract things like your mind, not by concrete things like tits. Real love is like that. Love based on superficial things like big tits isn't worth much. Love is about things you feel, not about things you see."

"Well, I like things I can see."

"The most powerful things are those you can't. I don't know if I should tell you this because it probably won't make sense to you."

She looked at him suspiciously.

"Everyone has a spirit who visits them in their dreams. This dream entity usually doesn't resemble anyone you know because it's an undeveloped part of yourself that is of the opposite sex. It's not an invention of your conscious mind, it's a spontaneous product of the unconscious. For men it's the anima and for women it's the animus."

Cool, she thought.

"Your animus serves as a link between your conscious mind and the much vaster world of your unconscious and the collective unconscious, the spirit world. He comes to you in your dreams and gives you information you need. If you ignore or misinterpret the information, your life can get a lot tougher. Part of my fascination with you is you resemble my dream anima. You feel like her to me, like she did when I was your age."

"That's interesting," she said. "Is there a special ritual or something you have to do, to like *conjure* her up?"

"For you it'd be a he, and he's with you all the time in your dreams and fantasies. All you have to do is learn to listen, and eventually you will understand what he's saying."

Tracy frowned. An evil man pursued her in her dreams, and anything he had to say she was sure would be the death of her.

KATIE'S AWARENESS of the cold, damp fog increased the closer they got to the path, as did her irritability.

"What did you do to me last night?" she demanded. "I don't remember a thing."

Spear signaled with his hand for her to remain silent. She'd been instructed to remain silent until they reached the path. The worst thing she could do under these circumstances was to ask questions, or complain. He'd learned the folly of asking questions from Sandoval, how it kept one from understanding answers. Leading only to more questions. Silence and observation were the best way to learn important things.

When they reached the path he scanned the area around it. Satisfied, he said, "You were purified and empowered last night. Don't waste it with petty concerns."

"Okay, great, fine," she said, testily. "Now tell me what happened. Please."

"You came here as Angelica. She was too unstable to withstand the impact of power so I had to shove her everyday awareness aside at a critical moment. It was a dangerous thing to do. Riley had drained so much of your personal power, I could not be sure she would be able to come back."

"What do you mean?"

"I pushed ALL of your personalities aside."

"Ahh!" she gasped. "You pulled Angel through."

Her response surprised him. "Yes," he said. "Can you recall what she said?"

She stared at him, breathing deeply, her face impassive.

"If you want to understand what happened, you must recall it yourself. You can do that. Do you want to?"

She hesitated, and then nodded.

"The nearest I can come to describing how to do that is, it's like a feeling in the eyes." He closed his eyes. "You recall with a feeling in your eyes." He moved his eyeballs under their lids. "Being stunned and lacking energy is what makes you hide your knowledge. The Earth, she gave all of you a boost. You have the energy to do it now." He opened his eyes. Hers were closed. "Riley's game. What did she have to say about it?"

She stiffened as she shook her head, her eyes still closed.

"Angel's a feeling in your eyes. Find Her. You know her feeling. Find it."

"Riley's trapped and desperate," she said when she opened her eyes. "I must not allow him to sacrifice me to break his spell of madness."

"And her decision?"

"To fire Riley?" she said, without thinking. "We had to fire him?"

"Angelica, the weakest link, fired him," said Spear. "Only her arrow could penetrate his armor. When she returns, all of you must now treat her with the proper respect. She is the key for you all to merge."

Someone let me in, I think the sky is falling, Seems I got lost on the way. All I want to do is to find myself. Come and let me look in your eyes.

Jake fell face forward onto his unmade bed and buried his face in a pillow. Cedar, his ex-wife, had designated this song as their song. She said it expressed how she felt when he looked in her eyes. "I wish my wife had been different," he mumbled. "I do, I do, I do, I do, I do." They would never listen to that song together again. She would never look for herself in his eyes again. Nor would he ever again see the beauty in hers.

"I loved," he sighed. She would look into another's eyes. The other would look into hers. Her memories of their love discarded, decaying into a distant past. Not worth her remembering. A mistake. Their love, fading into a kind of death.

His love had been real and so much a part of him, of who he was. It was not something he could rip out without causing himself serious harm. He wanted to release it, to let it go. It haunted him. All it took was that song, her song, to flatten him.

He loved seeing the beauty in women's eyes. But for as long as his pain remained, when he looked into a woman's eyes who said she loved him, he would hold back, not trusting either her or himself. "I wish," he moaned, wishing things had turned out different. "I do. I do. I do," he muttered through clenched teeth. "I wish I could let it go."

But wishes to let go had no more traction than wishing things had been different. He recalled telling her early in their relationship, the song he felt best expressed what he saw when he looked in her eyes came from *The Sound of Music*. He remembered singing it to her. *Somewhere in my youth or childhood I must have done something good.*

Then he thought about what she meant, and what he meant. She found herself in his eyes because he reflected back an image of herself she loved. It had little to do about him personally. His song reflected his regarding her as a reward for having done something good. The foolishness of people in love.

Tap! Tap! The window in the front door.

Jake picked a t-shirt up off the floor and wiped his eyes with it, then made his way through the living room to the front door and opened it.

Four-year-old little Vera stood there, outside, alone, staring up at him with a mischievous grin on her face. "Hello, Jake-o-lantern," she giggled.

Jake knelt down with open arms. "Veeeeee-Raaa! My best goil!" He picked her up, and hugged her. Then Jazz and Joaquin stepped out from behind his truck.

"Who are these people, Vra?"

She twisted her body to look then said, "Daddy and Jasmine." Her body tensed. Jake planted a kiss on the top of her head then carried her inside. Something was bothering her, he sensed as he gently stroked the top of her head like he used to do when she was a baby. Little Vera relaxed, going limp in his arms. He figured probably a reaction to an argument between her daddy and Jasmine.

"We were in the neighborhood so we thought we'd drop by and annoy you," said Joaquin.

"You got some meat?" asked Jazz, mimicking a freeloading friend of hers who always asked that question whenever she came over to her place.

"No," Jake said. "But we could order a pizza."

"Order a pizza," said Jazz. "Extra large!"

"All right." He went to the phone, hesitant to let Vera down, feeling she needed more comforting. "I have to put you down, Vra, okay?" She tensed as Jake placed her gently on the floor, giving him a furtive little smile.

Jazz took a bottle of red wine from the liquor cabinet then rummaged through a drawer in search of a corkscrew. By the time he finished ordering the pizza, she had filled three glasses with wine.

"Jake-o-lantern, I wanna go in the hot tub," Vera said.

"In a minute, honey," Joaquin said. "Jazzala, tell Jake about Dr. Ben."

"Oh, yeah!" Jazz laughed. "You remember Ben, the little troll what was coming on to everybody? He's been calling, saying he fantasizes 'bout me all the time being his love slave. Ha! Ha! And he came to my concert, not like some people I know, dressed in African clothes. You should've seen how ri-dic-u-lous he looked, Ha!"

"Maybe he's the one who stole your panties," Joaquin said, laughing.

She shook her head. "He don't know where I live. One thing for damn sure, I don't let no crazy people know where I live. I'd be asking for trouble."

"How'd he get your number?" Jake asked.

"I told him."

"You gave *him* your phone number?"

"He might be useful. The boy's loaded. Showed me a shit load of cash."

"He offered to finance a video of the group," said Joaquin.

"I was thinking maybe I'd get him to switch brokers. Oh, damn!" She hit herself on the side of the head with the palm of her hand. "My damn ear hurts. I'm gonna have to get it drained again." She hit her head again. A small ball of wax popped out. "That's better." She picked up the ball. "Look at this, Jake. I told you I knocked these things out of my ears and you didn't believe me."

"Let me see! Let me see!" Vera cried. Jazz showed it to her. Vera made a face.

"You want to get in the hot tub?" Jazz said. Vera nodded. "Okay, I'll get in wif you. Let me know when the pizza gets here."

"You coming, Jake-o-lantern?" Vera asked hopefully.

"Not now, pumpkin. I have to be ready for when the pizza comes."

"Ohhh, Daddy can do it."

"Come on, Vera," Jazz said. "I'll play wif you."

After the ladies left the room, Joaquin said, "What's the scoop on tomorrow?"

"Well, Janus has a guy doing camera for nothing. She can't afford to pay."

"What happened with the teenybopper? Did you pork her?"

"You know, I dreamed about her all week. I was so turned on I could taste it."

"Welcome to the real world," Joaquin chuckled. "How was it?"

"Strange. Her body's tight, smells and tastes great, but I've never had sex with anyone so sexually out of sync. We're talking loose connection, no depth. She was awful at everything except cocksucking." He thought a moment. "A weird thing, though, I somehow kept imagining her as Cedar. A teenage Cedar transported into Tracy's body. I wondered what I'd do if that actually were true?"

"If she's anything like your ex-wife, you'd best stay clear of her, boy. You got to exorcise that witch from your mind."

"Anyway, she is star material. I can't make anything happen for myself, but I know I could make something happen for her. Know what I'm saying?"

"The old self-esteem ain't up to speed," Joaquin said.

"I have personal trust problems. I feel like no matter what I do for myself, I'll be ripped off. So why bother, right? On the other hand, it's a hell of a lot easier for me to protect somebody else than to protect myself."

Rrrrring!

Jake picked up the phone. "Hello," he said.

"What're you doing?" Moira asked suggestively.

Jake glanced furtively at the hot tub. Jazz looked back, suspicious. "I have some friends over. It's not a good time."

"I thought we were getting together tonight. Can I come over?"

"No," he said quickly. "I've got a shoot tomorrow. I'm taking it easy tonight."

Jazz got out of the tub and wrapped herself in a towel.

"Oh," Moira said, disappointed. "Why can't I join you and your friends? I could get you nice and relaxed for tomorrow."

"I'd rather not," he said evasively. Jazz sat at the table and stared at him.

"Have you heard again from your friend?"

"My friend?" Moira said. "Oh, yeah, him. He's the reason I need to see you tonight."

"What happened?"

Jazz filled a glass to the brim with wine.

Moira was silent for a moment. "The guy's scary. Now he says I'm a *temptress* in league with the devil. Yeah, right. Called me Satan's Snare. Creepy."

"You didn't follow my advice, did you?"

"How can you *not* react to something like that? Like he said he was going to *unmask* me and reveal my *evil*."

Jazz lit a cigarette, crossed her legs then blew smoke in Jake's direction.

"You remember Dr. Ben the psychiatrist. Short rodent-like guy in the orgy scene?"

"Yeaaa-uuh."

"My friend, Jazz, you remember her, right?" he said. Jazz spilled wine on her white towel. "He's been harassing her on the phone, too. Maybe he's—"

"Hell, no," she said. "Not a chance. I'm telling you this guy has a very distinctive quality in his voice. A weird English-like accent. Whoever he is, he wasn't at the shoot."

"Have you talked to Mindy about it?"

"No."

"You should do some detective work, see if we can figure out who it is. Joaquin's here with me, I'll go over it with him."

No response, just the sound of paper rustling. "Hello?"

"I wrote a poem about you," she said. "Want to hear it."

Jake rolled his eyes impatiently, mostly for Jazz's benefit. "Sure," he said. "Of course." Listening to lady friends' poetry always made him uncomfortable.

> "*Your eyes,*" she began. "*hidden*
> veiled
> The red lining of a dream
> In between the movie machine
> cut

one cut two
the bleeding photograph magnetize
sympathize your serious intensified
civilized hermitized
tongue flaps
incompleted novels throbbing with the
he who has been hurt yet, still
ready (un)willing chilling
and
thrilling
racing the words to love again
perhaps in the peak of winter

Come coming her face
will shine in the goblet
of your so called imaginary fingers when the amorous aroma
still lingering
will sing mocking cheeks
whispering desire…
desire…
desire…

Silence. He had no idea how to respond. The peculiar intensity in her voice had made it difficult for him to concentrate on what she said.

"I want to see you," she said.

He could not think of a safe way to answer that in the presence of a glowering Jazz.

"Why do you have to be such a jerk?" Moira said sullenly. Then she hung up. "Okay," Jake said slowly. "I'll see what I can do." Then he hung up.

"And who was that?" Jazz demanded.

"Moira, the brunette in the video we were in," Jake said.

"And what did *she* want?"

"Someone's harassing her on the phone. He's accused her of being a devil in disguise and threatens to tell her parents about the video. I thought it might be Ben."

"No, it's not Ben-ja-min," Jazz said. "Just because he's a shrink don't mean he's crazy. So why is she calling *you*?"

"Come on, Jazz. She's trying to find out who it might be. She wanted help."

"And why would she want *your* help? And how did she get your number?"

"I didn't give it to her. I suspect she got it from Mindy."

"I'll have you know I do *not* appreciate your telling your bimbos my personal business!"

"What? What?"

"You talk to me before you tell people about Ben-ja-min botherin' me, got it? And I don't appreciate you talking to your girlfriends period while I'm a guest in your house. That is uncalled for and insulting. I wouldn't do that to you."

"What do you mean my girlfriend? She has a problem I'm helping her with."

"Don't give me that shit," she said contemptuously. "I know you. You wouldn't use your soft voice wif that bimbo unless you be fucking her." She stood up. "Don't bother denying it, I don't want to hear it." She got up and went back to the hot tub, muttering, "Damn fucking liar."

"Woooo!" Joaquin whistled softly. "That true? You fucking Moira, too, you horn dog?"

"Forget about it," Jake said. "I'm concerned about the nut that's bothering her."

"That is weird. I can't imagine who'd be doing that."

"Worthingham?"

"Na. Listen to you, boy. You always suspect shrinks or sharks. Where's the motive? He got her the job in the first place, and he's her uncle."

"He may have mentioned it to the wrong element."

"Yeah, but anybody could've done that," Joaquin said, re-filling his glass. "Less likely a shark or a shrink since they supposedly know how to keep their traps shut, right?"

Jake rubbed his chin thoughtfully. "We may not have the whole picture here. Moira's got a weird side to her."

"Now, bro, have you ever known a woman who didn't?"

"We sure know how to pick 'em, don't we?" Jake said, glancing in Jazz's direction.

"Don't we, though," Joaquin laughed. "Let's face it, boy, we're attracted to fucked up women. But it's damn near impossible to get far in this life without getting fucked up."

Jake sighed. "Seems like women used to recognize paying their fair share was part of being equal. Now they treat men like cash cows yet demand to be treated as equals."

"I don't think women have changed all that much. Back in our day the young women who hung out with old farts expected them to pay for the privilege, as well. I think we glossed over their basic hostility because women's lib was fashionable and we were young and dumb and full of cum. I bet they weren't all that much different from the angry young women we put up with today."

"Right," said Jake, ironically. "Like little Vera's mom."

"Mary Jane? You're right, that woman's definitely out there. She *is* crazy. Runs in the family, you know."

"I never could understand why you hung with her so long."

"Mary Jane was a stupid, destructive addiction. We met during a time when I was crazy and down on myself. You remember the ulcers, all that crap."

"I remember. Used to call you the Flying Dutchman back then."

Joaquin laughed, then said, "I forgot what you meant by that."

"You, and I, are doomed to an endless search for the ideal woman to give us what we lack. We don't know what that is but it's something mommy should have provided but didn't. We'll never find this woman because we're drawn to women who have our mother's weaknesses, so they can't give us any more than she did. But we keep going, like moths to a flame, hoping somehow this time things will be different and we'll find in them what we're missing. That's the message behind the myth of the Flying Dutchman and the ghost ship."

"My mother wasn't that crazy, but I do love to suffer, though, don't I?" he laughed. "It's amazing something as wonderfully sane as little Vera could've come of all that."

"So much for our old feminist idealism. Still, there's got to be stable non-hostile women out there."

"Sure there are," Joaquin said. "But they're not interested in neurotic old farts like you and me, bro."

"Maybe our standards are too low and women with high standards have no use for men with such low ones. Since Cedar left, I don't give a shit anymore, and that draws wicked women like flies."

"What are you whining about?" Jazz said, adjusting her robe as she entered the room.

"About lust," Joaquin said.

"Oh, really," she sneered. "And just who might he be lusting for?"

"Pizza," Joaquin said.

"Ha! Ha!" Jazz laughed, waving an empty wineglass. "Where the fuck is that pizza?"

"Any minute now," Jake said.

"I need some meat now!" She sat down, jostling the table.

Little Vera came in, wrapped in a towel as she climbed up on the chair between Jazz and her father.

"You didn't use one of your stupid coupons, did you?" Jazz snapped. "No wonder it's taking so fucking long to get here. You better feed me now!"

Jake looked at little Vera. From the intense expression on her face as she stared at Jazz, he knew something was bothering her. He glanced at her father. Joaquin looked serious, concerned, while he listened to Jazz's rant. Jake looked back at little Vera.

She glanced up at him and smiled.

"Ra!" said Jake.

PART FOUR

The Underworld

Because the foolishness of God is wiser than men;
and the weakness of God is stronger than men.

For ye see your calling, brethren,
how that not many wise men after the flesh, not many mighty,
not many noble, are called:

But God hath chosen the foolish things of the world to confound the wise;
and God hath chosen the weak things of the world to confound the
things which are mighty;

and base things of the world, and things which are despised,
hath God chosen, yea, and things which are nothing
to destroy what the world thinks are important:
that no flesh should glory in His presence.

— Corinthians (1:25-29)

9

Playpen of the Damned

The sun was beating in and out of the trees on a curvy back road in the wine country. Jake inhaled the warm aromatic spring air when he downshifted.

"I've been thinking about a stage name," said Tracy, breaking their silence. "I want a single name like Madonna, Jewel, Cher, like that."

"Okay," Jake said. "Any ideas?" She shrugged.

"Well, how about Anais?"

"Oh, that's gross!" she grimaced. "I want something serious. I like city names, like Paris or Dallas, but something sexier."

"Akron?" he suggested and she groaned. "Billings?" She frowned, annoyed. "Sparks?" She shook her head. "Salem?"

"Salem? I like that. That's something to do with witches, right?"

"Yeah, but I don't think it's you. Why a place name? Why not something like Vanity or Charity or Chastity?"

"Chastity!" She stuck out her tongue. "Give me a fucking break."

"How about Destiny?"

"Destiny?" she shrugged. "Sounds like a hippy kid's name."

"Yeah, you're right. But the tension of opposites is the essence of eroticism, so, if…."

"Sounds dumb."

"So did Madonna at first. Anyway, we can always change it later."

"Okay," she shrugged. "No more Tracy. I'm Chastity!"

"There you go! Now let's construct a reality for Chastity. This is important because an alter ego will help shield you from the confusion of sudden fame. It's not a bad idea to keep the people who know Chastity separate from those who know Tracy until you learn the fame game. Only allow those who prove worthy of trust to know both."

"Trust!" she said with a wide-eyed innocent look.

"Chastity's a happy, wholesome kid from the Bible Belt who's been lured into the dirty business by me. Okay?"

"Wholesome!"

"No one in the industry is to know you've been a prostitute or an anorexic or have had any problems of any kind. If you let them see you as troubled, they'll treat you like trash. I want you to be treated with respect. You won't need my protection once you've learned to distinguish those who have your best interests at heart from those who don't. As long as I represent you, you must trust me and do as I say. Understand?"

"Respect!" she chirped then she pouted. "I'd rather be like Madonna, wild and tough."

"All in good time, my dear. But for now stick to the wholesome script."

"I don't know where you got the idea I'm a cry baby or need protection. I can take care of myself."

"Trust me, hon, you don't know what you're getting into. Tough guys have crumbled under the burden of fame and fortune. It can happen to you if things happen faster than you can take. Today, you're Chastity, a sweet, happy, wholesome, mid-western student."

"Happy!"

"And I, a Svengali-like pimp, am solely responsible for your debauchery. In reality, Tracy is tough and wild and does as she damn well pleases, and I'm just her humble servant. You understand this is just an act?"

"Of course I do," she grimaced. "I'm not stupid."

"All right, then. You're a brilliant co-ed from Grundy Center, Iowa. You were working as a waitress when I seduced you with promises of fun and easy money in Porno World. You've never done anything naughty in your entire life before you met me, right?"

"Purity!"

"Pure as the driven snow." Jake studied her. She was reflecting a personality with no depth. A comic book character. Then he spotted Port Wine Lane, a narrow potholed road obscured by dense foliage. He turned onto it. "This is it."

"Jake," Tracy said, nervous. "Are you sure this is cool?"

"Not to worry," he said, confidently.

"I mean, I haven't seen a script. I have no idea what to do. I'm going to blow it. They're not going to like me."

"Hey, no problem, sweet Chastity. That's how porn's done these days. In my day, I gave performers scripts and expected them to know their lines. That rarely happens anymore. Most directors wing it. You'll do fine, better than most, trust me."

"I don't want to do better than most," she said as they turned up an incline. "I want to be the best."

"You will be," he said as they pulled into a large circular driveway. He parked behind a black Cadillac limo, some distance back from an ordinary ranch house.

Tracy looked at the expanse of thick forest on one side of the house and the bluff bordering it on the other. Isolated. *No one would hear her scream!* A red-haired young man in cut-offs stepped out onto the front porch. He looked her way then yelled into the house. An older man and a teenage boy around her height, five foot five, joined the red-headed guy on the porch. She gripped Jake's forearm.

"It's okay for Chastity to be nervous," Jake said softly. "After all, she is wholesome and innocent. The more innocent she is, the more nervous she'd be, and the more they'll want her. Remember, I'm your protector. If you want to leave, tell me and we're outa here. In reality, this is all about you, and you're actually the one in control. Got it?"

"Okay," she said, her face stiff with tension, her eyes watchful.

The three men started toward her. The short teen had a cute, tough boy look. The red-haired kid, early twenties, had the disorientated look of an addict. The old guy was older than she thought up close in the sunlight. Like grandpa old, dressed in weird old people clothes. Drawstring pants, smoking jacket and yacht shoes. A frowning fourth man, tall, muscular, dressed in a black uniform, came out of the house, following them from behind. She fumbled in her purse, feeling for her sunglasses to hide behind. *Chastity!* She put the sunglasses on. *I'm Chastity!* Jake got out and went to her side of the truck.

"Yo, Dude," Redhair yelled. "We were worried the chick chickened out. Excellent! She's a babe!"

"Yo!" said grandpa, raising a hand in greeting.

What a dork, she frowned, safe behind the sunglasses.

"Chastity, this is Dr. Benjamin Adler, a head shrinker," Jake said. "What's up, doc? What brings you to this neck of the woods?"

"Janus invited me and a business partner of mine," Ben said. "The tall man in black here is his chauffer, Christian Chastain. I call him C. C. Ryder."

"Seth's my name and smut's my game," Redhair said with a smirk. "The little geek's Cody." Cody grinned at her.

"I'm Jake and the lady here is Chastity," Jake said, opening the car door for her. Chastity nodded, in control behind her dark glasses. She slid calmly out of the truck, stumbling only slightly when her feet touched the ground.

"Chastity?" said the red-haired Seth. "Are you a lesbian like Cher's daughter?"

"Yeah, right," she sneered. "Not."

"Young and tender, don't offend her," said Cody.

"I've always considered chastity the most unnatural of sexual perversions," said Ben.

"So where's the Holy Terror?" Jake said, putting an arm around Chastity. "Janus?" No response. "Janus Terror?"

"What was it you called her, Dude?" Seth asked Ben. "Janutalia," said Ben. Cody and Seth laughed.

"Oh, I get it!" Christian said. "Like genitalia. Har! Har! A real cunt."

Jake gestured to Ben for an aside. "Chastity's a bit nervous," Jake whispered. "I'd appreciate it if everyone took it easy on her until she acclimatizes."

"I'm fine," she said, her face flushed. "I don't like not knowing my lines, that's all."

"Hey, we're all clueless in that department," said Ben. "Janus has been waiting for a miracle to save the day."

"Cool, dude!" Seth pointed at the Gold Rush era engraving on Jake's belt buckle of a miner boxing a devil, his second holding a vial of holy water in one hand and a cross in the other, and the devil's second holding a bottle of whiskey. "Boxing devils, heh!, heh!, heh! I like that. What does it say?" He leaned in close to read the inscription. "San Francisco Asylum. Licensed to perform exorcism. No way! For real, dude, you can do that? That's cool. I could throw some business your way. Heh! heh! heh!"

"That's more like Dr. Ben's department," Jake said when he spotted Janus on the deck. "Excuse us, gents." He took hold of Chastity's hand and walked off toward Janus.

"Shit, I'm glad you guys made it," Janus said in a stage whisper as they approached. "I was sweating bullets. I don't like getting riled up but the other girl turned all wishy washy after jacking me around all night with how desperately she needed work, then she doesn't show up. Now it's too late to find a replacement, which makes you guys the only game in town. If you hadn't shown, I'd be alone with these raving maniacs. I don't give a fucking shit, I could close my eyes and just do it, it's part of the job, but I'm not crazy about shooting something I'll lose money on. Still these guys came all the way out here expecting something, and all I had to offer is me."

"I wouldn't leave you twisting in the wind, you know that, Janus." Jake glanced at Tracy, who was nervously listening to the laughter of the men by the limo. He turned back to Janus. "Sorry. It took longer than expected to find the place. So what's the plan?"

"I figured I could come up with some fuckass routine. I mean, how hard could it be? But I'm drawing a blank." Noticing the men coming toward them, she rushed into a hurried whisper. "It's really not funny. I've never directed before. I don't know how to handle these mother-fuckers. I was hoping you might come up with something. Let's talk private somewhere."

"What about Chastity?"

"Ben!" Janus yelled. "Could you show Chastity around?"

"You okay?" Jake asked Chastity. "I'll be back in a moment."

Chastity shrugged. "Yeah, I'm fine."

"Watch yourself around Dr. Ben," he whispered. "He's a wolf in gnome's clothing. Don't let him touch you."

"Allow me, Goldilocks," said Ben, offering her his arm as he approached. Jake and Janus walked into the house, through the dining room and out a sliding glass door onto the backyard deck. Janus stopped by a large hot tub.

"I can't handle this," she said. "Would you take over? You know, direct it?"

"I thought the point of your doing this project was to direct?"

She sighed. "It's a bloody mess. Ben's been talking all kinds of nonsense. He set me up with this free location from Peter Hakim, a cameraman and two young studs and brought along a fat slob he hoodwinked into investing in a blood and guts horror flick. All of it, at no cost to me. All I had to do was to provide a couple of cute girls. Fine, except the boys are crazier than bed bugs, probably patients of his. Seth, the scrawny one, I wouldn't let him fuck my worst enemy. He has to be disturbed to shave off all his body hair, right? I'm telling you he's from another planet and they don't want him back. His buddy Cody has needle marks and tattoos all over him. They certainly aren't the answer to a maiden's prayer. I was about to get my John Henry out of here when you showed up."

"You do tend to attract certifieds, Janus."

"Well, there are some sad stories out there, and they come to me for help. What can I do? I grew up in a small town with an older sister who was schizo, for real crazy. I had to take care of her, and take the heat for all the shit she did."

"Then you ought to know by now, nutcases feel compelled to inflict their pain on others and to punish those who help them."

"Tell me about it! Don't I know. I got this one nutcase who—"

"Janus," he interrupted. "What did you have in mind to do?"

"You mean the sex? Low voltage bondage and some light S and M, which these kids don't know shit from shinola about. They can talk the talk but they can't walk the walk."

"Well, that's your specialty, I don't play that. What makes you think I can direct it better than you?"

"You know what I do. Bird dog, take out the garbage, but I don't direct. I thought I could, but I can't. Please, could you do it for me?"

"Well, I don't know the rules of the genre, what's acceptable for the amateur B and D market. I'm sure distributors have restrictions on what can and can't be done, right?"

"Yeah, you know, nothing too heavy. No whipping while the girl's tied up, that sort of thing."

Crazy kids, B&D, S&M, Dr. Ben. He considered terminating the deal, but if he did Tracy would be upset. Unless she agreed with him. She's nervous, so she might.

"All right, I'll do it. But on one condition."

"Sure. What?"

"Don't say anything about it to Jazz, or to anyone who might pass it on to her. She's very jealous and there'd be hell to pay if she connected me with Chastity."

"Jazz is jealous?" she said, puzzled. "I thought you weren't lovers anymore?"

"It's complicated. There's no need to make it more complicated."

"That's too bad."

"Yeah, it is. Let's go back inside." He started toward the house. "Any story ideas?"

"No," she frowned, following him. "I thought maybe an orgy?"

"I saw some musical instruments in the living room. Let's make the boys punk musicians who're into bondage, and she's a groupie. Call it *Playpen of the Damned.*"

"Playpen of the Damned?"

"The damned are damaged kids, eternally acting out," he said as they entered the dining room. "Porn, B&D, S&M, heavy metal and punk are playpens. And this group sure looks damned to me."

"We don't really need a title. It's just a fuck scene." She pointed at a tall, pale, fat man with a big belly, dressed in black, by the kitchen counter. "The big guy's John Booth. He's a Playboy photographer, but what he really wants to do is direct. He got a shot at it when he replaced Riley Theirault as director after he and Ben worked out a deal with Theirault's crew to switch to a Playboy flick. The Arab looking at Booth's portfolio, that's Peter Hakim. He's loaded, but don't ask me where he gets it."

"Yeah, I know Peter," Jake said.

"Peter said he'd put the money up for the soft core Playboy flick providing they did a hard version of it, too. Booth has no experience with porn, which is why he's here. He said he'd let me work his project if I let him observe mine. And he wants to talk to you."

"Okay. I'll go introduce myself."

Jake approached Booth and Peter. "Hey, Peter! Like your place. Very private."

"I just bought it a few months ago," Peter said, as if apologizing for not inviting him over earlier. "I'd like to introduce you to John Wilkes Booth. John, this is Jake Zakheim."

"Pleased to meet you," said Booth, extending his hand.

"John Wilkes Booth?" Jake said as Booth squeezed his hand with bone crushing intensity, immediately putting him on edge. His father considered a firm handshake manly, a sign of character, but Jake found it overly aggressive and off putting. "You use that name with Playboy?"

"That's my name."

"You're putting me on. What American mother would give a kid a name like that?"

With a I've-heard-it-all-before look, Booth said, "A Southern mother would. I was raised in South Georgia and the name wasn't a problem there, or in law enforcement."

"Law enforcement?" Jake said, raising an eyebrow.

"I was a sheriff in Georgia, like my pappy and his pappy before him."

The big belly hanging over his belt fits the image, Jake thought. "What brings one of the South's finest to beaver films in the bear state?"

"My last job was as a vice cop in Chicago. But I changed my mind about the sex industry after I got to know the Playboy people. Would you like to see my portfolio?" He slid an album over and opened it on nude shots. "I thought perhaps we could do business."

"What kind of business you got in mind?" Jake turned a page.

"I've seen your films. You could use a better class of women, better make-up and styling. I create the total look." Booth spotted Chastity, *sans* sunglasses, as she entered the room with her entourage. "She has potential. I could make something of her. I'd like to use her in a feature I'm doing for Playboy."

"Sounds good, but I have to get this production going. Let's rap after we've wrapped."

"I have business in the City tonight." Booth handed him a card. "Give me a call if we don't have a chance to talk before I leave."

"Jake!" Chastity said grinning from ear to ear, feeling like a star. Important people had come in a limousine to see her, and they liked what they saw. *Her!*

"Ah, sweet Chastity," said Jake. "I'd like you to meet John Wilkes Booth. He's a famous photographer for Playboy."

"Really?" she said, impressed. "You know, I think I've heard of you."

"And this is Peter Hakim, an up and coming film producer," said Jake. "You met him at Hasib's."

"Pleased to see you again," said Peter, looking very pleased indeed.

"Likewise," beamed Chastity.

"Mr. Booth says he'd like to use you in a Playboy movie he's doing," Jake said. "Why don't you take a look at his portfolio."

"Look at the hooters on that babe," Cody said pointing at an un-blemished beauty.

"Awesome, dude," Seth drooled. "You shot her? I couldn't a kept the camera still if it was me, man."

"Oh, no," Chastity said, closing the portfolio. Their flawless bodies were more attractive than hers could ever be, and her admirers knew it. "I don't look like them."

"You could," said Booth. "No one's born looking like that, you have to work at it. It's an art form. First thing I'd do is fix your hair and send you to a tanning salon to even out your coloring. You need different make-up. What you've done to yourself is strictly teenager."

"But I am a teenager! Besides that's what guys want. When you're twenty, you're too old."

Booth stared at her for a moment. Then he laughed.

"I like teen babes," said Seth, noticing her blushing.

"DID I BLOW IT?" Tracy asked, alone in a bedroom with Jake.

"Na. Chastity's a bit naïve and innocent," said Jake. "It's appropriate that she makes mistakes. You didn't blow it."

"Why did he laugh?"

"Because you're wrong. Most men don't take teenagers seriously. Teens are like junk food. A man wants a woman, not a little girl. If there's an ideal age it's more like twenty-five to thirty, because the personality's more developed and the body's still youthful."

"That's mean," she pouted.

"Let's go outside." He lead her through a bathroom to the hall to the front of the house. "Anyway, you are special. You'll have 'em eating out of your hand. By the time we're through, Booth will want you for the lead in his feature."

"No he won't. I don't look at all like those women. I'm stupid and clumsy and I don't know anything. I can't be like them."

"Believe me, it's no big thing. You have what it takes and you'll succeed in spite of what you think, because you're a natural. You can't fail."

"So what am I suppose to do? What's happening?"

"Well, you're in luck, I'm now the director and the writer. The story involves S&M and bondage. Got a problem with that?"

"No," she said. "That's great. I'm taking S&M classes."

"They teach S&M at the College of Alameda?"

"No, it's a night class in San Francisco. Wormyham enrolled me."

"He what? How many have you gone to?"

"Not many. It only meets once a week. Each time they have a different speaker talking about different things. You should come with me."

"You go alone?"

"No, I have a friend, a nice guy. We're not lovers or anything. He's the only guy who's never tried anything on me."

"Well, great, I'll go with you next time," he said, leading her to the limo. "Okay, the plot is Cody and Seth are members of a heavy metal group. I'm their agent and you're a groupie I picked up at a concert. I'm bringing you to them in the limo on the pretense of introducing you to Rotten Robbie, the lead singer. Of course, I want you for myself. Eventually we end up in an orgy scene with light S&M and bondage. We can't do both at the same time because if we whip you when you're restrained the distributor could get in trouble."

"Which one's Rotten Robbie?"

"Oh, uh, Cody, the short one."

"That's cool. Seth's too creepy. I don't mind fucking Cody. He's kinda cute."

"You don't have to fuck either of them. Just me, remember?"

"Okay," she shrugged. "I wouldn't mind if it were Cody is all. So what do I say? Do I get a script?"

"No, we have to wing it. Don't worry, though, I have a sixth sense about this. You're a natural born improviser."

"What do you mean, improvise? I can't do that. I wouldn't know what to do!"

"The kids don't have experience either. You're better than them."

"But I'm not! I'm going to look like a jerk!"

Jake put a finger to his lips. "We'll go through it so you can get the feel of it. When the camera's on, you'll surprise everyone with how good you are, including yourself."

"No! I need more time."

He opened the door to the back of the limo. "Get in." He got in after her and pointed to the front partition. "The camera will be there. We'll do whatever feels appropriate for our characters. You're a nervous, insecure, underage girl, intimidated by everything. We'll start with your behaving like a jerk. Think you can do that?"

"No," she pouted. "I don't know what to say."

"Neither does your character. All you need to do is be yourself. Let's give it a try."

"No! I'm not ready!"

"Camera rolling, the limo's in motion. You're a sweet innocent underage groupie and I'm a seedy agent giving you a lascivious grin." He grinned.

"Lascivious?" she giggled, nervously.

"The scene is happening, I give direction, you do as directed. Camera's on your face, the dirty old man's leering at you. You're en route to Rotten Robbie's mansion, a heavy metal star you worship. You're excited, right? But nervous. That's it, you got it. You don't know anybody and you don't know what's expected of you. It's all so very strange. Good, now I'll get in character." He curled his lips into a smirk and lowered his eyelids halfway. "You're a very pretty little girl."

"Thank you," Chastity said, averting her eyes.

He placed a hand on her thigh and she flinched. She looked so frightened, he wanted to comfort her. "Robbie's going to like you."

"I hope so," Chastity said, trembling.

"Excellent! That's all there's to it. Doesn't matter what we say as long as the atmosphere gets across. Let's get the crew."

"No, wait! I'm not ready. I want to go through it a few more times."

"We don't have the time, hon. It's not necessary, just follow my lead like you did and we'll be done with it."

"But I want to do it right. I can do better."

"If you blow it, we do another take, no problem. Let's do it," he said. She gave him a look of panic. "Look, you'll do just fine. Even if you prove me wrong, which you won't, I won't be mad or disappointed. Just means I was wrong, and you were right. Then I'll try it your way. Deal?" He got out and yelled for the crew.

She watched Jake approach Freddy, the frumpy quiet old man with sad eyes who had stared at her while she toured the house. He had the *camera!* Freddy was the cameraman! They treated her like she was special. Now they were going to laugh at her. Her stomach *queeeeasy.* What was she suppose to say? No way could she do it. *I'm not like those girls!*

"I'm going to hurl," she moaned, shoving open the limo door facing the cliff. The colors outside, too bright. She stared down at the gravel. The pungent odor of weeds. Buzzing insects. She imagined everybody laughing at her stinking chunks on the ground.

The front car door opened. The cameraman slid in.

Jake slid into the back with her and looked at her. "You're a real pro, hon. You stayed in character. That's the look I want. I think we can do it in one take. Just follow my lead and do what feels natural for your character. I'll tell you when we've arrived at Robbie's, then we get out and walk to the house. After that, we do cutaways, if we need them. You know, some famous stage actors get so nervous before they go on stage they actually throw up. You're doing fine. So without further ado, let the games begin!"

Chastity's mouth fell open. Jake placed his hand under her chin and closed it. "Camera, ready?" he smiled.

"Ready," said the cameraman.

Jake removed his hand. "Let's rock and roll."

"Rolling," said the cameraman.

Chastity stared in panic at Jake. *I must look so stupid!* His eyes, distant, cold. *He's angry.* His smirk *mocking her.* She trembled.

"You're a very pretty little girl," he said.

"Why thank you, sir," she replied. *Horrible! I'm horrible!*

Jake looked her over, feeling like a dirty old man.

She stiffened when he placed his hand on her thigh. She bit her lower lip, wondering what to do. *Push it away? What?* He withdrew his hand. She looked at him for signs she had done the right thing.

"Robbie's going to like you," he said with a smirk.

"I hope so," she sighed, resigning herself to the necessity of many takes and ridicule.

"We have arrived," he said in a pseudo-hip voice. He raised her head up and moved in close. "You are about to meet Rotten Robbie, little girl. Nervous?"

"A little."

"Good." He took his hand away. "He'll like that." He opened his door and slid out.

She looked around, uncertain what to do. *This is so wrong. They should stop. Why don't they stop!*

Jake gestured for her to get out. Fumbling, she got out.

"Madame," he said as he took her hand, and lead her to the house. When they reached the front door, he yelled, "Cut!" then to Freddie, "How'd it look?"

"Terrific," said the cameraman.

"No problems with light shifts from inside to out. Focus okay, no obstructions?"

"No, it's fine. Suppose to be amateur anyway."

"Okay, then, on to the next scene," Jake said.

"Wait!" Chastity cried. "I was awful. I was clumsy. I was terrible. We gotta do it again."

"Sweetheart, you were superb," Jake smiled.

"No, I wasn't!"

"Hey, kid, you were great. You were fantastic," the cameraman said. "You had me so convinced. I wanted to send you home to your parents."

"Hon, I won't let you look bad. We got a lot more to shoot and that was top drawer. I'd be delighted if the rest of the movie went so good."

"But, but..," she groaned, following him.

"JANUS!" Jake called out as they entered the dining room. She had stripped down to the same leather underwear she had worn at Mindy's. "Let's do the deck scene before we lose the light. Follow me, you're in it."

Chastity watched Janus as they walked out on the deck. She'd never seen an outfit like that before, openings for tits and cunt. *Way cool.*

"Here comes heaven," said Cody from the hot tub in which he and Seth were naked.

"Hey, Chase-tity, I'm wanna chase your titties!" said Seth. "Hey, dude, I'm ready for a piece of that action."

Jake rubbed his chin. "Cody, you're Rotten Robbie, a rock star, Chastity's idol."

"All right!" Cody whooped. "That means I get to pork her!"

"Hey, dude!" Seth said, upset. "I get to bone her, too, don't I?"

"No, no, gentlemen. That's not the way it's going down. Nobody porks her but me. Cody, you're not in this scene so you have to get out of the hot tub. Seth, you stay in."

Cody winked at Chastity then stood up to show his tattoos.

Seth reacted by standing up as well, hoping to impress her with his shaven genitals. Her apparent disinterest darkened his mood.

"Hey, director dude," Seth said. "Who am I suppose to be? Like, what's my name?"

"Terrible Herbst," Jake said. "You're Robbie's sidekick."

"Oh! Fab-u-lous. That sucks big time. Totally bogus, dude."

"Sorry about that." He scanned the set. "When Chastity and I come into the shot, I want all eyes on her. No one looks at me."

"That's easy, dude," Seth sneered. "Who'd want to look at you."

"Janus, you think she's underage so you give me a contemptuous look when I get close enough. I'll make with introductions then you ask her if she's ever played before." Jake turned to Chastity. "And you have no idea what she means by that."

"That's easy," she said. "What does it mean?"

"She's asking whether you've done S&M or B&D before." He turned to Janus. "Tap her with the whip to dramatize the question, okay?" Then to Chastity. "You reply something like 'that's what I'm here for.' Of course, you have no idea what she's talking about. Got it?"

"I don't know if I can remember all that," Chastity said.

"Not to worry. If we don't lose the light, we'll shoot from different angles so they can pick the best takes. So," he turned to Janus, "after she says that's what I'm here for, lift her shirt with your riding crop and show us some tit."

"All right!" Seth yelped. "It's about fucking time, dude." Chastity smiled self-consciously.

"And tell her to undress," Jake said.

"Chastity, try to stay in the sunlight," said the cameraman.

"Right, the shadows are getting longer. No time for a run through. Okay, after the first glimpse of tit, Janus leaves the scene and I undress her."

"Woof, woof, woof, woof," cheered the two young men.

Smiling shyly, Chastity scanned the faces. One, two, three, four, five, six, seven, eight. *Eight guys watching her! Cool.*

"Okay, let's do it. Janus, lean against the railing and watch as we enter. Chastity and I will wait for a cue from the camera to enter. Let us know when you're ready, Mr. Cameraperson."

"Fred," said the cameraperson. "My name's Fred."

"Thanks, Fred," Jake said.

"Action," said Fred.

Jake looked at where the shadows were on the deck, then entered the shot with Chastity in tow. Janus stared at them with a blank smile.

"Ms. Rachet," said Jake, "this is Chastity, an avid fan of our pugnacious protégé, Rotten Robbie. Chastity, this is Hortense Rachet, the famous record producer."

Janus smiled. "How do you do, Chastity?"

"I'm fine, thank you," she answered shyly. "I think your work on Robbie's albums is, um, top drawer."

"Why, thank you," said Janus.

"I brought Chastity here to play," said Jake.

"Oh," Janus said, looking confused, then, "Have you ever played before, little girl?"

Chastity glanced down at her breasts, waiting for them to be exposed. Then she remembered she was supposed to say something. *What?* "Uh, uh, no," she said. "Not with Robbie, I mean. But that's what I came here to do."

Janus glanced at Jake then tapped Chastity with the whip. "Maybe you better warm her up a bit first," she said, then exited.

Jake caressed Chastity's face with his fingers. "You seem very tense, little girl."

"Yeah, I am … a little," she laughed nervously.

"Ever been naked in front of a bunch of men before?"

"Huh?" she said, surprised. *What am I suppose to say to that?* "Sure. Sure I have. I guess."

"Good, then you won't mind showing us your tits."

"Excuse me?"

"Show me your tits," Jake repeated.

"I..." she stammered, looking at the anticipating faces.

"You want to play with Robbie, right?"

"Uh huh," she nodded.

"We're playing now. Do as you're told. Show us your tits."

"You heard the dude. Drop your laundry, blondie," said Seth, standing in the hot tub. Chastity looked at him. Her startled look prompted him to fondle himself. "Don't be a wanker, babe. Show us your hooters."

Jake motioned impatiently. Too much resistance. Was she really frightened? Maybe he should ask her, off camera.

She slowly unbuttoned her blouse, then opened it.

"Holy fucking ... SHEEE-IT!" Seth gasped at the sight of her large pointed tits, while Cody and Christian clapped.

"Hey, you guys, quiet!" Janus yelled.

Looking a sweet, healthy pink in the dying light, Chastity angled to give them a better view, Telling herself, *don't smile, I'm supposed to be nervous.*

"Take off your pants," said Jake.

Cody silently waved his fists in excitement as she unbuttoned her jeans and squatted, pulling them down as she stood up.

"Oh, Lord, take me!" moaned Cody. "I've died and gone to heaven."

"Thou sawest it, and did rejoice," said Ben. "1 Samuel 19:5"

"Twat you say?" said Seth. "Cunt hear you."

"All right, my little beauty," said Jake. "Let's go meet Rotten Robbie."

Her audience cheered and broke into applause.

"You're a most excellent babe," Seth said, hopping out of the hot tub with an erection. "I wanna fuck you."

The naked Chastity beamed at the excited men gathering around her.

"I can't believe those tits!" said Ben. "Can I feel them?"

"Sure," said a grinning Chastity.

"Unfucking believable," said Ben, cupping her breasts.

"Hands off, guys!" said Jake, uncomfortable. The idea of these people watching him fuck her bothered him. Letting Cody take his place made sense, although he didn't like the idea of him touching her either. Of course, she did say she wouldn't mind.

"Check this out!" Cody said, pointing at his stiffy.

"For me?" Chastity giggled.

"Hey, what about mine!" Seth pointed at his. "His is a carrot, mine's a beer can!"

"What do you think, Mr. Booth?" asked Chastity. "Of my, uh, performance?"

"You are beautiful," said Booth. "And an excellent actress. Very real."

Her face glowed. *They loved her! They wanted her! What a wonderful feeling!*

"Nice touch, Jake, naming the boys after cheap gas stations," Ben whispered. Then, looking up above the trees, he asked, "Have you felt it? Something extraordinary?"

"Janus!" Jake yelled, gesturing for her to come to him. He had felt something that seemed to have energized him, but he did not want to disrupt its flow by thinking about it.

"Letting go involves connecting with an image without any kind of grasping from the perspective of the ego," said Ben.

Annoyed by what Ben just said, he chose to ignore him by addressing Janus as she approached. "I want you to stay close to Chastity, don't let anyone touch her. Take her and Fred inside to wherever you want the sex shot, then let me know when you're ready. I'll be out here, thinking things through. Meanwhile, no one touches her, got it?"

"Sure, sure, okay, got it," said Janus. "No one touches her."

"Go, go!" Jake said, motioning with his hands.

"Yeah, you do that," Ben said after she walked off. "Think things through. Build barriers between your personality and its unconscious matrix."

"Oooooh-kay," Jake said as he sat down on a lawn chair, not wanting to address whatever Ben was driving at. "Sex is obviously something I'm supposed to deal with in this lifetime," he muttered, watching the pack following Chastity inside.

Ben watched him closely, and Jake felt obliged to add something relevant. "What Buddhists say is when we die, anyone who penetrates the unconscious with purely biological assumptions falls prey to sexual fantasies and gets stuck in the instinctual sphere. Sexual energy then pulls them back into a womb." He looked up at Ben. "Back into this, as they say, inferior world. If so, it seems to me sex must be some kind of trap."

Ben laughed as he looked down at Jake. "Stuck in the instinctual sphere. I like that. Reminds me of what Jung said about Freud. And I quote: *If Freud had given somewhat more consideration to the psychological truth that sexuality is numinous —both a god and a devil— he would not have remained bound within the confines of a biological concept."*

Jake nodded then looked away, not wanting Ben to sense how his coming up so quickly with a quote like that had impressed him.

"Helping the damned caught in sex-related karmic loops is what you may call my area of expertise," Ben went on. "Come to think of it, you might even know a couple of my damned. Riley Thierault, for instance, or his niece Katie Seabolt."

"I know who they are," Jake said, still avoiding eye contact. "Haven't met them."

"If anyone, as you so elegantly put it, penetrates the unconscious with *purely* biological assumptions, it's Riley, although he wouldn't admit to it. Katie, on the other hand, lies on the opposite end of the spectrum." He paused. "Remember what I said about church and family, professional and patriotic allegiances, and moral and ethical rules? That they're not conducive to the true spiritual welfare of the human soul. They're more likely to be the very shackles that keep us from our true spiritual destiny, which Gnostics believe is to unite our divine spark with the Divine hidden beyond the world we see."

"Yeah," Jake said, not remembering having heard him say that. "I remember."

"Well, Riley can only sense his divine spark when he sees Katie's spark. He believes if he could somehow manage to get her to focus her spark on something he refers to as *a little kernel of satisfaction* while in the midst of biological pain pleasure, which is how he sees her fits, he'd be able to meld his assumptions with hers and free the divine spark imprisoned behind his mad façade." He paused. "When Katie was little, he encouraged her to retain her childhood imaginal thinking, for use as a grown-up to help her find and focus on that little kernel. You know what imaginal thinking is, right?"

"Uh, yeah. Thoughts clumped like images. Poetic vision. No words."

"Not so much thoughts. It's more like a picture, with everything in it adding up to an image, all of which you experience at once. If you were to think about parts of the image, you'd lose the feel of the image. You'd lose its magic. In imaginal thinking, you hold the image intact. As I told your lady Esad, you have to know what you're doing. Riley believes his ability to invoke the amoral, energetic forces of nature unfettered by inhibitions and intellect, means he knows what he's doing. That his commitment to error, darkness, suffering, ecstasy and passion would somehow enable him to ascend to the realms of light, guided by the transfigured Sophianic spirit of his niece."

"Sophianic?" Jake said, trying to convince Ben, as well as himself, that he was capable of understanding what Ben was saying.

"Sophia. The primeval element of light. The Cosmic Challenger to the primordial shadow that becomes chaos. The Gnostic concept of the Holy Ghost, or Spirit. The anima of wisdom. Sophia, the veil between the Immortals and mankind."

"Oh," said Jake. "I was thinking sophistic. You know, clever-sounding and plausible, but based on dishonest thinking or flawed logic, with the intent to deceive."

Ben laughed, knowing Jake was messing with him. "That's Riley, alright! The trouble with dishonesty is it's one-sided, so you end up deceiving yourself, as well."

Jake glanced up at Ben who appeared to be distracted by something above the trees.

"Riley seized an opportunity to meld with Katie during his last project," Ben said in a tentative manner that hinted he was about to impart something important. "They both came out of it energetically mangled."

"What happened? I mean, how did he do it? The meld?"

"Katie's prone to sudden seizures that release immense surges of sexual energy. Riley grabbed hold of her head while her body was thrashing about, looking for the spark in her eyes. He found it, then he short circuited. It was too intense for him. Spear, his cameraman, had to pull him off her before he did them both serious harm. She came out better than he did, but she wouldn't have anything to do with him after that."

"They both sound like—"

"Yes, as Janus would say, certifiable," Ben interrupted with a laugh. "The mysteries can't be made to fit the limited scope of the personal mind. I warned him, but he couldn't listen." Ben looked up over the trees. "Are you sure you haven't felt anything out there?"

Jake sighed. "No, I haven't. Is there something out there I should feel?"

Ben shrugged. "I'll leave you with your thoughts."

JAKE watched the sky as the sun slowly sank below the tree line. He couldn't think. He just stared at the fading light, aware of his breathing and the approaching darkness. Gradually, he sensed a dark heavy tension above the tree line. He could not identify, much less describe it, other than it felt as if it had some sort of sexual edge. Although he couldn't tell what it was about the tension that made him think so, it also felt as if he were being judged by an incredibly powerful woman. He held his breath as he considered what Ben had said about his holding back. He was holding back now. Some part of him did not want to know if something was out there, much less what it was.

"Jake, could I have a word with you?" he heard Janus say. He looked up over at her.

"These guys really want to fuck Chastity," she said. "They're willing to put their money where their dicks are."

"What?" he said, acting surprised. "They think she's a whore?"

"I told them she gets fifty bucks to fuck you and they offered to match it for a crack at her. The boys want credit but I told them no way. I figured you don't want those brain-damaged cases humping her. Otherwise, it's a solid extra couple hundred for her."

Jake thought of Chastity when she was standing naked on the deck surrounded by the pack of horny wolves. No doubt the deal would delight her, but that didn't make it right.

"Who's idea was it? Dr. Ben's?"

"Huh? Oh, I don't know. Maybe."

"All of them? Booth? Peter? Dr. Ben? The cameraman?"

"Well, not the cameraman. He's got to shoot it. Christian's the fourth. Oh, and they insist on wearing disguises."

Chastity and the wolves appeared to be in high spirits together. But Ben? If he said no to Ben, he'd have to say no to them all. It was his call.

"I figure what the hey," said Janus. "No skin off my nose. I get more action, she makes more money and you wouldn't have to do any sex if you didn't want to. She gets that fifty either way. Everyone gets what they want. Win-win, eh? Think she'll go for it?"

"No. Maybe if I asked her if she'd be willing to do an expanded scene for more money, you know, since the other girl didn't show. If she goes for it, I don't want her to know the guys put up the bucks. That would scare her." He sighed. "For the story line to work, she should fuck Rotten Robbie, not me. Send her over."

"Sure, thanks," she said, then walked off.

He had been responsible over the years for many people getting into the business. It'd never bothered him before. Porn was not something he took seriously. It was an adventure, and like all adventures, had an element of risk. This, though, felt wrong. He felt a virulent certainty *this* was wrong, that he must not allow it to happen. He must prevent her from selling herself. But why? And why did he feel it now? She wanted it. Everyone wanted it. Except for him. *Why* this gut feeling? Why did it feel so wrong?

"Jake!" Chastity beamed. "This is so great! You're right, they like me. They really *like* me! It's so great I can't believe it. I love it! I want to be a star!"

Jake smiled. "They like you so much they've offered to cough up an extra fifty bucks apiece for the privilege of fucking you."

"Really! Fifty dollars each? God, that's what, um, four hundred dollars! They're going to pay me that! They really, really like me!"

"It's more like an extra two hundred bucks. Cody and Seth don't have the money and the cameraman has to tape it."

"An extra two hundred dollars!" she squealed. "I only got $25 on the streets, and these guys aren't disgusting or anything! Three hundred dollars! This is so much fun! I want to be a star!"

"Wait, wait, wait! I don't want anyone to know you've agreed to this. You're Chastity, a star. You're not a prostitute. As far as everyone's concerned, Chastity thinks I negotiated more money for a bigger scene. She doesn't know the guys put up the bucks themselves so they could fuck her."

"What's the difference?" she groaned with a look of concern that he was going to lecture her.

"It's the Fourth Wall, separating performers from the audience. If you fuck the audience, you shift from being an entertainer to being a harlot."

"Oh, Jake, I don't care about that."

"Listen, give me your attention!"

"Okay, okay. I'm listening."

"You *are* a star. You must be treated like one. You're not a whore anymore. When they fuck you, it makes a difference. I told Janus to tell each and everyone one of them you think you're being paid more to do a bigger scene, that you don't know whose money it is because if you did, you'd be offended, being a wholesome girl and all."

"That's stupid! I want to be a bad girl, and I want to fuck Cody and whoever else I want. I don't see why I have to pretend."

"Because you are a professional. In this business you can't afford to be trash; at least not until you know what you're doing, which you don't. Think of yourself as special and people will put up more than just money for the honor of fucking you."

She studied him a moment then said with a little girlish lilt, "Professional! That's me! So what's next, Mr. Directorman?"

"Tell Janus and Fred to prep the scene, and to let me know when, or *if*, she needs me. You can do Cody, because the story requires that. But don't let anyone else touch you unless you're paid for it, and it's on camera."

"Aye, aye, sir," she saluted and walked off.

HIS MIND, numbing down, drifted into the twilight darkness and the rising of the full moon. He felt an odd pressure, a tension outside himself tugging at his attention. Suddenly he felt threatened, as if he were being shamed. He considered what Ben had said about a numinous charge being both a god and a devil. Why shame? Because he'd sent Chastity off to jump into a pit of wolves? No. More than that. But what? Why did he feel so bad? Why this sense of mortal danger? Then he felt a presence. Like a force emerging from another dimension, watching, judging; that if he were to offend, there would be consequences beyond anything he could ever imagine. *Why* was it here *now*?

The tension seemed to expand as it descended, coming directly at him. He instinctively turned toward it, speaking in a respectful voice, "I don't understand. I want to know what I should be doing, if what I'm doing is wrong, against nature. If porn's wrong. If I *knew* it was, and why, I wouldn't do it. Somehow I know, but don't know. Help me understand, so I can do what is right. I won't know how to do that if I don't know what I'm doing. Show me. I want to know." He paused. "Just don't be too rough with how you go about doing it, please." To his surprise the tension faded away.

"Wow!" said Ben, applauding. "Un-fucking believable!"

Startled, Jake turned around and found Ben standing fifteen feet behind him. "Asking *stupid* questions of an archetypal power is asking for trouble," Ben said, shaking his head. "Is porn wrong? Is it against nature? Help me understand! Don't be too *rough* on me! You should never try to engage power with a display of weakness, especially if you have no idea of who you're dealing with." He squinted, as if in pain. "No fucking idea of who you just asked to instruct you, much less the position you've put yourself in. *And* the answer to your questions is so freaking obvious. You covered that earlier, remember? Buddhists say biological assumptions get dying people stuck in the instinctual sphere where they're vulnerable to sexual energy pulling them into a womb. Caught in sex-related karmic loops. Born again into this inferior world. Porn re-enforces dirty minds, like an addictive drug, yet you —"

Jake interrupted. "Did you instigate the fifty-dollar-a-head deal to fuck Chastity?"

Ben looked surprised. "I did. Figured one way or another, you'd let her go for it, and that your doing so would activate the archetype I'd sensed the moment you arrived with her. Chastity has a vulnerable underage girl vibe about her, which led me to believe the archetype was Artemis, whose mental and spiritual growth had been arrested as a prepubescent. She's a tomboy who never grows up, a virgin who, among other things, is a merciless slayer of sexual transgressors. Not someone you can bargain with."

"Chastity's not underage. She's nineteen. I checked her driver's license."

"Booth will want to see her IDs. He has his doubts. Says she smells too young." He smacked his lips, then went on, "Myths are useful for understanding the effects of different aspects of archetypes. Greek and Roman myths started out as stories composed in attempts to understand archetypal experiences, a task you've just committed yourself to, as well. Artemis, as a vengeful aspect of the anima archetype, would not have gone peacefully into the night with your lines of crap. You asked *Her* not to be too rough on you!" He shook his head. "Considering your attraction to angry Artemisian women, I thought for sure She'd be the one activated tonight." He looked up into the darkening sky. "Aphrodite has a vengeful side, as well as one of grace. Could very well be Her. The longing in your voice. She could have responded to that. To your being a Pothos figure."

"Pathos?"

"No, that's an aspect of Greek drama. Pothos is the seeker of the unattainable, the incomprehensible. The idealization which is attendant upon all love, and always beyond capture. The driving force behind Eros. Oh! Of course. Looking at what you said in that light, that's what you were actually asking for. Wow! Hmm. If so, you've just set yourself up for a mythic chase after impossibilities and the fictive goals you must set for yourself."

"Aphrodite?" Jake said, skeptical. "The Greek goddess of love, beauty and lust."

"Yeah, I know it sounds a bit too convenient. I didn't consider Her because Artemis made more sense, especially after you cut Chastity loose. However, a vengeful Aphrodite could be appeased by your being aware enough to sense Her descent, and your looking directly at Her as you addressed Her in a respectful, longing voice. And, of course, there is your offering yourself up for an impossible quest." He chuckled. "Who knows, since your sex films have been mostly comedies, She might actually take on human form, like She did with Aristophanes. If She does, She'll announce Her presence with laughter. Homer referred to Her as *the sweetly laughing Aphrodite*. But that doesn't mean She's going to be sweet with you. Think of it more like a rattlesnake's rattle."

Before Jake could respond, he added, "Or, and I hope not for your sake. She could be Hekate who, as the Queen of the Underworld, is the shadow of Artemis." He fidgeted, grunting a few times, then spoke with a sense of urgency in his voice. "Hekate sometimes manifests Herself as a three-headed goddess, working in tandem with Aphrodite and Artemis. You may have just made a nonsensical pact with a pack of she-devils."

10

Shocks to the System

"I want a Bloody Mary," Jazz snorted as she entered Jake's house. "Better not be out of tomato juice." She headed for the liquor cabinet and noisily extracted a can of juice and a bottle of vodka (*snort!*), then jerked open the freezer (*snorf!*), grabbed a tray of ice and tossed it on the counter. A cube popped out and fell on the floor, (*snort! snorf!*).

"Gimme a cigarette," she snapped while slicing a lemon. She stuck a slice in her mouth to suck on while she mixed a Bloody Mary, some of which splashed on the table when she spat the lemon wedge into an ashtray. She took another cigarette from Jake, and glared at him while he lit it for her. She sucked in the smoke and slowly blew it out the side of her mouth as she said, "So where were *you* yesterday?"

"You talked to Janus?" He opened a bottle of brandy and poured it neat, knowing doing so would disturb her, having never seen him drink liquor straight before.

"That's right," she sneered, as if she knew what he was doing. "I talked to Janus."

"So then you know," he shrugged, taking a sip.

"So?" Her nostrils flared. "So you lied to me!"

"I did? How?"

"Don't play poor, innocent White boy with me! She told me what a *beautiful* couple you and your little blondie bimbee make, how you be lining up all kinds of work for *her!*"

"So what brought on this conversation with Janus?"

"Doesn't matter *what* brought the damn conversation on, it happened. I was talking to Janus, period! She told me the little White bitch worships you, hangs on your every word like she was your perfect little slave!"

"Why were you talking to her?"

"I can talk with Janus anytime I please! It's a free country. I've known her longer than I've known you so why shouldn't I talk with her? We talked, all right!"

"Yeah, right, like you and Janus are friends. You wouldn't talk to her unless you had a reason. What was it?"

"All right! She called to ask if I wanted to be in a video."

"I thought you were against doing porn."

"And I thought you were gonna let me *know* when you did one!" she snapped. "Anyway, it's not hard core or nothing. All I had to do was shave my pussy. Don't have to fuck nobody. They just film me shaving my damn pussy. Satisfied? Now what about you and your little slave?"

Jake sipped the brandy. "She's a teenager. I didn't take them seriously when I was one, and I'm not about to start now. Remember what you were like as a teen?"

"Why you giving so much of your precious time to get *her* a job and can't be bothered to do a damn thing for me?"

"Well, she has definite commercial appeal, no doubt about it. That could benefit me."

Her eyes narrowed as she blew smoke at him. "If this be so damned innocent, why didn't you tell me before?"

"As I've said time and again, because you're jealous. Look, we're no longer lovers. We're occasional fuck buddies. Even when we were lovers, you fucked around. You've always fucked around, yet you're still jealous of what I do. I don't talk to you about other women because you read shit into it, then fuck with them and me. You no longer have the right to know about my other relationships."

"I *do* have the right! I'm in love with you *and* you told me you love me! That *gives* me the right! So, did you fuck her?"

"I'm sorry, I'm not going to answer that."

"So tell me, was she better than me?"

"She's no threat. She's a kid. Her loyalty will shift to the first guy that comes along with more to offer who takes an interest in her. Helping her helps me focus on making things happen, something I haven't been able to do for a very long time. I hope our association will last long enough to be worth the trouble."

"And how long would that be?"

"Six months, if I'm lucky. But, in reality, I'd be surprised if it lasted a month." He hoped he was wrong, that Tracy valued him more than that.

"So, did you fuck her?"

"I can't be frank with you on these things, but..."

"Just answer the damn question! Did you fuck the damn bitch or not?"

"Well, since you put it so nicely. No, I did not. You can ask Janus, she can confirm I did not fuck her," he said. Rotten Robby had done it instead.

"Liar! You're a goddamn liar, and I hate liars!"

"All things considered, it's on you since you're a jealous, vindictive woman. I don't want to give out *any* information, so don't count on accuracy if I'm pressured to."

"I am NOT jealous! I'm *mad* because you're a low life liar!"

"And you're not?"

"That's right, I'm not! I may be a lot of things but I'm not a liar!"

"You're telling me you've never borrowed things from me, promised to return them, then turned around and pawned them?"

"I *said* I'd pay you back!"

"Well, you haven't and until you do, you're a liar. Intentions don't count for shit."

"I needed the money," she sneered, "and I knew you wouldn't give it to me so I had no choice."

"You're right, I wouldn't have, considering you already owe me a few grand."

"I was hungry and had to do what I had to do. I *said* I'd pay you back and I will, but *you* have no cause to be a damn liar." She looked away and took a quick puff off her cigarette. "I didn't get any sleep last night and I don't need this shit!"

"Okay, then just forget about it. I'm not interested in relationships. Not with her, not with you, not with anybody. I've got too much on my mind."

"You want a relationship, all right," she scowled. "All your precious little White girls have to do is snap their fingers and you'd go running on back to them."

"You still don't get it, do you. I will *never* go back to my ex, because I *lost all my trust* in her. Why can't you grasp the importance of trust to me? I can't and I don't trust you, and it's not like this is the first time you've heard me say that."

"You can trust me!" she screamed at him, her eyes full of hate. "You can trust me because I love you."

"Yeah, right. More harm's been done in the name of love than in the name of hate."

"Damn it! I'm divorced, too! People do shit to each other and there ain't nothing you can do about it except be happy as long as you can then curse the muthafuckers and be done with 'em."

Jake stared at her a moment with a dumbfounded expression.

"What?" she snarled.

"You going to say something?"

She looked at him askance. "You're a sorry ass muthafucker."

"We're not lovers anymore," Jake said softly. "If you keep this shit up, we can't be fuck buddies either. Maybe not even friends."

THE NIGHT'S residue of rain hissed against Jake's tires as he turned onto Folsom Street. The pale yellow streetlights cast a vaguely sinister air over the glistening streets of San Francisco's S&M district. Tracy's leather jacket would be appropriate here, he thought.

Tracy pointed at the entrance to a large building. "There it is."

There were several available spaces. Even on a stormy night he'd expected to have trouble finding a place to park. He pulled into a spot, and they got out of the truck.

"How long you been interested in leather and bondage?" he asked as he checked to see if she had locked her door.

"I've always liked the way bondage looks," she said as they walked toward the building. "It's way cool. And leather's fresh. I like the way it feels and smells. But I don't know anything about it, that's why I'm taking these classes."

"You never practiced before, then?"

"Oh, sure. Anyway I imitated the look, but I never actually did anything serious before I met Wormyham."

"What did he do?" Jake said, trying to mask his discomfort.

"He uses a soft leather whip that doesn't hurt much. And he ties me up and takes pictures, which was something I'd never done before. I wouldn't have thought I'd like being tied up and helpless and everything, but it was cool. Also, he talks dirty and hurts me a little."

"Yeah, well, at least he didn't cuddle you."

She rolled her eyes and pushed a buzzer on the side of a large glass door. "I hope we're not late. I'd hate to miss a meeting, especially this one since it's specifically about S&M. Oh, and next week's should be excellent, too. It's on tit torture. And after that there's a class on balls torture." She looked at his crotch. "I can't wait for that one."

He grimaced, remembering the searing pain of his nuts being twisted in the stockade.

A short bald man with thick glasses looked suspiciously through the glass door. "Hi!" Tracy waved. "I'm on the roster upstairs for the S&M class. He's my guest. I hope we're not too late?"

The little man glanced at Jake then opened the door. "We run on Pagan Standard Time here," he said. "It'll be a while yet before they start. We're expecting a few more stragglers. That'll be ten dollars, sir."

"Right," said Jake. He took out his wallet and opened it. *Only six one dollar bills!* There should be over three hundred dollars in there! Where could the money have gone? Tracy could not have taken it. She would have had to pick his pocket on the drive over. He put the six dollars on the little man's desk. "I think I'll get rid of some change."

He dumped his coins on the counter. The little man separated four dollars in change from the coins then handed him a receipt.

Tracy talked about the previous week's class while they waited for the elevator. Jake searched his memory for an explanation for what could have happened to the money. Then he froze. Jazz! *Revenge.* She was hurt, she needed to hurt him. They had talked of *trust.* A guest in his house —*a friend!*— violating his trust by taking money from his wallet. *Sick.* There must be some other explanation. It shocked him to think such a thing of a friend, yet he knew it was true. And it was not the first time.

"What's wrong?" Tracy asked. "You look so serious."

"Oh," he shrugged. "I was thinking about some unpleasant business. Sorry. I should keep my mind here."

"That's right, mister," she said, placing her hands on his shoulders.

Jake pulled her to him and gently kissed her forehead. She smiled contentedly, closing her eyes as he put his arms around her. *Such a sweet face shouldn't be here.*

"My bad girl doesn't like hugs and kisses, eh?" he said.

"No, I don't," she said, smiling.

"Well," he whispered, "that's what we're doing and you seem to be enjoying it."

She opened her eyes and shoved him away. "That's not fair! You tricked me!"

The little man opened the door for two obese lesbians, one of whom was in a wheelchair.

"You liked it, didn't you?" Jake said.

"I did not!"

The elevator door opened. They moved aside to allow the lesbians to enter first. They looked Tracy over as the elevator slowly crawled noisily up. The woman in the wheelchair winked at her partner. Tracy watched the floor numbers until the doors opened on the hall across from the classroom.

Tracy looked pale and nervous under the classroom's fluorescent light. Or was it excitement, Jake wondered. He scanned the room for anyone who looked under thirty. No one, except for an effeminate man with long hair. Two men in their sixties in the front row looked perfect for the part of Satanists. He wondered how these people looked to Tracy. Intriguing? Worldly? Maybe she just feels at home with any group that accepts her in their midst.

An obese, middle-aged woman near the podium, stood up.

"Hello," she said. "My name's Zenobia. Before I introduce to-night's speaker, I'd like to say a few things for the benefit of those of you for whom this is your first experience with Advanced Spiritual Workshops. This class is part of an on-going program of instruction in the fine art of Bondage and Discipline and S&M. There are a great many misconceptions about our crafts so we tend to emphasize the spiritual side of the disciplines since, after all is said and done, they are very much spiritual experiences."

"Amen!" said the woman in the wheelchair, while others in the audience chuckled in agreement.

"We're talking about *spiritual* power exchange," Zenobia said with an empathic gesture and beatific smile. "We create magic!"

"Amen!" said a Black woman around Jake's age.

What is this, a revival meeting? thought Jake, uneasy.

"The emphasis has always been on this exchange," Zenobia continued. "Both partners in a bondage and discipline or sado-masochistic relation-ship are giving and receiving power. Neither partner is superior to the other. In fact, for those of you here who are practicing, you know in spite of appearances the submissive partner is, if anything, the one in control."

"That's right!" said the elder of the two elders.

"More often than not, they hold the position of power in the relationship."

"Do they ever," said the woman in the wheelchair.

"Tonight's lecture concerns power exchange and our guest speaker comes to us from the Pagan community." She gestured to an effeminate youth sitting to her right. "In addition to power exchange, Ganymede will be discussing the importance of ritual and the connections S&M has with religion and spirituality. So without further ado, I turn the floor over to Ganymede."

Ganymede stood up to a spattering of applause and approached the podium. "Thank you, Zenobia," Ganymede said. "How many of you are familiar with Paganism? A show of hands, please." A third of the audience raised their hands.

Jake's mind drifted, trying to avoid thinking of the pack of she-devils. Instead he focused on Cedar, his ex, and her involvement with Pagans the year before she left him. He blamed them for the rapid deterioration of her integrity and grasp on reality. Her fascination with rituals had drawn her to them, whereas his distrust of it prevented him from recognizing the power rituals held over her. Whenever he went with her to one, he would wonder what an educated, ambitious, beautiful young woman from an upper class Southern family could possibly have in common with these people.

"Most people aren't aware of the connection between Paganism and modern Bondage and Discipline and S&M," said Ganymede. "To prove the point, of those of you familiar with Paganism, how many of you are aware of the connection?" Two people raised their hands. "That's good, that's good. Think about it, everybody. Can you see it? Think pain and restraint. Visualize the rituals. There you are, a few more hands. Good, good, good. You see, the connection is *very* real and, in fact, ritual pain and restraint," he raised a finger, pointing to the heavens, "is very much a part of *all* religious rituals."

Could the ritual Pagan, bondage, pain thing have a parallel between Tracy and Cedar? No, Cedar was adverse to restraint and pain. For herself anyway. Perhaps she fostered a secret desire to inflict it on others. Maybe rituals generated some kind of hypnotic power that tempts beautiful women to seek the company of trolls.

Ganymede called for a volunteer from the audience. He selected a young man in back, a straggler Jake had not noticed earlier called Trevor. He asked him to remove his shirt so he could demonstrate how ancient fertility rites used ritual flogging.

He then tied the nervous (or was it excited) youth's wrists together.

"Fertility rites were concerned by their very nature with death and resurrection, frequently requiring the bonding of victims, both animals and men. If the victim were human, as we have here, he would be *symbolically* killed or *symbolically* tortured, and the severing of his bonds would symbolize his resurrection, the return of the fertile season. In Christian rites, Christ on the cross, as a symbol, combined both sado-masochism and bondage. Christian art glorified Christ being flogged, his humiliation, the spear in his side, the crown of thorns. Oh! The crown of thorns!" Several people laughed. "And then there are the *saints!*" The audience laughed appreciatively. "Did any of the martyrs have a simple execution?" More laughter. "No. They had to be bound and exquisitely tortured. The importance of sadomasochism and bondage in the early Church was so strong that many a mad monk assumed the spectacle of flogging and bondage pleased their Lord and Master. Consequently, they designed elaborate forms of restraint and torment for heretics, infidels, as well as for themselves. Bondage and pain, as a favorite Christian motif, evolved into an experience of personal spiritual ec-stasy and redemption which, in turn, developed into modern S&M. But like all Christian ideas, the essential concepts pre-date them. The Christians borrowed heavily from Pagan rites."

Ganymede took a knife and cut the youth's bonds then faced the audience.

"Who *really* had the power? The Romans who nailed Christ to the cross, or Christ? The folks who martyred the saints, or the saints? What sort of power exchange took place? Who was redeemed? The *image* of suffering leading to redemption is the essence of the sadomasochistic experience. From this equation, the one who receives the pain is more empowered than the one who gives it. In spiritual ceremonies, the con-gregation identifies with the dying king, not with those who kill the king. In his death, they are re-born, cleansed of their sins. The one who inflicts the suffering is no more than a vehicle, albeit he is God's instrument and as such he does God's bidding. There is *power* in that, but no redemption."

Jake's attention drifted again. *Pain relieves guilt?* Cedar didn't like pain. But this is a symbolic expression of pain. Redemption by ritual-ized torture and restraint.

Ganymede told the youth to sit down then stepped behind him.

"We are now going to do an exercise in power exchange. Don't look behind you because you're going to entrust your sacred head to whoever is sitting there and the exercise works best if you don't know who it is. Most of you will have the opportunity to return the honor since you are the person behind whoever is in front of you. Allow me to show you how this works. I'm behind Trevor and I take his head by the neck, like so." Ganymede took a stranglehold. "Looks threatening, doesn't it? Trevor submits to me and I have the power to do *what*? But behind me, someone has me by *my* neck. In this position, you'll see whether your thoughts are dominated more by the one you oppress or by the one who oppresses you."

A woman in her late thirties turned to look at who was behind her. A forty-something male dressed like a kid. She grimaced like a trapped animal, baring her buckteeth. Jake gave her what he thought was a reassuring smile. Alarmed, she turned away.

"All right, everyone take hold of the head in front of you," Ganymede said. "Abandon your head to the hands of whoever takes it. Open up to the energy of both your oppressor and your victim."

Jake expected Horse Face to pull away at his touch. She shuddered and stiffened but did not move away. He flinched at the sudden sensation of hands on his neck, touching so lightly it would be easy to ignore. In contrast, his grip on the grimacing woman was firm, mostly due to his response to her tense muscles. What kind of person was touching him? Male? Female? Gay? Young? Old? Why should he care? A strange indifference to the woman he was touching, and to whomever was touching him gradually settled in.

His mind drifted, tuning out Ganymede's talk on energy transference. He no longer had any feeling, good or bad, for the spiritually homeless who resurrect ancient beliefs on which to project their needs, seeking redemption in a society that rejects their lifestyles by re-inventing a religion of atonement and ritual to absolve responsibility. Seeking forgiveness for being human. The Church of Consenting Adults.

When he was an adolescent, he and a friend had created their own religion. He invented the myths for the God No-doze and his prophets. His friend, who divined the rituals, actually came to believe in their religion. He remembered wondering at the time, *could he be serious?* That was how he now felt about the Pagans.

"Set free and be free," Ganymede said, taking his hands away from Trevor.

Jake glanced at Tracy, who was smiling, obviously pleased with the class. The person behind him stood up. He turned to see who it was. A tall effeminate man with long auburn hair who smiled at him as if they knew each other.

"Let's take a fifteen-minute break," Ganymede said. "I hope no one here smokes, but if you must, do it downstairs, please."

"Wasn't that great!" Tracy said. "Come on. I got to have a cigarette. Let's go downstairs."

"Do you know him?" Jake asked, pointing at the tall effeminate man.

"No," she said. "Should I?"

"He looks familiar."

"I've seen him before. He's been at all the classes I've gone to. He's kinda hard not to notice, being a guy with tits and all."

"Lars!" Jake said, remembering Mindy's video. "Let's talk to him." He took her arm.

"Why?" she said, resisting as they went to the door. Jake looked up and down the hall. Lars was gone.

"Let's get a smoke," she said, heading for the elevator. "You can talk to him after class." She pushed the lobby button. "I got a problem."

"What kind of problem?" he asked, as the elevator jolted down.

"Well," she sighed guiltily. "My roommate kinda told me I had to move out by the end of the month."

"By the end of the month? Why? What happened?"

"Oh, all sorts of things. Partly it's because a friend of hers is coming on the first and she'd rather live with her than with me. Partly it's because I smoke. And partly it's because of my friend, you know, the one I told you about."

The elevator door opened and they stepped into the lobby.

"What are you going to do?" Jake asked.

She looked down. "Wormyham wants me to move into his place."

"Is that your only option?" Jake asked stiffly.

"I don't know," she said with a little girl expression. "Maybe I could move in with you instead?"

Jake froze. "Is that it? Me or Worthingham."

"Well, yeah," she shrugged. "I mean, I haven't got the money to move anywhere else."

"What's your relationship like with him?"

She frowned. "He wants me around all the time. He wants to control me and tell me what to do. He's always lecturing me about things."

"I could be accused of those things, too, except for wanting you around all the time."

"That's different. He never listens to me. He doesn't take me seriously at all. I don't think he's interested in me personally. I'm like some *thing* to him and I'm not some *thing*."

"Okay, I know what you mean."

"If I were living with him he'd always be talking at me and wanting me to do things with him. And he drinks too much and gets like really stupid when he's drunk."

"So why were you attracted to him in the first place?"

"Please! I wasn't attracted to him. He's interesting and has a lot to say about things. I thought he could help me, you know. But I got tired of him. He's always saying the same things and he treats me like he thinks I'm really stupid or something."

"Where's your cigarettes?"

"Oh! I forgot." She took out a cigarette and lit it. "Could I have a puff?" he asked.

"Not unless you let me move in with you," she teased.

"If you don't give me a puff, I won't let you move in."

"Okay, but you hafta spank me tonight for being a bad girl."

"You definitely deserve a spanking. You've been a horrible little girl. Absolutely dreadful."

"Oh!" she moaned. "What'd I do, daddy?"

He took the cigarette from her. "Little girls shouldn't smoke. Stunts their growth." He took a drag.

She snatched the cigarette from him, took a drag and blew the smoke on him. "You're going to have to spank me extra hard tonight then because I'm going to smoke the whole thing right in front of you."

"Don't talk back to me, young lady, or I'm going to get you but good."

"Oh, yeah? Like what're you going to do?"

"I'll kiss you."

"No! Yeeeeech!" she stuck out her tongue.

"Then I'll tie you up."

"Mmmmmmm!" she smiled.

"Then I'll snuggle up and cuddle you and whisper nice things in your ears about how smart and beautiful you are and…"

"Stop it!" she protested.

"I'll plant loving kisses on your sweet cheeks!"

"That's disgusting!" she grimaced. Her face became serious. "You wouldn't really do those things, would you?"

"No, no no no no," he reassured her. "What do you think I am? A pervert?" She looked at him, uncertain. "There is one thing, though. Before you move in with me, you need to decide whether I have the right to love you."

"Oh, that'd be okay," she said.

"This is serious. Giving someone permission to love you is serious business."

"I know that. It'd be cool. I like it, just as long as it doesn't make you be too nice to me or anything."

11

Tempting the Fates

The dread and resistance which every natural human being experiences when it comes to delving too deeply into himself is, at bottom, the fear of the journey to Hades.

— Carl Jung, *Psychology and Alchemy*

GOING down to the men's room in the basement of the Market Street strip club had always been a low point for Ben, where doubts concerning his judgment and integrity would threaten to overwhelm him. He knew insights into the Underworld were more accessible at low points. One such low point was looking for a stall in the men's room in the bowels of a strip club to change his soiled underwear (a result of coming in his pants during a lap dance). The stalls down there were usually occupied, giving him time to stew among the men standing around looking for someone to suck their dicks. Time to tap into his discomfort and disgust, to prepare for his descent into the Underworld where he would attempt to see through to the sources of his fixations.

The men in the dimly-lit basement were unaware of the goddesses behind their compulsions. Unaware this was a place of worship. Unaware of the ritualistic nature of their perversions, that their desires (the source of all suffering) compelled them to gather here, worshippers oblivious to the reality of their being worshippers, unaware of the goddess they worshipped, or of absolution either sought or received. Unaware that they could not escape the psychic significance of what they did there. Just the sort of place for him to seek to see through into the hidden libido in the shadows.

Whenever Ben tried to isolate and grasp the content behind his overwhelming urge to seek out exotic young women willing to sell their Big Butts, he fell victim to the urge that had activated the compulsion. Eventually he realized he should be able to find a way to see through to the hidden image he sought from the vantage point of the Underworld energy represented in a place such as this. A place where goddesses were sure to notice the sole person capable of recognizing them for what they were.

From his training in archetypal depth psychology and his dealings with sexually deviant patients and prostitutes, he'd gained a great deal of insight into the Underworld. Enough to know he was running out of time, and that there'd be hell to pay if he failed.

Some years prior, Father Flanagan, a priest who'd referred patients to his clinic, told him of his interest in Galen, the Greek physician in the court of the Roman Emperor Marcus Aurelius. Galen's writings compiled the best of classical medicine and provided the form through which science was transmitted from the medieval period to the Renaissance. What intrigued Father Flanagan about Galen was his belief in the magical potency of the poo (*Flanagan's word choice)* of twelve-year-old boys. Galen used it as an ingredient in treatments for various afflictions. The priest also noted that up into the nineteenth century, most Christian ascetics ate human excrement, and that the practice had continued into the present day.

Flanagan admitted to having experimented with boy poo, even to having developed increasingly elaborate rituals in his search for its magic. Until he noticed something had gone horribly wrong. He couldn't sleep. He had strange fevers when his body temperature was low and was frequently disorientated in time, slipping into trance states. He stopped his rituals, disposed of his freeze-dried boy poo and went on retreat. His prayers calmed him, and he felt fine for a time, but inward pressures would build up again and again, until he became convinced he'd been somehow forsaken and was losing his mind.

Ben offered rote advice on obsessive thinking, wrote a prescription then penciled in an appointment for ten days later to allow enough time for the medication to kick in. Mostly, though, it was to give him time to decide what to do. He felt as if a bomb had gone off in his head, shattering everything that was him. Some part of him observed himself handing Flanagan the prescription, offering him encouragement.

When he returned to his body, he looked at the priest, feeling a kind of amazement Flanagan had been utterly unaware of his absence. He'd taken on his case largely due to the intensity of his resistance to taking it on. Something important in Flanagan had died.

Working with psychosexual deviants wears on the immune system. His patients were so charged with invasive energy, Ben had to construct and maintain elaborate shields and outlets. To help these patients, he had to establish connections with them, something that over time had gotten too risky for him, especially in his current frame of mind.

There was something in the way Flanagan had described the moment he realized he'd opened what he called the gates of Hell. Not so much what he said, as the feelings in his voice. Ben tried to explain how in the Underworld, the land of the dead, moral judgment does not exist. Neither does punishment, nor reward. But, Flanagan's literal consciousness and complexes held such sway over him, his world would shatter should he try to let go.

At that time it had not yet occurred to Ben that he, too, had been blinded by his own fixations. It did not occur to him until after the priest had walked off in a trance, after a morning mass, and met death under the wheels of a dump truck. That death could come for him in a similar fashion hit Ben hard. An unintended suicide.

All his knowledge and beliefs would provide no more protection than Flanagan's faith had given him. Ben gasped when he fully realized that among the methods he'd used to free himself from what he regarded as false identities, several of them had possessed him. He also realized, and had made a point of forgetting, his missing wife left him because she knew his obsession with the Underworld was poisoning her. He'd managed to convince himself once again he was immune because he did not want to fear his fixations, like Flanagan's Magic Poo, made him vulnerable to the undertow of the Underworld. Then came the disaster of the last hour of Riley's splatter movie, when he realized he was not immune.

Riley's degeneration, and those of other patients over the years, had inflamed his sense of running out of time. On his sixty-fourth birthday, Ben realized his time for transformation was now, or never. Flanagan was sixty-four when he died. Den master Franz was around the same age when he mysteriously disappeared.

The idea of what he might have accomplished, and of how little he actually had, sickened him. So much time spent obsessing over Big Butts, knowing full well it put him at risk of his instincts failing him by impairing his judgment at a critical moment. The charge he got from buying Butt was an addiction he really didn't want to let go of.

To ultimately break the hold Butts held over him, he had to return it to its source. Suicide was an occupational hazard for depth psycho-therapists who dealt with the depths. Riley's murderous descent had served as a warning. Murder, suicide by proxy. Riley had, by losing Katie, his outlet, lost control of his pathology.

He feared his own fate, should he short circuit as Riley had, would be a sudden seizure of the spirit and the threat of an impulsive suicide .

Upstairs, Jezebel the temptress awaited him.

Ben had sensed the part of Jezebel that dwelled in the Underworld. His description of the Underworld as a realm of essences, invisible eter-nal factors that are very much a part of life, had intrigued her. He told her the Greeks believed that to have depth and soul requires a relation-ship with the Underworld. Some part of us must feel at home there.

Jezebel told him some part of all the club's dancers dwelled in the Underworld. One way or another, Ben had to find the part of himself that was in the Underworld. From that vantage point, he'd be able to observe his catastrophes with a dark wisdom that expects little else. He felt the part of Jezebel that lived there would come to her, as well. When it did, they'd both find the place where they could lay their compulsions down.

JEZEBEL/CHANTAL sang along to a song blasting through the plugs in her head, unaware that Willow had entered the cramped dressing room.

> I have no excuse, just want you to use me.
> Take me and abuse me.
> I have no taboos to make a trade with you
> I'll do anything you ask me to
>
> Money talks, money talks, dirty cash I want you, Dirty cash I need you.
> *The trashy mood*, the bad girl rush from pulling off something spectacularly outrageous.

Control! Make them beg! *Traaa—sssssshhhhh!!!*

Then she saw Willow and the smudged eyeliner around her pale blue eyes. Jezebel pulled out her earplugs.

Everything about Willow was pathetic. Her limp hair. Her slumping shoulders. Her once fine tits and ass, crack had sucked the life out of. Garbage. The difference between *garbage* and *trash* was control. *Power!* Losers were garrrr-bahhhge.

"You're getting yourself pumped for the streets, aren't you?" Willow said. "You always listen to that song before you hustle."

"I have a date, as if that's any of your business."

"A *date?* Is it that old dweeb you spent the entire shift with last night?"

"You'll find out soon enough," Chantal said, annoyed. "He'll be here any minute."

"You can get fired for dating a customer, you know," Willow said, frowning.

"Hasib isn't going to fire me," Chantal said, examining herself in a smudged full-length mirror. "He knows a good thing when he sees one."

"If you gonna hustle, don't do it here. That way they can't find you if you don't want them to. My date turned out to be a religious psycho."

"If I get any kind of religious crap off a guy, I'm out of there. Your problem is you hang around. That's why the pervs, who get their jollies punishing people to save their souls, are drawn to you like flies."

"I didn't know he was religious," Willow whined. "He seemed normal to me. I sat on his lap for hours taking his money and he never once said anything weird the whole time. How was I to know?"

"You don't know what to look for. If you wait for them to start talking Jesus or Satan and crap like that, it's too late. Men are such idiots. One way or another, they let you know pretty damn quick what they're up to. If!!! you pay attention. I use my stage name, Jezebel, to spike the religious nuts so I know right off to avoid them. But speaking of pervs, what's with the tall tranny I saw you hanging with last night?"

"I've known him, I mean her, for like years. It's not like we're dating or anything."

"Well, *he* gives me the creeps." A knock distracted her. "You sure know how to pick 'em," she mumbled as she went to the door.

"Ready to rock and roll, Jezebel?" said Dr. Ben with a grin.

> It's in your bloodstream, it's like a bad dream. Money's a fiend, you know what I mean, I mean, I mean?

BEN AND JEZEBEL approached the limousine, double parked in front of the theater.

Ben swung the limo's door open. "John, this is Jezebel. Jezebel, Jonathan Booth."

"Pleased to meet you, Jezebel." Booth gestured for her to come in.

Jezebel sat beside Booth, then glanced over at an Indian, in an olive single-breasted linen sports coat, sitting alone on the seat facing her. Ben sat next to her.

"Penthouse, Christian," Booth told the chauffeur. Then, to Jezebel, "Ben tells me you're the hottest dancer in the Bay Area."

"And he told me you're doing a feature for Playboy," she said.

"He jumped the gun a bit there. My backers stipulated I do a hard core version first."

"Wait a damn minute!" she said. "This is porno?"

Ben touched her hand. "With a soft version for Playboy." Just a matter of money. Temptation. His for her Butt, hers for his Bucks.

She glared at him. "I said no porn. Is there something wrong with my English?"

"An unforeseen complication." Ben raised his right hand, fingers spread. "But the girls who do the X version get preferential treatment for his legit features."

Jezebel placed a finger on his chest and pushed in. "I don't like surprises." He looked her in the eye. She frowned then turned to Booth, shifting her hip back against Ben.

"We're going to my building," said Booth. "I want you to see our operation. This gentleman," he indicated the Indian, "is Douglas Spear. Best cameraman in the business."

"Where are you from?" Spear asked. "Where you were born."

"Saudi Arabia. Lived there till I was ten." Strange man, she thought. He seemed to be focusing on something behind her.

"She's a princess," said Ben, his fingertips touching his nose and lips as if in prayer. He enjoyed her fantasies, especially her being an exploited princess in a dark world, who's being forced to sell her Butt to a Jew (him).

"My father was a prince, but he was assassinated."

"My expertise is giving women the look," said Booth. "Douglas photographs them. What we do isn't pornography. It's beautiful."

The warmth of her hip against him reminded Ben of how she'd exposed an open wound under her hard shell with a look she gave him the first time she told him to stay away from her butt hole. He'd lusted right then and there to penetrate that psychopathic hole in her psyche. The urge, just thinking of it, made him flush.

"Could I have a moment alone with Jezebel?" Ben asked Booth as the limo pulled in front of a four-story building.

"Don't take too long," said Booth, getting out. "It's late."

When they were alone, Ben took a zip lock bag full of hundred dollar bills from his jacket. An odor like parmesan cheese wafted from the bag when he unsealed it.

He watched her hungry eyes. "I love your ass." His hand shook as it pulled out a bill then placed it on her lap. She cringed, as if smelling it with her eyes. He took out another. "I love giving you money, but you won't let me do what I want." She screwed up her face as he placed the second bill on the other. "I want your butt. I want to buy it."

"What is it you got in mind, baby?" she said, staring at his bag of bucks.

"I want to dig into your butt."

"No can do," she said, brushing the money off her lap. "My asshole's sacred."

"That it is, indeed," he smiled, thinking of her dance on stage, how she gave her audience a chance to worship her sacred portal by wiggling it in their faces. Child of Hecate, the goddess of the Temple of Temptresses who make sacred the waste of life.

He extracted another hundred dollar bill. "I want to buy your hole," he whispered as he placed it on her lap. She squinted at the bag, as if waiting for him to take out another.

She licked her lips. "You want your bone inside me?" She snatched the bag away from him then quickly gathered the rest of the money up and stuffed it all in her purse.

"I won't hurt you." He waved a finger at her.

"Got that straight," she said, rubbing his crotch. "Because you're not going to put your bad boy in my butt."

"Oh, you badass slut!" he moaned as she opened his pants, taking his stiff member between her warm palms, her active fingers stroking it stiffer.

She stripped down to her panties then, slowly turning her butt to him, she stretched herself out on her side on the seat. He stared at her nakedness, tinged a luminous blue from the street lights filtering through the tinted windows. He parted the lacy crotch of her panties to finger the wet mouth and lips of her sex. *Hades compels arousal.* Then he pulled down her panties. *Seizing souls through sexual fantasy.* He spread her legs, preparing to open her psychological gates. *RAPE, the entrance to the Underworld.*

"You piece of shit," he muttered under his breath as he sniffed her orifices.

Urgent blind passion, sullen and violent, building up into a sudden furious arousal to assault her false outer self. TO PIERCE! *Hecate, Dark Angel, silent witness of violation of the soul's struggles. Goddess of the Underworld, guide us to where she lives.*

"You can play with my butt cheeks, baby. But no touchy my asshole. Off limits."

"I bought your butt," he gasped through clenched teeth as he moved in close, seeking the invisible meaning in the sexual act glowing in her orifices, radiating need, lust and resentment, all the wavelengths in the spectrum connected to her soul. "Your butt's so beautiful," he gasped as he positioned his fingertips around her lower openings, silently chanting as he spread her cheeks. Presenting his tongue as he spread her holes open. *All of our life force, including pornographic desire, are reflections of the Underworld.*

"No way!" she yelled, tensing her butt cheeks and grabbing at his hands.

"Yes, way!" he exclaimed, forcing a finger up into her butt. As expected, something inside. Burnt offerings to the gods. No doubt the idea of people admiring her loaded Butt turned her on. *Child of Hecate. The Myth in the Mess.* A perfect image for initiation into the Underworld where the depths are not revealed to sight or touch, but to smell.

Only the sense of smell can discriminate amidst what is hidden. Bowels, the seat of the soul. Perceiving intangibles by intangible means.

The true nature of things, hidden in the most vile and rejected.

"Get your fucking finger out of my butt!" she exclaimed, jerking at his arm as he worked another finger in. Two fingers, deep in the mess, corkscrewing and thrusting in ways a penis could not. *To arrive at the basic structure of things, one must go into their darkness.* Visibilities are never enough for the soul. Invisible connections are stronger than the visible. Working a third finger in, he exclaimed in a heated whisper, "I want to pay you!"

"Get your goddamn fingers out of my fucking butt!"

"As you wish, milady," he said as he pulled them out. A smell like seaweed and algae rotting at the bottom of a pond. "Here you go, my dear." *What was held back comes forth* (his fingers moving toward her mouth) *released into the repressed, to set us free.*

"Mmmhmm," she grimaced, lips sealed shut, both hands fighting to keep his filthy fingers from her face while his free hand positioned his prick at her *Underworld Hole.*

"No, don't!" she pleaded through clenched teeth, his fingers moving between her lips.

"Your ass is mine," he grunted as he shoved his stiff staff against her tense aperture.

Rape, the central initiatory mystery in the Eleusis myths. Overwhelming violation. The initiation rites of the Eleusinian mysteries into the Underworld, a phallic parade where acts that seem shamelessly pornographic, or raving mad, are all held in secret. Something profound. Covered in shame. Hidden and invisible.

She shuddered as her mouth gasped open when he thrust himself into her below, clawing at air in mute protest as his filthy fingers slipped into her mouth.

He knew she'd entered her secret garden, where the part of her in the Underworld dwelled, when she started sucking hungrily on his filthy fingers.

"Grab hold and hang on tight!" Ben growled in an intense but low voice as he rolled her over onto her belly, "whilst I prod your filth!"

Gagging on his grasping fingers, she began to sob like a frightened child, moving her wet face back and forth while he furiously pumped his manhood into her.

When he turned her back over, face to face, she clutched and pressed herself so hard against him it felt as if they were no longer two people. They were so inter-penetrated they had become one wild, crying creature. "I own your fucking ass!" his hot breath huffed into her ear as he slammed himself into her. "Bought and paid for!" *Merge with it!*

"LET GO!" he screamed as her mouth clamped down on his fingers, her face on his, her salty tears washing his face as she wept. "*LET GO!!!*"

Then she exploded, and he *saw* the reflection of the disruptive element hidden in the mess and felt himself veering on the verge of knowing everything, the key to all initiatory mysteries! *All* the hidden events in the soul! He saw how the soul both wants yet resists being twisted into unnatural shapes. Something in it wants to remain in a fantasy of balance and harmony; but the moment a soul enters the natural world, the natural is not enough. Soul comes with an urge to make something of it. This urge to twist out of the natural is experienced as perversion, a shock of deformation.

Bringing an image close to death makes it live again, to perturb the soul to excess.

This was it! The point where they could both lay their complexes down!

He tightened his grip on her lower jaw then pulled it down, her hot foul gasping breath on his sour fingers. She was away, flowing in the wake of her waves, which were mounting and falling back behind his momentum. There was no time. She was about to hang again. He could feel it. That moment of hesitation between the past and the present, the habit and the adventure.

"You filthy, little Arab slut," his horrid breath hissed into her ear.

That whipped her over.

The first wave hit, a second spilled, the third and fourth and fifth came breaking over, and finally she was away, loose in the water, spraying liquid all over him, drenching him.

He was about to come when suddenly time stopped, and everything came at him at once. He saw the twist in his psychopathic hole and winced at all the information that came with it and what it implied.

"I know," he moaned, squinting as if in pain.

Then Jezebel bit down on his fingers and he screeched. His body went rigid, and he went blind. In the darkness he caught a glimmer of a shadow, a fantasy in the moment, like a shadow play. Caught in a desperate panic of possession that made him feel reckless, his body sobbed, and he poured himself into her. Pounding! Pounding! Then pain.

Then there was a void, where all the heat had been. He felt himself falling.

Losing interest in sex was a common feeling for him after an orgasm, but this was different. A vast vacancy. He could remember having been aroused, but not how or why. Reduced to words, not feelings. Images devoid of feeling. Words stripped of meaning.

"Get the fuck off me, you disgusting little weasel," Jezebel barked, shoving him off.

A light like a candle flame leaped in his gut, making him feel like a crouching, guilty small boy again. "Shit, that can't be good," he muttered, realizing she'd missed her moment. And by having merged with her, he was now vulnerable to her poison.

Hearing her noise, but not her words, he pulled a packet of wipes from his jacket and offered them to her. His complex had been laid down, but not the urge to twist. Which is normal. Jezebel, however, seemed significantly more hooked on biological assumptions. The weakening depth of her resolve to transform may have *offended* Hecate.

He'd been so sure of the strength of the child's resolve within her, of her inner eye of self-recognition. So certain if pushed far enough to where she felt small and ugly, she'd reach that merciful moment where reflection is possible, when a reversal of the stream of energy which now flows away from the idea and towards oneself where insight into projections is then a simple matter. The most painful part of this process is the recognition that through the previous attitude or behavior one has lost valuable time or has even, through one's sacred convictions, been guilty of serious misdeeds. He'd honestly thought it was her time, that she knew she would die should she fail.

Her anger appeared to be building, so he reached into his jacket for another envelope then handed it to her. A sulfuric scent greeted her when she opened it, but its contents pleased her, and she stopped bitching. She did yatter on and on, but now in a conciliatory tone while wiping and spraying herself with perfume and smoothing out her clothing.

How could he have been so damn stupid? Unbelievably stupid. Riley Theirault kind of stupid. Well, that is, after all, the nature of being possessed. Don't know your ass from a hole in the ground. Amongst the things he saw in his twist was how he blew it when he saw what appeared to be the shadows the priest had told him about. He'd gone blind just before his orgasm, when Jezebel bit him. It was in the darkness that followed he'd seen the jump of the shadows. His fear they'd come to possess him was the twist that made him vulnerable. What he saw of it concerned him, that he may have laid down the wrong complex, leaving him trapped in biological assumptions.

"I said, why aren't you getting dressed?" Jezebel yelled. "Hey! Anyone home?"

When Ben looked at her. He knew he should not be around her, nor anyone else, for that matter. He had to get away.

"I'm sorry," he said with a soulful expression he could not mask. "You go on ahead. I'll stay and clean things up in here." He realized, as he gathered up his piss drenched clothing, his eyes were tearing up. "Tell them I…" He froze, trying to adjust to letting things go the way they will without any further twists from him. "My presence isn't necessary. If they ask, tell them I went home. Is that okay with you?"

The look she gave confused him. She appeared to be a completely surface, no-depth material girl, yet he still sensed a recognition from the part of her that dwelled in the Underworld. A hidden depth behind the surface superficial sheen in her eyes. A flickering pattern within her physical reality. A reflection of his perception looking back at him through a looking glass. It did not want him to abandon her in the Underworld.

"Doesn't matter," said Jezebel, as if in response to what he was thinking. "Woman or man. Anyone with cash in hand. I want your money. It's in my bloodstream. It's like a bad dream. Money's a fiend. Know what I mean? Do *you* know what I mean?"

JAKE WAS SURPRISED by what he saw. Worthingham, a wealthy lawyer with a multi-million dollar real estate portfolio, lived in a run-down concrete apartment complex with a concrete wall around a concrete yard, where a cheap picnic table, lawn chairs, barbecue equipment and various tools were spread around on faded astroturf.

"Come on in," Worthingham called from inside. "Door's open."

Inside, the stench of cats, mold and dirt assaulted him. Old, cheap furniture and ticky-tacky bric-a-brac cluttered the living room. He'd met other wealthy eccentrics who lived like slobs, but they'd been somehow consistent, whereas Worthingham's expensive taste in clothing and personal hygiene would not have lead him to expect *this*.

"You own the building?" said Jake.

"No," Worthingham said as he entered the living room wearing old Bermuda shorts and a tattered t-shirt. "I've rented this apartment since law school. Over forty years."

"Really?" Jake said, looking around.

"Rent control. Three hundred a month. Can you believe it? I charge more than that for an hour of my time. Care for a beer?"

"Sure."

"Have a seat." He gestured at the couch and continued talking as he went to the kitchen. "It's not my only home. It serves a purpose, a kind of permanent impermanence." He returned with two cans of beer and tossed one to Jake. "Nothing here's worth stealing. Just the place for strays to stay."

Jake opened the beer. "So you don't live here?"

"I'm a busy man," Worthingham laughed, sitting down. "I don't live anywhere. Our girl says she plans on staying somewhere else. Could that be by any chance with you?"

"Yeah, could be."

"Could be?"

"I told her I didn't think it was a good idea."

"But you didn't say no?"

"I suggested she stay with you but she said she didn't want to because you don't listen to her."

"She's a kid, it's natural for her to feel that way. Tell me, Mr. Zakheim, are you fucking her?"

"Don't worry about me, she's interested in some kid who's in some kind of trouble."

"Eric Lehto? The motorcycle kid?"

"I don't know his name, but she says he's the reason she has to move."

"That's the one."

"Anyway, she's not the kind of woman I'd want hanging around. I'm in the midst of a divorce and I have no use for more grief from women."

"That's the difference between you and me, Mr. Zakheim. You see, I don't care what she does as long as I get her for a couple of years. After that, she can do whatever she wants and I'll replace her with another kid." He took a drink. "I want her to stay here."

"Look, she'll be able to afford her own place in a month or two. She thinks if she moved in with you, it'd be a problem because she'd owe you."

"Talk to her for me. I'm not expecting much from her, regardless of what she thinks. All I want is time, we can negotiate how much."

"Sounds reasonable. I'll talk to her, but before we get down to business, I'd like to discuss your niece. She has a problem."

"What kind of problem?"

"Some nut's been making threatening phone calls. Apparently he knows about the video and he's accusing her of being in league with the devil for being in it. He's threatened to tell her parents and have her declared an unfit mother to keep her from her baby. We don't know who he is but I suspect he's someone from the shoot."

Worthingham grinned. "A phone sicko, huh? Well, Moira has a strange relationship with phones." He went to a bookshelf and pulled out a cheap photo album. "This might shed some light on the subject." He opened the album and pointed to a newspaper article taped beside a photo of a three-year-old girl with haunted eyes. "Read this."

CRYING CHILD FOUND SITTING ON BODY OF SLAIN WOMAN

SAN JOSE — A crying young girl was found sitting on the body of a dead woman in a field Wednesday morning, police said. The body and child were found about 7:10 a.m. by a man in a parked car near the field and a woman bicyclist in the area. The man went for police while the woman waited with the child. The dead woman was clothed but lacked shoes and was lying on her back, said police Lt. Sedona Silver.

"It appears she was killed at the scene," homicide Lt. George Gross said. He said the woman had multiple wounds and extensive bleeding, but he would not discuss what caused the injuries.

The child, believed to be two or three, was sitting on the body, covered with blood, saying "Mommy, Mommy," police said. The girl was taken to Children's Hospital for treatment of hypothermia, then turned over to Santa Clara County's Child Protective Services.

"Good god!" Jake muttered. *Child covered with blood, sitting on her mommy.* Mommy! Mommy! All night. Freezing. "That kid went through hell."

"Yes, she did. Hell on earth. A very special child."

Jake pointed at the photo. "Is this her?"

"Want to see more?" He turned the page to a series of photos of her at different ages.

The child looked strangely familiar. "Moira?" he said.

"She's entitled to be a bit peculiar, don't you think?"

"Oh, my god," Jake muttered, chilled.

"She would be an unfit mother indeed, if she had a child. Her kid and the demons who pursue her exist only in her mind."

"She didn't say anything about demons," Jake said, trying to focus. "No demons. Just some religious nut accusing her of desecration."

"Mr. Zakheim, what do you think demons are?" he said with a little smile. "They're God's cops, His prosecutors. Satan is His chief of police and attorney general, whose job it is to tempt and trap sinners, then convict them and send them straight to hell."

"How could you allow *her* to do a porno?"

"When my sister saw that article, she was bound and determined to adopt that child, and she did. Sis may have indulged her a bit much, but as you can see, Moira's a very special girl. She's been to hell, and if she came back with a few demons in tow, no surprise there. Even if this nut does exist and he calls my sister, nothing he has to say would make a difference."

"Her parents know about the porno then?"

"Let's just say they wouldn't be surprised. You seem to have taken an interest in my niece. A word to the wise, my friend. Don't get yourself involved in her fantasies."

"Could you excuse me a minute." Jake rose unsteadily to his feet. "I have to use the bathroom." He *was* involved in her fantasies. "The beer went right through me." What an unholy mess.

"First door to the right, down the hall."

The doorknob in the warped hollow core bathroom door was loose. Screws missing. Inside, a mess of discount lotions, creams, soaps and cosmetics scattered across the toilet tank, the edge of the grimy bathtub, the sink, and along the bathroom window.

The sickeningly sweet scent of cat shit and hair burned his eyes.

A flea jumped on him as he lifted the toilet seat. He averted his eyes to avoid looking at the thick ring of scum in the bowl and piss stains on the floor.

Moira grew up with demons, and this man, her *uncle*. He did not want to be a part of her nightmare. He lacked the energy, as well as the conviction he could make a difference. The time he could and would have helped had passed.

"I don't want you to get the wrong idea about what I said, Mr. Zakheim," Worthingham said when he returned. "If you want to fuck my niece, go ahead. That's entirely up to you both. But Tracy is a different matter. When I sent her to you, I placed my implicit trust in you as an honorable man not to fuck her."

Jake did not sit down. "*You* can tell *her* what to do and jump her butt if she doesn't do it, but don't take that stance with producers. I told her not to fuck anybody in the business without my say so because things have a way of getting out of hand, but it would never occur to me to tell producers not to touch her. It would embarrass everyone concerned, including her."

"You finished? Good. We were going to discuss my investing money in your project. You have the budget breakdowns?"

"I don't feel right about this. Having an investor with emotional baggage is dangerous business. When she's a star, she will lose interest in both of us and you may hold me responsible for that. I don't need the grief. I can't control her."

"Excuse me, Mr. Zakheim, but I'm beginning to think you are fucking her."

"Think what you like, but for me this is an issue of control. In entertainment, control is everything. I can't have people threatening and ordering me around. If you can't control her, that's your problem. Don't expect me to control her for you."

"There are plenty of girls out there just like Tracy. I can introduce you to some who so outclass her it's not funny, and I wouldn't care if you fucked them all. I'll send them to you as a favor, gratis. All I ask in exchange is that when I send you a special girl, special to me, I want to trust you not to fuck her."

"Don't send me your special girls. This business is for consenting adults who make up their own minds what they do. I can't be bothered by jealous husbands or lovers."

"She's not worth it. I've found her to be a liar. She's selfish and she's frigid. She's a bit crazy herself. A little pervert. Can't enjoy normal sex. But then you would know that if you fucked her, wouldn't you?" He glared at Jake. "Did you know she's a Satanist?"

"No, I did not know that." He felt pretty sure she wasn't.

"Have you checked her for disease?"

"No. Why?"

"She's okay as long as everyone wears a condom. Her crazy boyfriend claims she gave him venereal warts. And she probably has herpes, and lord knows what else."

"You knew all this when you sent her to me?"

"I told her to tell you so you'd make sure everyone wore condoms. I would have told you myself but she really should be the one to do that."

"Well, that's the sort of thing that has to be made clear up front since if she passed on a disease it'd kill her career. So, tell me why would you want to hang with a kid with so many problems and diseases?"

"Oh, I'm not worried about disease. I don't fuck her. There are things I want to teach her, things she wants to learn, things she must learn. You got me wrong, Mr. Zakheim. I know better than you how smart she is. Believe me, you don't want her. She's more trouble than you can possibly imagine."

"I HEARD YOU dated a customer last night," Hasib said, pulling into his parking space.

Jezebel released her seatbelt. "Willow tell you that?" she muttered. "She's just trying to get back at me."

"Sweetheart, I don't care about that. What I do care about is hustling. It makes you look bad, and that makes me look bad."

"I wasn't hustling! He's a talent scout for Playboy. He took me to meet a producer who offered me the lead in a movie."

"What's the name of this producer?"

"John Booth."

"Booth. I've heard of him. He's a vice cop."

"He's an *ex*-cop."

"Certain types become cops. Lower class control freaks and power junkies who lack the brains or guts to get their fix any other way."

"That's why he quit. He's into class. He lives in a penthouse on Nob Hill and has a limo and a chauffeur. I had to see him last night because they start shooting Friday."

"Cops are always pushing because of some urgent business that can't wait," said Hasib. "A vice cop who quits to do porn, I don't like the sound of this."

"You said I could be in movies if I wanted," Jezebel pouted.

"Are you working a full shift today?"

"Yes, of course." She leaned forward for a kiss.

"You heard me," said Hasib. "I don't want you dating customers. If you bring shame on me, I will not put up with it."

"YOU'RE DISGUSTING!" Willow hissed at the face in the grimy mirror. An artificial eyelash had fallen off. Her natural lashes were so sparse her eyes looked enormous without artificial ones. Did they fall off on stage? *God, I look crazy.* She slapped herself. "People hate you! They want you dead!" She punched her face with her fist. "I hate you! Hate you! Hate you!" she screamed, striking her face again and again. "Die! die! die!" She stopped, then squinted at her swollen, lopsided face in the mirror.

"What happened to you?" Jezebel asked when she entered the room.

Willow wiped the other eyelash off her cheek with a dirty towel, saying, "Oh, some crazy person attacked me."

"WHY THE FUCK you driving so slow?" Jazz said as Jack slowed down a block from his house.

"Looking for a parking place." He scanned the quiet dark street.

"Not back here, you ain't. I'm not carrying nothing that far. Double park if you have to but we gonna unload this sucker in front of your damn house." She glared at him. "Why you looking at the roof? You planning on parking on the damn roof?"

"Uh, I was thinking about something," Jack mumbled.

"Well, keep your damn mind on the road. Wait! Wait! Stop the damn car!"

"What's the matter, Shredder?" He stopped.

"That's your house, ain't it? Let's unload the damn groceries and you go park while I start the salad."

He placed a hand on her thigh. "Wait a minute."

"Well, come on, spit it out."

"I'd rather we stayed together."

"What is it, old man? What's wrong?"

"Nothing's wrong. I'd just like to go in with you."

"Don't fuck with me, Joaquin. What's wrong?"

He sighed. "I'll tell you later."

"Now! I want to know *now*, damnit!"

Joaquin parked a half a block away and shut off the engine. He took two of the three bags and handed her the third then scanned the other cars on the street.

"You in trouble?"

"No." He opened the door, avoiding eye contact.

"You're in some kind of trouble," she said as he got out.

When they reached his door, he said, "Hold one of these while I unlock the door."

She took a bag and watched him fumble with his keys. "You gonna tell me what's going on?" The phone rang as they entered the house. "You gonna answer that or what?"

He motioned her to stay put. "The machine will pick up."

"*Click.* You've reached White Line Productions. You may leave a message for Joaquin Spannamaker or Julie Jodorowski. *Beep!*"

"'Allo, Joaquin, old bean," a male voice said through a background of static. "I see you are 'ome non-alone. A mutual friend asked me to play you this fine melody."

You say you're going to leave me, tonight's the night. You say you're ... Jack shut the machine off.

"That was the worst fake English accent I ever 'eard," she snorted. "Sounded more German or Russian, one of those."

"You have to help me load the guns."

"Help you what?" she said as he pulled her toward the bedroom. "You better tell me what the hell's going on." He unlocked the gun cabinet and tossed two shotguns, a 357 magnum, a rifle and two small pistols on the bed.

"You expecting them to kick down the door or something?"

He dumped the contents of the ammunition drawer on the bed.

"No," he said, opening a shotgun.

"Then slow down, take it easy." She picked up the magnum. "This baby's mine."

"You know your friend, the one who said I had a PhD in crack?"

"Oh, no!" She put the gun down. "I'm not getting mixed up in no drug fight."

"Look, Shredder, you're the one who took me to that house."

"You're a crazy muthafucka! What the fuck did you do?"

"Nothing!" he snapped. "Nothing! Your friend, Rodney X —"

"That low life nigger's no friend of mine. Don't tell me you did business with him again after what happened the last time."

"No, well, yes. All right, it was a stupid thing to do but I was low on cash and he gave me credit. Here he calls me Doctor Crack then unloads crap on me. I refused to pay until he made good."

"Old man, you wanna die, don't you! Damn fool, you expect me to die wif you? You bent, Jack!"

"Let me finish! What happened was Rodney got busted trying to break in. The neighbors called the cops. Turned out he had a couple outstanding warrants so they locked him up. Couple months go by then this jerk with the phony accent starts calling saying Rodney's out looking for me."

"Man, I told you, didn't I? Don't be doing no business with low lifes. They rip you off then dog you like it was you who ripped them off. Low lifes on dope are crazy, and you crazy doing business wif 'em. You stand out. You white. You old. You got a new van. When they sees you coming, they gots to rip you off. If you want to get yourself killed, fine, but leave me out of it!"

"They're out there. They'll grab you if you go out. You have to stay the night."

"What you talking about? It's you they want, not me. It's your own damn funeral."

"Shredder, I've been there for you. I take you where you want and stick by you."

"There!" She snapped a magazine into place. "I helped you load your damn guns. There's nothing says I gots to shoot the damn thing."

"Look, there's more to this then the dope thing."

"What you mean?"

"I mean, no one's mentioned it."

"Yeah, like they're going to talk dope on the fucking phone."

"It's a feeling," he said.

"How's this for feeling, I feel you should call me a cab."

"Shredder, they saw us come in together."

"Then they can see me leave." She stood up.

"He claims he's the devil."

She sat down. "He's fucking wif you."

"Don't you feel something?"

She looked towards the living room. She sensed an oppressive aura of danger in the silence. "Okay, I'll stay, but you owe me, old man. And keep the damn safeties on. Don't want nothing going off by accident."

"Don't you think it'd be a good idea to leave a couple..."

"No, I don't think it'd be a good idea!" she said. "I may be crazy but I'm not stoop-id."

12

The Hard Way

Jake shuffled through the clutter in his section of the garage then stopped when he came to what had once been Cedar's work area. Strictly off limits. He'd left it the way she'd left it the day she moved out. Empty, except for a few cans of paint, a jar of body filler and assorted garden paraphernalia. Accepting her spirit had departed was painful enough, but accepting her space was now his to do with as he pleased tormented him.

She used to call him her Lard and Messer and, no doubt, expected him to revert to being a slob without her around to keep him in line. To prove her wrong, he'd kept the house in order, until it finally sank in that she no longer cared what he did or did not do.

She would never drop by. Their life together was over.

He kicked a battered box of film cores from his space into the emptiness under her workbench. Then he spotted a single little beige glove on a shelf with leather bands on the knuckles and a hole at one of the fingertips. Cedar liked beige. Beige clothes, beige car. He picked up the glove, seeing her coming in from the garden to snuggle, smelling of sunshine. Pulling off her gloves. Looking at him. Her beautiful eyes. Her bright smile. His happiness and trust was so intense he believed their love would last forever.

His face tightened. They would never do anything together again.

"Oh, God!" He grabbed hold of the workbench to steady himself as an onslaught of pain shattered any illusion he might have had he could control those memories.

Crying will let off some of the pressure, he thought as he sank down onto the cold, dirty floor. *Let it be.* He rubbed his damp face against the dank cement, inhaling dust, struggling to let go of the pain, to turn away from hurtful things. He had misjudged, seeing depth when there was only surface, believing in something that wasn't real.

He felt himself pulling away, as he had when he let go of the part of him that had once been Cedar, going to a place where a detached part of himself could watch his writhing body from a safe distance.

Rrrrrring! Four rings and the machine would pick up. He re-entered his body and attempted to get up. Rrrrrring! He was up! Two more rings. *Hurry!* Rrrrrring! He moved quickly, hoping whoever had broken the spell would not hang up if the machine picked up before he did. Rrrrrring! He grabbed the phone.

"Hold on! I'm here!" He turned the machine off. "Hello?"

"Hi-eeee," said Moira. "How are you? I haven't heard from you in a while."

Oh, Christ, he thought. "Hi. Been busy. Trying to get something going. Got to make money sometime, you know."

"Did you talk to Mindy?"

"No. Why?"

"The creep called her."

Jake sat down. "What'd he say?"

"He said she was unfit to be a teacher."

"He knows she's a teacher?"

"Lots of people know that. What's really scary is he's calling producers, telling them I'm diseased and unreliable and I have a doper boyfriend. Now no one'll hire me."

"Don't worry about it. Who pays attention to anonymous lunatics."

"Wrong! I've already lost a gig because of him. Would you hire someone you didn't know who's being stalked by some sick-o?"

"Well, depends on the woman."

"Precisely," she said.

"Okay, maybe we should arrange a meeting with this guy."

"Are you kidding? He's crazy. No telling what he'd do."

"Meet him in a public place where I just sort of happen by and join in on your nice, pleasant conversation."

"He'd never fall for that," she said, impatient. "Jake, I need to see you. Can you come over? You don't have to stay long or anything. I know you're busy, but please."

He thought of the poor, frightened, abandoned child in the article. Now he was part of what was happening to her.

"Jake, please! I'm scared because...," she hesitated.

"Yes?" Could he be of any real help?

"Oh, Jake, it's too weird. I'd rather, I'd feel better telling you face to face."

"Hint me."

"Then you'll see me?"

"I'm not sure when. I'll call back as soon as I know."

"Today?"

"What's your problem?"

"All right! All right!" she said. "He said he's sending a demon to my house."

Jake remembered what Worthingham said about her demons and delusions. He wanted no part of this. "And you believe him?"

"What does that matter? We're dealing with a sick-o here. That's enough to make me afraid to leave my apartment."

"Well, maybe it's time to call the police—" He stopped, realizing his mistake.

"The *police?* You serious? You ever deal with the *police?* If they did anything it'd be to put me in some institution."

"Okay, then, get him to arrange a meeting."

"He won't go for it. That's not what he wants. Please come over. Please!"

"Okay, all right, I'll call when I can," he said hurriedly.

"Okay," she said meekly. "Love you."

"Bye," he said and hung up. *I don't need this.*

He looked up Mindy's number and dialed. The phone rang several times. "Hello?" Mindy said.

"Good, you're home. I just had a talk with Moira about some nut who's harassing her. She said he called you as well."

"He's done more than that. He convinced Channel Seven a public school teacher, me, makes porn films and they sent a news crew over to the high school."

"Whew! I bet that went over big with the administrators. What happened?"

"We denied it, of course," she said, matter-of-factly. "Sounds like a crank call to me."

"They believed you? The administrators?"

"Sure, why wouldn't they? There wasn't anything to go on except for an anonymous tip."

"Aren't you in the least bit concerned about what might happen when the video's released?"

"Jake, if I worried about what lunatics might do, life would be hell. Besides, he'd have trouble proving anything since, unlike Shannen, my face doesn't appear in the video, and no one wants the kind of exposure they'd get from being a witness."

"Are you saying he bothered Shannen, too?"

"You don't know? He tracked down her parents and sent them a video with her in it. The bastard sent one with her in a triple pen."

"Jesus." He imagined her devout parents seeing their daughter with pricks in her mouth, cunt and ass at the same time. "What a flaming shit heel. I remember her saying the only thing that worried her about doing porn was her parents finding out. How the hell did he find them?"

"Who knows. Apparently he's resourceful."

"Moira said he threatened to send a demon after her. Did he say anything like that to you or Shannen?"

"We didn't give him the chance. Figured he was a crank and hung up."

"What about his voice? Could he be someone who was at the orgy scene?"

"He didn't sound like anybody I know."

"Perhaps he knows somebody who was there, like Worthingham?"

"Worthingham?" she said, thoughtful. "He's twisted but ... I don't think so."

"Twisted? What do you mean, twisted?"

"He's into kids. Goes to Thailand a couple times a year to be with kids."

"Oh, brother," Jake groaned.

"Apparently plays around with local runaways, too. He asked Janus if she could get porn work for a fifteen-year-old."

He felt a jolt. "When was that?"

"When he asked her? I think within the past month or so."

"That's sick," Jake stammered. "Yet you don't think he could be involved in this?"

"He's one sick puppy, I admit, but he's too clever and has much too much to lose to get involved. I mean, why would he?"

"Sick puppies like to roll in shit. Anyway, give it some thought and call me if anything occurs to you. I have to go." He hung up, his heart pounding as he took Worthingham's card off the bulletin board and dialed. He stared at the card while the phone rang. Berkeley number and address, name, no reference to work. A calling card.

"Hello. Don't hang up!" said Worthingham's voice, mimicking a Hungarian accent. "My name is Boris Meatloaf and I bought the space on this message from the gentleman who lives here. Relax. The beep is coming up and you can leave your message for him in a moment. But first I'd like to say a few words about cemetery plots."

Jake hung up. "Is this guy nuts, or what," he mumbled as he fumbled through his phone book. "Chickenhawk." He dialed Janus. The phone rang several times.

"Hello?" Janus said in the small tentative voice of a person accustomed to receiving unwelcomed calls.

"Hi, it's me, Jake. You sound tired. Did I wake you?"

"Oh, no," she perked up. "I thought you might be somebody else."

"Sorry to disappoint you."

"Oh, no, I was hoping you weren't him."

"You heard about the nut who's been harassing women involved in Mindy's video?"

"No, no, this is something different."

"Not related?"

"Yeah. Personal."

"I've been trying to figure out whether Worthingham's involved. He could be putting somebody up to it."

"I don't see why he would."

"I heard he asked you about finding porn work for a fifteen-year-old girl. Is that true?"

"Yeah, but he didn't say she was fifteen. He put her on the phone and she said she was."

Jake covered the mouthpiece of the phone with his hand to avoid breathing into it while she spoke, remembering how Cedar use to breathe into the phone when she was tense. He took his hand away to say, "Remember anything she said that might help identify her. Like measurements, hair color, height, uh, background. Anything?"

"No. She told me right off she was fifteen, or whatever, and after that I didn't want to hear any more. I was furious with Will for putting me in jeopardy. Who knows who could be listening in."

"Yeah. I think we should be suspicious of him, keep him at arm's length. Don't give him information on anybody, especially me. If he is involved in this harassment thing, he'd make use of any scrap of information he got his hands on. You clear on that?"

"Yeah, sure."

"You already let me down by blabbing to Jazz about your video. Don't do it again."

"Jasmine got mad?" Janus said, surprised. "I thought she'd think it was exciting."

"I told you not to say anything. That means, *no* information about me good, bad or indifferent to people I consider jealous or crazy. Right?"

"All right."

"Okay, thanks. Got to go. Bye." He hung up and considered Tracy's peculiarities. It was possible. She could be fifteen. That would explain a lot. Rrrrrrrrinnnnng!

He picked up. "Hello?" he said, tentatively.

"Jake?"

"Yes. Who's this?"

"John Booth. I'm calling about a couple of things. First, I got the funding for the Playboy feature and I'd like to talk to Chastity about being in it. Could you bring her over tonight?"

"I'd, uh, have to see if she's available." *Breast implants. A doctor should know the difference between a fifteen-year-old and a nineteen-year-old, right?* "What time?"

"Anytime between seven and eight."

"Sounds good. I'll give you a call if she can't make it."

"Come anyway," said Booth. "I understand you do scripts. We could discuss that."

Jake inhaled slowly. "Okay." "Excellent. See you then."

He stared blankly at the bulletin board until the dial tone prompted him to hang up. He couldn't think. A little while ago his energy had crashed but now he felt on the verge of exploding. The mood swings bothered him. Another crash could incapacitate him.

Oh, fuck! Jazz was coming over! He planned to confront her over the three hundred dollar theft. Four thirty, she would have left work by now, would be on BART on her way over. He could take her home on his way to see Booth, as long as Tracy was not with him. Of course, first he had to be certain Tracy was of age. He dialed her number. Odds were she would be out and that would be that.

"Yo!" Tracy said.

"Tracy?" Jake said, hesitantly.

"Yeah? Jake?"

"I have to ask you something important. Promise me you'll tell me the truth."

After a long pause she said, "Okay."

"Janus told me Worthingham had an underage girl call her for work in porn." He paused. "Was that girl, by any chance, you?" Her silence chilled him.

"Yes," she said.

Jake closed his eyes and leaned against the wall.

"But he told me to say that," she continued. "I'm nineteen, like I said. You can check my ID, it's all legit. I don't know if I should say this because he has helped me out. All right, well, Wormyham has this thing for little girls. He liked pretending I was twelve, that was before my tit job. He thought I'd make more money passing as underage, plus my parents would never find out since it's illegal and all. When that didn't pan out, he lent me the money for my tits."

Jake sighed. "That's true? You're telling me the truth?"

"Of course, it's true! I wouldn't lie to you, honest. I couldn't anyway because you'd find out eventually. Besides, I'm a college, not a high school student."

"All right, I believe you. There's something else. Wormyham told me you have venereal warts and herpes."

"Oh!" she growled. "He's doing this because I wouldn't go out with him last night. Look, I had warts but the free clinic took care of them, but I have to go back to be sure they're gone. I don't have herpes, it was just some kind of rash, and I don't have any other diseases either. I was checked for everything. That's why I got all those condoms, so I won't get any."

"Right," he said, thinking it unlikely she'd got them to protect anyone else. "Booth called. He got the money from Playboy and he wants me to bring you by tonight."

"That's great!"

"Bring all your IDs. Everything. California ID, college ID, social security card, birth certificate, passport. Whatever you have."

"Okay. When will you be here?"

"Around six, if traffic's no worse than usual. We'll go straight to Booth's."

He hung up and went to the bedroom to change. What to do about Jazz? He could leave her alone in the house while he went about his business, or put her back on BART, or leave before she arrived. Disorientated by adrenaline, he found himself staring into his closet trying to remember why he was staring into his closet.

Must focus my energy! Okay, get dressed, that's it! He scanned his wardrobe but everything looked wrong, unacceptable, and the harder he looked, the worse everything looked. Rrrrrrinng! He breathed faster. He could let the machine pick up. Since she stole from him, why concern himself over leaving her at BART?

He picked up the phone, hoping it wasn't Jazz. "Hello?"

"It's me," Jazz said. "Come and get me."

"YOU WERE QUICK for a change," said Jazz as she got into his truck. "Something must be up." She wore a black t-shirt with *You're Twisted, Perverted and Sick. I Like That in a Man* scrawled across it.

Jake stared at her, drawing a blank on what to do. He started back to his house. "You're quiet," she said. "What's wrong?"

"There was at least three hundred dollars missing from my wallet after your last visit. Did you take it?"

She laughed. "You came right to the point for once. Must be because there's money involved."

"Did you take it?"

"Yes," she said.

"God!" he groaned. "Why in the hell would you do that?"

"You hurt me and I wanted to hurt you back the only way I know that works. Hear me and hear me well. If your precious little wife hadn't taken so much of your money, you'd've forgotten all about her by now."

"Don't give me any of that crap," his voice thick with emotion. "This is about trust. A basic violation of trust."

"Well, if that isn't a statement in of itself," she said defiantly. "The one who's violated trust here is you. You're a damn liar! A liar's worse than any damn thief."

"You will return that money," he said barely containing himself.

"I can't," she said. "I spent it."

Jake breathed heavily, trying to compose himself. "You came into my home as my guest, you slept in my bed and while I was asleep, you took money from my wallet and then *spent* it! You've done some awful sleazy shit, Jazz, but this is too much. You crossed the line. You tell me over and over how I can trust you, and you do something like this! Have you got shit for brains? How in the hell can I trust anyone who behaves like that?"

"You don't have to *yell!*"

"I wouldn't have to yell if you'd pull your damn head out of your fucking ass! I am sick and tired of your not hearing a word I say. For once in the bloody fucking hell I'd like what I said to register! Do you hear me, bitch!"

"Don't you *ever* call me bitch!"

"You're so fucking full of crap." He pulled into his driveway, got out of the truck, unlocked the front door and glared at her. He sensed she was intimidated but she walked right in, head held high.

"I need a drink," she said.

He went to the liquor cabinet, took out a bottle of his cheapest red wine, uncorked it and glanced at the clock. Not much time. He put the bottle on the table, grabbed a couple of wine glasses and placed them by the bottle. He tossed a pack of cigarettes at the ashtray then sat down and stared at the kitchen floor until his anger subsided.

He had no real urge to punish her, to inflict suffering, whether she had wronged him or not. He could never be what she wanted him to be so he would always be a source of pain for her; therefore, by her logic, deserving of her vengeance. She lit a cigarette, blowing smoke into the room when she exhaled.

"I'm going out until I cool off," he said, getting up. "We'll talk when I get back."

"Oh, no," she said. "You're not leaving me here alone!"

"Get in the hot tub, watch TV, smoke, drink, whatever. I've had an extremely bad day. My energy's all fucked up. I'll be back as soon as I calm down."

"No!" she said. "You're calm enough now."

He stood up. "I'll be back." He went to the door.

"Come back here!" she yelled after him.

He slammed the door behind him, hoping the sound would tell her to leave him alone. He got in the truck and fumbled with his keys.

Jazz came out just as the motor turned over.

"Wait a fucking minute! You can't just snap your fingers and be done with this!"

The neighbors, he thought, putting the truck in gear, backing up. Crunching into first, he took off, hoping she would not dwell on his hasty departure while she sank into a drunken haze.

She glowered at the retreating truck, remembering his glance at the clock. He was hiding something. Evidently he had no idea who he was dealing with.

Slow learners learn the hard way.

TRACY'S EXCITEMENT when she let him in over being part of the glamorous world of Playboy somehow reassured him. When he was fifteen, he would have been terrified.

"I didn't expect you to be early," she said. "The way you went on, I figured you'd get here more like around seven. I haven't even begun to get ready."

"Well, do it as fast as you can. We're supposed to be there between six and seven and it's almost six thirty."

"We'll make it," she shrugged.

"Mind if I use your phone? I'll call to let him know we're on our way."

"Sure," she said, gesturing to the phone on the floor.

He glanced at the textbooks on her desk. No fifteen-year-old runaway would be taking college courses in chemistry and calculus. He watched her go through the few items in her closet. Now *that* was strange. A beautiful nineteen-year-old with no clothes to speak of. Then he blanked out. He was about to do something. Oh, right. Call Booth.

"Go ahead and use the phone. Something wrong? Are you upset with me?"

"Uh, no," Jake mumbled. "Tense day."

"What happened?"

"Worthingham, for one."

"Oh," she smiled. "You still think I'm fifteen?"

He studied her confident face. "There's something odd about the way you make love. I can't quite put my finger on it, but it seemed possible, yeah."

"Thanks a lot," she laughed. "Like what do I do that's so bad?"

"Little things like your reaction to having your pussy licked."

"Oh, come on. That's not fair. Lots of people think that's gross."

"Well, that's true, but that's beside the point. It's *how* you react, like you don't have a clue why anyone would want to lick you there. A nineteen-year-old with your level of experience should be more sophisticated than that."

"What's wrong with my reaction? I mean, that's where I go potty from and blood and all sorts of gross stuff comes out of there. Why would anyone want to lick it?"

"That's right from a kid's point of view, but not from an experienced adult's."

She shook her head as if she thought *he* was out of his mind.

"There are other things, too, but I figured maybe you were slow in sexual maturing because of childhood trauma or from having had sex so early."

"Well, I am *not* fifteen," she smiled, waving a finger in his face. "I'm sorry if I'm so weird." She turned away to examine a sweater. "I wish I had something nice to wear. This sweater is the nicest thing I have. Could you help me pick something to go with it." She pulled the sweater on over her head.

He looked at an open box on the floor of her closet. Pants. "No dresses?" he asked.

"Uh, uh," she shook her head. "Should I wear these?" She picked up the jeans she wore at Janus's video. "Or something different? Problem is everything else is kinda dirty and not in such great shape."

"Those are fine."

She held the jeans at her waist, studying her reflection in the full-length mirror leaning against the wall. Then she pulled down her shorts. No underwear. Probably all dirty, he thought. Then he saw his reflection in the mirror. He'd forgotten to change!

At home alone, he usually wore things he'd never wear in public. He was wearing an old dirty pair of out–of-fashion bellbottom jeans, tennis shoes ripped along the sides, a polyester disco shirt with the middle button missing and an embarrassingly out-of-fashion wide collar. He sat down and covered his face. How he could explain his attire without making himself look like an even bigger idiot?

"I'm so stressed out, I forgot to change. What do you think? Do I look pretty awful?"

She looked him over. "You look normal to me." She hesitated. "Except your socks don't match."

He looked down at his feet. One green sock, the other orange. Yet another of his bad habits, wearing orphaned socks around the house. To make light of it, he said, "No, this is how they're meant to be. I have another pair at home just like them."

"Oh," she said, scrutinizing her face in the mirror. "Should I put on make-up? I don't know much about make-up."

"Na." He tried to remember how he came to possess an orange sock. "Let's just go." He hoped the bellbottoms would hide the socks. They should, as long as he didn't sit down.

THEY DROVE in silence until they were on the Bay Bridge where Jake asked, "Have you spoken to Wormyham since last night?"

"Have I?" she laughed derisively. "He keeps calling, complaining about my not spending time with him since I met you. Like I'd want to spend time with him if I didn't have to. Not!"

"How did you treat him?"

"What do you mean?"

"I mean, were you polite or irritable, noncommittal?"

"Polite, I suppose," she shrugged. "Why not? He has helped me. I told him I have finals coming up and have to study, which is true. And I have to make money, which is also true. I don't have the time."

"Good. Be polite, but have as little to do with him as possible."

"Does that mean you don't want me to move in with him?" she said, delighted.

"Yeah. Anyone stupid enough to even pretend to involve himself in kiddie porn is someone to stay away from."

"I'm glad I don't have to stay with him. He was weirding me out."

"That's good because I wouldn't want to know anyone who'd want to hang out with that pervert. And another thing, don't say anything to him regarding our business or personal relationship."

"How can I do that? I mean, he'd be suspicious."

"Be careful. Don't volunteer anything. Whatever you do, don't let him or anyone who knows him know where you live. We don't want to piss him off, so be careful."

"I don't think he's dangerous or anything. So he likes little girls, lots of guys do. That doesn't make him dangerous."

"You don't think there's anything weird or gross about child molesters?"

"Not if they want to be molested. I was with lots of old guys when I was a kid and I didn't feel bad about it. It was something I had to do. The guys were nice and they paid me well. Anyway, what's the difference if he does it here or in some other country where it's considered natural?"

"In this business, you have to stay clear of anyone who fucks jailbait. Justice is blind when it comes to pornographers, and I mean that in the worst possible way. Believe me, I'd be found guilty by association, so I can't afford to be associated with anyone like him. Furthermore, kids simply are not emotionally mature enough to protect their self-esteem. They can be severely damaged without realizing it. Most adults do not understand the needs of kids. If they did, the last thing they'd do is molest them."

"All right," she pouted. "Sorry I said anything. You aren't going to talk at me all the way into the City, are you?"

"I need to clear some things up before we get to Booth's," he said. "Why won't you talk to your parents?"

"I don't want to talk about it," she frowned.

"I have to know."

"I have called them, okay? And it was awful, all tears and begging. My dad's okay. I don't think he cares one way or the other. But my mom, she wouldn't stop crying. I can't stand it."

He sighed. "Did you send her the Mother's Day card I bought?"

"Yeah, I sent it," she mumbled. "And I wish you wouldn't sigh like that. It reminds me of my mother."

"You sent it?"

"Yes!" she said. "I even wrote some nice things on it. I just hope it gets to them."

"Why wouldn't it?"

"I told you. I haven't talked to them for over a year. They might have moved."

"It'd be forwarded."

"*If* I remembered the right address."

"It would be easier for you, really, in the long run, if you made peace with them."

"I don't need to fucking hear this! Those people never listened to me or cared for me when I was with them. I could never please them. Anything I did they'd find fault in it. If I had a report card with five A's and one B, they'd only talk about the B. In the car, it was always like this, something was always wrong with me. I should be doing this or I should not be doing that. Never did I hear that anything I'd done was worth a damn or was I ever right or—I've had it, I don't want to hear any more!"

"I'm sorry."

"No! No! Don't start! Don't explain! Leave me the fuck alone!"

When he met Cedar, she had just moved from Atlanta to San Francisco and knew no one. Her parents, like Tracy's, were demanding and her self-esteem was low. She fell in "love" with the love she saw in his eyes and came to believe in the image of wondrous and worthy beauty he projected on her. His belief built her up, but all his support would crumble in her eyes if he criticized her. Then, like Tracy now, she would shut him out.

TRACY WATCHED Jake check the truck door lock, then accompanied him in silence to the entrance of Booth's building.

He pushed the button to the penthouse. "Nervous?"

"A little," Tracy said.

"Yes?" said Booth's voice from the intercom.

"Jake and Chastity," said Jake.

"The elevator's to your left at the end of the hall. It'll take you directly to our suite."

A loud buzz signaled Jake to push the door.

A pale young Black with long, stringy hair entered the hall. Tracy stared at him. "Is that Michael Jackson?" she whispered.

Jake knew Booth also booked concerts for pop singer look-alikes, all of whom lived in his building. The man passed by without acknowledging them.

"That was Michael Jackson, wasn't it?" she said, excited, looking after him.

"Yeah," he said, not wanting to spoil her fun.

"What's he doing here?"

"Booth's also a concert promoter. And *you* are Chastity, his beautiful starlet!"

"Chastity!" she exclaimed gaily.

They entered a mirror lined elevator. "Talk about vanity," he said, amused. "His performers must really like themselves."

"I can't believe I'm riding in an elevator Michael Jackson just rode," she said, fidgeting. "This is so cool."

Jake scrutinized his image in the sparkling clean mirrors on the elevator doors as they slid shut. Missing shirt button. Splotches of paint on his pants. Frayed cuffs. Maybe they wouldn't know what to make of him, so they'd make nothing of it.

Then he noticed his messy hair and tried to smooth it into place with his hand.

A peal of crystalline laughter greeted them when the elevator opened onto a large room full of plush trendy furniture and attractive strangers, most of whom were gathered around the wraparound kitchen counter. He looked in the direction of the laugh as they stepped out onto a thick white carpet. A strikingly beautiful woman with an unusual hairdo (ancient Greek style) caught his eye. Her body seemed to light up when she laughed. For a moment he forgot everything, except that he was looking at a truly beautiful woman. Then her laughter suddenly stopped, and she looked directly at him.

He looked away to Chastity, whose anxiety-laden face prompted him to scan the room for signs of disapproval. The only other person looking at them was a young woman lounging on a couch who appeared to be bored. Everyone else, at least a dozen people, had gathered in the kitchen area around either Booth or the beautiful woman. Standing next to Booth was the bejeweled blonde who'd refused to sign a release at Mindy's shoot. She briefly glanced at them then looked away, as if dismissing them.

"Don't worry," Jake whispered. "If there's anyone they won't like, it'll be me not you."

"Why?" Chastity muttered. "I'm the dorky one."

"Ah, you have yet to grasp the nature of glamour, grasshopper," said Jake, trying to remember the bejeweled blonde's name, or if he'd ever heard it. "Glamour comes from an ancient Scottish word for a magic spell that creates an illusion of beauty where no beauty exists. Entertainment is all about image, which is why they say an ounce of image is worth a pound of performance. And you have both. Believe me, Booth wouldn't have asked for you if he didn't want you."

"I can't be like these people." She averted her eyes. "I'm too dorky."

"You have no idea how shallow it all is. Don't worry about it. That's my job."

He scanned the kitchen area for the blonde's twin brother but stopped when he noticed a tall Indian, towering over the beautiful woman. They were both staring at him. Indians had made him uncomfortable since he learned at age six he was a quarter Indian. He felt guilty in their presence, as if his being mostly white was some form of betrayal.

"Jake! Chastity!" Booth gestured for them from the kitchen counter. "I'm glad you both could make it, because we start shooting Friday, so we need to tie things down fast."

"Are you serious?" said Jake, noticing the Indian and the beautiful woman approaching them. "Friday?"

"I have access to a closed health spa until Monday. It's as quiet as a sound stage and the main room's perfect for constructing sets. I have a crew waiting to start. All I need is to be sure I've got the girls."

"And a script," said Jake, aware of the woman and the Indian standing behind him.

"Could you have one ready by then?"

"Yeah, a basic acting script, not a shooting script."

"The most I can pay is three hundred bucks. My investor hasn't given me much to work with so everyone has to make sacrifices. I intend to make up for it on the next project."

"This is porn, right?"

"It's an explicit erotic movie I'm making to Playboy standards so I can sell them the soft version. If it were up to me I'd dump the hard version altogether but, being as I haven't had much directorial experience, my investor insists I cover his ass with a porn version in case the soft doesn't pass muster. Can I count you in?"

"Yeah, sure, as long as Chastity's in it."

"No problem there." He looked at Chastity. "Did you bring your IDs? I need to make photostats of them."

"Sure." She pulled them out of her purse. "Here's my California ID, Social Security card and college ID."

"Good, two picture IDs." Booth scrutinized them. "Application forms are on the kitchen counter. Please fill one out while I do the stats." Then he walked off toward a hallway to the right of the elevator.

"I'll be back in a few minutes, okay?" Jake whispered to Chastity.

"Okay," Chastity nodded. "I'll fill out the application."

"Excuse me," said the bejeweled blonde after Jake left. "My name's Kenyon. I hope you don't mind my asking, but are those for real?"

"My boobies?" Chastity said. "No."

"Oh, they are nice," Kenyon said. "Truly amazing."

"Hi, I'm Catherine," said the truly beautiful woman. "I'm make-up, wardrobe and hairstylist."

"Oh, hi," Chastity replied, conscious of being deficient in all three. "I'm Tracy, I mean, uh, Chastity."

Catherine giggled. "Chastity?"

"Chastity's my screen name," she said. "Dumb, huh?"

"No, I think it's great," she laughed. "Very appropriate."

"Well, I don't like it," she said, irritated. "It was Jake's idea. He's a famous porn director so he thinks he knows everything."

"Jake's the fellow who brought you in?" Catherine grinned. "A famous porn director? Oh, that's good."

"Would there be a problem changing it?" said Spear.

"Huh?" said Chastity. His height and deep voice intimidated her.

"This is Spear," said Catherine, pointing at him with her chin. "He's the cameraman. He comes from a long line of shamans who performed curing rituals called Ways to take care of mental, physical and spiritual problems. He's an expert on the Hard Way."

Spear took hold of Catherine's wrist and squeezed it.

"Jake said I could change it if I found one I liked," she said without looking at either of them. "I want something that's just one word. You know, like Madonna." Overly aware of Catherine being the best dressed, most attractive person in the room, she added with some irritation, "I feel silly with my stupid name, and my clothes, and not putting on make-up before I came over, and everything. I would've done it but I'm not any good at it. I must look really awful."

"No, you don't. You look real," said Catherine. Chastity grimaced. "You have a natural beauty that looks better without make up or ornamentation. That's a rare gift."

"Natural beauty?" Chastity said, looking at her to see if she were putting her on.

"Waverly," said Spear.

"Huh?"

"Your name," he said.

"Oh, I like it," Catherine nodded. "Very good, Spear."

JAKE found Booth in his office, standing by the Xerox machine surrounded by shelves of one-inch video masters, examining a copy of Tracy's IDs. "Could you make copies for me, too? I've been meaning to get some for my files."

"No problem." He pushed a button for another copy.

"Ben told me you expressed some concern she might be underage. Could you be sure to check her IDs to verify they're genuine before we start filming."

"Why? They look fine to me, and I'm an ex-vice cop. Do you think they're fake?"

"No, but I'd feel better if they were verified. I'd rather be safe than sorry."

"Okay, I will have it looked into."

Relieved, Jake then asked, "How many more ladies do you need?"

"Originally, I didn't plan on using any porn actresses. I intended to use the beauties I have on file for Playboy, but they all bailed as soon as I mentioned porn. All except for one. Olga, a nineteen-year-old Russian immigrant. Did you notice her on the couch?"

"Well, yeah, sort of," Jake said, sounding dubious.

"I think she's attractive," Booth responded. "Not Playboy material, but she has an unusually beautiful pussy, and she'll do all three days for

$200. She also has my cameraman's seal of approval. He knows what looks hot on tape. It's not easy finding beauties for $300 a day tops. The guys, I don't care about. I can get them on deferral."

"You know, my cameraman's good at keeping people motivated on low budgets. He'd probably work for a lot less than your man."

"No can do. My investor on Riley's projects insists on using his cameraman and make-up girl as part of the deal, so my hands are tied there."

"Uh, what kind of role do you have in mind for Chastity?"

Booth shrugged. "She's too young for the lead, as far as that goes. We'll have to see where her potential lies."

"Do me a favor, will you? Treat her special tonight. You know, flatter her, make her feel good. She likes that."

"Of course. Performers are like children. That's the only way to treat them."

"YOUR performance the other day was extraordinary," Booth said as he scanned Chastity's application. "Jake says you had no previous acting experience. Amazing, truly amazing."

As Jake watched Chastity, he sensed the beautiful laughing woman watching him. It felt as if she were passing judgment on him based on how he looked at Chastity. He turned to see if she was watching him. A jolt shot through him the moment their eyes met. He froze as he watched her eyes go through a series of changes, each change layering one upon another, until her eyes were like cold tempered steel.

Then she motioned for him to follow her away from the group.

"Are you her agent?" she asked, her full lips emphasizing each word.

"Uh, yeah, more or less," he said, sensing the Indian moving up behind him. "You must be the lead. I'm the scriptwriter. Maybe you, uh, might have some ideas. You know, what you'd like to do. Character, or whatever." Then he sensed he'd said the wrong thing.

"I'm make-up," she said with a penetrating look that seemed to darken her voice. "Why are you doing this, Mr. More or Less?" she asked in a voice that felt to Jake as if it came from a level of depth that downright intimidated him.

Jake froze, suspecting this strange woman was toying with him. He had a frivolous thought of how he always seemed to clash with make-up ladies. Never used the same one twice. Then it occurred to him, she must be Riley Thierault's *crazy niece!* The make-up artist.

"Uh, playing it as it lays?" he answered, weakly. "What is it you think I'm doing?"

"You're playing with surfaces, and you shouldn't be. You will find no answers there. You must overcome your fear of the depths to see what you're doing. You seek answers. To find them you must be willing and able to receive them. You are neither. You will run yourself and others through crap traps until you're ready to realize the obvious. That's what you're doing."

Jake stared at her for a moment. All of his make-up ladies had been judgmental. This one, apparently, was no different. Maybe nuttier. No point discussing anything with judgmental women, but he felt as if he had to say something. He had an urge to make light of it, then heard himself say, "TerrrrrrrEEEEEEEEbluh."

Her eyes flashed, and the Indian turned her around before she could respond.

"Excuse us, please," Spear said, guiding her away.

Jake watched them move through the gathering up to the bay view window in the living room. It struck him strange how they seemed to do so without drawing attention, as if they were now somehow invisible to everyone but him. His off-the-wall response to what she said reminded him of his off-the-wall reactions to Ben's spiels about archetypes. What Ben and Katie had to say was worth considering, yet his reactions had been off putting. Why did he do that? While he watched the Indian talking to her, he remembered what Ben said about Riley seeing Katie as an angel, and of Aphrodite announcing her presence with laughter.

Then it occurred to him, they were in an archetypal field!

"WHAT are you doing?" Spear asked, scrutinizing Catherine's smoldering eyes. "You marked him. Why?" The intensity in her eyes flickered out.

"I don't know, something happened when he looked me in the eye," she muttered. "Maybe Josephine?"

"No, no. Giving advice. Crap traps?" Spear said. "Not her style."

She considered this, and said, "Yeah. Maybe something else spoke through her?"

"Or, through you. What was it about the way he said terrible that upset you?"

"That's how Josephine talked to Riley when I was a kid. A parody of Joseph. That's how she got her name. Jake talking like that, like he knew her, was a foolish violation."

Spear remained silent for a moment. "Jake, he is a wild card. Aware, yet not aware. Involved, but flying blind. If you speak to him, you must be cautious with what you say."

JAKE FELT his normal thoughts return when he scrutinized the Russian on the couch. Nineteen. Broad hips. Small tits. Not Playboy material. Her face had the healthy milky complexion and ordinary features of a young East European peasant.

"I understand you're in the movie?" Jake said to her.

Olga shrugged. "I haven't been asked."

"You will be. You going to do it?"

She frowned. "I'm here, aren't I? I haven't left."

"It was suppose to be a project for Playboy, now it's not. Does it make a difference to you, it being changed to porn?"

"Why should it? What's the difference?"

"Well, porn involves real sex. You've seen porn, haven't you?"

"We have it in our country," she shrugged, looking bored.

"So you don't mind?"

"I need money. It is best not to mind. It amazes me how you Americans always feel free to ask of strangers such as these questions. So I'll make a question. This girl," Olga motioned toward Chastity, "She is with you?"

"Yes," he said. "I represent her."

Olga studied her. "A very sad child. And she wants this?"

"Yeah, she does." Watching her intense blue eyes, he understood the attraction. She had an aura of depth. "Makes her feel important." He felt uncomfortable at the thought of her perceiving him as a pimp.

Olga shook her head gravely. "I was like that when I was her age."

"But you are her age. You're both nineteen."

Olga blew air through her lips. "She is fourteen maybe fifteen, no more."

"Look, in America, kids aren't as sophisticated as Europeans," he said in a hushed voice as he sat down next to her. "They act like kids into their twenties. She's silly when she's nervous, but she's more so-phisticated when we're alone." Olga shook her head.

"I've got three sets of IDs. I checked them out, they're legal. DMV told me kids don't go to them for fake IDs because they require fin-gerprints and a birth certificate. She's going to college, I checked that out. She got breast implants a few months ago. You can't get that done at that age, and a doctor should know a fifteen-year-old from a nineteen-year-old, right? She has to be nineteen. I can't imagine it otherwise."

"She is clever, this one. Like myself, I see it. She thinks she punishes her parents with her stupid games. She knows of no other way. There is much a clever girl can do. You see me here, I am not Jewish, yet I got to America at seventeen by myself with no relatives or friends or job in this country. How can I do that? Powerful people with great influence can't do this, but I, a stupid clever little girl, can. Yes, I see her so. I left home at thirteen and made everything happen as I wish. False papers? College? False breasts? Is nothing. None of it is nothing to a clever girl."

"You can tell just by looking at her she ran away from home at thirteen? How can you do that? Are you psychic or something?"

"I have done this thing and I know it. I was a sad girl, like her. I survived. Maybe she will, too." She studied him for the first time, her eyes penetrating. "Tell me this, do you love this girl?"

"Yes," he said softly, his eyes guilty. He hastened to add, "I love her in the way that I want to protect her, nurture her, for as long as our relationship lasts."

"Perhaps then she will be luckier than I," she shrugged.

"If she's fifteen, she shouldn't be in porn. It's not good for any child that age, and it's against the law. Very much so."

"The law?" Olga frowned with contempt. "You must support her in what she would do, otherwise she cannot trust you, and she will do what she must. She's a sad girl. She needs guidance, but you must always support her."

JAKE TURNED the engine off and rubbed his eyes. He found it difficult to steel himself for what was to come. Jazz had been alone in his house for several hours. She must have heard him drive up and she would interpret a delay as a sign of weakness.

He got out of the truck and entered his home.

She glared up at him from the living room couch, sprawled out in a purple bathrobe. He glanced at two empty wine bottles, an ashtray full of butts and a crumpled cigarette pack all strewn across the coffee table. He waited for her to say something. Silence. Feeling her eyes on him, he took a bottle from the cupboard and poured himself a drink.

"Are you cooled off now?" she sneered, raising up on an elbow.

"Is your *energy* still fucked up?"

"I'm fine."

She made a raspy snort of disgust. "Aren't you going to check your damn machine?"

He glanced at the blinking green light.

"Some bitch called asking you to come and *pro-tect* her. You left the volume on so I heard every damn word. So, did you *protect* her?"

"Probably Moira. The butthead who's been harassing her threatened to send a demon over to annoy her."

She let out an unholy laugh that demanded attention. "Why couldn't you've been honest and took me home instead of going off to some bitch leaving me here all alone?"

"I didn't go to her. She asked me to earlier and I said no. I told her to call the cops or go somewhere else."

"Why did she call *you?*"

"What can I say, she must have mistaken me for someone who gives a damn. I bring that sort of thing out in women." *What a cruel thing to say*, he thought, going to the machine. Especially when he didn't mean it. "Do you mind if I listen to it?"

"What difference does it make? Go and listen to your little White bitch."

He rewound the message. "Jake? Are you there? Pick up the phone, please. Please! I'm really frightened. Could you please come over and ..." the sound level dropped. He turned it up and put his ear close to the machine to try to make out what she was saying.

"Did you pick up the phone or something?" Jake asked.

"No, I did *not* pick up the damn phone!"

"Must be something wrong with the connection."

"So why don't you call her?" she said, mocking.

"I don't want to get involved in her problems. I feel bad about her being scared but I don't need the grief."

"Something's up, or are you lying just to keep in practice? You don't *want* to get involved," she snorted, standing up. She winced in pain. "You care more about your little White whores and their damn problems than you do 'bout me."

"That's not true."

"Then why haven't you axed me about the band? Why haven't you axed how that's going, huh?" Her voice thickened. "You think you're so fucking sensitive but you don't give a damn about me!"

"What's wrong, hon?"

She shook her head defiantly. "Everything," she said with more authority than necessary, as though dismissing any further questions. "I don't want to talk about it."

"What happened?"

"I can't talk about it!" she shouted. "It'd drive me crazy."

"Sit down," he said, approaching. She shook her head. He sat down and picked up a half empty pack of cigarettes. He lit one and offered it to her.

"I quit the band." She exhaled smoke, eyes closed.

"You did! Why?"

She swallowed. "I was raped."

"You were? Who did it?"

"The manager." She shook her head. "I thought he was so fucking hip. I was stoop-id. I shoulda known. I was so drunk and fucked up I didn't know what was happening and didn't fucking care." She opened her eyes. "Until I felt him kissing and scratching on my booty. Then he tried to ram his long, fat Beer-Can cock up my ass. I fought back but I was too damn drunk." She paused. "Then I saw the blood on his face."

"Blood? What?"

"He cut my booty wif the edge of a scissors. Said he thought I liked it. They're small cuts but they hurt, damn it, especially when I sit."

He gathered the edge of her robe. "May I?" She shook her head *no* while he pulled back the flap. There were numerous short lines etched across her ashen skin. He visualized the creep slicing her then rubbing his face on her bloody booty.

"I thought he was going to kill me. It was horrible! Dirty! Filthy." She shuddered. "Said I axed for it. How dare he say I axed for that! I was fucked up and he took advantage of me!" She pushed his hand away when he tried to comfort her. "Don't touch me! None of 'em give a damn about me. They prefer their worfless manager over me. I'm just some lowlife axing to be cut up." Her face collapsed into itself. "That's the way you treat me, too. Why? Why you do that? What have I done to deserve this? All I ever did was love you. All I wanted was for you to love me back. Was that bad? Was that so awful?" she sobbed. "I hate you for loving you!"

"Jazz, please. We have to talk about this."

"Why?" she snapped. "So you can *lie* to me?"

"You don't understand, hon. I never said I would return your love. I said I *couldn't*. I'm too emotionally drained."

"No, *you* don't understand! I'm just your lowlife Black bitch, that's all I've ever been to you. That bastard cut me, raped me, used me. He hurt me! But *you!* You sap my soul, drain the life out of me, and you won't let me go until I'm either dead or you find somebody else to suck the life out of."

"Hon, it's not like that. You know I've given you love. I do love you, just not the way you want me to, but I do. What happened to you hurts me."

"Take me home," she said coldly.

"Why don't you stay the night."

"No! I want to go home. Take me home."

THEY DROVE in silence, Jake thinking of comforting things to say for her to remember later alone in her room. He pulled in front of her flat then turned off the engine.

"Little girl, we've stayed friends through many a fight. You've done things I'd never tolerate from anyone else. Think on that. We're no longer lovers because it hurts you and you hurt me. But we are friends. Maybe you can steal from lovers, but you don't steal from friends. Don't confuse the two." He watched her silent profile as he softly added, "There will always be assholes out there. Don't let them get to you. Let it go."

She turned and stared blankly at him. "All I ever did was love you."

Then she cried. She could not tell anyone, especially him, why.

She'd taken Dr. Ben up on his offer to buy her butt for two hours. What he'd done to her... restrained... gagged, saying he needed to do to her what someone had done to his missing-presumed-dead wife. She thought all along he was going to kill her, talking the way he did about taking her to the Underworld of the Dead. What he did, what he did ... she did not want to think of what he did. She went to the band's manager wanting to get fucked-up, thinking she could trust him. The fucking asshole treated her like a....low life.

Then he stole the ten grand cash Ben had given her.

IT WAS AFTER midnight when Jake got back to his answering machine. He stared at it, thinking of his callous remark about Moira. He did care. It was all just too painful.

But he would return her call.

"Hello?" said a faint apprehensive voice.

"Moira? Is that you?" he shouted. "I can barely hear you."

"Jake! Thank God!" Moira shouted back.

"I think we have a bad connection. I'll try calling back."

"No, don't! It won't help. The demon's blocking the sound."

Oh, Christ! The sound was unusual. The static's rhythm and pitch had a peculiar buzz. "You should call the phone company, get the line checked," he yelled.

"It's no use! Oh, Jake, it's so weird over here. My walls are oozing some kind of gooey stuff."

I don't want to hear this, he thought. "Okay, get out of there. Come over here."

"I'm afraid!" she cried. "He's trapped me in here. Please come and get me. I don't know who else to turn to."

"Jesus, I'm exhausted. Can't this wait until tomorrow?"

"No! This is serious. I wouldn't ask if I weren't so scared. Please don't abandon me!"

"Look, I'll send a cab over. Go down and wait for him."

"Jake, I ... I want you to come. I don't know who this cab driver is. You know, the demon could ..."

He groaned. "Okay, listen to me. I know how demons work. He's more likely to follow you if I come than if someone you don't know came. The cabbie will be all right. If you have any doubts about him, roll your eyes counterclockwise until you calm down."

"You know about demons?" she said.

"Yeah, sure. You'll be fine. I'm going to hang up now and call the cab, okay? Bye."

"Okay. Bye-eee."

He ordered the cab then rubbed his eyes, mumbling *trouble, trouble, trouble* as he ambled over to the hot tub. He needed to relax before Moira arrived. He stripped and raised the hot tub cover. Something was floating in the water.

He switched on the submerged tub light. A turd.

"Ah, Jazz." He sat on the edge of the tub and stared at his clothing on the floor. Getting dressed seemed too complicated, requiring much more energy than he could muster. He should put on better clothes. Something to face down a demon in.

"Shit." Decisions, decisions. Complex coordinated action. He had to do something about the turd in the tub. Then a song found its way into his mind.

I found out a long time ago what a woman could do to your soul.

Yeah, but she can't take you anywhere you don't know where to go.

"Yeah, but I don't want to go," he muttered as he gathered up his clothes.

What he wanted was to lie down and drift off to sleep. What he had to do, if he wanted to keep Moira's demon at bay, was to remove all evidence of Jazz having been in the house before she arrived. He disposed of the turd and dressed himself in fresh dark clothing, then cleared off the coffee table, sprayed air freshener all around and put things away until he heard a knock on his door. He smoothed his hair down and opened the door.

Moira looked at him with animal fear in her eyes and quickly entered the house. The cab driver watched until she was inside, then drove off.

"He took off like a bat out of hell," said Jake. "What'd you do?"

"The demon followed me," she whispered.

"Well, don't worry about it." He nonchalantly closed the door. "He can't get in here."

"How do you know?"

"The house was built by Shintos with spirits in mind. You've seen the shrine and the spirit wheel and spirit house in the garden. They're there to protect the house from evil spirits. Your demon can hover in the neighborhood all he wants but he can't get in here."

"Yes," she said, relieved. "I can feel that."

"Good," said Jake. Maybe now he could get some sleep.

He looked at her, imagining the child in her abandoned in a field, drenched in blood, her mother's body growing cold in the dark. No response to her cries. No help.

Then a jolt shattered his thoughts and he sensed a dark powerful presence, menacing, malicious, enveloping the house. He'd read somewhere that evil spirits feed on emotions. Afraid his fear could easily escalate into madness, he tried not to show any emotion.

"He's out there, though," she shuddered. "Can you feel him?"

"Yeah. Above the house." Realizing some part of him actually believed a demon had followed her worried him. To reassure both of them, he whispered, "But we're safe. He can't get in." Moira relaxed into his arms, amazing him at the ease with which she accepted what he said. She apparently believed he knew what he was talking about. It was in both their best interest she continue believing that. If she panicked, he might, too.

"What should I do if it won't go away?" she asked.

"Well." He mustered as much confidence in his voice as he could. "First of all, demons are not as powerful as you think. They feed on emotions, especially fear. But they are spirits. They can't hurt us physically. They can scare people to death, so don't let him do that. Consciousness rises from the tension of opposites, good and evil, truth and lies and so on. This demon's a manifestation of the dark side. The lie. So an effective defense would be to avoid lying to yourself or to others since evil spirits attach themselves to us through our lies."

"There was blood on my walls." She held out her hands. "Feel my hands."

He touched them. Clammy.

"I slime everything I touch. Look at this." She pulled her sweater up to expose a large red splotch on her back. "Scary. I don't know what to do. Can you make it go away?"

He felt a chill, a heavy pressure, as if she were summoning the malevolent spirit, and it would see his fear if he kept quiet. "I can protect you for now, but you have to learn to protect yourself. As demons go, this one's a wanker. He can do little more than wear you down by scaring you. You have nothing to fear but fear itself."

"I don't? But my welts, my clammy hands? The blood on the wall?"

"Look at me. I'm not impressed. I've seen worse. For all I care, let the blood flow." He stopped when he realized what he had just said. "Let's see if he has the power to override the house spirits and show us some blood." He pointed at a wall, thinking if blood were to run down it, he'd shit a brick. "You see, he can't do it. If you don't let him scare you, you won't get clammy hands. Now let's go to bed and get some sleep."

She grabbed hold of his wrist and closed her eyes. "I want you to hide out for awhile," he said.

"That's a drag," she groaned. "For how long?"

"A week or two. I'll arrange a diversion for your demon in the morning then Joaquin will take you somewhere. Don't let anyone know where you are, especially your uncle."

"Am I in danger?"

"I don't think so, but I want you somewhere safe until I figure out who's behind this."

"I'm okay as long as I'm with you," she said.

PART FIVE

The Myth in the Mess

…the rending pain of re-enactment
Of all that you have done, and been; the shame
Of motives late revealed, and the awareness
Of things ill done and done to others' harm
Which once you took for exercise of virtue.

— T. S. Elliot (Four Quartets IV.2)

Give me chastity and contingency
—but not yet!

— St. Augustine (Confessions)

13

Life Out of Balance

Jake was two hours late. Worried Booth had gone off to do exteriors leaving no one behind to let him in, he banged on the door hard enough to rumble the soaped-over plate glass windows. The lock clicked and the door opened a crack. Joaquin peered out.

"How's it going, eh?" Jake said with a guilty grin.

"Not even," said Joaquin, letting him in. "They're still constructing the set."

The club consisted of a four–hundred-foot room with floor-to-ceiling mirrored walls, the right half divided into three parts—the front, partitioned into three offices and a bathroom; the middle, an aerobics area where the jail set was being constructed by a three-man crew; the back, an enclosed area with showers, sauna and lockers. The left half, formerly a workout area, was empty except for a single leather–upholstered, leg-lift chair alongside the center support beam. Olga was sitting on the floor leaning against the mirrored wall in the back left corner near a card table with two folding chairs.

A loud familiar laugh echoing from the empty area drew Jake's attention to two men and two women across the room to his left. One of the women, a pale redhead, was jerking her free hand around while silently reading the script to herself, her lips moving.

"Tracy here?" asked Jake.

"Don't know," said Joaquin. "I've been hanging with the Indian cameraman. Let me tell you, bro, he's one strange dude."

"I couldn't reach her last night to let her know the show was on for today. Last time we spoke, I told her I doubted Booth could pull it off."

Joaquin shook his head. "Well, you were right. I've seen some disorganized productions in my day but this one takes the prize. He gets us here at six in the morning with no coffee or food waiting for us, the set unfinished, the carpenters not even scheduled to show for another four hours, with no idea of what he wants for his first shot. The talent arrived around eight with no make-up person and nothing for them to do while he hangs out at a deli across the street."

"I called Worthingham to see if he could help find her. Hopefully she'll show."

The man with the loud laugh turned sufficiently for Jake to recognize him as Joe. His hair was curlier and lighter and his sleeveless red t-shirt and turquoise workout pants were enough to make him unsure he was Joe. Standing next to Joe was a rugged, blond middle-aged man in a black jumpsuit with gold chains dangling on his shaven chest.

"Worthlessham knows her?" asked Joaquin.

"Uh, yeah," said Jake. "He knows her people, and I don't. How's morale?"

"All things considered, Booth lucked out there. The act persons seem to think this is some kind of big production; but let me tell you, we're going to be stuck here all goddamn night if something doesn't happen soon. Another fine mess you got me into, bro."

The two women were in their mid-twenties; one pale, one dark. The pale one wore baggy pastel colored clothing that obscured her figure. The dark one, her back to him, had a pleasing contour and crevice of buttocks in tight, faded jeans.

"Jake!" Joe yelled, gesturing for him to join them.

"Excuse me," Jake said to Joaquin.

"We've been going over your script," Joe said as he approached. "Let me introduce you around. The beautiful lady here is Jezebel." He designated the lady in jeans. "She's an Arabian princess."

"A princess?" said Jake, recognizing her from Hasib's office.

"A fallen princess," said Jezebel, indifferently.

"Everybody, this is Jake Zakheim, the famous director," said Joe.

"The script's a bit of a rush job," said Jake, wondering if she remembered Hasib introducing them. "Spent all of six hours on it. It'll improve as we go along."

"You're a director?" said Jezebel.

"A fallen director," said Jake. Jezebel glared at him suspiciously.

"I'm Kurt." The man in the black jumpsuit extended a hand. Jake met his firm grip. "I'm a director, too. Kurt Winslow. You heard of me?"

"Yeah," he lied. "But I don't think I've seen any of your work. Haven't kept up over the past few years."

"Mostly I'm an actor, but I have my own amateur line. I was in town scouting for talent when Janus said this guy needed help, so I figured I might as well check it out. Booth appears legit. You seen his equipment? Serious stuff, right? But I don't know, man. He told me if I gave him a break on price he'd give me a part in the legit flick he has on line for next month. What do you think? Do you know for a fact he is who he says he is? I mean, you know," he lowered his voice, "he was referred to me by Janus."

"Like you said, he has the props and he talks the talk."

"Yeah, that's it, right. He could be running a game on us."

"Probably no more than any other porn producer."

"Yeah," Kurt nodded. "So maybe he is, maybe he isn't."

"How well do you know him?" asked Jezebel. "He told me he was doing a movie for Playboy, then all of the sudden it's porn. I've turned down porn offers for a lot more money than this. No way I'd be here if I thought he was lying about the legit film."

"Same here," said Joe. "I'd do it, but not for the kind of money he's paying. Mindy's production pretty much filled my quota on promise and handshake deals. If the legit film's pie in the sky, I'd insist on being paid with the green, not the blue." He gestured skyward.

"Geeez," the redhead grunted, looking up from the script. "I don't care. I love porn. I'd pick a porn gig any day over sleazy soft shit. Porn's real, everything else is crap." She stared at Jake. "You don't remember me, do you?"

"Uh," said Jake. He had no idea who she was. "I tend to forget names. You look familiar but I can't say I remember where or when."

"I was in a movie that was shot at your house a few years ago."

"You were?"

"Yeah, and your wife was there. I remember her quite well. I asked you if she was into S&M and you gave me a goofy look."

"Is that right?" said Jake. He still didn't remember, but that was probably because he had avoided her. Remembering someone established a connection, an influence. "I don't remember that but I think I remember you now." He sensed she was unbalanced, not someone he would want either as a friend or an enemy. He decided to attempt a compliment. "You look different somehow. Better, younger."

"Thank you," she said with a malicious grin. "I wasn't healthy then. I had a cancerous tumor. It's been removed and I'm fine now. My name's Serena Hawke, the serene siren." She giggled. Jake, disturbed by its demented edge, grimaced.

"There's that look again."

"This whole production's unprofessional," Jezebel frowned. "I've been here for three hours with no make-up, no rehearsals, no food, nothing. What's the point of getting us here so early? It doesn't make sense. I don't think he knows what he's doing."

"He probably knows what he's doing," said Jake. "Just inconsiderate. What do you think, Kurt?"

Kurt snorted. "I think he should have spent more time in prep."

"He's hasn't had much directing experience," said Jake. "From the look of things, I'd say he has a problem delegating."

"What I'd like to know is, is this guy a for real Playboy producer," said Jezebel.

"Don't know for sure," said Jake. "The time to figure that out is before, not during production when everything depends on honoring your commitment. Anyway, being disorganized doesn't mean he's not legit. I've seen proof of that many times over."

"None of which means he has anything coming down the line," said Kurt.

"Hey, guys," said Joe. "As long as we're here, we might as well give it a shot. Who knows, maybe we'll hit something."

SPEAR SPOTTED Booth at the deli counter talking on his cell phone with Dr. Ben sitting on a stool nearby, his right leg shaking.

Booth glanced at Spear. "See what you can do, and call me in thirty," he said, then shut his phone. "That was my last hope. No way are we going to find an acceptable replacement at the last minute. Do me a favor and call Catherine and tell her to get her butt over here, at least for the day. She won't have to be on set if it upsets her. I'll send the performers to her. She just has to be here. That was the deal if she fired Riley."

"What did she say?" said Spear. "Her exact words."

"I don't know her *exact* words," Booth said, handing Spear the phone. "Some bullshit about a bad dream and waking up with the *position*, that was the word she used, that porn was wrong and she should have nothing to do with it."

"She said porn is *wrong*?" said Spear.

"No, but that's what she meant. She was talking about balance, how she couldn't afford to be found in the *wrong* position. Like I would know what the fuck that meant."

"I've always said the proper position for women in porn is prone," said Ben, looking uncomfortable after having said it. He had not intended to use that persona today.

"We'll lose more than Riley's name if she doesn't show," Booth said while Spear punched in her number. "She made a deal. She should stick to it."

"Hello," said Catherine, wearily.

"Seabolt," said Spear.

She exhaled, whispering in a tense voice, "Something's wrong. The omens are bad."

He listened to her heavy breathing into the mouthpiece.

"Doesn't feel right," she whispered. "Don't you feel it? Everything's out of whack?"

"As well it should be." He waited for a response. When there was none, he walked away from Booth and Ben. "Tempting the Fates," he said when out of their hearing range.

She tittered wistfully, then went silent. "Everything's wrong," she whispered. "I'm really not obligated to Peter, am I? Not-not-not ..." she struggled to find the words. "Too late. I *know* this one's destined to end badly. I feel like I'm being pulled into it by something evil. I can't take any more. I'm done."

"What is pulling you, *that* is why you can't walk away. To survive, you *must* face the chaos. You cannot properly face chaos by judging it." He paused again to allow her time to respond. "Don't react. Resonate. Then, hang on until you see through to the new order." Silence. "You know the drill." Then he gently added, "What you need to see, you can see only if you do not try to see it. It occurs without motivation, or desire, or knowledge of what may result. It is pure. It is what little children have. It is what the old masters regain once they have lost their minds and become children again."

Silence.

"John, he told me to tell you to get your butt over here."

"My butt, that's all?" she giggled. Then she sighed, "If I have to I will, but not today. Can't you talk him into putting it off? That shouldn't be so hard seeing as he's not ready."

"You're right, he's not. No surprise there."

After a long pause, she said, "Okay. But there'd better be food on the set when I get there or I walk. I agree to face chaos, not hunger." She giggled. "Time's a-wastin'."

"Is she coming?" Booth boomed. Spear nodded. "For the day or for the shoot?"

"She will do what she agreed to do," said Spear. "But she wants food on the set."

JANUS tentatively approached Jake. "Can I have a word with you?"

"Excuse me," Jake said to the group of actors.

"I don't know what's going on here," Janus whispered as they walked away. "Booth was supposed to have all these gorgeous women, but where the fuck are they? Jezebel's the only decent looker. Let's face it, the other two aren't exactly raving beauties. I don't know how he thinks he can get away with it if this is the best he can do. Where's Tracy?"

"Booth didn't confirm the shoot until the last minute and I couldn't find her."

"But didn't she know it was supposed to be today?"

"Yes, she did, but I told her I didn't think Booth would be stupid enough to start before he was ready."

"You told her we weren't shooting today?" she said, dumbfounded.

"I told her I doubted it, but I asked her to call me for confirmation, and she didn't."

"Oh, this is terrible! What can we do? Let's face it, we have to have her. Three other girls have flaked out as it is. We can't possibly do it without another looker."

"Even if she does show, that's still only four women, not enough to justify a project of this size. He should put it off anyway."

A pounding came from the street door. "I'll tell him about Jazz," she said, distracted. "I've seen black women on Playboy before."

"Don't bother. She wouldn't do it, not for what he's paying."

"Wait! Wait!" said Janus. "There's one of the vanished."

Jake looked toward the door. Julie, Joaquin's boyish assistant, let in a young woman dressed in a black jacquard top dress with matching pants and high heels. Julie pointed at him. He noticed Julie had changed the highlights in her short, spiked red hair, and that her crucifix was much larger. The two women walked toward him. He wondered what it was about the click of a woman's high heels on a polished floor that was so arousing.

"She's gorgeous," said Janus. "I hope she stays. It's awful how everybody's just standing around. I mean, where's the director? What's happening?"

"Hello, I'm Jake," he said to the newcomer. "I'm the writer and assistant director."

She gave him a slight smile. "Kenyon," she said in a soft deep voice, her glistening dark red, almost black lips not moving.

"Do you know what part you're playing?" he asked.

"No," she said. "John said I could pick."

"Okay, good. In my opinion, you should be Lacey, the lead. You have the prerequisite poise." He wondered what kind of force could drive a classy woman like her to be in a porno movie.

Her smile became ambiguous. "Could I see a script?"

"They're spread out on the counter over there," Julie said, pointing at a long counter outside the offices. She gave Jake a strange look that made him feel uncomfortable. "I'll take care of it," she snapped, then to Kenyon, "You have to assemble it, page by page."

"Let me know what you think after you've read it," said Jake. Kenyon gave him a sly grin then moved off in a gust of perfume, her resonant heels mocking him. "She'll make this movie work," he said to Janus. "Keep an eye on her. We don't want to lose her."

"What can I do? She ignored me on Mindy's shoot. I don't think she likes me."

Jake stared after her. Kenyon was the bejeweled blonde, only now de-jeweled and a brunette. "Get her to sign a release, then keep her busy. Most of all, keep her away from disgruntled actors. Watch her. Don't let her leave. Let me know if she tries."

He scanned the room. The actors had wandered off, but Olga was still at her spot on the floor. She looked up, disinterested, as he approached.

"Mind if I join you?" he said. She shrugged. He sat down on the floor facing her. "How do you feel about things so far?"

"Bored," she frowned. "I thought we would be getting this over with, but nothing. Absolutely nothing. I should have brought something to read."

"Movies are like that, lots of waiting around. It's part of what you're being paid for."

"I don't like it," she muttered.

"Well, to hell with movies then. What would you rather be doing with your life?"

She thought a moment and said, "I would like to write."

"Is that right? Well then, look at this as material for a story."

She looked around contemptuously and blew through her lips. "No, it is too boring."

"Ah, but there is a lot going on here. Different people, different dreams, desires, lies, lust. Everything a drama is made of is right here. All you have to do is look."

"It is cheap," she frowned. "Peoples such as these are stupid. Why should I want to write of them?"

"They're people, like everybody else."

"They are shallow, not interesting peoples. They think only stupid thoughts, of how they look, of fucking each other. What do such peoples know of responsibility, of beauty, of love, of deep aware? No, they are stupid. I would not write for peoples who cared to read of such empty peoples."

"Your stories have only smart, complex characters?"

"No, but the story would be about these, as you say, complex characters. The stupid peoples are everywhere, so why not also in my story. A story on these peoples," she motioned with her hand, "would be only a boring story of stupid peoples and their stupid concerns. That is not interesting to me."

"If you look close, without prejudging, you will find complex intelligent people here who are acting dumb. Lest you forget, you're one of the characters, too. The smart young Russian woman who has to deal with stupid Americans, making a stupid sex movie."

"I didn't mean that! There are plenty stupid peoples in Russia. Everywhere it is the same. I have said *this* is not an interesting story, that is all."

"Life is art, art is life. There's art even in a stupid person's dreams. Think about it, here we are. You and I have accepted being here. You have chosen to be paid to be erotic with the stupid peoples. You don't find anything surreal about that?"

"Surreal?" she said, confused. "What is surreal?"

"Sort of like a distorted dream. Look, everybody here is a genuine living being. They aren't all stupid. They act as if they are because they're trapped in their own illusions. If they can impress others, or con themselves, they validate the brilliance of their stupidity."

"I'm sorry," she said. "I don't speak English so well."

"You don't? You speak it well, I don't hear much of an accent."

"I have the ears of language but not the vocabulary. I have been here only nine months."

"Okay, sorry." He remembered his own confusion when attempting to understand foreign languages in Europe. "These peoples are not stupid—"

"Yes, I understand this. You talked too fast for me to understand. The end, I was lost, repeat that, please."

"I forgot what I said."

"It doesn't matter," she shrugged. "To me these peoples, what is the word, looking for, what they search is so small. Sex is sex. It can be big drama, magnificent, or beautiful, but here it is small, nothing, shallow, empty. I am finding it hard to find the words," she grimaced, frustrated.

"You did good. Very clear. But there is drama here nonetheless, and it's bigger than you imagine. A story by a woman with a big soul, such as yourself, on these peoples, would be worth reading. European readers would find your perspective interesting. Americans, too. Art is perspective."

"There is no art here. It is too shallow, with peoples who have no aware."

Jake sighed, thinking she had not lived long enough to escape the influence of the youthful idealism clouding her comprehension. She gave him a strange contemplative look that unnerved him. He realized she saw him as corrupted.

"All right," he said, slowly. "The extraordinary can happen to ordinary, boring people in cheap shallow reality. There is a kind of karma going on here. Everyone is here for a reason. We've all been chosen to expose our *selves* in this chaotic contrived fantasy reality. Something is happening, and you don't know what it is. So instead of acting bored, why not listen to these stupid people, experience their shallow lives as an artist would. This is life out of balance. Immense leaps of faith into the darkness, escapism verging on self-destruction. What seems shallow to you may be the result of your own focus on surfaces."

A loud rumbling from the front door distracted them.

As he watched Julie go to the door to open it, he wondered why Olga was being so rude to him. Then Tracy and a tall man entered.

"Your sad friend is here," Olga said.

"Her papers are valid. She is nineteen."

"I do not doubt her papers. She is much too clever to have false papers because she is, how you say, a ... fugitive."

"Fugitive?" he said, surprised. "You mean runaway."

"Runaway?" she said, thinking a moment. "Yes, that. A runaway. She would find new identity, a permanent name. She may have others."

"Damn it," he muttered. "She is nineteen."

Olga scornfully blew air through her lips.

"I'm serious. There are too many things that support her claim to being nineteen. You don't understand our culture. You can't judge our kids by Russian standards. It's not that simple for a kid of fifteen to construct such an elaborate charade."

"It is not such a difficult thing. When there is sex, a young girl can get what she wants even when she is not as clever as this one."

Tracy spotted Jake and started running toward him. "Keep this opinion to yourself," he said, standing up.

"Of course. It is not possible that I betray this girl."

"Jake!" Tracy wailed. "Oh, I'm so sorry. I'm so sorry! Wormyham told me I ruined everything, that you were through with me and Playboy would blacklist me because I'm unreliable and I'd never work again. Is it true? Have I ruined everything?"

He greeted her with open arms and a smile. "No, he's just being an asshole," he muttered, guiding her away from Olga. "Don't mention him again, all right? I asked him to help find you, that's all. He's the only person I knew to ask."

She stopped and gulped for air. "I don't feel well," she moaned. "My stomach's been tied in knots all the way over. I feel so awful. Hit me. Punish me for not calling you."

Jake hugged her. "No," he whispered, stroking her head. "I'm going to hug you and tell you how wonderful you are, and you're going to have to take it."

"No!" she groaned.

"Yes," he whispered. "You are lovable."

"Lovable," she chirped.

"Sweet."

"Sweet."

"Beautiful, desirable, smart, talented," he said, rubbing her back. "But if you keep fucking up, I'm going to kiss you on your lips and put my tongue in your mouth."

"No!" She pushed him away, and looked at him seriously. "Really? I'm not fired?"

"That's right. They're not even ready to shoot yet."

"Oh, that damn Wormyham! He made me suffer like that. That bastard! Oh! My tummy!" She gripped her stomach. "Where's a toilet?"

"There's one by the offices. I'll show you." He took her hand.

"Oh, just a minute. I gotta tell my ride."

He followed her back to the door where the tall man was talking with Julie. When they reached him, Tracy said, "Tom, this is Jake, my agent. The famous director."

"Pleased to meet you," Tom said, extending a large hand. Clean-cut, well dressed, in his mid-twenties. He looked like a door-to-door religious zealot. "I own a couple of your films. On video, of course."

"Really?" Jake said, noticing Julie was staring at Tracy. "You actually bought them?"

"Sorry," he winced. "I rented them and made copies. I realize that doesn't do you much good, but I can't afford to buy them."

"Well, it doesn't do me any harm either," said Jake, feeling Julie glaring at him. "Since I don't get royalties on anything."

"Really?" Tom said, surprised. "That's too bad."

"Which ones do you own?"

"Visions of Claire and Celebration. Did you know Celebration is the only film in existence of the first annual Gay Pride Day Parade? It's like a historical document."

"No, I did not know that. Good to know."

"And Visions is considered a classic Lesbian sex feature film, the one that got guys interested in watching girls doing girls."

"Yeah, I had to add a guy/gal scene after an audience in Colorado tore the seats out off the floor in a theater and threw them at the screen, protesting the mostly lesbian sex."

"Uh, I'm sorry guys," Tracy moaned. "But I really have to get to a bathroom."

"Okay. Thanks, Tom, for bringing her over."

"No problem," Tom said as they left.

"Oh, god," she groaned. "I don't know if I'm going to make it."

"You going to throw up?" Jake asked.

"No," she gasped. "I'm gonna shit my pants."

"Getting stressed makes you shit?"

"Oh," she groaned. "Like when I get really scared, sometimes I can't help myself."

"Hold on, sweetfart," he said. "We're almost there."

"Sweetfart?" She made a face. "You're sick."

Jake pushed open the door to the toilet and she dashed in.

"I read the script," Kenyon's husky voice said behind him. "Which character was it required poise?"

Startled, Jake turned to her and said, "Lacey, the lead."

Kenyon smiled ironically. "I didn't see what you called a prerequisite poise."

"You're right," he said, feeling self-conscious. "I had no idea who would be cast for the part so I skimped on details. With you in the part, poise it would be."

"Jake," said Booth, approaching. "Did you bring Waverly?"

"She's in the bathroom," he replied.

"Good," Booth said, relieved. "Then we've got everything we need to start. Glad you could make it, Kenyon. I will make it up to you."

"She'd be a perfect Lacey," said Jake.

"Lacey?" said Booth. "That's been promised to Jezebel."

"Jezebel?" said Jake. "Kenyon has more presence."

"It's a done deal," said Booth.

"Well, then what role do you have in mind for her?"

"Whatever she wants. We'll talk about it later, I've got to check on the set. Bring Waverly over when she's ready."

After Booth left, Jake asked her, "What sort of acting experience have you had?"

"Commercials, stage, bit parts," Kenyon said with a crooked smile. "No porn."

"Does it bother you?"

"No," she said, cocking her head. "If it's in good taste."

"Well, what do you think of the script?"

"I wasn't expecting much," she said. "It'll do."

Waverly, partially opened the bathroom door. "Jake? Could you come in here?"

"Excuse me, please," he said to Kenyon.

She turned and walked away in her filmy blouse, her high heels clicking.

When Jake entered the bathroom, he found Waverly on the toilet. "What's wrong?"

"There's no toilet paper. Could you get me some, please?"

He shook his head, annoyed at Booth for being so disorganized he'd forget something as basic as toilet paper. Then he noticed several individually wrapped rolls on a shelf.

"There's some right there," he said, pointing at the rolls.

"Oh, good," she said relieved. "I didn't see it. I mean, it doesn't look like toilet paper."

He unwrapped a roll, wondering how she managed never to have seen an individually wrapped roll of toilet paper before. "Feel better?" he asked, handing her the roll.

"Yeah," she said, wiping herself. "But I'm hungry. Is there any food around?"

"Not that I know of. Ask Booth. He wants to see you when you're ready."

"Oh, fuck!" she groaned. "Is he mad at me?"

"No. Don't worry about it. As far as he's concerned you arrived with me, so if you're late it's my fault, not yours."

"I want you to know I appreciate this," she said, flushing the toilet. "I want to do this right." She pulled her pants up, and buttoned them. "What's my part? I hope it's Lacey, she's got the best lines. She's the lead, right?"

"Well, Booth promised it to someone else. I'm trying to change his mind."

Waverly slumped, crestfallen. "Who got the part? That girl you were talking to? It figures."

"No. The Arab girl. You haven't met her yet."

"The Arab! I saw her when I came in. She has black hair and saggy tits. She's not even as pretty as me. That's not fair!"

"Oh, I agree. Doesn't make sense. You're much better suited for the part."

"Is she a star or something?"

"No. This is her first film."

"She's no better than me and she gets to be the lead! Why? What's wrong with me? Why doesn't he like me?"

"He likes you. It's just your age."

"Age? But I'm younger!"

"Yeah, that's right. He doesn't think a kid can carry the part."

"But younger girls are sexier!" she pouted.

"I'll remind him of that," he said, opening the bathroom door. He looked around for Kenyon. "Try being more mysterious." He noticed Ben talking to an irritated Jezebel.

"Mysterious? What do you mean? How do I do that?"

"Just be quiet and smile. Don't argue with him. Let me do that."

"You think I'm being stupid?" she asked, defensively.

"I think you get overexcited." He saw Jezebel walking away from Ben in a huff.

"Well, why shouldn't I! I'm much better than that ugly, old Arab! I should be upset."

"Well, don't be." He spotted Kenyon with Olga, another disgruntled actress, and Janus nowhere in sight. "Let me do the talking." *Come on, Janus! You space case, you should be watching her.*

"ARE YOU PART of the crew?" asked Kenyon.

"No," said Olga. "I'm a performer."

"You're Russian, aren't you?"

"Yes. So?"

"I had a Russian boyfriend once. I can't imagine him ever being in a porn movie. He didn't have the imagination for it."

Olga blew contemptuously between her lips. "There is no need for imagination. It is money."

Kenyon laughed. "That's just the sort of thing Vlad would have said. A glib dismissal, completely missing the point."

"What is to imagine? To fuck these stupid people? It is to do and forget."

Kenyon sat on the floor. "In spite of his lack of imagination, he was a good fuck."

"Why not? To make sex with these people in a stupid movie is not as you say a good fuck. Imagination is imagination, nothing more. It is not a good fuck." She studied Kenyon. "You do this because it gives you pleasure?"

"There are any number of ways of having a good fuck, but they all require imagination," said Kenyon. "A fuck can be an adventure. It can electrify. It can energize. Throw yourself into a group of horny men, and you have it all as long as you maintain control. Being an actress in a porn flick seems like a safe way to be the focal point of group lust. You're expected to vamp and absorb male lust. Sucking up male energy under those conditions is like shooting ducks in a barrel. Most men are so unaware, they give everything away without regard to cost."

"I don't need these people's foolish energy. Of what use is it?"

"Depends on how it stimulates the imagination. If their energy doesn't interest me, I leave."

"Mind if I join you, ladies?" Joe asked as he squatted down next to Kenyon. "Hi, I'm Joe." He extended his hand. She smiled at his hand then placed hers in his. He examined her long, shiny black fingernails and the single gold band covered with tiny diamonds.

"Kenyon," she said. "We're discussing boredom."

"I see life as experience, so I'm never bored," he said, raising her hand to his lips. She withdrew it before he could plant a kiss on it. "There are so many interesting and exciting experiences. Every moment is worth having been lived, and the memories of them will empower me long after I'm dead."

"And if the experience is foolish?" asked Olga.

"Foolish?" Joe laughed. "Life is foolish, but sex is the most exciting and worthwhile experience in life. What's foolish is limiting yourself to sex with just one person or one kind of person. It'd be like limiting the quality of life. I mean, really, what is there more exciting, more interesting than sex? What better way to get to know someone? Ultimately that's what porn is all about, and it's beautiful. I don't care if it's foolish, it's beautiful."

THE STREET door suddenly swung open and a group of men piled in, most of whom appeared to be in their thirties or forties. From their tool boxes and clothing, Jake figured them to be the long overdue set construction crew, except for a short meticulously dressed boyish twenty-something in their midst who did not appear to belong.

Jake approached him. "We're shooting a film here. I'm the assistant director. Are you in any way connected to the production?"

The youth gave him an odd grin of recognition. "Booth invited me over to hang out and watch," he said in a deeper voice than Jake expected.

"He didn't say anything about that to me," Jake said with a doubtful frown.

"That's how he does things," he said with something more like a smirk than a smile. "He likes having an audience of his choosing."

"Why did he choose you."

"Oh, for many reasons. Like, for my being a recovering mama's boy with an affinity for self-destructive women. I enjoy their company. But I don't fuck them. I do, however, rather enjoy fucking with their heads."

"Ooooh-Kay," Jake sighed, thinking he sounded more like someone Worthingham would have invited. "What's your name?"

"Trevor," he said with a grin and a wink, as if they knew each other. Thinking he was trying to mess with *his* head, Jake turned away to look for Booth.

"I WANT the sex scenes out of the way before the actors are too pooped to pop," Booth said as he inspected the layout of a small cell.

"I'll be ready whenever you need me," Kurt said, lifting up the gold chain around his neck. "This is my good fuck charm. You can count on me one hundred per cent to come through as long as I have it around my neck."

"I'm thinking a quick easy scene in here with you and Olga."

"No way, man! You're not paying me enough to pork her. I'll do it, but it'll cost extra."

Booth looked surprised. "What's wrong with Olga?"

"I don't like her attitude. No sense of fun. When it's not fun, it's work, and I expect to be paid extra for work."

"I can't pay you more. I understand if she doesn't turn you on, she doesn't turn you on. But if you do this for me, I'll make it up to you."

"Forget it. I'm a professional and I have limits. I wouldn't want anyone to know how much you're paying me as it is."

"I'll make a deal with you. I know you like Jezebel so if you fuck Olga, you can have her, too."

Kurt laughed derisively. "Tell you what. If the bitch will fuck me without a condom, I'll do it. Ordinarily I don't object to condoms but that was the first thing out of her mouth when we met. She went on and on about it until I walked away. If she lightens up enough to let me probe her guts with my sword unsheathed, you got yourself a deal."

Booth frowned. "She won't do that. Besides Jezebel insists on rubbers, too."

"I have no problem with Jezebel because that bitch is hot. And, you know, something tells me, and I'll bet dollars to donuts I'm right, she'll end up letting me do her without a condom."

"Maybe you'll have the same luck with Olga."

"I don't even want to think about it. If she'll do it without a condom, fine. If not, let Joe have her."

"I already asked him," said Booth. "He turned me down."

He laughed. "Then you have a problem, because only a pro could keep it up for her."

Booth ran his fingers through his hair as he watched Jake and Waverly approaching.

"Jake," Booth said, "we have to start soon. Make-up will be along any minute now, and when she is I need the actors prepared for sex scenes right away. The jail cells aren't ready for the group sequence yet, but we could shoot something with Olga in this one. Or maybe do a locker room scene. Which do you think we should do first?"

"I think we ought to do exteriors," said Jake.

"No, no. I want to nail things down with a sex scene."

"We have light outside now, we won't later."

"I don't want to dispel the energy, no," said Booth.

Jake shrugged. "Well, we could fake the alley sequence with a few props set against the black backdrop. It wouldn't take much time."

"Yeah," said Booth. "Set it up."

"I need to know which girls. Who's Lacey, who's Kimberly?"

"Jezebel is Lacey, Kenyon's Kimberly."

"John, I don't think Jezebel has the presence to be Lacey."

"It's a done deal, Jake. She said she'd do the picture only if she got the lead."

"If I could talk her into doing Kimberly instead, would you go for it?"

"Sure, if that's what she wants, but don't scare her off." Booth noticed Waverly's leather jacket and jeans. "That's all you got to wear?"

Waverly fidgeted. "I was in a hurry," she mumbled.

"Did you bring a bathing suit?"

"I told you she didn't have one," said Jake. "She doesn't have much of anything by way of wardrobe."

"We don't have a costume budget," said Booth. "She has to have a bikini for the boat scenes tomorrow."

"The weather may be bad tomorrow. Rain's been forecasted."

"No choice. That's the only day we have the boat, so we either use it or lose it."

"Oh, and I just saw someone called Trevor who says you invited him over to hang out and watch the action. Is that true?" Jake asked, with a a look of disapproval.

"Yes," Booth said, flashing a look of annoyance back at him. "He's the new owner of this facility. He plans on turning it into an S&M night club."

Jake's jaw dropped open as he realized Trevor was the young man Ganymede had used at the S&M lecture. Somehow he knew that must be significant, but he hoped not.

Then a loud pounding resounded from the street door.

"You ought to put this off," Jake said with unintended anxiety in his voice. "It's not coming together and you're losing money from the lack of organization."

"I second that emotion," said Kurt, somewhat distracted by the pounding on the door.

"I'd lose more money if I stopped. Everyone's agreed to a set price for three days and I'd lose those deals along with my locations."

Julie opened the street door. Catherine entered lugging a large metal suitcase. Once inside, she barked out a laugh that made the flesh crimp along the nape of Jake's neck, remembering the sound of her laughter when he entered Booth's penthouse, and their strange conversation after their eyes met. It also reminded him of what Ben said about Aphrodite announcing Her presence with laughter when She took on human form.

"Good, Catherine's here," said Booth. "Get the actors into make-up, and let me know when they're ready."

"You got it," Jake said as he started to leave.

"Wait a minute," said Booth. "I need someone to do a scene with Olga. Kurt and Joe are overworked. Could you do it?"

"That'd be great!" said Waverly. "I'd like to see that."

"Well, maybe," said Jake, hesitant. "I'd have to think about it."

"I'd appreciate it, and I'd make it up to you. The scene takes place here in this cell. Think about how you'd like to do it."

Jake, his eyes averted, nodded. "Well, okay. First, I'll check in on make-up."

He walked off with Waverly following behind, whispering, "What about me? The alley scene's the beginning of the movie and I'm not in it."

"We'll see about that. I'll try to work something out with Jezebel."

"You heard what he said," she pouted. "He gave her the lead because she said she wouldn't be in his stupid movie if he didn't. Do you think if I'd done that I would have gotten it instead?"

"It's a bit late to think about that now. I'll do what I can, but the natives are getting restless. I have to get this show on the road, or we'll have a revolt on our hands."

CATHERINE watched Spear approaching from the corners of her eyes while she opened her make-up kit. "Did you see what the former officer of the law hath provideth by way of nourishment?" she asked him. "Coffee and donuts. That's it. Just coffee and donuts."

"How are you feeling, Seabolt?" said Spear.

She bit her lip, whispering, "The bad ghost woke me this morning." Her eyes flared to see if he understood the significance of this. "I was dreaming about Adolf Hitler, like when I was a kid. This time, instead of letting him chase me, I asked him what he wanted." An unpleasant thought showed on her face. "Then he turned into Tarwater."

After a brief silence, Spear said, "The deeper you go in search of order or chaos, the more ghosts and monsters you will find. Or, they will find you." He waited for a response, then added, "We are just travelers here today. The meaning you find to see the underlying fabric of events must be done *without* questioning it."

She pointed with her chin at Kenyon, Olga and Joe. "Vamp."

Kenyon smiled at Spear when he looked her way. Her smile struck something deep inside him that resonated like an odd form of farewell. Then he recognized her. Ken, the enigmatic hermaphrodite, the all-female Kenyon's twin brother. His presence here as a woman was an omen of the sort that precedes the ascendancy of chaos. Signaling the crossing of a threshold. Signifying he must now trust his instincts to avoid confusing himself during the crucial transitional phases into chaos.

Turning to Catherine, he said, "Events, they have a force, a gravity of their own. You must be careful how you involve yourself in what happens. *Anything* you *do* or *say*, it can have serious repercussions. Power comes from *not* interfering. In that way, you can construct the meaning of every situation without asking questions. What we do here is not about talking or thinking or action. Today is *only* for watching. Watch everything. What you see, it will stir the forces in you that want out. You will let them out."

"I HATE TO break up the party," Jake said to Ken/Kenyon. "But make-up's ready and you're in the first scene. We need you in make-up."

"All right! Joe exclaimed. "It's about fucking time! I can't wait to fuck this woman."

Jake flinched at the crudity, concerned it might put her off.

Kenyon looked as if her mind were elsewhere, far away. Then a slight smile appeared on her face as she said, "I prefer to be made-up last."

"I DON'T KNOW if I can to go through with this," Jezebel muttered while she foraged through a box of donuts. "I don't like being jerked around."

"I know what you mean," said Kurt. "At least we have a choice, we can leave if we want to. What really pisses me off is being fucked with and not being able to do anything about it, like when I was in the navy."

"You were in the navy?" she said. "I was in the army, stationed in Korea, Airborne. Nobody fucked with me unless I asked for it. Once on the DMZ, I fucked a guy right where the North Korean guards could see."

"Is that a fact?" said Kurt with a twisted grin. "Things were different for me. This fucking Petty Officer, Adler was the bastard's name, jerked me round every chance he got. But I made damn sure I evened the score. When my discharge came through, I hung around until the ship was about to leave port then went to the asshole's quarters and took a dump on his pillow as a bon voyage gift. Left a note to let him know I'd taken all the shit from him I was going to and it was payback time. Nobody fucks with me and gets away with it."

"Jezebel," Jake said, approaching. "We need you in make-up."

"Finally. Where do I go?"

"Over there." He pointed to Catherine at the make-up table. "By the way, have you had any acting experience?"

"Acting? No. I'm a dancer, and I sing."

"You sing, too!" said Kurt. "Can you sing in Arabic?"

"Of course," she said.

"Oh," said Kurt. "I'd love to hear you do that."

"I need to go over the first scene with you after make-up," said Jake. "You have any problem remembering lines?"

"No," she said. "Why should I? They're pretty simple."

"Well, it's surprising how easy it is to forget simple lines and Lacey has a lot of them. As a dancer you may be more comfortable in a more visual part."

"No, I was promised the lead and if I don't get it, I walk."

"I understand. Since Lacey has more dialogue you see her as the lead, but dialogue takes up very little screen time. The lead is whoever dominates visually and the intent there is Kimberley. That's really what porn's about. Lacey talks, Kimberly walks. How she looks at someone has more impact than anything Lacey says. She has the juicier part."

"I want the dialogue. I've seen enough of this crap to know I can do it as good as anyone, probably better."

"Okay," Jake shrugged, seeing her mind was made up.

"Tell me, is Waverly your protégé?" she asked with a smirk. "Are you watching over her? Her knight in shining armor? Her rescuer?"

Jake was too surprised by her sarcasm to come up with a response so he busied himself with pouring a cup of coffee. "Let me know when you're out of make-up."

After she and Kurt left, he looked around for something to sit on. Nothing anywhere other than one exercise machine. He leaned against a counter as he swallowed a mouthful of coffee swilled in donut sweetness.

"Yo, Jake!" said Joe. "When's my scene?"

"Don't know," said Jake. "How're things with Kenyon?"

"Oh, that girl is hot!" Joe laughed. "Let me at her! You have to let me be Eric. He gets to fuck all the women."

"You're a regular horn dog today, aren't you?"

"Not really," said Joe. "I'm always like this. If I'm not fucking, I'm whacking off."

"Is that right? When pussy's not available, how often do you whack off?"

"Don't scare me like that," he laughed. "A day without pussy is like a day without sunshine. It's been years since I've missed a day."

"And yet you whack off every day?"

"Yeah. I always whack off first thing in the morning when I get up, like other guys piss. I'll do it even if there's a beautiful lady waiting for me in bed."

"Really? How many times do you jack off in a typical day?"

"Oh, I'd say eight times."

"What? Really? Eight times a day. You've got to be kidding."

"No, I'm not. I'd say that was pretty typical."

"Where in the hell do you find energy for anything else?"

"It doesn't take that much energy. It's not like I put much time into it. When I'm fucking, I like to fuck as long as I can, but whacking off I do quickly. Five minutes tops."

"Still that's forty minutes a day."

"So? It's better than reading a newspaper."

"Yeah, well, I suppose I could grant you that."

"Why you doing this, Jake? What's in it for you?"

"Like you said, a shot in the dark," he said, momentarily surprised by the question. "I have a feeling something will come of it."

"You mean like Booth's next project?"

"No. I don't take his future games seriously. It's a vague feeling, non-specific. Like I said, I'm thoroughly demoralized with X-rated projects. I expect no rewards."

"I can't understand that, man. What's your problem? You act like it's some sort of crime to do porn. You treat it like a dirty word. Listen to yourself. X-rated projects? The word is porn, man! Beautiful, exciting, fantastic, wonderful porn! When you say porn, smile!"

"It's not the sex. It's the business end. Distributors feel obligated to rip you off. They wouldn't be able to sleep at night if they didn't. Like they validate themselves when they cheat someone, as proof of their superiority."

"Sounds like standard business practice to me. My biological dad's in television and I have an uncle who's a defense contractor. Makes no difference where you go, that's the way it is. Business is not about intimacy, it's power. You play it as it lays, otherwise you don't belong in business, you're an employee and we all know what happens to them."

He slapped Jake on the back. "Lighten up, buddy. I'm going to go mingle with the ladies. Have me some fun."

FOR THE LACK OF a better place, Ben chose to sit on the bed in a jail cell while he scanned his Jezebel notes. There'd been so many twists and turns pointing at something he'd momentarily understand, but something always kept him from remembering what it was. The insight first occurred when he warned Jezebel her life would be at stake if she failed to make and sustain an important shift in perception. She'd snorted contemptuously, saying she'd been living on the cusp between life and death since the assassination of her father; and perverts tend to pick up on things like that, the tension of sex and death being a crucial part of her allure. He'd watched her closely, looking for signs of hidden depths beneath her surface sheen while he explained how feelings of impending death were signals from the part of her that dwelled in the Underworld. Her impatience made him rush through his explanation of what a destructive life was, how it pulled one toward an early death. She cut him off when he said it was a matter of her life or death that she develop her ability to see into the Underworld. She said if he wanted her to play that game, it would cost him a thousand dollars. He told her this was not a pay-to-play game, that it was in her best interest to prepare herself for the call of the Underworld.

Her response was, "Go fuck yourself!" She'd cold shouldered him ever since.

"Could I have a word?" Jake asked as he entered the cell.

Ben looked up at him with a grimace, concerned Jazz may have told him of what he'd done to her. "Take a load off." he said patting the bed mattress thinking it was bad enough Julie was upset with him for what he'd done. He could not afford to lose Jake, as well.

"This won't take long," Jake said, uncomfortable with the idea of sitting next to him on a bed. "You said Aphrodite would let me know when She's in human form by laughing. Could you go into that in a bit more detail?"

Ben breathed a sigh of relief. "Well, if only you can see or hear Her, She'll get right down to business. If She speaks through someone else, that person will laugh when She enters your presence. However, she may not speak through Her host right away. Might just pop in and out. If She does speak through Her host, no one else will hear Her, or so much as notice either of you talking, unless She intends them to."

"Katie made a strange laugh when she came in today. I wouldn't have thought anything of it except she did the same thing when I entered Booth's penthouse. When our eyes met, I got a powerful jolt and she got all judgmental. Telling me what I'm doing, what I should be doing. Then today, when she laughed, I got an intense vibe off it."

"Numinous charge, yeah. Katie's a multiple with eight personalities that I know of, two of which are definitely archetypal. They've both been used as mouthpieces."

Jake sat down. "So, you're saying a goddess may have possessed her to talk to me?"

"No, no, not possessed, *per se*. Katie's sensitive to archetypes and, on occasion, they *influence* what she says. Sort of like an oracle."

"She didn't speak in riddles. She criticized and advised."

"I said, sort of like an oracle," Ben said, staring at him. "Gods use riddles because They do not exist in a literal world. If you are to understand Them, you must free yourself from taking things literally. Literal thinking traps mortals in surface ego-driven realities."

"But this goddess thing, uh, talked to me. I don't know how not to take that literally."

"As far as archetypal psychology is concerned, gods are neither believed in nor worshipped. Our concerns are with attitudes. The fundamental principle is *all* psychological events and behaviors have an archetypal likeness to which they *can be* led back. We act, think and feel as permitted by primary patterns. The task of archetypal therapy is to discover archetypal patterns. The idea being, *all things desire to return to the archetypal originals,* of which they are copies. When a pathology *returns to its source* it feels as if *you've come in direct contact with a god* in a super-charged reality outside of time and space. You have a sense of understanding everything, which comes from likeness. It feels more real than anything you've experienced in ordinary reality."

"I don't have the sense of understanding anything, except something talked to me."

"Well, yeah, but an anima figure won't tell you anything you don't already know, albeit you may not be aware you know it. She points at patterns then shrouds them in mystery and confusion. Your objective should be to *not* allow confusion to set in. And be sure to remember, what's happening here today is not just about you. When an archetype's activated, especially if more than one is, events form into mythical reality. *Skopos.* The thematic unity of intention. Something like the internal necessity and fittingness to each part of a work of art. Everyone here tonight, whether they know it or not, is under the direction of their guardian spirit to play a part."

"Is that why you've been so subdued today? To avoid confusing yourself?"

"Let's just say I'd rather not attract any more anima attention than necessary. I've been screwing with anima women's heads for decades. Mostly patients, to determine what aspect they were under the influence of by planting feeling images via vanity irritants."

"Ohhh-kay."

"Basic psychic alchemy. The right feeling image applied to an appropriate woman's vanity spikes emotional content, increasing the odds of drawing attention from archetypes. Whether or not an archetype is activated depends on the explosive factor of the emotional content. If one does descend, some form of possession *could* take place. One has taken residence in you, for example, by way of th impossible quest you set up for yourself." Ben paused. "Sorry about that. After what happened on Riley's shoot, I should have been more careful."

"Uh, what exactly happened on Riley's shoot?" Jake muttered, reluctant to address the idea of a goddess establishing residence in him.

"Several archetypes descended. Igniting complexes in everyone there. Then everything went haywire. I tried to stop Riley from feeding the frenzy, but he was out of control. I'm somewhat concerned something similar could happen here, tonight."

"So, you're saying there are several activated archetypes here?"

"No, no. There are at least three here, only one of which is active but not yet activated. With all these mirrors around, and most of the people here harboring ignitable complexes, apparently under the influence of Aphrodite-Hecate-Artemis, I'd say everyone is at risk. What concerns me most is what I might do if all three of them were activated."

JAKE LOOKED around for Kenyon, until he spotted Waverly with Kurt. Seeing her with him made him uneasy. She waved innocently at him.

"Jake, guess what! Kurt's does videos, like the one Janus did, and he wants me to do a couple of them. Isn't that great? I'm going to make a lot of money!"

"That's good." He scrutinized Kurt.

"It's amateur," said Kurt. "So there's not much money in it. I can't pay more than seventy-five bucks."

"That's okay," she said. "I mean, he says it won't take as long as Janus's did or anything. Only a couple of hours, right?"

"She'll be considered pro after this production," said Jake, "which will disqualify her from amateurs."

"Hey, my video'll be out long before they finish editing this sucker. I want you to know this here little lady's hot. I mean that. I've worked with big stars and she's hotter."

"Yeah, we know. Could you excuse us? I need a moment alone with her."

"No problem," Kurt said and walked off.

"Watch yourself or he'll have you for breakfast," said Jake.

"But he's so nice. He said I was the hottest girl here."

"Well, you are. But still it's a come on. Don't let these guys get to you, Wavy."

"But I like it! It makes me feel wonderful."

"Okay, just don't get too cozy. If they realize a compliment is all it takes to get your attention, everyone here will be all over you."

"That'd be great!"

"No, it wouldn't, because you're a star and you should have more dignity than that."

She looked at him as if he were talking nonsense. "If I'm a star, I can do whatever I want."

"You're in this for the long haul, Wavy, and I intend to do my best to prevent premature burnout."

"Premature burnout." She made a face. "I just want to have fun."

"Fine, fine, but be more mysterious, will you? You're acting like a bimbo."

"A bimbo? I'm being beautiful. Beautiful people don't say things like premature burnout. They're just happy and everybody wants them. Like Joe. I mean, he's cute and he's smart but he doesn't do any of this professional mysterious stuff. I want to be like him. I want people to want me, to like me. They don't like serious people."

Jake rubbed his chin, wishing she could learn from his mistakes, as if her having to learn on her own reflected badly on him. He sighed.

"Don't do that!" she said.

"Do what?" he asked.

"That sigh! I hate it when you do that."

"Sorry."

"It's like you're disappointed in me, like you're my dad or something."

"All right, I got it. But sighs are involuntary, I don't think about them. I'll try my best to avoid them in the future."

"Good, do that," she pouted. "I want the lead. I read it for Kurt, and he agrees with me. I should have that part."

"Wavy, the decision's not up to me or him."

"You got to make Booth see! I mean, he hasn't directed before. You're the only real director here. He should listen to you!"

"Well, that won't necessarily land you the part."

He looked around for Kenyon, thinking, *Janus, you better not have let her get away.*

"HAVE YOU EVER wished you hadn't done something to someone even though they sort of deserved it?" Jezebel said while Catherine applied mascara.

"I've done things I wish I hadn't," said Catherine.

"Sometimes I sort of get carried away. There was this boy who thought he loved me. In his eyes I was the most beautiful woman in the world. He worshipped me, gave me anything I wanted. He wasn't rich, he was only a couple years older than me, but he made it too easy to take from him. Let me use his bank accounts, credit cards, everything. I couldn't help myself. I felt so awful about it one day I cleaned out his accounts, $20,000. Then I maxed out his cards and disappeared. That was six months ago. It's been bothering me ever since, and I don't know why. You see, he made it so easy, I couldn't not do it. How can you respect someone like that? I couldn't shake the feeling I'd done something wrong so I gave it all to some people who needed it, but that didn't help. I still felt bad."

"Your thoughts are out of balance with who you are," Catherine said in a serene voice as she put the make-up aside. "You've been infected with Ghost Sickness."

"Huh?" said Jezebel, startled by her sudden change of voice and a charge in the air, like when you suddenly realize you're with a crazy person. "Ghosts?"

"Negative, destructive feelings. You will have to change this soon, or you will die."

Jezebel suddenly sensed the presence of Amira, the long dead part of her that dwelled in the Underworld.

"The things you need to know, you won't be able to understand because your thoughts get in the way," said Catherine. "You must find a way to turn them off."

Trying to regain her composure, Jezebel muttered, "How do I find a way?"

"Let go of who you think you are. See through the eyes of death."

OLGA WAS STILL sitting on her spot when Jake asked if she knew where Kenyon was.

"I think she left," said Olga.

"Left? Where did she go? Is she coming back?"

"I don't know where. Home maybe."

"Why? I thought she decided to be in the movie."

She shrugged. "Maybe she was not impressed by these peoples. I don't think she trusts Booth."

"Why? What happened?"

"He makes promises too quickly."

"Oh, brother." He sat down beside her. "You know, uh, Booth asked me to do a sex scene with you. What do you think of that?"

"What's to think?" she shrugged.

"I thought we might discuss it, you know, what you think would make a good scene?"

"We do it and finish with."

"That's not a very imaginative approach for two creative people to take."

She glared at him and said, "This is not interesting."

"Win, lose or draw, whatever happens out there will be interesting," Jake said slowly and clearly. "We are two characters in a life out of balance, coming together in a moment in time, each with peculiar attitudes and motivations, to perform a sexual act for the entertainment of others. You're a writer, think of the implications. We can be entertaining or we can be boring. You, the artist, as a character in your story, will choose, one way or the other, either to be entertaining or to be boring before these stupid peoples. It may not be worthwhile either way; but it is, nonetheless, a choice."

"You Americans always look for opportunity where there is none." She thought a moment. "I think maybe I will do this. I will try. For me erotic is slow, soft rhythm. Seductive touch with, how you say. She looked at him. "Timing? Yes? Can you do this?"

Jake smiled. "I would love to give it a try."

"HI," Jezebel said in her sexiest voice, grazing her fingertips across Spear's hand as she passed. He did not acknowledge her.

Touching strangers was a White custom Spear found difficult to accept.

"Wow," said Joaquin, watching her as she walked off, hips swaying, her clothes lisping and teasing. "How can you resist a hot honey like that?"

"Practice," said Spear.

"I wish I had the opportunity for that kind of practice. I get hit on now and then, but by corporate types. What do you think draws them to you? The Indian thing?"

"I'm something to keep them on their game. I am not available. I am a challenge."

"How do you do it?"

"What they're selling, I'm not buying. They reduce a sublime act meant to bestow life to a physical urge."

"I know what you mean," said Joaquin. "I love fantasizing a child being the end result of what I do. That's a real turn on. But I also know there'd be hell to pay if I got someone like Jezebel pregnant. Believe me, I know. Been there, done that."

"That's not what I meant. The only real energy we have, it is life bestowing sexual energy. It takes a great deal of energy to withstand the pressures of the unknown. To achieve depth. I would not waste it on frivolous sexual encounters."

"I wouldn't go so far as to say sex with Jezebel would be a waste of energy but she does bring to mind that old saying. Never play cards with a man named Doc, never eat at a place called Mom's, and never fuck anybody who has more problems than you do."

"Her personal life force, it would impact on you in ways you can't imagine."

"You mean other than getting a disease, or something like that?"

"Have you considered the possibility that by merging with someone like her, you would be infected by her darkness?"

Joaquin cleared his throat. "I suppose you're right. God knows, women like her make you pay for it one way or another."

"JANUS, we have a problem," said Jake. "Kenyon's gone."

"What!" Janus gasped. "She can't do that!"

"Of course she can, and she has." He signaled Waverly, who was talking to Trevor, to come to him. "Could you phone her and try to lure her back?"

"I, I, I," Janus stammered. "I can, but I'd probably just get her answering machine."

Jake hugged her as he said, "Calm down. It's only a movie. It's nothing. Give her a call, and if it doesn't pan out ask Joe if he has any idea where she might have gone."

"Okay."

He released her then motioned with his hands, "Go! Go! Go!"

Then he said to Waverly as she approached, "You're in the opening scene."

"You did it!" said Waverly. "That's great! Lacey's role, right?"

"Well, no, but Kimberly has more screen time, so if you play it right the audience will assume you are the star. Meanwhile, get your butt into make-up."

"You mean like right now?"

"Yeah, now."

She trotted off toward the make-up table.

Jake approached Trevor to ask him, "Where's Booth?"

"I'll take you to him," Trevor said, squinting in a manner that made Jake suspect he was stoned on something.

"Ohhhh, Kay," Jake said, immediately aware Trevor had taken offense with his tone of voice. He followed Trevor past the lockers, through the bathroom to the sauna adjacent to the showers where he found Booth with Spear and Ben. Trevor stayed to listen in.

"John, we have a problem" Jake said to an annoyed looking Booth. "Kenyon split."

"She left!" he said with an accusative tone. "Why?"

"I don't know," said Jake. "Olga thinks she was put off by the lack of organization."

"That bitch," Booth muttered.

"It's no loss," Trevor said with a delighted smile spreading across his face. "She's a hermaphrodite. The real Kenyon's twin brother, Ken. Still has his pecker"

Before Booth could respond, Jake said, "Look, we're down to four women, only two of which are up to snuff. That's a far cry from the seven beauties called for in the script. Let's call it a day and do some serious talent scouting from the pro porn pool."

"No money," said Booth. "We'll shoot anyway."

"We don't have enough women," Jake insisted.

"We'll make it work," said Booth.

"How?"

"Atmosphere. It'll work. Trust me."

"All right," said Jake.

"I'll set up the first shot with Waverly in Kenyon's part."

"Put Serena in," said Booth.

"Serena?" said Jake through his teeth. "Why?"

"Waverly's too young and I don't want to lead with my two best cards."

"John, Serena can't act for shit and I doubt you'll get much out of Jezebel either which could make the opening scene a joke."

Booth frowned. "All right, do it. Let me know when you're ready."

"Hold on, Jake," Ben said, following him into the main room. "I'd like to go over something with you."

Jake turned to Ben, who appeared to be distracted by the mirrored walls.

"Remember what I said about Aphrodite and Aristophanes the playwright?" said Ben. "Ari specialized in the intimate relationships between Eros and Chaos. The peculiar connection between the worst inert sludge of human nature in Chaos and the attractions of Eros. The fixations in our lives between the erotic and the psychopathic. The idealizations of Eros and its affinity for Chaos."

Jake winced an impatient grimace. "Okay, okay. Your point being?"

"I'm trying to prepare you for what is likely to happen. Chaos is like a gap, an emptiness. Eros has a predilection for the psychopathic holes in the psyche." Ben paused to glance over at the wall mirror behind Jake. "I suggest you pay particularly close attention to relationships between the Erotic and Chaos."

"Oooo-kay. And how exactly am I suppose to do that?"

"Feel into the entanglements, and they become reflections of archetypal patterns. The Eros in the Chaos will lead you to the archetype behind a pattern. Once there, you are played into myth after myth. Mythical awareness and enactment is the payoff."

"'Entanglements,'" Jake muttered as he turned aside to see what Ben was looking at. He saw a reflection in the mirror of an oddly dressed old man observing Katie and Olga.

"Just remember," Ben said, looking at the same reflection. "When you *feel* Chaos, *look* for the Eros. Don't think and you will know what to do." Ben turned away to see if he could find Oliver outside of the mirror. For a moment, he thought he had. Then he didn't.

"Katie's working on Olga," said Jake. "I better check to see if she's done Waverly."

"We need each other to get through this, don't forget that," Ben said, following him. "Oh, and let me know if you've see an old man in a tweed jacket hanging around."

Jake hesitated for a moment to decide if he should tell Ben he'd just seen the old man in the mirror. It somehow felt odd to him that he felt he had to decide, so he said nothing.

"I NEVER LIVED on a collective farm," Olga said while Catherine brushed her hair. "I knew peoples who had been and they think of it as prison. The peoples there were, how you say, of small minds. Everything, always the same, no ambition, except maybe small ones, like to have a new refrigerator. I think in such places it can be no other way."

"Depends on the people," said Catherine. "I was raised on a hog farm. And for a couple of years a group of people lived there with us, sharing everything in the middle of nowhere. As I remember it, they weren't of small mind."

"If it is their choice. But I would not chose it."

"Of course, it was by choice. Everyone, except us kids, could leave whenever they liked." She stopped brushing. "Some of us resented that."

"You mean the parents left their children?"

"Everyone was considered a parent." She resumed brushing. "We weren't left alone."

"I don't think that would work good," Olga shrugged. "Your parents left you alone?"

"If he could, my dad left mom behind, because he knew I didn't like being left alone."

Then Catherine saw Jake and Ben approaching.

"Olga's not in the first scene," Jake said, firmly. Catherine's startled look set him back. This was not the woman he met at Booth's. "Have you finished with Waverly?"

"No," said Catherine. "She's up front with Joe rehearsing. I reckoned I might as well start experimenting with Olga's hair. I could see it's going to be a problem, it's so thin."

"Could you leave us please, Olga," said Ben.

Catherine stared at Ben, her eyes narrowing.

"I'm not here for myself," Ben said. "It's Jezebel. She needs to be warned —"

"She has been," a dark voice answered.

Jake now recognized the Catherine he'd met before.

"She's aware then that—" said Ben, looking her directly in the eyes.

"She knows."

"By you?"

"By the other."

"Any advice for what I can do to help her?" Ben said, maintaining eye contact.

"Tell her to ride the mood to enter the mythic drift."

Ben frowned as he nodded, then he said to Jake, "Let's go."

"I'll send Wavy over for make-up," Jake said as they walked off.

"Ride the mood," said Ben. "To ride the mood is to hold its image. To enter the mythic drift, look for the Eros in the Chaos. Like I said, they don't tell you anything you don't already know."

"What did she mean by the other? Who's the other?"

"That'd be Katie's Angel's persona," Ben said, distracted by Julie's glaring at him from across the room. "I should tell you something about Julie. After you and the lovely Esad left Mindy's shoot, Worthingham violated Julie's boundaries in ways that got Artemis's attention. Julie is uncomfortable having Artemis hanging around, as am I. I told her she had to re-establish boundaries. Why this should be of interest to you is I also told her whatever action she took in that regard, it would more likely succeed if she did so in tandem with you. That's why she's here, to hook up to establish boundaries with you."

"Wha—? Are you kidding me? I don't think she's even so much as said hello to me. What possible reason did you have to tell her that?"

"It just came out of my mouth. I have no idea why." Ben shrugged. "Most likely, Artemis made me do it. Remember, this *is* mythical reality. You don't question it."

"Really? Give me a mother freaking break," said Jake, his irritation bubbling over. "I have no fucking idea what you're talking about. How in the goddamn hell can I to do anything to help anyone deal with something I know next to nothing about?"

"Remember back when we first met, you said you had a problem turning your back on damsels in distress. You said when you had to, you felt compelled to tell them why, but your reason was you'd come to the conclusion they were hopeless crazies. You couldn't tell them that, so you gave them other reasons, usually along the lines of they were driving you crazy. You asked me for my opinion. Do you remember what I said?"

"I don't even remember the conversation," Jake said, irritated but confused because it did sound like something he'd say. "I have no idea why I'd say something like that to you."

"Well, you did, and I told you it was pointless and cruel to tell them anything because emotional women, especially if they think they are in love, will not process what you say if it does not conform to what they want to hear. So, save yourself the pointless trouble. Say nothing."

"Okay, okay, but what the holy fuck does this have to do with Julie?"

"She's a damsel in distress, and I've convinced her you're the only one who can save her, your being by nature a distressed damsel saver. The fact there's nothing personal going on between the two of you is an advantage to you both. So, when the time comes, and it will come, ride the mood with her and enter the mythic drift." Then he added, "Oh, and the man in the tweed jacket I mentioned earlier? He's her father. His name is Oliver, and he has a knack for making himself invisible. Except for in mirrors. He's here somewhere. Watching us, right now. If you see him face to face, don't speak to him."

JAKE FOUND Waverly and Joe in an office rehearsing. "Where's Jezebel?" he asked.

"She went to get something to eat," Joe said.

"Christ! She has to stay on the set. She's up next."

"You want me to go get her?" Joe asked.

"Please."

"No problem. I'm out of here." Joe left the room.

"Why aren't you made up?" said Jake.

"They're ready for me?" she said.

"Yeah! Didn't I tell you, you were next for make-up?"

"Gosh, I'm sorry. I didn't think it mattered since I have to practice anyway."

"It matters. Following instructions matters. Professionalism matters. We must focus energy to make this thing happen. Now go to make up."

"Okay, okay!" she grumbled.

Janus and a Filipino woman appeared in the doorway.

"Jake, I found somebody!" Janus announced triumphantly.

That somebody was Paola Passionata, a thirty-two-year-old Filipino nymphomaniac who specialized in doing bachelor parties. Her act consisted of smoking cigarettes with her cunt, picking her tips up off the floor with her cunt lips, and shoving her hand up into her ass. Her alluring Asiatic features and firm, youthful body was somewhat put off by her saggy tits and an enormous smile that bared her buckteeth to the gums.

"Nice to see you again, Paola," he said as if speaking to a child. "Do you remember me?"

Her smile wavered as she attempted to place him. "You worked on a video for Roger Jolly at my home a couple years ago." She grimaced, trying to remember. "Serena was there." She squinted. "You were in a three-way with an older woman and a transvestite. You had to leave before the scene was over."

"Oh, yeah," Paola said uncertainly. "So sorry. You look different. What you do with yourself?"

"I look better or what?" said Jake.

"Better. You seemed sad then. You making this movie?" Her smile flashed back on.

"Me? No, I'm the writer and assistant director."

Her smile disappeared and she looked away. The ease with which her face expressed her thoughts amused him. She was an awful actress, but that could change if she could grasp how expressive her face was.

A short Japanese woman with a long-lens camera stepped into the doorway.

"Where is the director?" Paola asked Janus.

"I'll take you to him," said Janus.

The two women walked past the young Japanese woman without acknowledging her.

"Hello," the Japanese woman said. "You Jake?"

"Yeah," he said.

"I'm Marika," she said, bowing slightly. "Mr. Worthingham, he said you gave permission for me to be here. Okay?"

"The photography student?" He vaguely remembered Worthingham saying something about a photography student. He couldn't remember agreeing to one coming on the set. "Yeah, I remember."

"I want to thank you for making it possible for me to be here," Marika said, bowing.

"You're welcome. What do you plan on doing with the photos?"

"I submit to magazines in Japan. Maybe use for classes, also."

"This must seem strange to you," he said.

"Strange?"

"Westerners making a porno film?"

"No. I have been on movie sets before."

"I mean the sex part. We are doing a sex movie. Do you make them in Japan, too?"

"Not like this," she nodded, smiling effusively. "We have large sex gatherings. I have been to in this country as well."

"Yeah, okay," Jake smiled, dismissing her.

"Jake Zakheim, right?" blurted a short burly man in his mid-forties as he breezed into the room. "My little pardner here," he gestured at Marika, "told me she was looking for you." He extended a beefy hand, saying, "Lou Mingarella." He squeezed Jake's hand. "Doing a spread for Hustler. John said he'd have a pack of foxes here."

"What do you think of what you've seen?" Jake said. "Foxy enough?"

"The little blonde's a stunner. By the way, your zipper's down."

Jake glanced down at his open fly and zipped it up. Marika smiled.

Mingarella laughed and said, "Marika asked how to find you and I said look for a guy with his fly open. Someone told me you liked going around with your zipper down."

"Who told you that?" Jake asked, embarrassed.

"A good journalist never reveals a source. I collect stories about various purveyors of fine smut. I got the zipper story from several sources. One actress said it's intentional, but she has no idea if you do it because you think it turns women on or because it turns you on. Or, could it be a source of inspiration, a creative lightning rod, so to speak."

"You're looking for a quote?" Jake asked, trying to mask his irritation.

"Oh, no, no, no," he shook his head. "Just curious. You're regarded as something of an eccentric, you know. So am I, in my own humble way. As one eccentric to another, why do you go around with your pants open?"

Jake scrutinized Mingarella and his loose wrinkled skin. His clothing smelled of cigars. "All right. I have a tendency to put my hands in my pockets and occasionally, not always, that causes my zipper to fall down without my being aware of it."

"So you're just," he grinned, "detached, so to speak."

"Yeah, that's right. Not quite fully in the material world."

"Yes, yes, from another planet," Mingarella laughed. "So I've heard. I remember your first films, I've seen them all by the way. Not an easy thing to do considering your penchant for changing your name. Your sets were awful. Unintentionally, I suppose?"

"I used what locations I could get as they were. I did not choose to alter them."

Mingarella laughed. "The original hippie pornographer, that's what you were. Hey, don't get me wrong, I was a hippie back then, too, and you were like my fucking hero. In fact, it was because of you I decided to get into the business. So you see, I owe you a debt of gratitude."

Jake stared at him, dumbfounded.

"I have seen, too," Marika meekly added.

"What I don't get is why all the different names? Kinda puts a damper on overall name recognition by the general public."

"Being anonymous is a kind of freedom. I don't want to be singled out by that kind of fame."

"Yeah, right," said Mingarella, grinning. "So, you getting back in the biz then?"

"If the money's right. I'm perfectly willing to sell out, but nobody's buying."

"That's a shame, a legend like you. You were the first to put girl-girl scenes in features back when distributors thought guys didn't like that sort of thing. Way I hear it, you started the ass fuck trend as well."

"That's not exactly true," said Jake. "When I started out, films were mostly cock sucking, which I find boring to watch, and when they did insertion shots they avoided showing assholes. I like women's butt holes, so I showed them. Maybe I influenced that trend. I did the first ass fuck features, but only because that's what my investor wanted."

"Hey, you know, maybe I could do a piece on you that would help. You know, a glamorous article in Hustler you could show around to investors. Just might impress somebody enough to cough up some dough."

Jake attempted to hide his skepticism, figuring Mingarella would waste his time without producing the article. He couldn't imagine himself showing an article to investors to raise money. It would make him look like an amateur.

Then, too, he was not sure he wanted any further involvement in the business anyway.

"Think about it," Mingarella said, reaching into his jacket. "Here's my card. Call me. I'd like to go over this with you."

"Will you be around for the entire project?" Jake asked.

Mingarella looked around, frowning. "Nah, don't think so. I'll hang out for the juice shots tonight. That should be enough. Frankly, blondie's the only decent babe here."

"What about the Arabian princess?" Jake asked.

"She's an Arab? That a fact? That's interesting, but I prefer lighter skin. You know, blondes, big boobs, that type. Blondie's perfect."

"Here comes trouble," Jake said, as Waverly entered. "She's upset the princess got the lead instead of her."

"She's not the lead?" Mingarella said, surprised.

"How do I look?" Waverly asked, smiling.

"Like a million bucks," said Mingarella. "Jake just told me you're not the lead. Booth must be out of his fucking mind."

"Waverly, this is Lou Mingarella from Hustler," said Jake. "He says you're the only reason for him to hang around."

"Really?" Waverly beamed.

"That's right," said Mingeralla. "I originally planned on staying for the entire production because John said he had seven beautiful women. From where I stand, he's only got one."

"Really?" Waverly flushed, ecstatic.

"John can think whatever he wants, but the real star of this movie is you. Distributors decide who's the star and who isn't. As a long time veteran in the business, I'll be damned if they don't pick you for the box cover."

Really? I'll "be the box cover girl?"

"I'd bet my life on it," said Mingarella.

14

Shreds of Dignity

"Change of plans." Booth thrust a jumpsuit at Jake, interrupting his conversation with Olga in the locker room. "We're doing your sex scene first."

"Oh," said Jake, conscious of Olga leaning against a locker, staring at him. He examined the SWAT logo on the jumpsuit. "Good. I'm really not up for a late night."

"Have you worked out your routine?" asked Booth.

"Olga wants me to seduce her," said Jake. "Slow and easy."

"Not too slow, we're behind schedule."

"John!" Janus said, entering with a nineteen-year-old blonde, blue-eyed boy. "This is Johan! Isn't he drop dead gorgeous?"

"Johan?" said Booth. "German?"

"Yes," said Johan. "From Pforzheim, in the near of Stuttgart. I am to understand I need no paper for work here?"

"That's not a hundred per cent. I require proof of age but you don't need work papers since I'm not paying you."

"No pay?" said Johan, puzzled.

"That's right," said Booth.

"Surely something?"

Janus flashed a desperate look. "I told him he'd be paid something. He's beautiful. It'd be criminal to let him get away without using him."

After a long pause, Booth said, "All right, I'll pay you something, depending on how you perform."

"Please, how you mean perform?" he asked.

"That means you have to get it up, you fuck whoever I tell you to fuck and come when I tell you to," said Booth. "If you do all that for me, then I'll do something for you."

"I must the sex completion and then paid?"

"That's correct."

"May I ask, please, how much?"

"I will determine that at the appropriate time."

Johan looked to Janus. She gave him an encouraging smile.

"All right." He offered Booth his hand. "I will do this for you."

Booth looked at the extended hand then shook it. "Good, let's get started." He glanced at Jezebel. "Jezebel, this is Johan. You'll be working with him."

Jezebel scrutinized Johan. "Has he done porn before?"

"I don't know, have you?" Booth asked him.

"No," said Johan. "I have not."

"Then you can forget about my working with him."

"Why not?" Booth asked.

She moved close to Johan. "Because he's a kid, it's his first time, and he'll have problems." She poked him in the chest with a finger. "I only work with pros."

Janus rubbed herself against Johan. "He won't have any problems," she said. "I'll get him ready for you."

"Doesn't matter, I work only with professionals." She looked Booth square in the face. "I thought this was a professional project."

Booth turned to Janus. "You're a guard, Johan's DEA. In this scene cops are fucking prisoners, not each other. To get around that, we start with you eating Jezebel, Johan comes in, starts fucking you and you keep on doing what you're doing."

Jezebel tugged on Booth's t-shirt and motioned to the men's room. "Excuse me," Booth said, irritated, and he followed her.

She walked up to the sinks, then turned to face him. "It's bad enough you expect me to fuck some kid still green behind the ears, but to expect me to fuck a woman with mint oozing out of her gills is way out of line. No way would I ever let that bitch's mouth touch me. Who knows where the hell it's been."

"She's safe. She gets checked for AIDS every other week."

"She disgusts me."

"So fake it."

"You couldn't pay me enough. Besides we're both dark, we'd look awful together."

"Well, if that's the case, you'd look great with the kid."

"He's *too* light. He makes me look practically black."

"Waverly's just as pale but you want to work with her."

"That's because we'd look great together, and she's so sweet. Anyway, he's a tourist."

"John, we have a problem," Janus said, entering the room with Johan and Jake. "Now what?" said Booth.

"Johan can't stay," she said.

"I must in two hours back in Berkeley," said Johan.

"No, you can't do that. You have to stay here for as long as we need you."

"Then perhaps I go now and back later."

"No, no, stay," said Booth. "We'll shoot your scene now. In fact, let's get started."

Jake liked the sound of that. Gawkers were always at their most attentive during the first sex scene. Relieved his would not be the first, Jake left the room.

"How long time is my scene?" Johan asked as they entered the locker room. "Depends on how long it takes you to fuck," said Booth signaling.

Johan watched Jezebel approach. He did not want to have sex with that angry woman. He scanned the others. A Japanese woman looked at him with an amused smile, as if they were co-conspirators. A pale redhead with a ring in her nose gave him a demented smirk. A Filipino licked her garishly red swollen lips.

"I must now to chose a woman?" Johan asked Booth.

"No, Janus will take care of you," said Booth.

Johan winced. Janus worked her fingers up from his thigh to his crotch. She looked like Frau Steimle, his English teacher. Click! The Japanese woman's camera. Pointed at him. Suddenly the reality of the situation struck him.

Pictures being taken! Millions of people would see!

Janus unbuttoned his fly, reached in and fondled his flaccid cock.

What if Frau Steimle saw it? What would she think? he thought as Janus pulled down his pants. *What if she told his mother?*

"Let me help!" Paola grinned, her breasts lying like pouches of milk against her fingers and thumbs. Then she reached for his cock and her red lips engulfed his balls.

How could these women want his body yet not be aware of how he felt. Click!

"No photos while the camera's on," Booth warned Marika.

Johan looked at the little, blinking light on the camera.

"Don't look at the camera," Spear said softly.

Joe, watching Johan, remembered his first video. His career in an industry he believed he was born to be a part of began with a hooker on his eighteenth birthday. Taped by a friend, sold to an amateur video company. For six years he'd *never* had an erection problem, until the day he discovered erections were not automatic. That discovery led to a string of failures. His tail between his legs, he returned to San Francisco, determined not to allow the doubts that dogged him in LA to haunt him here.

"What's wrong?" Waverly whispered. Why isn't he hard?"

"Haven't you seen a limp dick before?" said Joe.

"Sure," she said. "But shouldn't he be hard?"

"He's too nervous."

"Has he come already?" she asked.

"Don't tell me you've never had a problem with a guy getting it up?"

"No."

"That's great!" he laughed.

"Quiet on the set!" yelled Booth.

"Let's go to the sauna," Joe whispered in her ear.

JOE CAREFULLY pushed the sauna door open. The door squeaked shut behind them as he took her into his arms. "They can't hear us now," he said as he started to kiss her.

"Don't do that," she grimaced.

"What?" said Joe. "You don't like the way I kiss? Does my breath smell bad?"

"I don't like kissing, that's all. Besides I don't know if I'm supposed to be doing this."

"The kid's not going to get it up. By the time they figure that out, we'll be ready for them."

"Then we're supposed to be doing this, right?"

"That's right, pretty lady," he laughed, unbuttoning her blouse. "Fan-fucking-tastic!" he said to her tits, then he dropped his pants.

"Wow!" Waverly gasped at the sight of his long, fat, enormous erection.

"You like it?" he said, brandishing his staff.

She took hold of it and pulled. "Shouldn't we let them know you're ready?"

"In good time, all in good time." He guided her face to his rod. "We'll keep ourselves in a state of readiness until they come for us.

Oh, you're good," he moaned. "Very good."

The door swung open. "Hiya, kids! Hiya! Hiya! Hiya!" boomed Mingarella. "Don't mind me, I'm looking for some action and nothing's happening out there." He aimed his camera. "Pluck his magic twanger, girlie."

Click!

"You guys know what photonasty is?" said Mingarella.

"Isn't that what you're doing?" laughed Joe.

"It's how light affects the positioning of growing plants. So what I need is for you to position yourselves closer to the overhead light so I can take some nasty photos."

He got a whiff of Waverly's body odor when they moved. He lowered his camera and moved in close to her buttocks, sniffing it in short bursts.

"Hey! That's gross! He stuck his nose in my butt!"

"Stick to the photonasty, buddy," said Joe.

The sauna door swung open and Jake came in, glancing at Joe's stiff staff in Wavy's hand, then at Mingarella's camera pointed at her butt. Waverly gave Jake a guilty look.

"Nothing's happening out there," said Mingarella. "So I came to where the action is."

"Okay. I'll let John know," said Jake.

WHEN JAKE stepped out, he found himself face-to face with the man in the tweed jacket, his steel blue eyes glaring directly at him. He had a thick gray mustache, white goatee and professionally styled, salt and pepper hair. Probably pushing seventy. It took a moment for him to realize the man had somehow *grabbed him with his eyes*. His eyes, now a startling grey, reflecting a cold intelligence, tightened their grip. Julie's father. He instantly knew the man, knew Ben had set him up with his daughter, and that he was somehow being scanned by him. All of the fathers of his wives and lady friends had disapproved of him. With that thought in mind, he realized Julie's father disapproved of him more than all the others combined. That frightened him, because he sensed this father could easily squash him like a bug just by looking at him.

BOOTH WAS NOT on set when Jake returned. Paola and Janus were still working on Johan's limp dick while the crew stood around talking.

"Non-essential personnel clear the set," said Jake."Everyone else, please be quiet."

"Who's non-essential?" asked Serena.

"Anyone who's not in the shot or on the crew," he said, heading for the men's room.

Booth was with Ben by the sinks.

"Joe's up and ready," said Jake. "Why not give the kid a rest?"

Ben said, "We're taking a breather to give him a chance to get it up."

"His chances would be a hell of a lot better if you shot someone else for awhile," Jake said to Booth. "A break says we're waiting, and that's a lot of pressure for a novice."

Booth rolled his eyes. "The kid can't stay. He has to leave in an hour. Meaning if he doesn't get it up soon, we lose him."

"You should shoot as long as you have wood," said Jake.

"Wood?" said Booth.

"Shoptalk for hard on," said Jake. "It's late, we need to build sexual tension. Shutting down for a limp dick this early in the game disrupts the flow."

"If I brought Joe in, it'd be like telling the Kraut he can't cut it. I might as well just kiss the kid goodbye and save us the trouble."

"It's an orgy scene. Tell him you'll shoot whoever's hard when they're hard. Reduces the pressure. If he can't handle that, you can wait 'til hell freezes over and he still won't come through."

"Mr. Booth!" Paola shouted triumphantly, her lipstick smeared in a large splotches on the corners of her mouth. "He's up!"

"There you go," said Booth.

"It won't be for long," said Jake. "She broke rhythm trotting off to fetch you. One of the crew should have—"

"Stop being so damn negative!" Booth snapped then walked off.

JAKE WAITED for Booth and Kurt to leave before he said to Ben, "I saw the man in the tweed jacket. He locked his eyes on me. I don't think he likes the idea of me and Julie—"

"Don't worry about his approval," Ben interjected. "Power like his aimed at anyone would feel threatening in and of itself. He was scanning your weak points to shore them up, not to tear you down. He's actually an ally, not an enemy. I was hoping he would help you, which is why I mentioned him to you in the first place."

"You said you and I need each other to get through this tonight. Why?"

"Because of the senex-puer thing you got going," said Ben.

"Senex, the wise old man. The puer, the eternal youth who never grows up."

Ben grimaced. "It's more complicated than that. You understand they're polarities?"

"Yeah. I had an English teacher in high school who was into polarities, archetypes, mythology, all that stuff. "

"Okay, then. What struck me about you when we met at Mindy's was your puer and senex were not in conflict. Tension, yes, but cooperative mutual acceptance. I need to be around that kind of energy tonight. They were balanced in me, too, until the Riley episode knocked me off. Guiding you through will help keep me from confusing myself."

"You think for sure something will happen here tonight?"

"Oh, yeah, definitely. Probably around the midnight hour. But, always remember, the gods do not exist in a *literal* world, and it's easy to lose yourself trying to understand Them because there's so much behavioral crossover. Hekate will manifest as a three-headed goddess tonight, with Artemis and Aphrodite. Your destiny must be accepted sooner than later, or your further growth will be destructive. You need me to help you see through what happens tonight, and I need you to help me retain my balance and focus."

JOHAN'S semi-hard penis softened in spite of Janus's heroic efforts to restore it to life when Booth returned. Booth gestured at Paola to take over and she stared blankly at him.

"Get him hard," said Booth, under his breath.

Paola glanced at Johan's flaccid cock, seeming to fail to grasp that it was not erect.

Kurt approached Booth. "Send me in," Kurt whispered.

"I need you later," Booth said, without looking at him.

"As a stunt cock. Substitute my cock for his. I do it all the time. Shoot in close and nobody will know the difference."

"You're in the scene, it'd be noticeable," said Booth.

"Hey, this shit happens all the time. Shoot around it."

Irritated, he headed back to the men's room, Kurt following. Dr. Ben was smoking a cigarette when they entered. Booth said, "Where's Jake?"

"Probably with Olga or Katie," said Ben, running water over the tip of the cigarette.

"The little jinx's getting on my nerves," said Booth. "Seems like every other word out of his mouth brings us nothing but trouble, like he's planting ideas in people's heads. I need the support of my key people. What I don't need is some no talent jerk's incessant whining. He's not clever enough to do a mind fuck, but that big mouth of his is sabotaging our movie by pornofying it. Christ, I'm beginning to talk like him."

"Hate to be the one to break it to you, John," said Kurt, "but this is porn."

"No, it's not! Don't even think that. This is an erotic motion picture and will be one as long as I keep it from being trashed with porn platitudes. Did you read his idiotic script?"

"Of course I did." Kurt stiffened as if he had been called an idiot.

"I can't use this crap!" Booth slammed his fist on the script, and he picked up a page to read from it. "Lacey, takes off pack as if *her* were the most valuable object on earth." He looked at Kurt. "What the hell is that suppose to mean?"

"A typo?" said Kurt.

"Sloppy," said Booth.

"What do you expect," said Kurt. "He wrote it in a day."

"All right then, dialogue," said Booth. "Girls, we are about to *embark* on a summer vacation that will *exceed* our wildest dreams! We won't be *constrained* by the miserly $25,000 summer allowances our parents gave each of us. No! We're going to turn that money into real money!" He looked at Kurt. "Give me a fucking break."

"Reminds me of a story about a third-rate actor doing Hamlet," said Kurt. "He's so bad the audience yells at him to get off the stage and they keep at it till he can't take it anymore. So he stops and says: Hey, what're you blaming me for? I didn't write this crap."

Booth glared at him. "What the fuck's that suppose to mean?"

"Geez, man, it's porn. It's not meant to be *Gone With The Fucking Wind.*"

"That's just it. This," Booth shook the script, "is porn. That's not what I do. He has a tin ear for dialogue. I can't tell one character from another. He says shoot whenever we have wood. That's what he wants. Wooden sex, wooden dialogue, wooden movie."

JAKE WATCHED Catherine, sitting with her eyes closed under the make-up table, her chin at her right shoulder. He didn't know who he might encounter if he interrupted her meditation. She inhaled and slowly moved her chin to her left shoulder as she exhaled.

He decided to risk it. "Excuse me," he said, gently. "You're needed for touch-ups."

She looked at him as if searching for some person in hiding just behind himself. "Strange things have happened to you the past few days."

"What do you mean?" he said, absorbed in the different looks she got in her eyes one after another, from sparkly to sad to a kind of soulful light.

"A tension in the environment," she said, still working him over with her eyes.

He wasn't sure what to make of that. "A friend of mine is being pursued by a demon."

She got out from under the table and stood up. "Moira," she said, her voice normal.

"Yeah, but how did you know that? You know her?"

She closed the make-up kit. "She was in the last film I did with Riley."

"Do you know what's going on here?"

She looked at him, shifting in quick glances from his face to his hands, to her feet, then back. "It's a balancing act," she said. "Follow the clues, and do what you do."

Jake felt the atmosphere around her shift, and his thoughts turned off.

"You've grown accustomed to evil influences and no longer fight them."

The calm, nonjudgmental clarity of her voice gripped his attention. "This is the result of a weakness in your character. Although you are able to properly nourish yourself, you rely on inappropriate methods or people to fulfill your needs. This has created an unhealthy state of mind. You've lost your way. The more action you take, the farther afield you will stray. Begin again at another time." She picked up her kit then walked away.

Had she just warned him off from this project? Then he noticed a paperback on the table. *Archetypes and Strange Attractors*. He opened it at a page with a corner turned down and saw "Hit by God!" scrawled in the margin. He read the highlighted text. "... order occurs when the chaos in one of its dimensions is matched by chaos in another. ...Trying to avoid chaos prevents us from becoming a factor in its dynamics. We become its pawn. Only by resonating with it, allowing ourselves to become part of it, do we force chaos to take us into account. We establish self-similarity across scale. Chaos becomes orderly when it finds its reflection. To open oneself to chaotic dynamics ... is to offer oneself as a potential fractal dimension of those dynamics."

"This entire shoot's one holy mess," Mingarella said, breaking Jake's concentration. "A glass eye in a duck's ass can see Booth doesn't know what he's doing. I'd a been out of here long ago if I hadn't promised to watch over Marika. And wouldn't you know it, she wants to stay the whole nine yards. Reasoning with her is like trying to convince an eight-year-old sex is more fun than a chocolate ice cream cone. Hey, Jake-o, know what the Japanese consider the precise moment of highest erotic arousal?"

"Uh. No, what?"

He watched Jake's face. "The second before the loss of innocence." Then he laughed. "You look like you've just seen a ghost, Jake-o."

"So you got all you need on Waverly, then?"

"Got more than I'll ever need," he winked, "considering I can't use any of it."

"What do you mean? Why not?"

"You guys are small potatoes, you may get away with it, but a nude shot of an underage girl would bring Hustler down in a New York minute."

"What! Well, surprise, surprise, she's not underage. She's nineteen, almost twenty."

"Hey, I haven't been surprised by anything since I found out girls don't have weenies."

"I've seen her IDs, they're legit, I know, I—"

"Fuck IDs, man. Wanna know how I know?" He touched the tip of his nose. "The nose says she's fifteen. See, adolescent girls are my thing. Know why? Their smell. Nothing on God's green earth smells as divine as an adolescent girl. Alls I gots to do is sniff their butts. A green pepper smell tells me she's underage. That, along with other body odor nuance, will tell me within six months just how old she is."

Jake sat down and stared at his feet.

Mingarella chortled. "You actually believe she's nineteen?"

"Yes! Of course, I do. Booth wouldn't have hired her if he thought otherwise. He's an ex-vice cop, for Christ's sake. He should know an underage runaway when he sees one."

"Yeah, yeah, whatever," he laughed. "But if I were you, I wouldn't be too quick mistaking a cop's caution for responsibility. They're great believers in their own excuses and besides, in the end, they're above the law. And the ex-cop's the worst of the breed. They quit the force thinking the world's their donut. They take from everybody."

"I WANT your beautiful cock inside me," Janus whispered in Johan's ear while Paola pumped his inert penis as though trying to start an engine by churning its little handle.

"No!" he said. The attitude in Janus's voice disturbed him almost as much as the chafing motion on his cock. "I cannot."

"Yes, you can, sweet baby," Paola cooed.

"No!" Johan sat up. "I cannot. I must to my appointment."

"Fine!" said Booth. "Bring in Waverly and Joe."

"They're a mess," said Catherine. "I have to re-do their make-up."

"No time," said Booth with a why-is-everybody-doing-this-to-me face. "This is hard core sex, they should be a mess."

"What about me?" Serena asked. "My make-up's fine."

"You're not in this scene and I can't afford to pay you for an extra sex scene."

"I'm hot," she moaned. "I feel bad. Real bad."

"Fifty bucks is the best I can do."

"Okay, but you do it my way," said Serena.

"How's that?" asked Booth.

"I want Janus to use my knife."

"What do you think, Jake? Can I get away with it?"

"Maybe, since it's a woman doing another woman."

Serena pulled a switchblade out of her handbag. "You know how to use this?" She pushed a button and a blade snapped out. Janus jumped back.

"On the other hand, a switchblade's a bit much," said Jake.

Catherine stared vacantly at the knife, breaking out into a sweat as the air round her took on the steaming stink of fresh dung.

"I want the knife or I want more money," said Serena.

"It'll play in Europe," said Booth. "Let's do it." Then he muttered, "At least we won't have to worry about hard-ons."

Serena handed Janus the knife. "Hold the blade against my face, baby, and order me to strip."

"No time," said Booth. "She's already naked and you should be, too. We'll shoot tie-ins tomorrow when everyone's fresh. Take off your clothes."

Serena removed her blouse, the light whitening her skin. Janus traced the blade around her breasts, over the tiny veins crazing its tissue and the dusting of pale hairs and moles scattered like flakes, to the rings dangling from her nipples.

Spear noticed a flicker of alarm in Catherine's eyes, and her fingers curling into her palms. "Spell me," he said to Joaquin, handing over the camera.

Janus inserted the knife tip in Serena's nipple ring. Catherine's fists jerked up to her chest.

"It's very sharp," said Serena. "Like a razor. I want you to cut me. I want you to lick my blood."

"You can't do that," said Booth. "You can't even say it."

"Okay, so don't lick my blood. Just cut me. Draw something on me."

"Cut!" Booth yelled. "No cutting."

Joe laughed in the background.

Catherine sucked her breath in with a twisted sound, like a whimper. Her complexion took on a bluish hue as she absently stroked her hair.

"*You can only kill things with guts,*" she gasped.

"Seabolt?" Spear whispered as he grabbed hold of her hands and held them down.

"Rolling," said Joaquin.

"Cut me, baby, cut me!" Serena groaned. "Carve your name on my belly!"

"Oh, God," Catherine gasped, *evil thoughts flowing into her head!*

"Come with me." Spear squeezed her hands as he guided her toward the door.

"Let me take the knife away from her and threaten her with it," said Serena. "I know how to handle it so she wouldn't be in any danger."

"I don't know," Janus grimaced.

"Oh, you'll love it, baby," Serena smiled.

"Seabolt, you with me?" said Spear, *talking her into existence with the magic of his voice.* "What were you seeing?"

"My dad," she moaned, "gutting a pig on the farm."

Serena moved the blade slowly across Janus's neck.

"The evil ghost puts words in my mouth," Catherine gasped.

Spear slapped her gently but firmly midway between the hip and ribcage then shoved the door open to the main room.

"Is she all right?" asked Kurt as he and Ben followed after them.

"She will be," said Spear, leading her to the outside exit.

Ben stopped when he saw Jake reading a book over at the make-up table.

"What's the matter with Katie?" Jake asked Ben when he approached.

"She shouldn't have been on set," said Ben. "The arrangement was if we needed make-up during sex scenes, the talent would be sent to her."

"Why's that?"

"She's susceptible to sexual epileptic seizures. That may sound strange to a layman, considering she's a virgin."

"A virgin?" said Jake, now noticing Kurt approaching. "Really?"

"That's a symptom for her type of epilepsy, no sex drive. But her fits make up for the orgasms she missed out on. The one she had on Riley's last shoot was so intense she lost control of her bladder, bowels, everything. How are things going between you and her?"

"Well, I don't know what to think."

"When it comes to anima women, don't think. You'll just end up confusing yourself. They're transparent. The objective is to see through them."

Then, as Kurt approached, Ben excused himself.

"It's going to be a long night," Kurt said after Ben left. "The way things are stacking up, Catherine won't be the only one having a shit fit."

"Yeah. I'm worried about Waverly," said Jake.

"Hey, don't be. She's young, she can take it and then some."

"I don't mean the long hours. She's inexperienced and I don't want her taken advantage of."

"You mean like a gang bang or something? Hey, this is a fuck flick. Besides she'd probably like that just fine."

"She's a kid. Do you remember when you were a kid?"

"Yeah, and I would have loved it."

"Come on, Kurt. Get real. I know when I was a teen, in spite of my bravado, I was actually pretty damn vulnerable."

Kurt considered this. The memory that came to mind was of his mother, how she used to say whenever she got angry she was leaving and would never come back, and how that made him feel.

"Whether she wants to be trashed or not," said Jake, "it's the wrong thing to do."

"You're playing daddy to a pretty tough customer. You in love with her or something?"

Jake hesitated, reluctant to express his feelings. "I care about her. I care what happens to her. She doesn't always behave as flakey as she has today. She's actually quite smart, with a lot going for her. She's no bimbo. It annoys me that she likes to act like one."

"Hey, man, she doesn't come across any dumber than the other girls. Women are like that. You know, sort of like the way guys act tough. Acting clueless is their thing."

"Well, that's not the way I see her. I don't want her acting like trash or being treated like it. To tell the truth, I'd just as soon split and be done with all this, but I'm worried what will happen to her if I leave."

"I hear you, man," said Kurt. "Look, if it bothers you that much, I'll watch out for her. I'll make sure she gets home without anybody taking advantage of her. What she does when she gets home, hey, even you can't control that, am I right?"

"Thank you," Jake said, sensing Kurt liked him. He wondered why.

"There's something I'd like to ask you. You know a lot about women, right? I mean, you've been married and have had long relationships and all, whereas I've never been in a relationship that's lasted more than a month. What I'm saying is, you have a different take on women than I do. Maybe you understand them better. One thing's for sure, I don't."

"Lord Byron, the most famous of romantic poets, once said it is easier to die for the woman you love than to live with her."

"Ain't that the truth," Kurt snorted. "But what I was wondering was, did your wife ever call you into the bathroom to talk while she was taking a dump?"

"Well, no," said Jake, surprised.

Kurt thought a moment. "Maybe it's just the women in the industry. But then you've been in the business a long time so maybe you've had the same thing happen to you. Sometimes when I get something going with an actress I'm working with, she'll come up with some lame excuse for me to be in the bathroom with her while she's taking a dump. Has that happened to you?"

He considered Waverly's toilet paper issue. "No. Does that happen to you a lot?"

"Yeah, enough to make me wonder why the fuck they do it," said Kurt. "It's not just me, other actors told me it's happened to them, too. Why do you think they do that?"

"Well, uh, I don't know. Maybe since they're uninhibited, they don't think about it."

"No, that's what I thought at first but I don't think so. You know what I think it is? Hostility, like they're dumping their shit on me. Some sort of power trip, making me smell their stink."

"Well, I don't know," Jake stammered. "Doesn't make sense. If anything, it should be embarrassing to them, like losing their last shred of dignity."

"That's good! I like that!" Kurt laughed. "Their turds are shreds of their dignity, which is about right with those bitches. But, you see, that's why I asked about your wife. I figure, you know, I really don't like women and women know that about me. You, on the other hand, they know you like them. So I figure, me they'd give their shit to and you, maybe not."

"Whew," said Jake. "Could be they do it to me, too. It wouldn't necessarily occur to me to think anything of it. I don't remember. Women think different than we do, you know, and maybe they figure their reason for asking you in was, uh, a good one."

"Yeah, right," said Kurt, "except it's always some stupid thing that could've waited. Let me get this straight, you're telling me if a beautiful woman you barely knew invites you into a room to talk while she takes a dump, you'd think nothing of it? Don't you think that's a bit strange in itself?"

"Well, it's business, the situation, I, uh, I wouldn't necessarily remember it."

"I'm sure they're telling me something. And whatever it is, I don't think it's nice. You know, like eat shit and die."

SPEAR GENTLY GUIDED Catherine to a vacant bus stop bench.

"I'm cold," she whimpered as she sat down. "I hate being cold."

"A childish woman or man, they do not arouse a mature erotic response, Angelica," he said softly, as if addressing a child. "They usually fall into some form of prostitution."

She furrowed her brow. "Pros-ti-tu-tion."

"In the sense of misuse of sexual energy. A too easy sexual submission to another. Autoeroticism."

"Mas-tur-ba-tion," she whispered.

"Or, the woman who feels having sex with a man is to bestow on him an invaluable gift. Or, the man who sees sexual prowess as his measure of worldly success. These patterns would not continue on their destructive, egocentric way if their victims were mindful of the deeper processes of growth. Sexual problems, they arise from unconscious processes that have not been dealt with."

"Pro-ces-ses," she muttered, shivering.

"There's a pattern called Moth Craziness. It's associated with incest." Her eyes flashed. "The symptoms are nervousness, fits of uncontrolled behavior, convulsions, violence, rage. And the kind of fit you are prone to. It's called Moth Craziness because the victims are attracted to their destruction, like moths to a flame."

"Ah, ha, strange attractor," she whispered.

"The Moth Way myth, it involves Begochidi, one of our Holy People, the Creator of life. He made all living things by having sex with everything in the world. He's all knowing, yet He's a mischief maker and a gambler. He can change into any form. Water. Rainbows. Wind. Insects. As master of insects, he would send swarms of them to bite the other gods until they met his demands. His name means One-who-grabs-breasts, because He likes to sneak up behind young girls and twitch their breasts, shouting, "Bego, bego!""

She giggled. "That's silly."

"Sometimes, He appears as a worm or insect crawling in the dust, representing something obscene. He favors procreation and sex, because He is the Creator. He's also a transvestite. Dresses like a woman. The Creator is the essence of paradox, combining lowest and highest. Rampant sexuality and sexual transcendence. Lascivious trickster and mystic unity with god." He paused to give her time to frame a response. "In the Moth Way myth Begochidi, he lived among the Butterfly People as a berdache."

"What's a berdache?" she asked with a look of intense interest.

"A transgendered being. Half-man, half-woman. Usually stressing spiritual over sexual behavior. Begochidi, he would grab the Butterfly Peoples' crotches yelling, *Bego! Bego!*"

"Why did he do that?" she said, a mixture of curiosity and excitement on her face.

"The Creator *is* sexual energy. Energy demands negative and positive charges. Life springs from sexual energy. The Butterfly People, they were particularly susceptible to temptation. Begochidi would not let them marry as long as He took care of their needs. One day when He was away, they committed incest and went Moth Crazy. They jumped into the fire. Had to be forcibly separated from each other. After He gave them the cure, butterflies flew from their mouths, vanishing through the sacred hogan's smoke hole."

"Butterflies," she sighed, closing her eyes as she nestled up against him.

The contact startled him. His hands gently moved to comfort her, as if it were the most natural thing to do. Her open mouth breathing caught his attention. Angelica, a frightened child seeking a safe place, needing to be comforted before she could let go. He felt her body relax, then she moved out of his embrace. She looked embarrassed.

"Seabolt?" He waited for a response, a sign that she was ready, that some part of her would understand what he was about to say. She nodded, and he began.

"Each movement of growth has its own particular ebb and flow. Its shifting of alignments of forces, they cannot be stopped. They can only be felt into. Responded to. Worked with. The unknown can come to you at any time. You must brace yourself to face a force that will sweep you away from language. There is no way to describe adequately what is going on. This force, it will disintegrate the foreign patterns attached to you. It will pull you away from their rules."

She nodded.

"You will need sobriety and fluidity to face what will come. To do this you must free yourself of expectation, fears and hopes. In silence, look for an interplay of energy accompanied by a strong emotion, and an interplay of hues. To interpret this, your true mind must emerge. Then the Spirit, an outside source, It will guide you."

Her lips formed the words *true mind*.

"To leave the comforts of a shelter to walk exposed into chaos is one of the hardest tasks one can face. Let the masturbatory, heavy purposelessness, self-pitying, self-indulgence of the negative feminine principle disintegrate. The moths within you that want out are being stirred. You will let them out, and ride in their wake to restore balance."

"Why *this?*" she asked. "Why horror films? Why porn?"

He smiled, then whispered in her ear, "Bego! Bego!"

SERENA'S RED MANE shook furiously, as she buried her face in Janus's genitalia.

"Oh, shit!" Janus gasped, stiffening. "Oh, shit, oh, fuck! Shit!" Vibrating and contracting with each spasm, she screamed as if she were being stabbed. "Aaaaaaaah!!!!"

A gush of liquid shot out of her cunt into Serena's face.

"Cut!" said Booth.

"Thank you for being so strange," a wet faced Serena said to Janus.

"All right!" said Joe, straddling a bench with Waverly sucking him. "Janus, the electric lady, comes through! Hey John, check this out. We're ready to cock 'n crow."

"Great stuff, you guys! Rub that stuff on your face, Serena," said Joaquin. "Let me see it. Lick it off her pussy. Camera's still rolling. Believe me, you'll thank me later."

"How's Catherine?" Booth asked Spear as he reentered. "Fine," said Spear. "The knife upset her."

"That's it? Just upset? She's all right?"

"She's fine."

JEZEBEL swallowed a large pill as she examined her reflection in the mirror. She looked healthy and alert, considering the long hours and neglecting her medication. Then she noticed someone else in the mirror. Marika, a big smile on her face. Motionless, in the doorway. Like a statue. No telling how long she'd been there watching with her camera.

She put the pill case back in her handbag then turned. "What are you doing here?"

Marika's smile disappeared. "So sorry to have disturbed." She lowered her head. "I come to use toilet."

"Did you take a photograph of me in here?"

"No, please, I did not."

Jezebel looked closely for a sign of deception.

"You better not have. No pictures are to be taken of me unless I sign a release. Understand? And for that you have to pay me, got it?"

Marika nodded. She'd known treacherous Asian women as a child. But this one, no older than herself, did not appear to be one.

"What's your connection to Jake?" she asked in a kinder voice.

"Connection?" Marika looked up. "Mr. Worthingham said Mr. Jake would allow me to make photos of a pornography as it is made. I never met him before this day."

"That's it?" Jezebel said, suspicious. Marika nodded. "He didn't ask for anything in return? Does he want copies? Are there restrictions on what you can do? There must be some conditions."

"No, nothing," Marika said, puzzled, wondering if she had been misunderstood.

"What's the point? Why are you here?"

"Point?" Marika smiled, thinking of a point being like on a target. "I find this interesting. Very American. I look for images. It is very, I don't know how it is said in English, special? No? Unique? Yes, a unique way of doing."

"Are your photos going to be in a book or gallery or what?"

Marika looked as if she didn't understand the need to show the pictures. "I don't know what I do with them. Perhaps if I make a good photo, it may publish."

"What you're saying is you don't expect to make money off them, right?"

"Oh, no," Marika laughed as if it were a foolish to think so.

"I think I'm gonna hurl," a naked Waverly said as she headed for the sink.

"What's wrong?" Jezebel asked, touching her shoulder.

Waverly stiffened. She'd heard Jezebel wanted to do a sex scene with her. "I have a problem with women doing women, okay?"

"What sort of problem?" Jezebel asked.

"I tried not to look, but that old woman screamed like she was being stabbed or something. So I looked to see what's going on, and all this stuff shot out of her cunt, like right into the redhead's face. Ugh! I'm going to spew!"

"What about a woman doing you?"

"No way!" Waverly grimaced. "That's so weird."

"Women are much better at it than men," Jezebel said.

"Well, I don't like it when guys do it either, but at least I can understand why a guy might want to. But a woman? I mean, a woman knows how gross it is."

"Then you're a virgin."

"A virgin? Me?"

"You've never been with a woman before," Jezebel said, her dark eyes fixing on Waverly's bright blues.

"No, I haven't," Waverly stammered. "Because I don't want to! And I never will!"

"Oh, you will," she purred, gently squeezing her arm. "And I'm going to be the first."

Waverly winced, but Jezebel's lust had begun to work its magic, transforming her in Waverly's eyes from adversary to admirer.

JAKE SLIPPED into a jumpsuit. All it would take for him to be naked was a simple down zip of the zipper and a shrug of his shoulders. He reached for his shoes.

"Don't bother," said Booth as he entered the room with Trevor who seemed to be trying to swallow a laugh. "We won't see your feet. It's late and I'd like to get this over with as soon as possible. I'm not going to use much of it in the final product."

"You might change your mind. Olga wants it to be erotic."

Trevor sniggered. Obviously stoned.

"Erotic?" Booth made a face. "You mean like romantic erotic? You're a cop, you're taking what you want, that's all there is to it. Romance has nothing to do with it."

"Well, anyway, it could be done with some sensitivity."

Trevor pushed his lips together tightly, his face turning red from his efforts to swallow his laughter.

"Look, I don't care what you do as long as the scene's over and done within thirty minutes," said Booth.

"Sort of like wham, bam, thank you, m'am," Jake said as he slipped on a shoe. Trevor giggled out loud, then covered his mouth with his hand, transferring his laughter to his eyes.

"What can I say? Things haven't worked out as planned. I didn't get all the people I need so now everyone has to do extra scenes, including Waverly. I added a girl/girl scene with her and Jezebel. Since girl/girl scenes aren't sex scenes, she won't be paid for it."

Taking his hands away from his mouth, Trevor laughed out loud.

"What! What do you mean it's not a sex scene!" said Jake. "She's repulsed by lesbian sex. Refuses to do it. To her a girl/girl scene is more work than sex with a guy. I won't advise her to do it for nothing, I'll tell you that right now. No freaking way!"

"Freaking way!" Trevor snorted. "Are boy/boy scenes not sex scenes, too!"

"I need your help, Jake," Booth said, ignoring Trevor. "Will you help me, or not?"

"Not!" Jake said, standing up. "You're short two women you budgeted for, you could use that money to pay for the extra work expected of your people."

"No can do," Booth said. "My budget's gone to hell. I can't spend any more money. We'll talk about this after your scene."

Jake walked off shaking with anger. He took in a series of deep breaths, trying to dispel the anger as he exhaled. Failure to do so would be fatal to an erection.

"MY FATHER was epileptic," said Olga, sitting on a jail cell bed.

"Is that why you ran away?" said Catherine, brushing her hair.

"No. He was a drunk and a bastard, and he did not care for me. What did the peoples on the farm think of your seizures? You had them there, yes?"

"I don't know what others thought, but my father was embarrassed."

"Are you frightened? You seem somehow frightened. My father, he was crazy before, sometimes for days. Usually some hours before the seizure he thinks peoples are threatening him. Are you like this?"

"It's people, not peoples," Catherine tittered, pulling nervously at her own hair with her free hand. " People is plural. Many."

Olga looked up at her. She jerked her hand down.

Jake entered the cell, too distracted by his anger to notice Catherine's discomfort or her swift departure. He needed Olga's help to reign in his rage, otherwise he might as well forget about obtaining, much less maintaining, an erection.

"Excuse me," he said. "I wish I weren't but I am irritated. Not at you, but with John and this whole damn mess. There's no way I'm going to be able to give a sensitive, erotic performance." She shrugged. "We need to flesh out an alternative, something fast paced."

"That's not what I do," Olga said.

"Never? You've never been carried away by passion?"

"Yes, sure, but not so fast. I must, how you say, contact the person. The passion, it must be built. It is stupid fantasy someone comes to prison, says stupid things and suddenly I am full of this passion. I am not so simple."

"Yeah, okay, but you have to help me out here. Remember, I'm the one who has to get it up if we're to get out of here any time soon, and I'm not going to be able to do that if you don't play along. Can't you use your imagination to build up passion, you know, think of me somehow in that way? Fake it if you have to? Imagine someone else."

She frowned. "I cannot turn passions on because you ask it. I need time."

"We don't have time. We must find a way to heat things up quickly to make it easier on me to get it up, otherwise it'll be unpleasant and demeaning work for both of us. If you'd seen what happened to the

German kid, you'd know what I'm talking about."

She made a hopeless gesture with her hands. "This is not some game I play with you. Passion for me is either real or it is not."

"All right then, not. Do a half-assed job, or fake it, but give me something to work with. The simplest thing is for me to be a jerk who takes advantage of you."

"Then I will fight you."

"No, no, no! Don't do that. You can resist a little, but I am the law. Give in and let me do it. Trust me, it requires less of you than of me. I'm the one who's doing the work."

"This is not a game. You attack and I will resist."

"For Christ's sake, it is a game! We're actors! I am not actually doing anything to you. And I am not in the mood to play games! We are co-workers, help me do our job."

"I will respond to what you do."

The lights clicked on. People started to gather around the set. Olga frowned, and when she did he saw how easily she assumed the expression, as though disapproval came naturally to her and was part of her face. He desperately sought ways to fan any kind of desire to sexually touch this woman that would work without her co-operation. Narrow it down! Exotic teen, deep soul, powerful life force — FEMALE!

"Here's what we do," said Booth. "Jake and Janus walk up to the cell, she unlocks the door, Jake goes in, interrogates Olga and Janus watches. Keep the prelims short, I don't need dawdling around getting undressed. Let's get this thing over and done with quick."

"See what I mean?" Jake said to Olga. "We're expected to rush through this. That means I'm expected to get it up and keep it up pretty damn quick. I *need* help from you."

"I will respond as I would respond, that is all."

"Come on, you have to cut me some slack or it ain't going to happen. You don't get it, do you? Hostility is not a turn on for me and, believe me, this is a lot harder for me than it is for you." He shook his head and walked out of the cell. "Okay, let's do it."

"Go over to Janus and wait for my signal," said Booth.

Janus was at the edge of the set, dressed in a police jumpsuit, hair pulled back tight in a bun. She looked tough.

"Action!" yelled Booth.

Startled, Janus glanced at Jake for help. Jake walked back to the cell and waited for her to join him there. She approached, her face frozen, then hesitated by the cell door until she remembered the loop of keys hanging from her belt and fumbled with them.

"Any key will do," Jake whispered. "Fake lock."

Janus nervously shoved a key into the lock, awkwardly flung the door open and stepped to one side, out of the shot.

"Give me a few minutes alone with the prisoner," Jake said, approaching Olga. He wondered if she were disgusted at having to work with him. No, he must narrow focus to what works or hang it up. Churn the fantasy. Her holes, her matter. Her, *her*, HER!!!

"Are you going to tell me where the dope is?" he asked, menacing. She answered by spitting air out between her lips. "No? Well, then, take off your clothes."

"No!" she said, disdainful.

He turned his back to the camera, gave her a pleading look and she gave him one of contempt. He rolled his eyes and continued. "I have to search you for the dope. You *must* take off your clothes."

"No," she shook her head.

"All right, then, I'll take them off for you." He reached for her and she hit his hand.

"You touch me again and I'll scratch your eyes out," she snarled.

Jesus, he groaned to himself. *What a royal pain in the ass!*

"I don't want to get rough with you," he said out loud, "but if you resist, you will regret it. Now take off your clothes!"

"Fuck you, you piece of shit," she spat.

"All right, here goes nothing," he said lunging for her. She grabbed at his hands and fought back. He froze a moment and whispered to her, "Come on, we can't do this."

"You stupid swine, get your hands off me!" she yelled.

Jake let her go and turned to the camera with an exasperated expression. "Come on, John, you can't use any of this crap. Cut it."

"Cut!" Booth yelled, after which Trevor let out a loud snigger.

Jake turned back to Olga. "Rape and violence is unacceptable in major markets. You have to co-operate or forget about it!"

"He's right Olga," said Booth. "When he tells you to strip, do it."

"That's not realistic," Olga insisted. "I wouldn't let a cop do that to me."

Booth covered his eyes. "I can't believe what I'm hearing." He looked at her. "Look, I was a cop and you would, all right? But that's neither here nor there. We cannot have a lack of consent. If it's not clear you are willing, I can't use the footage."

"Then he must explain why I must strip in a nice voice, with a nice smile. If he treats me bad," She shook her head emphatically, "I will not cooperate with him."

"Okay, okay, Jake, be polite," said Booth. "From the top!"

Kurt chuckled as they resumed their positions. "She's deliberately sabotaging him so you'll have to fuck her," he whispered to Joe. "No way he's going to get it up so here's your big opportunity to show Joe the stud's back on track."

"Rolling," said Spear.

"You'd save us all a lot of trouble if you'd tell me where the dope is," Jake said in as friendly a voice as he could.

"I know nothing of this dope," Olga sneered.

"Okay," Jake nodded compassionately. "I'm sorry but you are under arrest on suspicion of smuggling so I must ask you to undress for a full body cavity search."

"I don't think it's so that I must for a man do this."

"That's why there's a woman officer present. Now please remove your clothing." She stood up with an angry glare and slowly stripped.

Booth shook his head, annoyed at the time the scene was taking as she undressed.

Jake looked for something to focus desire on. The bluish veins in her breasts made them look as cool as marble. The smooth whiteness of the skin with a suggestion of pale hair around the russet-brown aureole made her thick nipples look like the cut stem of a fruit. Her whiteness made her seem all the more naked. He liked that. He told himself to focus on nakedness, *her* nakedness. Tits and ass! Take it!

"Lie on the bunk, please," he said.

"Why should I do this?" Olga said, suspicious.

"For a full body cavity search."

"Forget about that, tell her to suck your dick," said Booth.

"You got to be kidding," said Jake. "Just like that?"

"Do it! And be polite about it," Booth snapped.

Trevor sputtered a barely suppressed laugh.

"Yeah, right," said Jake. "Pretty please with sugar on it."

"Camera back for a two shot," said Booth. "All right, be serious folks. Action!"

"Tell you what," Jake said to Olga. "I have a very effective lie detector device called a peter meter. If you can make it spurt that means you're telling the truth and I'll have to let you go. So please insert the meter in your mouth so I can check out your story."

"I am not such a stupid person to believe this," said Olga.

"Please, m'am. I realize it's hard to believe but I'm just doing my job. You know how it is with officials and government. The peter meter is an essential devise for cutting red tape, yes? You understand cutting red tape, don't you?"

"You are a bastard," she said. "Very well, then, if I must, I will take this test."

He watched her steel blue eyes as she took hold of the zipper and opened his jumpsuit. In a cool professional manner, she extracted his flaccid penis and he closed his eyes. He thought of the hand touching him belonging to the big Soul naked woman.

Something cool and slimy. His eyes shot open. She was slipping a rubber on his cock! *As if I didn't have troubles enough as it is!* He needed real contact to churn fantasies. The lubricated condom was hanging loosely off the tip of his limp tool when she placed it in her mouth, sucking gingerly to keep it from slipping off.

Concentrate! He tried visualizing his loosely covered cock in her mouth. Into her, inside her. *Concentrate, dammit! Naked! My cock in her mouth, for whatever the damn hell's that's worth!* He felt her teeth rubbing against his shaft. This had to be the worst blow job of his life. Why was he putting himself through this? There was nothing in it for him. Nothing! No possible way would anything worthwhile ever come of it. Even if he could through some miracle obtain an erection, there'd be hell to pay maintaining it.

He pulled away and jerked off the condom. "To hell with it." He stuffed his prick back in the jumpsuit. "I'm out of here." Then he walked off toward the locker room, hearing Trevor's childish giggling that seemed to be aimed at him.

Spear zoomed in on Olga's expression of disbelief, then turned the camera off. He glanced over at Catherine sitting on a folding chair looking up at Jake who was looking down at her, interested in what she was saying.

"Ultimate meaning you will never find," she said. "It's kept forever beyond the reach of man. The only choice you have is action. Not understanding. Not words. You must make the right choice, but you tend to let events chose for you then get angry when you don't like the outcome. You must now choose, know that you have chosen, and act. Then, accept the consequences of your actions."

After Jake left, Spear considered reminding her not to interfere in this Archetypal Field. But now there was no longer any point to say anything more, except to warn her.

"He will leave with the other," he said, softly. "Then your time will come."

"Implications of the enigmatic fragmentation of the cosmos," she whispered.

Spear knew then he had to shift tactics. She was trapped in her web of events.

KURT SIGNALED Joe. "As I said, golden opportunity. If you can get it up for the ice queen after fucking all day, if that ain't proof you're back, I don't know what the hell is."

"Man, I don't know," said Joe. "It's quite a come down from where I've been all day."

"Hey, man, make sure he pays you up front. Make the bastard squirm. Five will get you ten, one way or another, he'll try to game you into boning her for nothing."

"Not a chance," Joe laughed. "No way I'm going to let him take advantage of me."

"We'll see about that, here he comes," Kurt whispered as Booth came out of the men's room. "Just remember when it comes to giving, some people stop at nothing."

"Joe, I need to talk to you," said Booth. "I'm in a bind. I need somebody to finish this scene and I don't have any money. If you'll help me out on this, I'll make it up to you."

"Excuse me, guys," Kurt chuckled, walking off.

"ARE YOU LEAVING?" Dr. Ben asked Jake in the locker room.

"Yeah," Jake said as he tied his shoes. "This whole thing's a fucking mess."

"That's Chaos. The very nature of sex. Ride the mood."

"I didn't see no fucking Eros in the Chaos. Nothing. Nada. Zero. Zilch."

"That's because you're thinking. You can't *see* or properly *feel* when you think. Turn off your thoughts. Be silent, and observe. This moment, *now*, is the crossroad. Hecate's intent. Her answer to show you. I screwed up on Riley's shoot because I got involved like you did when you involved yourself with Olga. Your attention should have been directed at Julie. From here on out, do not do *anything*. Just observe. And ask yourself now, are you absolutely certain you want to walk out before Hecate finishes Her drama?"

Jake stared at the floor. "Well, maybe I got the point."

"Is that *may-be* good enough?"

"Katie said I had to make a choice, and I have. I chose not to be part of this charade."

"No, no, no, oh god, no!" Ben gasped, looking shocked. "This is *no* charade," he hissed. "You cannot leave when *She* is about to answer your request. You *must* not. And, what about your protégé? How do you think Artemis will react to your abandoning Waverly here alone with these hungry wolves after what happened on her first project?"

"I haven't got a sense that it's the wrong thing to do," he said with a grimace.

"The right choice involves everything and everyone, not just you. Before you remove yourself from the entangling dilemmas Hecate has set in motion, I suggest you seriously consider saving yourself decades of torment by hanging around long enough to see this challenge through to the ambiguity which is the identity of the opposites involved."

"Uhhh. Say what?" said Jake, shaking his head, looking both confused and annoyed.

"Maybe I should have mentioned this sooner. I didn't because you need to be in the right place, like up against the wall, in order to grasp what I'm about to say. You made a *serious* mistake when you asked Hecate to help you understand, because you *cannot* understand this stuff in the way you want to. No human can. The Greeks believed mathematics was the language of the Gods. Not words, but numbers and equations. Which is why early Christians believed mathematics to be the work of the Devil. Understanding as you know it, is at best, like when you try to remember a dream. It loses its magic then disappears. Literal understanding is not up to the task of multilayered polytheistic meaning. Hold the image, and let it speak to you without prejudging. No trying to make it into something you can understand. The objective is to see through. What you see will be graspable in a non-literal form, and loaded with meaning."

"Man, my brain's way too fucked up to deal with that kind of crap right now."

Ben made a painful wince. "Yeah, well, so is mine. But the show is right here right now, and *you* know it. Whatever's fucking with your head will be shoved aside once the shit hits the fan. Then we'll be in the thick of it. And believe me, you'll have no problem keeping your mouth shut or observing the feelings and connections and moods that will lead you to what's hidden. What you seek to know is here, and you *will* see it, and you *will* grasp its meaning. Do it now! Tonight! Because, if you don't, it's going to cost you in every conceivable way for the rest of your life."

"Hey, Jake," said Kurt as he approached.

"Ambivalence. Ride the mood," Ben stage-whispered. "Enter the mythic drift. Stick with it. Later could take torturous decades, until death do you part." Then he left.

"That's one stone cold bitch," Kurt said to Jake after Ben left. "Even I couldn't have pulled that one off, not even with my charm. She hasn't a clue on how to turn a man on."

"Yeah, well, I could have done it if I weren't so fucking pissed," said Jake, concerned his decision to leave may have been based more on anger than gut reaction. "The last thing I wanted to do was fuck."

"What're you so pissed about?"

"Well, for one, Booth's trying to take advantage of Wavy by not paying her for a lessie scene with Jezebel, claiming it's not a sex scene. But there's no shortage of things to be pissed about around here. He is the most inconsiderate timewaster I've ever had the misfortune of dealing with, and that's saying a lot. He's a fucking user, and I'm fed up with it. Man, I don't want to be here, but I'm worried about leaving Wavy here alone."

"I hear you. Hey, like I said before, I'll take care of her and make sure she gets to where she has to go. Go on home if you want."

Jake considered this for a moment. It felt right to him, that Kurt would watch over her. "I'll check to see if it's okay with her. Make sure she's sent to my place when she's done. That way we can be sure she'll be back tomorrow."

"You're leaving?" Julie asked Jake as she entered the locker room with her gym bag strapped over her shoulder.

"Yeah," said Jake as he picked up his bag.

"Take me with you."

"Uh," Jake grunted with a look of surprise. "Where to?"

She gave him a boyish grin as she said, "We'll cross that bridge when we come to it."

15

Wicked Games

By the time Jake opened the door of his truck for her, he'd decided to say nothing until Julie said something. When he got to driver's side, he found she'd unlocked it for him. He got in, started the engine, then backed up and out of his parking spot and headed for the Bay Bridge, all the while conscious of the weight of her eyes focusing on him.

He'd felt the weight of her watching him from the moment he arrived at the shoot. He remembered what Ben had said about her, and of his advice to say nothing to damsels in distress since they only want to hear what they want to hear. Does that mean silence was the right thing for now? Yes. Yes, it does. Was he Riding the Mood? He did not know for sure how he knew, but he knew he was. There certainly was a mood here, and he was riding it. Enter the Mythic Drift?

"Are you in the drift?" He heard Julie whisper, then glanced over at her and nodded.

"Do you sense the entanglements?" she muttered. He nodded again. Then she said in a louder whisper, "Take the Treasure Island exit, then pull over where I tell you to."

JULIE, apparently listening to the rumble of overhead traffic, waited for a long time after they parked under the bridge to say anything. He found the noise distracting.

"Do you want to beat me?" she asked in a barely audible voice, not looking at him.

"What?" That was the last thing he would have expected her to say. "No!"

"You have a lot of anger in you," she said looking at him. "You wanted to beat Olga."

"No, I did not. I don't *want* to beat anybody, no matter how irritated or angry I get, not even if they asked me to!"

"Not even…," she said in a soft suggestive whisper as she leaned toward him, the tips of her fingers lightly touching his thigh. "…to spank them? For being naughty?"

Jake hesitated. *What is she doing?* The rumble of overhead traffic seemed to grow louder, making him feel as if their sound waves were actually shaking his truck.

"Well. Maybe," he volunteered. "If they asked me to. Nicely. Said pretty please."

"You're in Eros," she whispered, barely audible below the rumble. "Now, feel for the Chaos in the Eros. It's a gap. An emptiness. Find it." Then, as she moved closer, looking him directly in the eyes, she asked in a loud breathy whisper, "Would you spank my bare butt if I asked you to? It's a nice firm, perfectly smooth young butt. You could do with it whatever you liked. You'd like that, wouldn't you? You know you would."

Then her hot breath whispered in his ear, "Spank me. Pretty please."

He pulled back, dumbfounded. Then. She. Scree-ee-ched!!! and kept on screeching as if she were being raped and torn asunder by rabid demons! Until his mind stopped. Then she went silent. All he could hear in the darkness was the hypnotic rumble of overhead traffic. When her voice came back on, he knew he was in an altered state, under her control. "You're in Chaos. Now, enter the mythic drift by looking for the Eros in the Chaos. Feel into its entanglements. Focus on the reflections of archetypal patterns until you see through them into what's behind them all. That will be your Myth. Your Fate."

The reverberating overhead traffic drowned out his thoughts, leaving only her words.

A COLD BREEZE outside his front door buffeted Jake. He had a strange feeling Poochini was waiting for him behind the door. Cedar had taken the dog with her, so why was he feeling Poochini's presence now? Then he remembered standing in this very spot years ago, listening to her barking inside behind the door on Christmas Eve, thinking how fortunate he was. He was not alone. He had a wife and a Sheltie who'd greet him joyfully when he came in. Poochini's happy face, her tail wagging. Cedar's bright, funny smile and her hugs that fit him so well. Looking into Cedar's eyes made him feel worthy. Clean. After so much suffering, he'd found love and happiness. He remembered thinking at the time, he would never forget this perfect moment. And he never did.

From childhood on, silent voices had told him things that, in retrospect, turned out to be true. As a teen, after having heard of people who remembered past lives, he came to believe his silent voices were from previous lives. The most persistent voice he suspected came from his previous life. It did not want him to repeat mistakes that had resulted in his dying alone as an old man in a cluttered, filthy house. Whenever this voice warned him to avoid certain people, he'd regret ignoring his warnings. The voice had forcefully warned him to stay clear of Cedar from the instant he noticed her at a party, with visions of betrayal and being haunted by his mistake for the rest of his life. The virulence of this warning made him curious because he saw nothing about her that would have otherwise prompted him to speak to her. He briefly spoke to her, and then wrote her off. Nonetheless, his curiosity stuck. Two weeks later he got her number and asked her out. While on Fisherman's Wharf, listening to stories of her trip to San Francisco from Atlanta, he spontaneously looked into her eyes. Then the most extraordinary thing happened, he saw her soul spark, and it was the most beautiful thing he had ever seen. They were both caught in the beauty of his vision. He loved her spark, and she loved the way his love made her feel. Until she didn't. He no longer had access to her spark, and she had done what she could to devastate his beautiful memories. Even if he died as a lonely old man in a cluttered, filthy house, he knew he would always have the memory of the one perfect moment. Standing outside his front door. With love waiting for him inside.

"I loved," he whispered. "And was loved. Once upon a time," he sighed as he unlocked the door. "I wish my wife had been different."

THE HOUSE was dark, except for the green light blinking in the answering machine. He stared at the light, thinking of the green highlights in Julie's hair, of her intense silence while he drove through the confusing back streets to her apartment in Oakland, of the look of concern on her face when she warned him for the last time to prepare himself for a visit from Hecate. She advised him to trust his silent knowledge to know what to do when She came. Then, as if to punctuate the importance of what she'd just said, she gave him a boyish grin that made her look like an entirely different person. He'd felt as if he were unraveling. Could she be a prepubescent boy? When she started talking in a boyish voice, he could not process what he or she was saying, as if it were in an unknown language directed at an unknown part of him. He felt as if he were being hypnotized.

JAKE SWITCHED on an overhead light, then pushed rewind on the machine and stared at the sagging bottom of the nearby wicker chair until he heard a *Beeeep*.

"Jake? It's me." Jazz, dark, impatient, drunk. "Are you there? I know you're there. Pick up the damn phone!" Pause. "I just want you to know what you did was the last straw, and you better call me back or I'm going to talk to your sweet little wife's attorney."

She laughed maliciously then slammed down the phone.

He sighed. She had made that threat, and others like it, many times before. When in pain, she needed to inflict pain on someone she loved.

Beeeep! "Jake?" Moria, barely audible under static. He turned up the volume. "I hope you're there. Um, I was so stupid. I went back home and the demon," the static got worse, "was here. He won't let me out. I'm so scared. Please come and get me. Please."

The image of her as a child, alone for hours in a cold dark park with her mother's bloody body, chilled him. He wanted to sleep. Moira would certainly deprive him of that and what little energy he had left. And he needed to be home when Waverly came. He turned the machine off.

Rrrring! He closed his eyes then lifted the phone.

"Jake?" Moira's dim voice in a wall of static.

He grimaced. "Moira, I can hardly hear you. Can you speak up?"

"Oh, Jake," she said, relieved. "I got to get out of here. There's blood on the wall."

"Speak louder, I can't hear you!"

"You don't have to shout. I can hear you fine."

"Well, I can't hear you."

"That's because the demon's distorting outgoing calls. Please come over right away. I have to get out of here!"

"What are you afraid of? What do you think he's going to do?"

"I don't know! That's what I'm afraid of. I don't know! Please, you got to help me!"

Bonk! "Uh, excuse me, I have a call on the other line."

"Please hurry. He may not let me talk much longer."

"Hello," Jake said in a tired voice to the other line.

"So you're answering the phone now," said Jazz.

"I just got in. I have a call on the other line."

"You gonna call me back?" her voice accused.

"When I can," he said. "I might have to go back out."

"Oh, really? At this hour? What for?"

"Look, I told you I'd be busy over the next few days. Whatever you have to say is going to have to wait."

"No, it is not going to have to wait. We're going to talk about this right now! I've t—"

Jake pushed the button down to return to Moira. "All right, here's what I propose." He stopped. He didn't hear the static.

"Yes, I'm here," Moira answered faintly. "He hasn't cut me off yet, but he will. Please hurry over. Please."

"All right, but only under certain conditions."

She was silent then said in an even dimmer voice, "What conditions."

"If I have to come out there, I'm going to take you to a hospital for observation."

Bonk!

"You've got to be kidding. I thought you believed me?"

"I do, but that's evidently not enough. Demons feed on fear, so if you can't cap your fear you might as well go to a hospital because I can't be there whenever you need me."

Bonk!!

"I'm not afraid when I'm with you. "That's all I need. I can't go to some hospital. How can you even suggest such a thing!"

"If I come over there, I'm going to take you to a hospital for observation. Are you really so scared you'd go to a hospital, or can you handle it yourself?" *Bonk!!!*

Moira took several moments before she muttered, "Okay."

"Good," he said, relieved. "I knew you could do it."

"No," she said. "You can take me to the hospital."

Damn, he thought, sliding onto the sagging chair, hoping to come up with some idea to save him a night's rest. *Bonk!!!* "Are you sure? The doctors will ask a lot of questions."

"Yes, and they'll think I'm crazy. Been there, done that. Please don't do that to me. Just take me away from the demon."

"Look, I already did that once before. You didn't follow instructions." *Bonk!!!!*

"I will! I will this time, I promise."

Like hell she will, he thought. "You can either walk out of your apartment by yourself, call someone else or have me take you to a hospital." *She better believe it*, he told himself, *because there's no way I'm going to put up with this all night.*

"All right!" Moira yelled.

Jake suspected she would say whatever it took to get him there and he wanted to tell her so but something kept him silent. What was it? Compassion? *Bonk!!!!!*

"All right," Moira said, composed. "But please hurry."

He tried to think of a way out but the call waiting bonks were rattling him, and the thought of dealing with Jazz made dealing with Moira's demon seem the lesser threat.

"All right, I got another call," he said. "I'll come over when I'm done with it."

Bonk!!!!!!

"Don't be long."

"I won't." He turned on the answering machine and hung up. Then he stared at the couch, as if Poochini were there watching, judging him. He wondered what he should do. He had to be alert for tomorrow, yet here he was once again going back into the fray, risking disaster to aid yet another of life's inexhaustible supply of damsels in distress. In his twenties, midnight madness could have seemed like an exciting adventure full of exotic, erotic potential. In his thirties, it felt more like a duty. Now, in his forties, it was an imposition. A maddening imposition. As an adolescent, he used to wonder what he would be like at forty. That kid would not have understood this reaction.

POLK STREET was a magnet for transient homosexuals and runaway boys pedaling their youth. The last time he was on the street at night he'd felt threatened by its atmosphere. Tonight, at two a.m., there was only silence. The eerie stillness made him uncomfortable. Parking was always a problem on Polk, yet to his surprise he spotted a space right across from Moira's apartment. Then, suddenly, his mind was on fire. The demon?

He tried to remember how long it had been since he was last on Polk this late, but his thoughts kept swirling back to Moira's demon. He was overtired, he told himself, hence more vulnerable to creatures of the night. If it's really out there, he would magnetize its attention if he failed to keep the demon out of his mind.

Just get her out as quickly as possible. Get it over and done with.

He looked through a plate glass window into a deserted lobby. Threadbare carpet, grungy walls. Such neglect did not fit his impression of Moira's vanity. Perhaps he had the wrong address. As he scanned for her name on the board, a sense of unease like an invisible hail urged him to seek cover. If her name wasn't there, he'd look for a phone and call for the right address. Better yet, go home and unplug his phone. There it was! Her name, and a number to call on an intercom. He punched in her code, six six six.

"What kind of fucking game is this," he muttered, staring up the empty street.

Ring! Ring! No answer. His mind raced to find a justification to disconnect from this nightmare. The intercom broke his train of thought. Someone had picked up on the other side. "Moira?" Jake yelled into the intercom. "It's Jake. Are you ready?" Silence. Then he heard something that sounded like breathing. Labored, deep breathing.

"Come on, Moira! Either buzz me in or say something. I can't hear you." He closed his eyes, hoping things weren't about to go from stupid to insane. Then he saw Moira enter the lobby. She'd taken the trouble to put on jewelry, nylons and a designer dress. She looked as if she were on her way to a social ball. Her make-up, too, was impeccable, but her eyes were desperate, her smile frantic.

She flung the door open and hugged him like a frightened child. "Why didn't you answer on the intercom?"

She looked puzzled. "It doesn't work. I had to watch for you outside on the landing."

"What do you mean it doesn't work? Somebody picked up. They didn't say anything, just heavy breathing."

She looked worried. "I wasn't there. I started down when I saw your truck."

"All right, all right," he said, skeptically. "But I have to ask, what's with the six six six code number. Did you pick that out?"

"No. I'm on the sixth floor in apartment sixty-six."

"You know what six six six stands for, don't you?"

"No, what?"

"Really? It's the mark of the devil."

"Let's get out of here," she whispered, turning resolutely in the direction of his truck.

"Did the demon try to stop you from leaving your apartment?" he asked, following.

"Shhhhh! Not now."

He walked as nonchalantly as he could, determined not to show any concern. Moira fidgeted impatiently while he unlocked the passenger door. He made a gallant gesture for her to enter and, in a flash, she was in, reaching over to unlock the driver's side door.

"Let's go!" she said. "Let's go!"

"Where? Which hospital? Presbyterian is closest."

"Oh, god, no," she frowned as if no one with any pride would go to such a place. "If you have to be such a bastard, take me to French. You know where that is?"

"As a matter of fact, I do." He eased his truck onto the street, steeling himself against whatever she came up with to lure him into her labyrinth of self-destruction. He had followed far too many damsels into the labyrinths they'd rush into with such abandon.

"Why are you being like this?" she said.

"You really don't have anywhere else you can go?" he said. She shook her head no. "But you have family here, right?"

"Yeah, right. I should go freak out my family."

"It's not a bad idea. With family around, the demon would probably stay away."

"Just take me to the damn hospital."

"Wait, hear me out. If you're hospitalized your family's eventually going to find out anyway, so why not just give them a try now as a last ditch effort."

"If my lover doesn't give a damn, they're not going to either," she muttered pointedly. She scrutinized his faded clothes and dirty cap. If she walked into a hospital with him dressed like that they would think she was crazy for sure. "All right," she said tersely, as though snapping a handbag shut. "Take me to my parents."

"Okay," he nodded, relieved. "Should we call first? It's late."

"No, it's all right," she said, annoyed.

"Fine. So where do I go?"

"Berkeley," she groaned as if he should have known.

"Well, that's good," he said in a careful not to offend voice. "I have to go through Berkeley anyway to get home."

"Duh, like I don't know that."

"I want to be very clear about this. You will stay at your parents. If you want to go anywhere else, they can take you there, not me. So no

I-don't-have-a-key routine or some other excuse. I take you there and that's that."

"You don't trust me?" she said with a strange smile.

He said nothing, surprising himself with the strength of his resolve *not* to buy into another damsel's problem that only *he* can save her from. This was a first for him.

"Why are you doing this to me?" she said in a little girl voice, looking as if she were about to cry. "Why are you being like this?"

"I can't afford to get pulled into this. Especially now. I'm overwhelmed with crap." That felt like a whine so he tried to sound stronger. "It requires more time and energy than I can spare." *Still a whine.* "I know how it'd play out. I've been there before and—"

"No!" she yelled. "I am not like your past lovers. They didn't give a damn about you! They just wanted something from you. I love you! They didn't love you! I don't care what you say or think, they didn't love you. None of them did." She choked with emotion, and then continued. "You just can't abandon someone who loves you like I do. You can't! Not even if you don't love me." She sobbed. "Could you?"

Holy Christ on a crutch! Abandonment.

He'd seen the haunted eyes in a photo of her as a toddler. He would go through anything to help that frightened child, but Jazz's frightened inner child had exhausted him. In his teens he used to fantasize about receiving love, in some fashion, after saving a maiden. Rescues, though, were always illusionary and the reward, if there was one, took the form of a pale fantasy inevitably followed by the harsh reality of betrayal. He no longer believed in any other outcome.

"You're right." He glanced at her, trying to feel an attitude to adopt that might make a difference, as if she were a wild animal and he needed only to find the tone that would settle her down. "You are different. Everyone's love is different. Some of my lovers I'm sure loved me in their own way, much as you do in yours."

"What a wicked thing to say," she whispered. *How dare he put her on the same level as his past women.* The corners of her lips bent upwards in a cramped attempt at a smile.

"Look, I'm not saying anyone's ever loved me deeper than you, because it doesn't matter," he said, immediately regretting his wording. "What matters is they all pulled me into their problems then turned on me when I was no longer of use."

"I wouldn't do that because I love you. I couldn't hurt you."

"Yeah, well, I've found the memory of love and promises doesn't carry much weight when a woman changes her mind." *Too harsh*, he thought.

"What a wicked game," she said.

"What?"

"It's from a song." She stared into the night as she sang, " *World was on fire, no one could save me but you. I never dreamed that I'd love somebody like you.*" She frowned. "Boy, if that ain't that the truth."

"Yeah," he said, smiling. "We are an odd couple."

"What do you mean by that?" she growled.

"Oh, come on now. I mean, like you're into fashion, make-up and upper class crap that I could give a damn about."

"No, that's not what you meant."

"Well, we are from different generations. I like camping, you like resorts, so forth and so on and on."

"And I love you and you don't love me!" she said.

Suddenly, he realized his strength in resisting her pleas to enter her private hell came from somehow knowing, deep down, he lacked the strength to survive if he did. It was easier to avoid something he knew for certain he absolutely must not do.

"Why can't you let me in?" she asked.

"I don't know how to make you understand I've done that before and have been thoroughly trashed. I'm a mess inside and I don't want to be trashed again. I can't afford to love you. I'm just not strong enough to endure another—"

"I would never trash you," she said sweetly. "I love you."

He wondered if Cedar had reacted to his love pleas as he was now reacting to Moira's. He didn't really care enough, and perhaps, as a result, he didn't actually believe her. Then again, maybe she didn't mean a word of what she said. A constructed reality, Cedar's phrase for a vow or promise broken. Meaning, I meant it at the time.

"I wouldn't be surprised if everyone who's ever trashed me at one time or other didn't believe they'd ever do such a thing. Fact is, they probably thought they did me a favor and that I'm a butthead to think otherwise. It's amazing the hell good intentions bring on those who believe in them." He paused. Her silence insinuated itself like doubt, demanding he offer proof of what he had said. He tried to sound warmer. "I don't question your sincerity, but it's not enough. Before I could trust anyone again the way you want me to, I'd have to be sure they knew what they were doing."

Moira focused on his cheap watch and his jerky half gestures. Fortunately the watch wasn't digital, she could not have endured that. The imitation leather band, though, made it *sooo* obvious it was not a genuine Gucci. At least it wasn't one of those tacky Rolex rip-offs most phonies wore. Nonetheless, it made his gestures seem all the more dishonest.

How could an old fool like him not want her? She knew he did. He just didn't think he was worthy of her.

16

Figures in a Mirror

Jezebel closed her eyes to envision her naked image, something she always did before going on stage to expose her sexual secrets. Being the focal point of lust made her feel alive and present in proportion to the number of eyes fixed on her. Erotic dancing and hustling were like dream-images from which she could awaken, whereas photos and movie-images were frozen in time. They would long survive her. One day, they would be all that was left of her. People not yet born would watch her nasty nakedness, wondering what she'd been like in life. The idea of this prompted a gasp of excitement.

Her heart pounding, her face flushing, she closed her eyes to savor the feeling.

Ben watched how her expression seemed to have turned in on itself, as if everyone had magically disappeared when she closed her eyes. He feared the fires building up in her could suddenly flare up and ignite a frequency in him where desire and its object became indistinguishable, rendering him incapable of detachment at a crucial moment.

Jezebel, feeling all the eye energy focusing in on her body, quivered with excitement. So many eyes lusting to see her bare ass naked! All the men who'd come to the set to work had stayed. Waiting to see her naked. Wanting to see her get fucked.

She gasped for air.

"Emission accomplished!" Joe roared with a triumphant grin.

Her eyes flashed open, only to find all eyes and cameras focused on the splotches of semen all over Waverly's tits. Only a man could act like a conquering hero after making a sticky mess on a woman, expecting her to like it. No way would she ever do *that* on film!

She closed her eyes, listening to the Japanese girl's camera clicking, vowing to herself to never leave such images behind to haunt her in the afterlife.

"You're up next, Jezebel," said Booth. Her shut-eyed, faraway dreamy expression, followed by a crazed flash in her eyes when she opened them were the sort of things that indicated drugs, or some kind of craziness. Crazy women made him nervous.

She stared vacantly at Booth and muttered, "Body make-up."

"Not necessary," said Booth, tensing. "You're in the shower."

"Who's in the scene with me?"

Booth hesitated a moment then said, "Joe." She would want him.

She held her hands up in a delicate tentative way and shook her head. Joe could get anyone he wanted, whenever he wanted. *But not her.*

"You don't want to work with Joe?" said Booth, surprised.

"He just did a scene."

"All right, then, Kurt."

Kurt, icy blue eyes, old enough to be her step-dad. She nodded.

Ben noticed Booth's uneasiness, and Jezebel's toying with him, trying to infect him, to pull him into her orbit in some perverse way.

"Kurt!" Booth shouted at him across the room. "You up for a scene with Jezebel?"

"You kidding?" Kurt answered. "Does a bear shit in the woods? Why do you think I've been hanging around all day?"

Jezebel gave him a look of cold contempt as he approached.

"How old are you?" she said, fingering his lucky necklace between her index and forefinger.

"Let's just say I'm still in my advancing years," said Kurt.

"Still in your *advancing* years?" She tugged on his necklace. "I'm still at an age where I make advances."

"You have to wear a condom," she whispered, implying she *knew* he'd rather not.

"I've no problem with that," he said.

Her eyes narrowed. "And you can't fuck me in the ass." She moved her hand to his chest then pushed, as if to imprint on him her doubt he could control his lust for her butt.

"Hey, again, no problem." *Weird woman,* he thought. *What did he do to make her think he wanted to fuck her fucking ass?*

Any lingering hopes Ben might have had that Jezebel would not be the one to activate the archetypes were dispelled by the spectacle of her deliberately baiting Kurt.

Jezebel's attention then shifted to something behind Kurt. Her expression darkened.

Ben looked to see what had affected her, but saw nothing of interest, other than Joe had resumed fucking Waverly. The Japanese girl, the Hustler photographer and most of the men were hovering over them due to the live action cameras being turned off.

An icy determination came over Jezebel as she realized it did not matter to Joe if she, the star, refused him. She scanned the other men *(all of them waiting to see her naked, all of them wanting to spill themselves into her)*. They'd all flock to her when she was naked.

Her wicked grin caught Spear's attention. Ben watched his eyes locking onto her dark pupils, conscious of the intelligence behind them balancing whatever considerations she was weighing. To his surprise, he sensed she had somehow activated something in Spear.

"You need to undress for the shower sequence," said Booth. "You're starting with me naked?" Jezebel snapped.

"Yeah, so?"

"I'm the star, everybody's waiting to see me naked, then poof! I'm naked. Any dancer knows the real charge comes from anticipation, the tease. I can't just suddenly be naked."

Booth stiffened. "This is a much later scene. Anyway, the audience sees only what the camera lets them see. We'll tease them with angles and steam. Trust me, it'll work."

She considered this then grinned up at Spear. "So Dougie's doing the tease for me?"

Ben glanced at Catherine, sensing Jezebel's insinuation Spear's camerawork somehow made him an active participant in a sex act had activated something in Katie.

"That's right," said Booth. "He knows what he's doing."

"Oh, I'm sure Dougie does," said Jezebel.

Ben feared the presence of Artemis had prompted Jezebel to spin a web on Spear to trigger Katie's complexes. If so, when Jezebel ignited the archetypes, and he had no doubt she would, the three goddesses would descend to pull Katie into the resulting chaos.

"Good, I'm glad you understand," said Booth. "Now, would you please undress so we can shoot this thing and get out of here sometime tonight."

"All right, but you're not ready," Jezebel snapped. "When you're ready, I'll strip."

"Okay then, let's get at it!" Booth yelled. "To the showers, people. Make it snappy!"

Worst case scenario (and Ben took it for granted this would be a worse case), after the Big Bang, he too would be swept away in the avalanche of archetypes. Unless Spear had a plan to contain or direct the flow. Jake and Julie had been Ben's plan. Manipulating them would have provided him with the edge he needed to intuit hidden meaning. Their sneaking off together without his noticing clearly meant the archetypes had other plans. Without them to help focus his knowledge, he'd find it increasingly difficult to make sense of things, maybe to even remember basic tactics. It was possible Spear, too, was in their crosshairs. Or, already infected. If so, the resulting chaos could actually turn lethal.

Jezebel leaned against a cold mirrored wall, her eyes half closed, watching all the men scrambling for the shower room. They'd been waiting all day to see her naked. They'd all want copies of the movie so they could watch her being fucked over and over again for the rest of their lives. Now. The time was now. When it would all come to pass.

Ben saw Booth signal Spear for a conference. He moved to join them.

"Jezebel worries me," said Booth. "I think she's going to walk. She seems to like you. Could you talk to her to put her at ease. You know, whatever it takes to keep her here."

Spear considered this. "She's just jerking you around. Toying with you."

"She sees the world through tramp colored glasses," said Ben. "A slut like her doesn't feel right if she's not annoying somebody." He hadn't meant to say that, or even think it. Doing so didn't bode well for maintaining distance. He had better keep his mouth shut.

"Yeah, I know," said Booth. "But I can't get a bead on her."

"Let it ride," said Spear.

"Talk to her, will you?" said Booth. "Trust me on this."

"All right, but you're setting a dangerous precedent letting the talent get to you."

Ben remembered how Spear, the only one on Riley's shoot not infected by a complex, had managed to pull Riley off Katie before she sustained serious damage. Why would Spear allow himself to be infected? Does he even know? Of course he knows. He also knows Jezebel will be the catalyst. He's using her. He must have a plan.

Then his mind became a confused flash of associations. Hekate, his own Eros, and Spear's as well, all linked somehow to Jezebel. Ben grabbed on to that.

He would watch Spear, to see through his link. To ride his myth.

Jezebel sucked in her lips for a quick moistening as Spear approached her. Then with a subtle shift of focus, she looked up at him. "You will make me look good, won't you, Dougie?" she asked as she stepped away from the mirrored wall, leaving her smears on it.

Spear thoughtfully ran his tongue over his teeth. "That won't be hard to do."

"I want you to be hard when you do," she said.

Better, he figured, to say nothing. Just paying attention to her should be enough.

"You are really weird," she said. "Either that or you want me to think you are."

He did not know what to say to that, so he said, "Excuse me, I have to set-up."

She watched him walk away. He wants her. They all want to give her dirty cash.

> I have no excuse, just want you to use me.
> Take me and abuse me.
> I have no taboos to make a trade with you,
> I'll do anything you want me to.

Booth watched her. He'd seen that crazy look before, when he was a cop, on the face of a fourteen-year-old girl who'd just knifed her father to death.

Jezebel felt Booth's eyes on her. She had what he wanted, what he had to have. *Big Shot*, afraid she won't give it to him, because she's TRASH! *Big Shot*, doesn't know what to expect from trash. But she knows what he wants. What he really, really wants.

A smeary smudge of dirty *T-T-T-trrrr-assSSHHH!!!*

Ben caught her Eros/Chaos mood then held onto it, trying not to judge. Judging was what got him into trouble the last time. After all his years of experience, he still found it hard to keep his ego in check at critical moments. Judging was the most die-hard of ego defenses. He needed to be more like Spear to ride in his wake.

"We're ready for you now," Booth said. "Get undressed, and then go to the showers."

Jezebel glared at him. "I'll *strip* in there," she said, turning toward the shower room.

"Whatever," Booth muttered, following her.

JEZEBEL looked around the showers. Barely enough room for everyone to watch.

Booth pointed at a showerhead. "Would you please *strip* then get in position?"

Ben moved off to the side, his mind locked on her as she turned her back to Spear, slowly unbuttoning her blouse, letting it slide off, revealing a chiffon regal print crop top underwire with an intricate medieval floral print trim and black stretch lace. Arching her back, she then unfastened her top, letting it fall to the floor as she kicked off her shoes. At long last, she slowly worked her tight jeans down, exposing her black lace underwear slit open back and front, showing the shadowy folds of her sexual secrets.

She turned to see if Spear was watching as she worked her panties below the dimples at the base of her spine, then down over the firm fullness of her buttocks.

I know what they want, what they really, really want!

"She's staring right at you," Joaquin whispered to Spear. "She wants you, bro."

"She only wants me because she can't have me," he said as he zoomed in on her butt, then gestured for Joaquin to look at the monitor. "I'm a challenge."

"Mmmm, nice," said Joaquin, looking at her butt in the monitor. "Venus dimples.

"Stretch marks. Hard to hide with a dark complexion."

"They're not all that obvious," Joaquin said, now noticing them. Spear panned up to the stretch marks on her tits.

Ben, who'd approached them to see what Spear was up to, had never noticed her stretch marks before. But then, he'd never seen her naked under bright lights before. That Spear would bring this up at a critical juncture, knowing full well stretch marks could be hidden with body-make-up, signaled some sort of game change on his part.

"Those you are definitely going to see," said Joaquin. "Must have had a kid."

"Or lost a lot of weight," said Spear.

"You get a lot of that in porn," said Joaquin, "former fatties who became sex goddesses after losing a lot of weight. Reminds me of a girl I knew in college who was so fat in high school guys avoided her like the plague. The summer after graduation she lost fifty-eight pounds. Turned herself into a babe, then went off to a college where no one knew her and everyone wanted to. I was one of several guys who fell for her because she seemed so genuine and vulnerable, unlike most beautiful women. In the end, though, she ripped us all off because she figured we wouldn't have paid attention to her if she was fat." He laughed. "Thing is I like fat girls. I do, but she didn't know that. I like the way their bodies keep wiggling when they stop moving."

"Turn the showers on," Booth shouted. "Let's get some steam in here."

"That's going to be a problem," said Catherine. "The gas is turned off, so there's no hot water."

"That's great! Just fucking great. All right, we'll have to live with it. This is supposed to be a prison, not a dorm, so it'll be a cold shower."

"A cold shower," said Jezebel. "I don't think so."

"We'll make it quick," said Booth.

"So what happened to my sexy steam scene? I'm going to just pop up naked on the screen now, aren't I?"

"We know what we're doing," said Booth. "We'll handle it. Now get in the shower and lather up so we can get this over with. Are you ready, Doug?"

"You ready, Dougie?" Jezebel teased.

Spear signaled Booth for a conference, whispering, "We have serious T&A stretch marks," pointing them out on the monitor.

"What?" Booth snapped, glancing her way, his nostrils flaring. "These are the best women I could find willing to do porn."

"What's six inches long, has a head on it and drives women wild?" said Kurt. Booth shot him an impatient look. "Folding money. Money has more to do with the caliber of honeys you get then the fact it's porn."

"You're beginning to sound like Jake. Look, I know what I'm doing. Stretch marks will not be a problem because of the water on her body. Anyway, perfect bodies aren't as necessary in porn as in soft core. Her body's fine for what we're doing."

Joaquin realized he was wasting his time. Booth would never give him work on legitimate projects, unless it was to rip him off.

They're all passing judgment, Ben sensed. Could mean Saturn, the male god behind pornography. Soulless sex. Ben felt a sudden drop into hopelessness. He needed someone like Jake around to help him maintain balance, to remember what to do. He could not remember anything more about Saturn, except judgment. How could that be?

Unless Saturn is present. Oh, fuck! Damn! Shit! Totally unprepared for that!

"Rolling," Joaquin said as he spontaneously took over the camera.

Booth saw a medium shot of Jezebel in the monitor, stepping in and out of the cold water looking perturbed and shivering, trying to get wet enough to soap herself down.

"What are you doing?" Booth whispered.

"It's funny," Joaquin whispered as he moved in closer. "And real."

Booth hesitated for a moment, and then nodded. "Use the dolly. Where's Julie?"

"She left with Jake," Joaquin said.

"She didn't say anything to me," said Booth.

"She's been here since six this morning with no pay. Got tired of it, I suppose."

"She agreed to do the job. She's just shown I can't count on her for a major project."

"I'll do the dolly," said Joaquin, relinquishing the camera to Spear.

"Well, but get in there before she figures out what we're up to," said Booth.

"Hey, John," said Kurt. "What's my cue?"

Booth gestured for silence while Spear and Joaquin moved a half circle around Jezebel. Then Spear signaled Kurt to enter the shot.

"All right, bitch," said Kurt. "You're coming with me."

Startled, Jezebel turned. "What the fuck!" she said when she saw the camera. "You're shooting this!"

"Cut!" said Booth. "Great reaction, Jezebel. That's how I want the scene."

"You shot without calling action! You're not suppose to do that. I wasn't ready!" She turned to Spear and hissed, "We'll have to do it again."

"Looked good to me," said Spear.

They're screwing with her, Ben noted, trying to calm himself by shifting his attention from gods and goddesses to Spear, who seemed to have changed his strategy by centering himself as a factor in the dynamics, likely connected to his having Katie stay on the set.

"I wasn't ready!" Jezebel barked. "I looked silly. I need to be sexier."

"Okay," said Booth. "From the top. Be sexy. Roll tape."

"Rolling," said Spear.

Jezebel shook her head in disgust. "Just like that? You didn't give me any time to get ready."

"We're taping," said Booth. "Be sexy."

"No one said action."

"Action!" said Booth.

Wondering how the hell she could manage to look sexy in a cold shower, she braced herself then stepped under the cold water. Everyone watching, lusting after her, she thought as she tried to retrieve her trashy mood while lathering herself up.

"All right, bitch!" Kurt yelled. "You're coming with me."

She spun around with a ferocious look. "Who the fuck do you think you are, you piece of shit!" she yelled. They ruined the scene again, depriving her of time to get it right. "This is the women's shower and you don't belong in here." They would pay. "Now get the fuck out of my face!" She'd blow it and keep blowing it until they got it right.

Kurt was momentarily taken aback by her departure from the script. "What we have here is a failure to communicate," he growled, grabbing her arm. "I'll make it simple so you can understand. Me jailer, you prisoner. You're coming with me."

She jerked herself free. "You're the one who doesn't understand, you dumb fucking ape. You Samson, me Deliah. You come near me again and I'll rip your fucking balls off."

Kurt turned white, his eyes seeming to bulge out. No one calls him stupid and gets away with it. "What did you call me?" he said in cold fury.

"Stay away from me!" Jezebel yelled, backing off. "Stay away!"

Ben caught the fear in Catherine's image in the mirrors, and then he heard a croaking-grinding voice, arising from a terrible depth, crawling like an insect into his ears.

"*Boy,*" it said. Then he knew, the goddesses were about to descend.

"Dumb fucking ape, eh?" Kurt snapped, grabbing hold of her arms and shaking her. She'd been toying with him all day, as if he were too stupid to figure out she preferred Joe over him because he was smarter.

"You're hurting me!!!" she cried out when the tug on her right arm turned into a caveman yank.

Ben's heart pounded in his chest, pulsed in his throat, throbbed in his temples, while an intense yearning and a pitiful desperation leached its way into the deepest reaches of his inner being, as it had done on Riley' shoot.

Violence, so sudden, not what he'd expected. *"BOY!!!"*

Then an image, flittering over his reflection in the mirror, stabilized as that of a panicky bewildered naked eleven-year-old boy, strapped face down on a work bench.

"Going to tear my balls off, are you?" Kurt yelled, shaking Jezebel. The bitch held him in such contempt, she thought nothing of calling him stupid in front of everyone. "How's about I rip a piece off your fucking ass!" he growled, jerking her off her feet.

Jezebel moved with this man's willful, irresistible roughness, finding it turned her on.

Something flickered in the mirrors that caught Catherine's attention. Tarwater floating between her image and that of a disorientated Ben.

"Cut!" Booth yelled.

"Whoa!" Trevor whooped, joining in with the other men clapping and shouting. Kurt froze, suddenly aware of where he was, and that he'd gone too far.

"That was great," said Joaquin. "You scared the be-Jesus out of me, bro."

He let go of Jezebel. "Well, I like playing the heavy. Sometimes I even scare myself."

The look she gave him said the female in her was fascinated. A sensual tremor of fear had awakened a dark layer, a desire to feel the brutality of a man that could break her open and violate her. She needed that. Her not so secret, erotic desire.

Ben, having felt her desire for violation before, her burning attachment to it, realized the power driving the frenzied hammering of his heart was more excitement than fear. In fear dwelled a potential shift, either to awe and the possibility of transformation, or to excitement and a probability of possession. Balancing from the standpoint of excitement would be difficult, if not impossible. To avoid possession, he needed to tilt more to fear.

"On to the next scene," Booth said. "Back to the locker room."

Jezebel frowned. "Another scene on those stupid benches? That's totally hideous."

"It's a group scene. Everybody fucks on the benches."

"Boring," said Jezebel.

"How long before you're ready for us?" asked Kurt.

"Ten, fifteen minutes tops," said Booth.

"Good. That'll give me time to get hard."

"Wait a minute," she said. "We start out fucking?"

"It's late," said Booth. "We have an early call tomorrow. Everyone's tired. We're just shooting sex."

"I thought this was suppose to be a class picture! There has to be a story here."

"There is a story. Trust me. When you see the finished product, you will be pleased."

"Let's fucking do it," said Kurt, gesturing for her to follow him to a bench.

Ben followed Jezebel, watching her flexing butt cheeks in the harsh light as she strutted behind Kurt. Then a sudden fear permeated him, attaching itself like a shadow, disrupting his ability to free himself from an irritable itch of excitement that felt inflammatory.

"Let's start with you giving me head," Kurt said as he unzipped his jumpsuit.

"Let's start with you putting on a condom," said Jezebel.

"You want to suck a condom?" He pulled out his flaccid cock.

"It's better than catching a disease," she grumbled as she examined it.

"Hey, I'm clean. I get tested every month."

"Yeah, right," she said, rubbing his cock between her hands like a stick she was trying to start a fire with. "Like I should believe everyone who says that."

"Standard industry practice. You have to have tested clean within the past thirty days or you don't work." The friction on his cock annoyed him, but her confidence made him wonder whether there might be something to it. "Anyway, you can't get infected in the mouth unless you have an open sore."

"We need condoms over here!" Jezebel yelled as her song flowed through her like the blood swelling his cock. *Psycho killer in the streets, looking for someone to meet.*

Sensing Jezebel's delirium could suddenly shift to a level of frenzy with massive fluctuations between excitement and fear that could activate archetypes, Ben found it hard to think or decide, much less to act. He was in danger of spinning off into chaos, out of control. He needed time to focus his intent on something else, or to find a position from which he could trust his instincts. The image of the placard above the entrance to his uncle's hunting cabin came to him. A quote, in Latin, from Horace, *What you seek is here in this remote place;*

IF YOU CAN ONLY KEEP A BALANCED DISPOSITION.

Ben focused on the reflections in the mirrored walls, thinking of the old adage *know thyself,* how it morphed into *know your limits,* the point beyond which are powers that do not belong to humans. Outside those limits, the ego can no longer be any kind of hero. It becomes a watchman at the frontiers of a weak kingdom, dozing on the edge of madness, drifting among complexes in the night of their fantasies.

Catherine handed Jezebel a condom. She immediately ripped the package open with her teeth then slipped the condom on Kurt's hard cock faster than he thought possible, then started sucking his latex covered cock without a hint of distaste.

A pro. Kurt liked the idea of being paid to be serviced by a whore.

"Hey, John," Joe yelled, pointing at Waverly's moving up to the top and down to the base of his prick. "We have some hot action over here."

Jezebel breathed in the dense odor of middle-aged dick. The smell of *d i r t y cash!*

> Dirty cash I want you, dirty cash I need you, oh, oh, oh!
> Doesn't matter, woman or man,
> anyone with cash in hand. I want your money.

Kurt grinned, feeling the tip of his erection slide over the roof of her mouth. She may be smart, but his cock was in her head. He shoved it deeper down her throat as she swallowed to let it in, and then gagged when he shoved it deeper still. When she pulled back to avoid puking, the condom slipped off. Her tongue kept darting absently up and down his daddy dick, until she sensed the movement of strange shapes shifting in the mirrors. She heard the whisperings of the wings of the Angel of Death flapping, beating unevenly, as if in distress or pain. The figures in the mirrors becoming more and more indistinct as she felt herself starting to slide. Edges forming and reforming, like figures seen through frosted glass. Until she heard a scream.

"I WANT you to FUCK ME!"

She felt herself bending over a bench, her bulbous bare bubble butt wriggling while someone somewhere was screaming something.

Kurt grinned at her straining to receive him. Open, hot with liquid.

The bitch has gone over the edge, he thought as he slipped his cock into her.

BEN TURNED AWAY from Jezebel's mirror image to look at Catherine's, fearing Chaos would soon overwhelm her, as well. Her complexion had taken on a bluish hue. Finding Spear's reflection, he saw a glimpse of concern on his face. Scanning back to Katie, he found her shivering and absently stroking her hair backward and down, her legs rubbery. Back to Spear, he saw him signal Joaquin to take over camera. Ben found himself hoping Spear's effort to help Katie would somehow benefit him. He'd sensed the new order under the chaos, but he couldn't shift through the tumult for its meaning. If he found a way to see through, he somehow knew that would be enough to carry him through.

All he had to do was to empty his mind of everything to see the light.

"FUCK ME, TOUGH GUY! Show me what you got!" Jezebel yelled, her asshole twitching as if it, too, were saying, *Show me!* "Fuck me hard, you base-turd!"

Kurt scowled at being mocked, thinking she obviously didn't give a crap about him or what he wanted. Jezebel glared up at him. "Fuck me, damn it! Fuck me! Is that all you got! Well, I want more! Give it to me! Give! IT! to ME!"

Waverly stopped moving on Joe. "Is she all right?" she said.

"Faster!" she screamed. "Harder! Let me have it. All of it! Do it to me! Dooooo! IT!"

Joe grinned. "Oh, she's more than all right."

Ben felt the sensation of his thoughts swirling. "Shit," he mumbled, having realized he'd caught Hekate's attention. Whatever problems he had would be taken to an extremity where they'd no longer be living realities but become fantasies, reflecting their source in imaginal reality. Looking for a focal point, he moved closer to Spear and Catherine.

"Fuck me in my a-a-a—SSS!" Jezebel screamed, hanging by a thread over a dark place. *Ass, trash, dirty cash, anything you want.* "Fuck my ASS!-ss-ss-ss-ssss!"

Kurt stopped moving. "What the fuck?" he said.

"Ass! Asss-ss-sss!" she squealed as something small and bright separated from the darkness. "Fuck my fuck-ing aaaa-SSSS-sss!" A pair of bright, almond shaped eyes enlarged until they struck her. "Ass-ass-ass, AAAAsssssS!" Then everything fell away.

Kurt glanced at Booth with a *what-the-fuck-should-I-do* look.

No ground beneath her, nor air above. "Ass! ass! ass! Ass!" she howled, fragmented torments melting into her mind.

"She's acting, right?" said Waverly.

Joe laughed. "Guys marry women who fake it that good."

Ben, his teeth clenched, his mind blank, moved closer to Spear and Catherine.

"Listen to me carefully, Seabolt," he heard Spear whisper in her ear. "At the climax of your illness destructive powers, they will turn into healing forces. Awakened to independent spontaneous life, they will take over the guidance of something that is not who you think you are, and therefore beyond the reach of your personal will. In that moment, you will gain access to the sources of psychic life. And, the potential of a cure."

He's letting her go! Ben gasped as he staggered away up to the mirrored walls, thinking he should not be near them when he did.

Jezebel screeched when a throbbing pain surged through her gut. Then, as if a veil had been jerked aside at the moment of her death to reveal a cold black emptiness beyond, she screamed, "Ass in! Ass sin! AASSAASSIN!"

"I can't fucking believe this," said Kurt. "First she raises a stink about how she won't let anyone near her fucking shit shoot, and now she expects me to fuck her in the ass."

"So fuck her in the ass," said Booth.

"No," said Kurt. "I don't feel like it."

"I'll do it," said a glassy-eyed naked Trevor, suddenly appearing brandishing a surprisingly enormous erection for such a small man. "No charge," he giggled. "Because butt fucking is not a sex scene." He giggled louder.

Trying to tune out the pandemonium, Ben focused on a phantom figure in the mirror, which was his face. Bags under his eyes. Drooping eyelids. Then he heard a guttural voice say,

"*Boy!*" He flinched. The gravelly voice sounded urgent, eager. Then an image of a frightened naked boy strapped by his wrists over a work bench replaced his in the mirror. He felt the boy's fear, and his efforts to keep fear from his voice by not being able to speak at all. For a moment, he thought the boy was about to cry. His eyes wrinkling, lips quivering, his efforts not to cry showing on his pale face. Too scared to cry.

Then Ben realized there was something intimately familiar in his eyes.

"Oh, no," Ben silently moaned, having recognized his boyhood face.

Pale gray smoke rose up Catherine's left leg, and hovered over her as she realized she'd been staring at Spear, his skin the color of smoke, then she had a vision of an Indian with a feathered stick from long ago. And she remembered what he'd said to her many years ago. She tried to tell Spear this but the words were too deep inside her. When one finally came up, it carried her to the surface, making a howling sound that kept on resounding after she closed her mouth.

"What the hell?" Booth growled, glancing over at Catherine.

"Is she having a fit, too?" Kurt asked, interested.

"Never mind her, just get the scene done with," said Booth. "Fuck her in the ass."

"Ass, ass!" screeched Jezebel. "Ass in! Assassin! ASSASSIN! ASSASSIN!"

"She's out of her mind. She doesn't know what she's doing. I can't get off on that."

Booth glared at her with contempt. "All right, do what you got to do. Come on her fucking asshole, then poke your load into it."

"I'm ready! I'm ready!" Trevor exclaimed, flaunting his swollen staff. "Let me do it."

THE BOY in the mirror gasped. Ben could hear and feel him, and smell the grit on the work bench coming up into his nostrils, along with the sweet-sour fragrance of old motor oil stains and wood shavings. The crisp limy scent of cold concrete and turpentine. The faint lingering astringency of insecticide. And something like gunpowder.

Den Leader Franz. Punishing him for being a wise ass. *No more lies, Boy.* Teach him a lesson he would never forget. Get to the bottom of things. *Of all your dirty little secrets, Boy.* His long, long, knobby, hairy fingers digging into him.

Kurt pushed an inquisitive finger against Jezebel's clenched aperture.

"Assss!" She arched her back then pushed back against his finger. She felt only a heaviness, like a dark wet blanket over her consciousness. "ASS-ssssss-SSS-sss!"

"Fuck that shit, man," he scowled pulling his finger out. "She's got junk in her trunk."

"Alright already!" Booth snapped. "Just fuck her cunt, then come on her fucking ass."

"ASSASSIN! ASSASSIN! Butt! Butt!" Jezebel wailed, her eyes rolling back into her head, her face slick and pale, as if she were troubled by something she saw in her head.

"Let me do her butt!" Trevor exclaimed shoving Kurt aside just in time to shoot a massive load of cum between her cheeks, his frantic fingers working his load into her.

Spear took hold of Catherine's face, whispering, "Resonate with it," holding onto her head as her body thrashed about, "Let go. Roll with it. Let go."

A part of her was aware Spear was saying something. She struggled to hear over the echoes in her head. *Poo! Poo!* Unable to tell where the words came from. Whether she was thinking it, screaming it, or hearing it.

"Ass ass! Poo!" Jezebel screeched in tandem. "Poooooo-oo-oo-OOO!"

Joaquin panned the camera from one woman to the other, amazed at the spectacle of two beautiful women going into frenzy at the same time.

THE BOY in the mirror, caught in a virulent mixture of Chaos and Eros, had no frame of reference for these overwhelming forces. Ben, the adult, was considered an expert on Archetypal Fields, but he was not a Master like Oliver who could easily become an unobserved observer in a Field of Events. Ben had no answers, because words and thoughts had no power in Fields of overwhelming Chaos and mangled Eros.

Only action counted. He found himself frozen. Unable to act.

Then he remembered. Everything. The boy knew Franz forced "bad boys" to strip, then made them bend over and hold on to their ankles while he whipped them. Ben had refused to strip so Franz pulled his shirt off and tied him over the bench, then pulled his pants down and off. Ben the elder could hear Franz's voice and his heavy breathing. He saw how Franz looked at the boy, and felt the memory of his probing fingers.

Then the boy looked up directly at Ben, as Franz's filthy fingers reached up to his mouth.

Ben gasped, shocked, suddenly realizing *this* was the Hidden.

"Oh god, oh god, oh god!" Ben muttered, tapping his forehead against the mirror. The Myth in the Mess. The moment Franz had infected him with his diseased myth.

"Tellus, help me!" Ben cried out under his breath as he rammed his forehead against the mirror. "Persephone, mercy! Hecate, mercy! Artemis, mercy! Aphrodite, Mercy!"

This was the moment to return the myth to its source, but something held him back. He kept reeling with realizations of the damage he'd done. To Jezebel, Jazz and Julie. To his wife. His patients, and to so many others while in the thrall of Buying Butts.

The boy could not possibly have processed what had happened to him. The adult saw everything the boy did not want to remember, his wanting to make less of it than it was. A punishment. Not an evil. The boy as an Old Man was failing to seize the moment. He tried and he tried and he tried and he tried, tried, tried, but the boy *could not let go*.

"For god's sakes!" Ben cried out to the frightened boy in the mirror who was looking at him as if he were an infection he could not admit. That idea so disorientated Ben he lost any sense he might have had of knowing what to do. He was in Chaos, fearful of finding the Eros. He'd seen himself doing things to Julie's boyish butt that Franz had done to his. That was when he'd yelled at Will to shut the tape off, to shut the memory of having done or seen it out of his mind, to forcefully censor it from ever having happened.

"Blessed Queen of the Heavens, I beseech you," Ben exclaimed in Latin as he struck his forehead against the mirrored wall. "By whatever name, in whatever aspect, with whatever ceremonies you deign to be invoked." He pulled back. The images blurred, losing their outlines. "Have mercy on me in my extreme distress."

He smashed his head again, shattering the figures in the mirror. Turning them into sharp abstract patterns, flickering in a mass of dark edges set in an area that had a dull, painful light. "Restore my shattered fortune and give me back to myself."

Then he rammed his head full force into the mirror. An explosion of flickering, swirling colored lights suddenly shifted to revelations. He saw his missing wife looking at him with the same twisted enigmatic smile on her face as the one she had on the day they met, and on the day she disappeared. "I did love you," he whispered. The grace and compassion he saw in her eyes grabbed him, then he let go. He felt strangely cold and rigid, followed by a hot stupefying light ricocheting mercilessly. Then he saw Ollie, the boy, looking out at him from the mirror, repeating what he'd said in 1938.

"The choice you make right now, between trying to forget or trying to forgive, to let go, will determine the outcome of your life." Then the elderly Oliver appeared in the fragmented mirror. "To lay down a complex at its source, you must let go of it," he said. "To do that, you must forgive everything and everyone involved, including yourself."

Then the most extraordinary thing happened. Julie appeared in the mirror with a gracious smile. "I forgive you," she said. "Thank you for willing me here to do that."

Ben suddenly felt like a boy again, as he gently drifted off into a dream of bright blue love in another life.

THERE WAS A TREMENDOUS WEIGHT under Catherine's scalp, and on the back of her neck. Voices around her, soft as darkness. Jerking lumps fluttering underwater in curtains of dense cloth. Then the room tumbled, and she felt herself slide.

"There's something wrong with *her*, right?" said Waverly.

"Yeah," Joe said, standing up. "She's pissing all over herself."

Spear, kneeling beside her, chanted in Navajo while her body squirmed and squealed as she frantically rubbed at her genitals.

"WHAT THE BLOODY HELL!" Booth yelled, spotting Ben bloody and motionless on the floor below the shattered wall mirror. "Cut!"

"Cut, cut, cut!" Jezebel screeched at the speaking figures encircling her, gloating with powerful evil confidence, their dark bodies smeared with filth while she wailed, fending off their filthy hands. Trevor still digging into her, watching it all. Knowing he was in an altered state, unaware of his own laughter, or of the people yelling at him while he convulsed on the floor, having slipped and fallen in his own vomit.

Catherine stared blankly at the movements around her. Everything soft, as in a dream. Sounds exploding out of her as she began to spin. Feeling herself ascending, she caught a glimpse of her motionless body sprawled out on the floor.

The unintelligible voices of the people around her faded into silence as her ascension turned into a twirling descent into darkness. Profound numbness. Sensations of heaviness. Falling away.

Then, Darkness. Everything stopped. Then, nothingness.

Everythingwasover

17

Rude Awakening

Jake pulled up in front of what looked like a plantation mansion with white pillars and a veranda set back against a vast, manicured lawn.

"Is that it?" he said, thinking it couldn't be her parents' place because it was the most ostentatious building on the block.

"Yeah," Moira sighed.

The idea her parents had that kind of money intimidated him. He sat in silence with the motor running, hoping the sound of the motor would hurry her along.

"You seem lost in thought. And like most men you won't ask for directions."

"It's getting late," said Jake.

"I want to talk. I don't want to go in like this. Just give me a few minutes to collect myself."

He considered this. She would undoubtedly take her last best shot at changing his mind, an experience he could do without. The enormous mansion, though, weakened his resolve — probably part of her plan. He turned the engine off.

"Do you think pornography is satanic?" Moira asked.

"What?" said Jake.

"That's what that guy said. He said we're working for the devil."

"Well, a lot of people think the mob controls porn, but in all my years in the biz I haven't found that to be true. Nor have I seen any evidence that Satan runs it either."

"He said devils disguise themselves. They find ways to tempt you until you yield to temptation without knowing it's the devil's work. Then it's too late. He's got your soul."

Jake covered his face with his hands and rubbed his eyes, remembering a phrase Joaquin used to use. *Screaming Catholic girls on acid.*

"So," he said as he took his hands away from his face, "he preaches at you one minute then sends a demon to haunt you the next. He sounds more like a devil himself."

Moria breathed deep. "That's just it. He says he *is* an agent of the devil. He said I entered Satan's domain by getting involved in porn, and I must submit myself."

"Why didn't you tell me this before?" he said, thinking *this is fucking crazy.*

"It's not like he actually told me in so many words he was an agent of the devil. I just sort of figured it out."

"How did you do that, reach that conclusion?" He noticed rows of tall shrubs to the left of the great house that looked like a maze. "And to what are you suppose to submit?"

"He wants me to do whatever he asks."

"Like what?" He looked at her.

She frowned. "I didn't really pay that much attention, but I think he wants me to hurt people. You know, by sort of bringing them to him, like an offering or something."

"Bring people to him?" he said. He definitely did *not* want to get involved in this. "All right, look, devils are attracted to power. Business, religion, politics and law are much more alluring than something as banal as porn. A porn demon, if there is such a thing, would be strictly bush league. If you hear from the flaming shit heel again, give him my number. He knows where I live, right? Offer me to him." He stopped. He wondered what had possessed him to suddenly cast himself in the role of dragon slayer. Now, how could he get out of it?

"Oh, Jake," Moira sighed. "I feel so safe with you. Please, take me home with you."

"No." Feeling compelled to elaborate, he added, "We must separate until this is over. You must be alone when he calls you, and I must be alone when he calls me. It won't work if we're together." She looked doubtful. "I'll wait until you're inside."

She glared at him and said, "Don't bother."

"I'll wait."

"I'd rather you didn't," she said sarcastically. "It doesn't feel right."

"Why?"

"It just doesn't, okay!" She got out and slammed the door shut. She stood still, her back to him, waiting for him to leave.

He considered saying something more. Thinking he had already said too much, he turned the truck on, and drove off.

A DAZED JEZEBEL struggled with the deadbolt in her battered door. "Let me try," said Joe. "I have a pretty good feel for these things."

She shrugged him off. "No, there's a trick to it." She wiggled the key, feeling for the little give. "Damn-it," she mumbled. "I wish Yee would spring for a new lock."

Paola gave Kurt a little push. "What do you think?" she said. He gave her a blank look. "Should I call Bob? He's expecting me. He'll be furious if I don't show. I have to tell him something, but I can't tell the truth. He's too jealous."

Kurt shrugged, trying to look sympathetic.

"I don't know what to say," Paola persisted. "I've never had a jealous lover before. They all knew what I do for a living, that's how I met them in the first place. How can you be jealous when you know these things? But he is, and he doesn't believe me."

"Just tell him you're on location and won't be home until the picture's done and leave it at that," Kurt said with a touch of impatience.

Jezebel felt the give in the lock, and quickly followed through with the little twist that unlocked the door. Then she shoved it open.

Kurt scanned her studio apartment. Dirty sheer pieces of fabric hanging from the ceiling, thrift store pillows scattered around the floor. Halloween stuff, swords, hats, and a genie costume pinned to the wall. What was it about San Francisco that turned people into slobs? Everyone he knew who moved there seemed to end up slumming it. She'd offered her place as a location, saying it was like something out of Arabian nights. This so-called princess's monorail definitely does not go all the way to Tomorrowland.

Paola looked around for a phone. "Where's the phone?"

"I don't have one," said Jezebel, irritable, trying to concentrate.

"No phone?" Paola grimaced.

"There you go," Kurt said, pulling her to him. "You can't call because there's no phone." He kissed her, her tongue darting absently in his mouth.

"What you got to drink?" Joe asked Jezebel, noticing her discomfort. She obviously hadn't recovered from the dramas around her scene and their quick exit before the cops and medics arrived in the aftermath of Ben's head bashing and Katie's coma.

"I'll show you," she said. Joe followed her into the kitchen.

"Wow!" Joe said when he saw an old Amana refrigerator. "Far out. That's yours?"

"No." She looked at him as if he had to be joking. "It came with the place."

"There was an old fridge just like it in the flop house we stayed in when I was a kid. That's all I remember from that period, the old fridge and the strange stuff inside."

He looked inside. Wilted vegetables. Unlabeled bottles. "Any of these beer or wine?"

"Should be some wine left over here." She opened a cupboard and pulled out a half empty bottle of Chardonnay. "My stepdad's a devout Muslim." She handed him the bottle. "I don't bring alcohol into the house as a courtesy to him. That was left by a friend."

"How long ago?" He pulled the cork and sniffed. Sour.

"Not long."

The only game in town, he thought, taking a swig. He looked around for an ashtray. "Do you mind if I smoke?" he said.

She frowned. "No, but please open the window and blow your smoke out. My stepdad's allergic to tobacco."

"How often does he come around?"

"Never. He lives in Paris."

"Never? Then why make these rules? If he's in Paris, how could he know, or for that matter care?"

"You don't understand. It's something I do. He sends me so much money every month. I must respect his wishes."

"So much money? Pardon me, but this is no palace. You don't even have a phone."

She looked distant. "I don't choose to spend his money on a palace. It's filthy money and I spend it on filthy things."

"Filthy?" he said as he pulled a chair draped with clothing out from under the hand-painted kitchen table. "What do you mean, filthy?" He removed a box of threads from the seat and placed it on the table, then sat down.

"He raped me. He's buying me off."

Joe took out a cigarette. "That's fairly common, isn't it? In France. Dad's doing their daughters."

"Yes, it is. But he's an important man. He does not want me to talk of it. So he sent me here."

"Well, then, fuck the bastard." He lit his cigarette. "Your mom's still with him?"

"She's dead."

"Oh, I'm sorry." He opened the window and blew the smoke out. "How did she die?"

Jezebel looked away. "In a fire. It was terrible. So many people killed in a terrorist attack. So stupid. So very stupid."

"Terrorists, huh? What about your real father? Couldn't you go to him?"

"He's dead, too. Otherwise my mother would never have re-married."

"How did he die?"

"He was murdered," she said, angrily.

"Murdered?" he said, interested. He had never known anyone whose parents were murdered. "How?"

"What difference does it make? He was murdered."

"I'd like to know. A detail like that is fascinating."

"I don't know. I was very young and couldn't understand. It was something political, but no one knows for sure. My father was a very secretive man. They never found out who did it."

"Your father, I mean, your stepfather raped you after your mother's death?"

Jezebel nodded. "He was lonely. He said it was just him and me now and he needed me in that way."

"How old were you?"

"Ten."

"Fuck."

"I started acting crazy by the time I was sixteen, so he sent me to a doctor. Then he decided to send me out of the country."

Joe picked up a guitar leaning against the wall. "You play?"

"No. It belongs to the guy who left the wine."

He plucked the strings. "What do you know, it's in tune." He started strumming then sang:

"Jeze-bell-elle-elle-elle-elle
If ever a devil was born without a pair of horns, It was you. Jezebel.
    It was you.
If ever an angel fell, Je-ze-bel, it was you, Jezebel it was you.
If ever a pair of eyes promised paradise
Deceiving me, grieving me, making me blue.

If ever the devil's plan was made to torment man
It was you, Jezebel, it was you.
T'would be better if I had never known a lover such as you,
    Forsaken dreams, and all for the siren calls of your arms, Like
    a demon love possessed me and obsessed me constantly. What
    evil star was made that my fate's dream should be,
Jeze-bel-elle-elle-elle-elle, night and day, every way
Jezebel it was you."

"That's not who I am," Jezebel said, pointedly. "I'm not about to use my real name in a porno movie."

"What's your name? You know mine. I mean, I wouldn't feel quite as close to you if I insisted on being called Max Stryde."

"Well, that is a pretty stupid name."

"Precisely. And Jezebel isn't you, either."

She gave him such a serious look, he suspected she was trying to show him she had recovered from her fit. She'd been in a daze all the way over from the shoot to her place.

"Chantal," she said, her eyes looking haunted again.

"Chantal? That's your name? Sounds French. What's your Arabic name."

"I was very little when we moved to Paris. I've been called Chantal for as long as I can remember so that's who I am. My Arabic name doesn't matter."

Joe considered whether or not to believe her, just as he did when she told him she was going to law school. "Chantal's a pretty name. I like it. Can I call you that?"

"I prefer it not to be common knowledge," she said.

"Sure," he said. "Chantal."

Paola's sex cries came from the other room.

"Hey, let's party," he said. He'd never had an Arab before, and that was something he wanted to change.

"No," she said with a distant, exhausted smile, as if she weren't there. "Not after what I'd been through. My scene, you know, it took a lot out of me."

"I understand." He suspected she wanted him to seduce her in some specific way. All he had to do was wait for a signal as to how to proceed. That was how you learned a culture, play their games. "I'm exhausted myself."

Something like disappointment seemed to flit across her face.

"Yes, it's late and we have to get up early," she said. "Besides, we'll be doing that all day tomorrow anyway."

"Yeah, isn't it wonderful?" he said, although he doubted Booth would come through.

"I have to take a long hot shower," she muttered. "I stink."

JOE LAY in Chantal's bed waiting for her to come out of the bathroom while Kurt and Paola appeared to drift off to sleep on the sofa bed. He began to wonder if he, too, would fall asleep before she came out. Then he thought of her medicine cabinet and the little white bottles with handwritten Arabic letters on them, and all the pills inside.

"You look tense, Joe," Paola yawned. "Would you like me to suck you off?"

"Na, I'm cool," said Joe.

Chantal quietly came out of the bathroom, looking as if she were in a trance as she crawled under the covers, lying down on her side, her back to Joe.

"Let's sleep," she whispered when Joe slid up to her.

"Let's cuddle," Joe said. "You'll sleep better that way." Hearing her groan, he added. "Don't you like cuddling?"

"No, because men always get ideas."

"Like this?" Joe placed his hand on her open-crotch panties, his fingers fondling the folds of her sex. No response. "All right," he mumbled, turning away. "Good night."

"No," she whispered.

Joe moved back. "Excuse me?"

"No," she whispered, lower, making him come closer.

He whispered, "No what?"

"Don't touch me," she whispered, barely audible.

He waited a moment, then, breathing loud enough for her to hear, carefully pulled the bedding back. *So that's her game. Pretending to be asleep.*

Slowly, without touching her, he raised her nightie up to her armpits, draping it over her head, covering her face. Then he moved his fingertips to the waistband of her panties, one hand to her left, the other to the right, touching her only with his hot breath on her bare skin. He pinched her waistband, and gave her panties a tentative tug.

After a while, he lightly touched her hip with the tip of his nose. When there was no response, he opened his mouth, licking her with the tip of his tongue. She tensed. He responded by rising up, holding himself still until she rolled onto her back. She whispered something, or he thought she did. He moved in close. Her lips barely moved. A gasp, a puff, and a gasp, sounding like *Amira*. He whispered that word as if to a child to see if she were asleep. Her slight smile, and making like she had gone back to sleep meant he got it right. Her Arabic name. She wanted him to take advantage of the Arab princess in her, the hidden unnamed one. Who she was before the masks. Realizing, as he gingerly worked her panties down to her ankles, this could be serious business. He'd have to be on the lookout out for signs if he crossed a line. He touched her sex.

Wet. A good sign.

"What are you guys doing over there?" said Kurt.

"Shhhhh!" said Joe in a stage whisper. "Don't wake her."

"Don't wake her?" Kurt whispered back.

"She's *aaa*-sleep. I can do *any*-thing I want with her and she wouldn't know."

"Ohhhh!" said Kurt, catching on. "She's a-sleeeep."

"You guys, let her sleep," Paola murmured.

"Women should be obscene and not heard," said Kurt, holding a finger to his lips to shush her. "What are you doing?" he said to Joe.

"Juicing her cunt."

"I like the sound of that," Kurt said as he took a long vibrator off the bedside bureau. "You know, you could probably get away with shoving this up her butt."

"You guys are sick," said Paola. "Leave her alone. How'd you like it if someone did that to you while you were asleep?"

"You know what's better than honor?" said Kurt as he got off the sofa bed to join Joe.

"No, what?" Joe said, stifling a laugh as he slipped a finger into her sex.

"In her," Kurt said, watching Joe spreading her legs. "That's one sweet looking cunny. Why don't you split it open so we can have a good look-see what's up in there?"

Joe felt her tense in the detached way women do when in fantasy.

Amira squirmed back onto her side with a grunt, and lay there as if she were asleep, her left fist pressed tightly against her lips, intensely aware of people staring at her nakedness from her tits down to her pink striped booties and fuck-me panties clutched down at her ankles. All of which made her feel all the more naked.

"Come on, you guys," said Paola. "This isn't funny."

"Shhhh," shushed Kurt with a twisted grin.

Hidden behind her eyelids, Amira sensed Joe hovering over her like some sort of hungry, drooling beast. Then she felt his wet mouth pressing flat against her hip, gobbling her up in a most intensely hungry way. The sensations of his tongue and sandpapery stubble against her tender skin made her shiver . She cried out with little sighs, biting down on the tip of her thumb, and held her breath to stop all sound as a deep moan built up inside her. With a sound like surrender, she stretched to grip the top edge of the mattress, like a captive on a torture rack, while the nameless beast-man sucked on her lower parts with so much lust she curled up into a fetal position.

"I want to see her face," Kurt said, tugging at her nightie.

"Fine with me, just don't wake her," Joe whispered, watching to see what effect this would have on her.

"Come on, you guys, stop it!" Paola protested, plopping onto the bed next to Kurt. Amira didn't know what to do. She couldn't control her face.

Then Joe's mouth moved up, defining and bringing to life every part of her body. Lapping her belly, then up along her ribs. Sucking on her left tit then her right, like a wild baby trying to draw milk. She felt waves of sensation surge through her entire body with each foul touch of his mouth and scratchy stubble, until his body was fully extended over her. He was over her now in a push-up position, like a wild animal about to go for the jugular.

"You know what someone ought to do?" Kurt said to Paola. "Shove their tongue up in her butt, then try to work a hand up in there, like you do at the bachelor parties."

"You guys are sick!" said Paola.

Joe moved aside. "That's not my thing. Why don't *you* do it?" He winked at Paola.

Paola looked at him, confused.

Kurt then grabbed Jezebel/Chantal/Amira by her hips and jerked her up on her knees, her butt in the air. She stuck her fingers in her mouth, squeezing her eyes shut, the right side of her head flat against the bed, her knees locked together.

"She's asleep, dead to the world," said Kurt to Paola. "She's not going to know. Go on. Do it!"

"She's not going to know?" Paola looked doubtfully at Chantal/

Amira chewing on her fingers. Then, catching on, she said, "Actually, that's not such a bad idea."

"Shhh, not so loud," said Kurt, turning on a vibrator. "We don't want to wake her."

Paola again looked confused. Kurt put a finger to his lips to shush her with a grin. Amira cringed as Paola rose over her like some mighty lizard, feeling the grip of her claws on her butt, her hot wet tongue licking, drooling around her fingers as they dug into her. A buzzing-hum sound came closer and closer. Then! *SHOVED!* Deep into her! Her spine coming alive under its thrusts, its vibrations somehow connecting to the base of her spine, manipulating it. OOOOH, Ah! She shivered. Oh! Ah! Ah! Ah! Hard to control her breathing. *Sweet green musty pepper.* Hard to control her burning face! AH! AH! AH!

"Ah! Ah! Ah! AAAAH! Lah, lah, lah, lah, lah, LAAAAAAH!"

THE DREAMER approached a filthy, muddy hole. At the bottom of the murk, he saw his Lady. Immobile. Her whitish spines glowing faintly in the dark filth, like a spidery snow crab. He immersed himself into the poisonous murk, the taffy-colored darkness smearing his eyes, filling his mouth and nostrils until he could not move.

Then he saw the moon, whirling round and round, as if he were seeing it underwater from the vortex of a whirlpool. Around him, as far as he could see, was a plain of bluish-grey mud. He began to trudge toward the horizon, hearing nothing but the pulse in his ears. He was at the bottom of an ocean whose darkness he had taken for light. With this realization the darkness increased. He could barely see in front of him as he strode on through the dimness, feeling his way through a foul pond overgrown with scum, until he found the Golden Key. He then began pulling himself up a monstrous wall, barnacled and corroded with fissures, by grasping great stalactites of rust. At last, he broke through into a green light where he saw Everything with rapturous drowning eyes. Then he saw the Lady. He offered her the Golden Key.

RRRRING! RRRRING!
Dazed, Jake groped for the phone. "Hello," he said, trying to sound awake.
RRRRING!
Slowly, he tumbled back into the muck.

"Good morning, Mr. Zakheim," said Worthingham. "May I speak to Tracy."

"She's not here."

"Really? Then where is she staying these days?"

Jake sighed. "What do you want?"

"Tell her not to bother showing up for work. The gig is up."

"Okay, I'll let her know as soon as I hear from her."

"Tell her I don't appreciate being lied to and I don't like being used. I warned her about the limits and costs of our association. My time is valuable, but her I gave a special price — her time for my time. She owes me and she's ignored my collection notices so I'm repossessing what could have been hers."

"All right, I'll let her know." He glanced at the clock. Six A.M.

"I'm not through, Mr. Zakheim. I just got off the phone with Janus. I told her to inform Booth her IDs are fake. Turns out the little tramp's fifteen, and you're in one hell of a lot of trouble."

Jake sat up, wide awake. Tracy stirred. She noticed his anxiety. He signaled her to be silent. "I'd like to remind you, Mr. Worthingham, *you* sent her to me." His voice was shaky. "*You* told me she was nineteen. I had no reason to think otherwise." He noted Tracy's frightened expression. "*You* got her into porn, and now in a jealous pique you blow the whistle. If anyone's going to be in a hell of a lot of trouble, it's *you*."

"When the shit hits the fan, Mr. Zakheim, who do you think the powers-that-be will believe? You, a pathetic middle-aged pornographer fucking a fifteen-year-old, or the solid citizen who blew the whistle?" Worthingham laughed. "I checked you out, Danny boy. That's right, I know your real name. I know your military history. Deserter. Got the low down on your divorce. Cuckold. You're up shit creek in a wire canoe. All your dirty, little secrets are going to come out. Nothing's worse than disgrace, Danny boy. It's lonely and irreversible. Having to live through it is worse than dying."

"You're one sick sack of shit! A man your age expecting a fifteen-year-old girl to do whatever you say! There's no force on earth that can make an adolescent girl be anything other than an adolescent girl. And to show what an absolute idiot you are, you destroy her because she doesn't spend enough time with you."

"You don't know squat about kids, Danny boy. You know even less about power and control. Believe me, you don't know what you're talking about. There are plenty of little girls out there prettier, more clever, much more interesting than her. I know, I've been there many times. Tell our girl if she knows what's best for her, don't show up for work. The way I see it, she has two choices. She can come to me for protection and forgiveness, or she can disappear. She could have had it all, but she fucked with the wrong guy. Tell her I hope she learns something from her mistake."

"If you had a semblance of a brain, rather than put yourself and everyone else at risk you would have approached me honestly and directly with what you intended to do before you did it."

"Are you ever in for a rude awakening." Worthingham laughed. "That kind of involvement's more trouble than it's worth. Best option, cut your losses. The sooner the better. The longer you wait, the more dangerous the game. The ball's in your court. Let's see what you do with it."

Jake put down the receiver. Tracy stared at him.

"He told Janus your IDs are fake."

She covered her face.

"He said you're fifteen. Is that true? Are you fifteen?"

"I'm sorry," she sobbed. "Does this mean I'm going to lose all those gigs? Isn't there some way around it?"

"Please tell the truth. How long have you been fifteen? Be honest, please."

"Since December."

"How'd you come by the name Tracy Stockton? Will the birth certificate hold up?"

"No, it's fake. I got the name from a freeway sign. You know, the one that has both Tracy and Stockton on it."

Rrrrrrrring!

Jake picked up the phone and, in a relaxed voice, said, "Good morning."

"Jake, I have some awful news," said Janus. "I got a call from someone who says Tracy's IDs are fake. Could I talk to her?"

"She's not here," said Jake.

"I thought Mingarella took her over there."

"He did, but she didn't stay. Who said the IDs are fake? Anyone I know?"

"I can't tell you that. The person wants to be left out of it."

"Well, as long as it's not Worthingham. He's a nutcase. He fucks around with street kids, as you well know. He's been pressuring her to hang out with him, threatening her if she didn't. I wouldn't give a hamster's hankie to keep that jerk's confidences."

Janus was silent. "I already told Booth," she said finally. "Worthingham helped him put the project together. Why would he shoot it down out of spite? He said he checked her ID because he didn't trust you."

"He didn't trust me?" said Jake. "The son-of-a-bitch sent her to me. *He* told me she was nineteen. You remember when I called you about him?"

Janus was silent. "Booth believes him."

"Well, I don't. Doesn't make sense. Her tit job, college, everything."

"She needs to prove she's over eighteen, and she needs to do it right away. Will you call me the moment you hear from her?"

"Yes, of course, of course," he said, wondering how well Booth knew Worthingham.

"Oh, by the way, did you hear about Willow?"

"Huh?"

"The police say she killed herself, but I don't think so. I mean, a woman wouldn't kill herself by slicing her gut open. That's an awful way to die."

Jake felt numb. "Wh-what"

"Could have been her mother. They fought a lot. Maybe one of the creepy guys she hangs with but the cops are calling it a suicide so they won't have to bother investigating."

"Uh. Wow." Jake felt empty, blank, until he noticed the anxiety on Tracy's face. *She thinks this is about her.* "Uh, Tracy told me about Dr. Ben and Catherine. Are they okay?"

"I always thought Ben was a certified wacko. The people he hangs with, you know, birds of a feather. Would you believe he asked me just before you left to keep a watch on you and Julie to make sure you guys didn't leave. He was creepy about it, too, like it was a matter of life or death. I mean, how hard would it have been for him to do it himself? After all, there's only one way in and out. You know, he even offered me a couple hundred bucks if I could get you to come back. I mean, like, if it was so damn important, why didn't he just slip you a couple hundred to stay. You would have done it then, right? Julie sure would have. I mean, you guys weren't being paid to stay, so why stay?"

"Is he alright? And Catherine? Are they okay?"

"They didn't pull a sheet up over his face when they hauled him off. Booth said Will told him they have him on life support."

"Worthingham?" said Jake, surprised. "And Ben, they know each other?"

"Yeah, since they were kids. Ben was the one who introduced me to Will in the first place. I've met a lot of sickos through them. I'm not surprised he got his head bashed in. Just never figured he'd be the one who'd do it."

"Yeah," Jake said, distracted. "Yeah. Uh, listen. We'd better keep my line clear in case Tracy tries to call. Okay." Then he hung up.

"I'm sorry," Tracy sobbed. "I didn't think anybody'd find out. I didn't think Wormyham would be such a jerk."

"Did he tell you he'd do this if you didn't spend time with him?"

"No, he didn't tell me that. He said he could end my career faster than he started it, but I didn't think he'd actually go and do it."

He stopped himself from sighing, remembering how she hated it. He did not want to agitate her any more than necessary.

"Isn't there anything we can do, you know, so I can work?"

"No," he said. "Did you know he was involved in Booth's project? Did he say anything like that?"

"No. If he had I wouldn't have done it."

Neither would I, he thought. "Did he get you the IDs?"

"Yeah. And the tit job."

"What a fucking, arrogant fool," he said. "He's implicated in all these things, why in the hell would he risk everything by blowing the whistle on you?"

"I don't know, but I'm not the only one he's set up. All the street kids know, if he likes you he'll get things done for you."

"Listen. I, uh, can't keep you here. It's too risky, since I know you're underage. If the cops found you here, they'd lock me up and throw away the keys. What are you going to do? You know, school.'"

"I have to finish school, but I can't afford a new ID."

"So. We need to make this go away in a way that allows you to keep your ID. I doubt anybody's going to come after you. They'd be cutting their own throats if they did."

"Tell you one thing," she snapped. "I'm not going to let them put me away. They come after me, I'll do whatever it takes to stay out of the system."

"Like what?"

"Whatever. If they want me to say you guys forced me into it, I'll say that. Whatever it takes."

"No, no, don't do anything like that. You'd hurt a lot of people whose only crime was they believed you. Not a good thing."

"Look, they're a bunch of pornographers! It goes with the fucking territory! There's no fucking way I'm going to let them put me away again."

"What about me? I'd lose everything. I'd go to jail for a long time. It'd ruin my life. If you kept quiet, it'd be over in a few months and you'd have done the right thing. The pain you'd inflict on others would be so much more than any inconvenience—"

"I don't care! There is no fucking way I'm going to let them put me in an institution!"

Breathing shallowly, Jake looked down, trying not to display his devastating disappointment. He remembered when he first grasped the extent of his wife's betrayal, how he left her in the living room and went to his office to cry. What shocked him most was the realization she had no idea of who he was. He had been useful, a useful love, but she never had a clue as to who he was. Which meant their closeness, their intimacy, all of it was an illusion. Now, with Tracy, he felt a similar betrayal. He had taken risks, stood by her, helped her, yet she would not for a second consider the consequences of her actions on him. It didn't matter to her who he was or what his fate might be, she wasn't interested. He made himself available and convenient, and for that he would pay. Of course, whatever her name is, she was just a kid. It wasn't the same. It just felt that way.

"Couldn't we like tell everybody I'm eighteen but I can't give them my real ID because I don't want my real identity known, like because my parents are famous or something?"

Jake looked down, "I don't think they'd believe me, or you for that matter. Without a valid ID, I doubt they'd want to take the risk even if they did."

"They might believe Joe," she said, softly. "If he calls, let me ask him."

TRACY TOOK the phone from Jake. She sighed into the receiver.

"Hey, Tracy," said Joe. "How you doing?"

She snorted a laugh. "Fine."

"Pretty deep shit, huh?"

"Oh, yeah," she sighed.

"You feel all right?"

"Huh?"

"That we all still love you?"

She laughed sadly. "Really?"

"I still do. Can't speak for anybody else, but I still do."

She laughed nervously."Ah ha, man. I had a fucking dream about you and Kurt."

"Oh, really?"

"And you were just like on me, and like just terribly upset."

"Oh," Joe said thoughtfully.

"I mean I understand the situation you're in but," her voice wavered, "I'm not fifteen."

"I know you're not but, uh, the problem we have now is there has to be proof what you are."

"I know that," she said annoyed, like he'd said something stupid.

"I know you don't want anyone to really know who you are, and I respect that."

"That's the situation because you can't prove that I am, and I can't prove that I'm not."

"Do you realize what you're throwing away here? It's not the money, I could care less, I don't have any money invested. Booth's the one who's going to lose big and I could give a toidy bowel for him. But what you're throwing away is a career, the future. You've got people begging for you in different films. There are people in LA I've already talked to who want to use you. *And* the productions we were going to do with you in the lead. Is it worth it to throw all that away? All that money, all that fun, all the people you're associated with, everything? If you're eighteen and you can prove it, don't throw it away."

Tracy started crying.

"I realize it's really tough and that you got your mind set, and I don't want to talk you into anything you don't want to do. But I just want you to really think about what you're giving up. If it's worth it for what your giving up. Okay?"

"Yeah," she sobbed.

"Unless you got something deep, dark and nasty, don't throw it all away. If you're legally an adult, act like one. You can have some time to think about it, but you need to tell me what I should tell other people. I won't tell them anything you don't want me to tell them. You can count on me as a friend in that regard. But they're going to want to know something, and they're using me as the point person. They've all called me and said we've got this accusation, you're kind of friends with them and so what's going up. I'll tell them what you want me to, but they're going to want to know fairly soon."

"So what do you need?"

"Proof."

"Uh, huh."

"Of who you really are and how old you really are."

She sighed, "Jesus."

"That's what will get you back in the loop. Tracy, throw off the shackles of the past. Be what you want to be, don't let your parents win one more battle."

"Shit. I... I just can't."

"Okay. If that's what you really want then tell me what you want me to tell people."

"Well, I don't know. What can you tell them?"

"Well, as it stands now, if I were to tell them the truth I would tell them that the ID you have now is fake. You say you're eighteen, but you're not willing to prove it because you don't want people to know who you really are. That's the truth."

"Right."

"I usually start there and then modify it," he laughed. "Why is it you can't let people know who you really are? Can you tell me that?"

She groaned. "Because it'll get back to my parents. I can't give information on that."

"I don't see how it could get back to your parents."

"Well, uh, huh huh," she laughed sardonically.

"I mean are they actively searching for you? Hold on, I see Jezebel walking down the street."

"Okay," she said, handing the phone to Jake.

"Hello," said Jake. He heard Joe talking to someone in the street.

"Chantal, I mean, Jezebel wants to say something," said Joe.

"Tracy doesn't want to talk anymore," said Jake. "Uh, I was wondering. Have you heard anything about how Catherine's doing?"

"No, I haven't. The cameraman took off with her before the paramedics got there. She looked dead to the world to me, but Booth said she has fits like that all the time and the cameraman knows what to do. He didn't seem concerned."

"And Ben. Any word?"

"I'll ask Booth next time I speak to him. I take it you're avoiding him."

"Uh, no. He hasn't called me."

"You know what's going to happen. Booth has a bug up his butt."

"How's that?"

"Well, he's got ten grand on the line of Peter Hakim's money which is going to be nothing more than toilet paper if he can't get a positive ID off of her. I don't know if he's going to be satisfied with, well, she says she's eighteen but she's not willing to prove it. What that's going to do is torment him, and he's going to try to find out who she really is and how old she really is."

"Yeah, okay. I was hoping it'd be possible to put a lid on it, since nobody else knows about it. Because nothing's going to come out."

"Yeah, but you see my ass is in the sling if this goes to court. I'm willing to sling my ass a long way but I'm not willing to sling it into statutory rape. I don't think we can play ostrich on this. If she's under eighteen, there's enough evidence out there to put us away for years. *And* her ass is more in the sling than she realizes. People have got money down on her. They're going to find things out. I don't know to what extent Booth's willing to go to, but it's getting down to the wire. He's going to want to have some word from me and I'm going to need something to tell him."

"Okay. Then tell him she's fifteen." Hoping fear would put an end to it, he added, "And that *he* should have checked out her damn ID, like he promised me he would."

Tracy left the room crying before he had a chance to hang up. A moment later he heard the large oval mirror over the fireplace crash onto the hearth.

CATHERINE gradually became aware of a dazzling bright light pulsing like a big fluid diamond in the darkness. An intense light shining down, as if searching for her at the bottom of a dry well. The light pulled at her, enticing her up, out of the dark. Like a moth to a flame, she felt herself flying toward the diamond light. As she approached it, a howl exploded in her head and her skin ignited. She felt as if she were being flayed alive.

Then she stuck. The next thing she knew, she was in a bed. In a room.

What had been the dazzling light had turned into the sun, filtering through the branches outside a window. Someone was asleep in a chair beside the bed. He seemed somehow familiar, safe. She liked him. She tried to speak. His eyes opened.

"Don't try to talk," his voice clear, like water, fluid and warm. "Your mind is silent and clear. Let it stay that way." He moved closer on a chair with wheels, blocking the light between her and the window. "Everything depends on whether you have enough power to focus your unwavering attention." He looked into her eyes. "Your mind is sufficiently open to make the proper connections. But this kind of knowledge, it can be devastating." His irises golden, like some sort of animal's.

His eyes soothed her. Touching something undefined, deep within.

"Hypatia, she sought the Beauty rather than the practicality in what was to become physics. She was right in doing so. Because physics, it deals with Infinity. There is no end to it. It is a ceaseless process of transformation, clarification, and unfolding. To be in harmony with it, is to recognize its purpose. Which is Symmetry. Which is Beauty. To the Navajo, restoring one to health, is to bring them back to harmony. To walk in Beauty. Symmetry." He moved slightly back, allowing the window to emit a most incredible white light that spread around him like a silver aura. It was as though he radiated the light. She could see it glowing out the back of his head like a silver halo.

"Free from desire, you realize its mystery. Caught in desire, you see only its manifestations. Mystery and manifestations, they arise from the same source. This source is called darkness. Darkness within darkness. The gateway to all understanding."

He paused. "Until you develop your consciousness of the darkness in you, to the same proportions as the light, that darkness will nullify your best efforts."

She became aware of his breathing, then of her own breathing, that it matched his, that there were no boundaries. Then everything broke and went clear.

There was no her observing. There was only his and her bare essential presence filling the room, breathing together. As they breathed, she felt the room expand with their breath.

"If you heed the appointed time," he whispered close to her smiling face, confident some part of her was listening that understood now was the time. "If you have listened for its coming, and it has ripened deep within you, you can transform a meaningless fate into a purposive destiny. The goal of the Quest is the Quest itself." He took her hands into his. "Follow the restless longing upward. Let no small thing stay forgotten and unhonored. And remember, seek the formless mover at the center of the speaking movement."

Suddenly, she felt her raging past, her complexes of emotions, her personalities, all lifting and peeling off her like so many multi-colored butterflies, vanishing through the open window. And she felt at rest. With no desire to remember.

Yet there was just enough awareness left in her to feel the magnificence of it all.

JAKE ENTERED his house then took out the receipt he'd written on just before Tracy left the restaurant to catch the bus. He had wanted to say something because he knew he would never see her again, and he had somehow loved her. They'd touched each other's lives, and its ending should be honored. Or, at least acknowledged in some way. He had listened to her promises to call when she got settled, but he knew she wouldn't. When she looked to see if her bus was coming, he scrawled *Goodbye, Little Robin / Have a nice life* on the receipt. He felt his farewell was more important to him than to her, and this way he could make it and take it with him. His wish, the final act, here on a credit card receipt.

He would never see her again. He would never know how her life turned out and that saddened him. He did not return to his home. He did not want to answer or return phone calls. Instead, he wandered in nearby Wildcat Canyon until nightfall, thinking through all the strange things that had happened and of what Julie had said about Hecate's likely visit.

When he got home, it was dark, he saw there'd been many messages left. He was reluctant to listen to any of them. Then *RRRRRing!* A chill swept through him, as if this call were a bad omen. *Rrrrring!* He picked up.

"I understand you have offered yourself to me," blared what sounded like a computerized voice.

"Well, not really," he said, trying to sound nonchalant. "More of a friendly invitation for a pleasant little chit chat."

"Thought we might drop by for a wee visit. Say, outside, in ten minutes."

The line went dead. *We?*

Jake went to the foyer closet, took out an overcoat, draping it over his shoulders. Then he grabbed hold of the baseball bat he kept in the closet. Whatever was coming, it was looking for fear. He intended to show it something else.

He waited inside by the front door, his mind detached, working on several levels. On one level, he tried to remember the last time he'd felt threatened with physical danger, with death. At another, he considered what he should do. What to say. Why all this was happening. At still another, he felt simple animal rage — an instinct to kill.

He chose to focus on why this was happening. Wormyham was a common element. Moira's fake uncle, Tracy's fake mentor. Definitely behind the fall of Robin-Tracy-Chastity-Waverly, and probably the force behind Moira's torments as well. And, he had access to everyone's personal information. What was it he said? *You're in for a rude awakening.* He'd set him up to take the fall, using Moira and Tracy as decoys to lure him into being crucified for their sins. Why? Some sort of mind-fuck sport. Or?

The Ben connection. Jake considered the women he knew Ben had messed with. Jazz, Jezebel, Julie, Janus, Tracy and Catherine. And maybe, Moira (a patient?). Ben seemed to mess with everyone he came in contact with. He also considered the crazy spiritual stuff Ben had attributed to Riley. He could not recall in detail what Ben said had happened to Riley during and after his disastrous shoot, other than Riley had been hauled off *energetically mangled.* If so, Riley could be the energetically mangled demon. Moira was in the movie on the day he got mangled. He probably knows her history? Then it struck him. *Riley could be the one who killed Moira's mother! And Willow, as well?* Wormyham could have passed their numbers and personal information on to Riley.

Ben made it clear he needed Jake to play along in an archetypal game that could end up worse than the one that flipped Riley into madness. In fact, Ben flat out told him there'd be serious repercussions if he left before the goddess descended. So, Ben ends up seriously damaged because he had not done his part. Wormyham then outs Tracy and sends the demon Riley after him. If so, how much more freaking stupid can this get!

Everyone was supposed to play their part in mythical reality. In the end, it didn't matter because, as Ben would say, all the sound and fury, fuss and bother, vanity and profanity, all of it comes to nothing once the Goddesses in the Machine descend.

Suddenly his thoughts stopped. He felt the presence of an outside force molding his feelings. The same force he'd first felt a week ago, pulling him into a dream/vision, the outcome of which depended on his ability to grasp and deal with its hidden meaning. If he grasped it, the dream would end and he'd wake up. If he failed, all the ongoing chaos would implode into a nightmare, pulling all the dreamers in this drama into its sway.

He had to do something quickly. Time was running out. Once again, he instinctively addressed the force. "I don't know what I'm supposed to do, or the answer to anything. But, if you give me time and allow me to wake peacefully from this dream, I will not forget it. I will dedicate myself to grasping the meaning behind what happened by writing its story until I get it right." Then, to his surprise, the tension lifted, and he relaxed.

Somehow he knew the fallout from the day's events had dissipated.

He heard a car pull up outside. He lifted the place-mat over the small window in the door. A red Skylark stopped across the street. A dark, heavy energy oppressed him as he opened the door and scanned the area. No one around. Two people in the car. The driver, a woman. A passenger in back, a man. They remained absolutely still as he approached.

He recognized the driver. She was not a woman. Not yet, anyway. She was the pre-op transsexual Lars. The man in back he didn't recognize. Sixtyish. Big. Probably Riley.

Riley slowly powered down his window halfway, then lounged back against the door opposite as if he expected Jake to stick his head in through the opening so he could then push a fast window up button to catch his head, trapping him. An incredibly childish idea, yet somehow Jake felt that was exactly what Riley expected him to do from the way he wiggled his bushy eyebrows, tilted his head and lifted the corner of his mouth to wink, inviting him in. *Come to the window. Come to the window.* There was something out of balance in his movements. Shaky. Madness? Intoxicated? His scraggly beard and the smell of bourbon made him suspect the later. Probably both. Energetically mangled.

"What can I do for you, mate?" Jake said with what could pass as a friendly smile. Riley beckoned with his long fingers for him to come closer.

"I'm 'ere to even things out a wee bit."

"And just who in the Hell do you think you are?" said Jake.

"I am!" he said, "The God of Hellfire!" as he straighten up, lurching toward Jake.

"Well, good for you," said Jake, shrugging his overcoat off as he stepped back to raise his bat. "Hallelujah!" he yelled as the bat struck the car's roof, startling Riley who then jumped back. "Halle-fucking-lujah!" He swung at the windshield, cracking it. Lars's face flashing panic as he managed to jerk the keys out trying to start the car. "Hosanna to the bloody fucking Highest!" He shattered the half open window, sending shards of glass spraying toward the weird man who was staring back wide-eyed, grinning with delight.

"Hallelujah!!!!" Jake screamed all of his energy into the bat, smashing the door in.

"Go the fuck back to Hell where you belong, Riley!" he yelled as the car jerked forward.

The weird man's expression shifted to something that defied description. The words that came immediately to Jake's mind was he looked as if he had seen a ghost, but it was much more than that. Maybe, the core look of the energetically mangled.

The wheels screeched, and then the car took off.

A light went on in a neighbor's house. He stood still, wondering at the sudden rage that had possessed him. Now his neighbors, long suspicious of him, had something juicy to gossip about. Thinking he should get off the street, he loosened his grip on the bat, but anger kept him rooted there. He felt invincible, as if some kind of spell had been broken.

JAKE TOOK OFF his clothes then eased himself into the hot tub. The riddle on his mind was hidden somewhere in the meaning of the events over the past two weeks. To see it, he would have to understand what he was seeing. He wanted whatever was shaping events to know he was serious about grasping it. That he'd do whatever it took, for however long it took. He wanted to know, but he needed help. He needed a clue.

Rrrrring! He looked at the phone. He didn't remember bringing it to the tub, but there it was, as if in answer for the clue he had requested. He picked it up.

"Yes," he said.

"Good, you're answering your damn phone," said Jazz.

He furled his brow. *Jazz? She doesn't have a clue, how could she provide one?* He had so little patience left for her, he found it hard to do anything but steel himself against her. Taking her seriously would be a waste of energy.

"I want you to hear me and hear me well," she said.

He had committed to do whatever it took, so he knew he had to listen. Especially to those he did not wish to.

"You hurt me when you wouldn't pick up the phone to help me deal with my pain. You say you don't intend making me feel like a lowlife but I can't tell you anything in con-fi-dence without you using it against me. I admit my chemical problems with drugs, alcohol, things I'm proud to say I've overcome, but you won't let me forget it. You tell everybody, then anything missing, they say I took it, and you believe them. You think whatever you like but keep it to yourself. You won't make me feel like a lowlife because you're no better than me. Look at your own life."

"Okay," Jake said. She sounded drunk or stoned. Probably both.

"Why you so cold? Why can't you show some concern for me during the times..." She hesitated, apparently confused, and then started up again. "A person who confesses to love me, who enjoys and desires my body, someone who manipulates me and uses my body for his own sexual needs, then when I'd like you to be close and caring, when I'd like to feel you'd voluntarily give me extra attention, that never has come."

"Well, that's not exactly true," he ventured.

"No, don't you talk!" she yelled. "Just listen for a change. I know taking your money was not right but I did not justify it by saying I had a right to do it. You on the other hand been lying to me since I first met you. You feel it's okay to be a liar. It's okay to enter a relationship with a person, lead them on, deeply hurt them continuously, but feel you're not doing it on purpose so you say, well, if you don't like it you don't have to put up with it. But you let me put up with you, and I try to understand and work it out, but you're not willing to do the same. You're a one-sided person who only looks out for himself. I'm not perfect but I honestly felt we had a very special relationship going on. How wrong I was. Janus put it very eloquently when she said you're nothing but a washing machine. You use people until their usefulness is over and then toss them aside."

"A washing machine?" he said with a grimace in his voice.

"There! That's what I mean! You never give me the consideration or respect you give other people. You're aware of the deep love I have for you but you don't appreciate it. One day when you come off your mountain and stop judging others to make you feel superior over their faults you may be a decent person, your life may come together and you may stop having the problems you do, but until that time your life will always be in turmoil." She paused, breathing heavily. "This has been a relationship that will take me a long time to understand and to get over."

Jake covered the mouthpiece and sighed. He asked himself what he got out of her harangue other than he should have avoided getting involved with her in the first place. Then he realized his actions had come from the wrong place. Careful and sensitive observation with a gentle instinct for balance and harmony were what the situation had called for, things she must have felt him capable of. Then he realized why she thought that. He was like that with children, and when he addressed the child in her. He failed her when he related to the adult, as if the adult were an unworthy successor to the child.

"You there?" she said. "I know you're there. Say something."

"I'm here," he said.

Then Jazz sobbed, "All I ever wanted was for you to love me."

Oh, fuck, thought Jake, suddenly realizing the clue had to do with entanglements. What he seeks, lies in the Myth hidden behind the entanglements.

Acknowledgments

Many thanks to the friends and fellow writers who have read and critiqued earlier drafts or portions of this novel.

I am especially grateful to Steve Hoppe who offered technical help with files and organization of the text, and urged me to continue working on the book.

Karin Rohde read several drafts and also accompanied me on explorations of the southwest, providing inspiration and feedback for the Navajo customs described in the novel. As well, I am grateful to the work of the late anthropologist Ruth Benedict.

My thanks to Thomas Kellogg, whom I met over half a century ago while serving in the military, for years of encouragement.

And to Jo-Anne Rosen, also a friend of fifty years, who has never stinted in her support of my writing and, in this instance, copy edited and proofed the final manuscript.